The Saint's Second Life

A Saints & Sinners Novel

By A.M. Nordman

For all my little freaks with religious trauma who like to giggle and kick your feet while reading the dirtiest scene possible.
This one's for you.

Prologue

I was born with chartreuse eyes. A sign of divinity, the people once whispered. A mark of fate, others claimed. But in the end, all it ever meant was that I was doomed from the start.

The flickering candlelight cast dancing shadows upon the stone walls, and beyond the windows, the moon that drenched what remained of the former kingdoms of Etheria and Calbraxia hung in the sky. It watched over me as it had watched over my people for centuries, silent and unchanging. As I closed my eyes, I thought of the stories I once studied in my youth, the last tales of my people.

The goddess of the moon and the god of the sun, together, forged this land and blessed the first humans as their children. They wove the stars into the sky and filled the rivers with light, giving mortals the rare ability to touch the divine. All were equal under their gaze, all held a connection to the gods.

But power is a fickle thing in the hands of man. It was not long before the purity of their bond to the gods was twisted by greed and ambition. Through generations of war, pestilence, and corruption, only those with pure souls and the blood which cursed me retained the ability to channel the divine. Those few would bear the same chartreuse eyes that I had been told as a child were a blessing, the mark of the goddess.

They became known as the Divinials, vessels of the gods' will. They could heal, they were a link to the heavens themselves, but most importantly, they could wield an immense power. However, power always comes at a price. The purity of the soul was their tether, and to maintain it, they were stripped of their freedom.

For centuries, they were kept in cages, some physically, some mentally. To ensure their purity and ability to touch the divine, they were forced to live by the strictest moral laws. They were never to love, never to know the warmth of another's touch, never to bear children of their own. As a result, their numbers dwindled, and their existence was bound to cruel necessity. It wasn't until near extinction that the truly heinous practices began.

While the wealthy were raised in temples and monasteries, the poor would be bred like prized livestock, left to keep the population from dropping to nothing. It became trendy for nobles to have several Divinials in their company, almost as a show of wealth. Some would be purchased just to deflower, almost as a rite of passage.

They were farmed, their powers exploited, their voices silenced. This would continue for decades, even centuries. As their powers were exploited, their link to the gods weakened. The world feasted on their powers until they became nothing more than relics of a dying age.

Then, during a great war, the kingdoms of Etheria and Calbraxia both decreed an end to the suffering of my people. The practice of keeping Divinials was banned. With freedom to forge a new path, the once sought-after gifts began to vanish from the world. It was rumored that not a single Divinial was left who could obtain the divine, until my mother came along, of course.

A final, unintentional relic of a forgotten era, born from a union never meant to exist. My mother, the last Divinial capable of being bred, was sent to the king of Calbraxia, married before she had even grown. A last offering from a world that had used her kind until there was nothing left.

She bore two daughters: me and my sister, Margaret. Both of us share the same haunting stare as my mother, the silent burden of a dying people.

Once, there was some hope that we could repopulate our people, that we would not bear the burden of extinction by the hands of man, however after my imprisonment, and my sister's death, I was the last of our kind, and in my old dying age, I had made peace with knowing this curse would end with me.

There will be no more Divinials left once I die. No more children born into chains. No more prayers that go unanswered. No more pointless wars that have caused an end for so many innocent lives.

The moon shone brighter on the eve of my death than it ever had. As I closed my eyes, I imagined a world where I was never bound, where I lived and loved as freely as the winds that carried the voices of the gods. A world where I would still have my sister, and the monsters who created me would know nothing but the suffering that I had endured. Perhaps, in another life, I would have known such a world.

But not this one. In this one, I was born with chartreuse eyes. And in this one, I would die with them, too.

Chapter 1

I, Saint Silvia Stephan, once hailed as the Savior of the two Kingdoms, now lie fragile and withered upon my deathbed. My breaths came shallow and slow, each one a quiet testament to the seventy years I had suffered upon this earth. The candlelight flickered softly, casting long shadows across the sparse chamber; a far cry from the opulent palace I had once called home, and later, the battlefield where I had forged my legacy.

My gaze drifted to the ceiling, though my mind wandered far beyond it, traversing the labyrinth of memories that had shaped my life. I remembered the naive young woman I had been some fifty years prior, blinded by love to the machinations of those around me who saw me as a pawn. That fateful day, what was supposed to be my wedding day, still lingered in my mind like a thorn.

I had been promised to the Prince of Etheria on my twentieth name day, and even on the day we were to be betrothed, that promise had been honeyed and false. I had heard the stories of my people, forced to learn the history by tutors and scholars alike. If by the time I reached the age of thirty, while remaining chaste, my holy powers would bloom. The Prince, hearing of this, tricked me into a union meant not for love but for power.

When sent to Etheria to meet my husband, I wouldn't find a walk down the aisle, nor a husband or crown. Instead, I would find myself locked in a tower until I reached that fruitful age where I could be of use to the Etherian royalty. I would never be kissed, nor touched by anyone, to make sure my powers were at their purest form. I had found myself shackled by both marriage and circumstance.

The tower became my prison. Months turned to years, my cries for freedom echoed, unheard within cold stone walls. Yet, amidst the despair, I could feel my strength stirring within me; an awakening. On my thirtieth name day, my confinement would pay off. After the destruction of my homeland of Calbraxia and the subsequent murder of my sister, the world itself would tremble as my divine powers surged forth. The very magic that my captors had sought now flowed through my veins, unbridled and potent.

They celebrated my transformation, as I had now become a weapon to further their tyranny. My time away from civilization would leave me powerless to the changes that had been undertaken. Etheria no longer stood as a powerful kingdom, but an empire hell bent on control. For a time, I was their reluctant instrument, forced to wield my powers against the innocent.

But even the brightest flames cannot be caged forever. When I heard about the death of my mother, I woke from my shell. Slowly, I began to turn the tides, no longer using my gifts not to oppress, but to inspire. I became a beacon for the downtrodden, a symbol of hope for those who had long since forgotten what it meant to dream.

The rebellion I led was fierce and unyielding. The war would last decades, with me at the front of the battlefields. I watched as the vermilion colors of Etheria slowly dissipated until we finally succeeded in our mission.

The death of the Etherian crown culminated in the overthrow of the monarchy and the birth of a new Etheria. I had freed the kingdoms, yet the cost had been steep, a life of sacrifice, loneliness, and unending responsibility.

And now, that life was ending. The powers that had once raged on the battlefields now wavered in my body, leaving not even a spark. I felt no fear as the edges of my vision began to blur. Instead, there was peace, even anticipation. The prospect of rest after decades of struggle felt like a gift I had earned a thousand times over.

As my eyelids grew heavy, I whispered a quiet farewell to the world I had saved. "Finally," I murmured, "I can rest."

I was wrapped in a gossamer of warmth as the light that surrounded me grew brighter. I knew I would be venturing to the great beyond, welcomed by the Goddess Leticia for my years of hard work and sacrifice. I could picture her figure just out of reach, her smile would be welcoming me to my new forever home.

I closed my eyes in anticipation as I stepped forward to embrace the winged angel that I had seen so many times before in my dreams. Her words and power that had once flowed through my body and fought alongside me so many times before, emptied as I took my last breath on earth.

When I opened my eyes again, it was not to the serene haven I had expected, but to the soft golden light of an uncanny morning. The scent of roses wafted through the open window, and the sound of exuberant songbirds greeted my ears.

I lay in bed, frozen with one hand extended ahead of me, reaching for something I would never grasp. The other clutched the silken sheets beneath me. I felt the tears that stained my cheeks and swiped them away.

I sat up abruptly, my hands trembling as they brushed against skin soft as cashmere. Something was wrong. As my vision cleared, I stared down, expecting the familiar sight of worn, calloused hands. Instead, I found smooth, unblemished skin, untouched by time or toil. Hands that had never known a hard day's work.

I felt the trepidation rise in my body as I stumbled to the mirror across the familiar room, my breath caught as my reflection stared back at me. Gone were the wrinkles etched by time and toil, replaced by smooth, youthful skin. My midnight hair, once peppered with gray, fell in thick waves past my shoulders.

Seventy years of memories flooded my mind, clashing with the reality before me. The naivety I had carried on this day was gone, replaced by the wisdom and scars of a lifetime.

"No, no, no!" I groaned as I fell to my knees. "This cannot be happening. I was supposed to be dead!"

But deep down, I knew there was no escaping it. The path I had walked before was not immutable. Whether I liked it or not, the universe had decided I wasn't quite finished yet.

This had to be a cosmic joke. A trick of the gods. My mind reeled, grasping for logic where none could be found. I stumbled toward the mirror, feet unsteady, breath shallow, and placed my hand against the cool glass. It didn't fog. It didn't ripple. It simply stared back, solid and real and cruel.

The girl in the reflection was me, but not the me I knew. Not the one who had freed an empire, who lived a life of hardship. This version was untouched, unmarred, like the world hadn't laid a single finger on her.

Desperate to wake up, to prove this was all some fever dream, I pinched my cheek. Hard. Pain bloomed, sharp and immediate, making my eyes water. But the image didn't vanish. I didn't wake. My knees nearly buckled. No. This wasn't a dream. This was real. And something was very, very wrong.

As I began to process my indignation, the air around me shifted, growing warm, thick with reverence. A soft golden light spilled across the room, though there was no source, no flame, no sun. Just an all-encompassing glow that pressed against my skin like sunlight filtered through curtains.

Then came the voice. Gentle at first. Melodic. Disarming.

"Silvia." My stomach dropped.

It rang like a chorus of wind chimes drifting on a summer breeze. Familiar, serene, and far too calm. A voice I'd heard before only in dreams, in ancient scriptures, in the whispered prayers of dying priests. The Goddess Leticia.

"You've done so well in your past life," the voice continued, echoing softly from every corner of the space, as if the very walls spoke to me. "Truly, your deeds were remarkable. You brought hope to Calbraxia, liberated the oppressed in Etheria, and embodied my teachings with grace. As thanks, I have granted you the chance to live again. A chance to re-experience your legacy and ascend into my divine embrace once more—"

"Thanks for the offer," I interrupted. "But I would prefer not to. You can take me back into the light instead."

There was a long pregnant pause in the room before she decided to speak again. "...Really?" She asked. "You would refuse my reward?"

For a long moment, all I could do was blink, mouth open in utter disbelief. "A reward?" I finally croaked. "You think this is a reward?"

There was a soft hum of divine calm, infuriating in its detachment.

"I *wanted* death," I snapped. "I earned peace. I earned rest! And now you're sending me back? Back to this—-this nightmare?"

"There is no nightmare in a gift freely given," Leticia's voice replied, smooth and unwavering. "This is a blessing, child. A chance to walk the sacred path once more."

"I've walked it already," I hissed. "I walked it bloody and broken. I did the righteous thing. I played the martyr. I gave everything. I don't want another trial, I want bliss. The whole choir-of-angels, no-more-crying, eternal peace package!"

There was a pause, a thoughtful hum that vibrated through my bones.

"My sweet Silvia," she said, "Is the experience of your rise not more rewarding than a resting place in the stars? The growth, the trials, the purpose—"

"Nope!" I shouted, my voice echoing in the vast emptiness. "I want my reward. My *real* reward. Just end this and take me to eternity already."

A sympathetic sigh echoed softly.

"I cannot," Leticia advised gently. "In this life, you have not yet awakened to your divinity. You must walk the path again, face the trials anew, and prove yourself once more before you may ascend."

I stood frozen, slack-jawed. "You mean, I have to do it *again*? The betrayals? The pain? The godsdamned tower!"

"The path is yours to walk," her voice turned misty and distant, like the final note of a hymn drifting into silence.

"That's divine-speak for yes, isn't it?" I groaned, dragging my hands down my face.

"You already know what lies in your fate, it shan't be much longer," she whispered, soothing, so warm it almost made me believe it wasn't the worst news of my life.

The light began to dim. The golden glow slipped through my fingers like water as I lunged for it. I reached into the air, desperate, clawing at the shimmer, praying to catch hold of something. Anything.

"No," I whispered, a panic rising in my chest. "No, don't do this."

It was no use; the light offered no hand to grasp, no warmth to cling to.

"Please!" I sobbed, my voice cracking. "Take me with you! Please, just let me go!"

"My child..." Leticia's voice echoed faintly as the last tendrils of gold faded around me. "You have done it once. You shall do it again."

The glow dissolved, vanishing into the void like the last breath of a dying star. And I was alone. Cold. Mortal. Trapped in a life I never asked for, bound to a fate I would have to live through again.

I sat on the floor of that painfully cheerful room for what felt like an eternity, though time meant nothing in that moment. Whether it had been a minute or an hour, I couldn't say. The sunlight filtered through lace curtains like laughter I didn't want to hear, illuminating a life I hadn't chosen. My breath quickened, my hands curling into trembling fists as frustration surged through me, hot and aimless.

My eyes landed on the jade vase by the mirror. Ornate and delicate, overflowing with sickeningly sweet roses, as if mocking my grief with their perfection. I lunged before I could stop myself. With a sharp cry, my hands wrapped around the cool glass and flung it across the room. It shattered beautifully, violently, jagged pieces glittering across the polished marble like fallen stars.

The sound echoed, final and satisfying, but my chest remained tight. My stomach sank into a cold, gnawing void. And then came the sobs; raw, uninvited, ripping their way out of me. Tears blurred my vision as I gasped for breath, the kind of crying that left no room for pride. A sharp sting pulled my gaze downward. A sliver of glass had cut the flesh along my palm, and I watched numbly as crimson drops splattered to the floor like tiny red spiders, staining the white stone.

I was interrupted by the sound of creaking hinges. The door edged open, hesitantly. A pair of wide brown eyes peeked in, filled with concern.

"Princess?" a soft voice asked. "Are you... all right?"

I wiped at my face quickly, as if that could erase the evidence. "I'm okay..." I muttered, though my voice betrayed the lie. I squinted, studying her features. She was familiar in a way that sent a jolt through my spine.

"Excuse me," I asked, swallowing thickly. "What was your name again?"

"Oh! It's June, Princess," she said with a bright, practiced curtsy. Her voice held a lilting sweetness, and she looked as though she was trying not to intrude. "I've been assigned to you since last season."

June had been my maid in my past life as well. She had been a constant shadow at my side, one of the few who never expected anything of me except that I be well. A little scattered, a little too quick to trust, but her heart had always been kind. Honest. I hadn't relied on her much back then, too afraid that even the smallest dependency would tip the scales of my righteousness. Saints were meant to suffer. To endure in solitude. And so I kept my distance.

She didn't remember me, of course. Not the way I remembered her. And how could she? This was my second beginning. My curse to carry.

Her eyes flashed to my still bleeding palm, widening as she pulled my hand into hers. "Oh no! You're hurt!" She exclaimed, wrapping a thin piece of cloth around my wound. "Don't worry, we'll get this cleaned up before the party tonight—"

"What day is it, June?" I asked as I felt a sting of fear strike.

She blinked, clearly unsettled. "It's your twentieth name day, Your Highness."

Of course it was. My stomach churned as I sat in the soft quiet, haunted by the echo of a day I had already lived. In my first life, this had been the moment everything shifted. I remembered the stir of excitement that had filled the castle; the fluttering gossip, the rush of servants, the way the walls themselves seemed to buzz with promise.

The cavalry from Etheria would arrive that evening, unannounced and uninvited. They were a symbol of grandeur, of peace between two kingdoms. A gesture of courtship.

They would never ask to speak with me. Not once. They met with my mother behind closed doors, whispering things I wasn't meant to hear. I remembered the way she had emerged from that meeting, her expression unreadable, her smile tight. She'd told me the prince was enchanted by my reputation, that this was my fate. That he had chosen me. And I, the naïve idiot that I had been, would accept, thinking it was a fairytale come true. Instead, it had been the beginning of a nightmare, one that ended with me locked in a tower on my wedding day, forever waiting to meet the charming Prince.

"Princess?" June's voice broke through my thoughts like a soft knock on a locked door.

I looked her up and down. "Help me up, June."

She did without hesitation, slipping her arms beneath mine and guiding me carefully around the shards of broken glass scattered across the floor. I leaned into her for balance, more than I needed to, maybe. But the anchoring presence of another person helped calm the static in my head. She settled me gently into the cushioned seat at my dressing table before scurrying to the door. I heard her whisper something quickly to the other maids, and within moments, a quiet flurry of brooms and hushed voices filled the corners of the room as the mess was swept away.

June returned to my side, brushing through my hair with practiced fingers. She worked with care and intention, her hands gentle but efficient, easing each knot as though they were fragile antiques. I let my eyes close for a moment, surrendering to the simple rhythm of it. For the first time since waking in this strange new-old world, I felt calm. Or close to it.

She had done this for me before, in my first life. But back then, I'd barely spoken to her. I kept my distance, afraid to grow close to anyone who might make me form some sort of attachment. Afraid that forming bonds would weaken me. And when I was taken from the palace, when I was locked away and left to rot, she had vanished from my life without even a goodbye. I'd often wondered what became of her, if she missed me, or if she ever thought of me at all.

Now, watching her fuss over my hair with that same innocent focus, I felt the ache of that wasted closeness. I hadn't known her before. But I could. This time could be different. This time, I could choose who stood beside me. And gods knew, I needed someone. Someone who wasn't wrapped in prophecy, politics, or royal schemes. Just a girl with a good heart and kind hands.

"What do you think makes someone a saint?" I asked suddenly, my voice too sharp in the quiet. June startled slightly, the brush pausing mid-stroke.

"A saint? Why would you ask such a silly thing?" she said with a breathless laugh, as if the question had come from nowhere.

I shrugged, eyes drifting back to the mirror. "I've been thinking about what I want to do with my life."

June giggled again, a musical sound that filled the room with a warmth I hadn't expected. She was young for a maid, barely a few years older than me, and sometimes spoke with such wonder it made her seem younger still. But there was something in her that drew me in, a lightness I hadn't let myself be near in my former life.

She was technically my attendant, but more of a ghost flitting about the edges of my world. I hadn't asked much of her, hadn't dared invite joy or connection into my days. After my engagement, they took everything from me. Every pleasure, every friend, every tether to the person I was. And June had been one of the first to disappear from my side.

"And you're thinking sainthood is the right fit?" she questioned, working out a particularly tough knot. "Why not marry someone? Maybe even a prince?"

"I think I'm fated to," I muttered, shifting in my chair and gazing out the window.

My mother had cultivated a massive, twisting rose garden in the palace yard. Each bush meticulously maintained, the flowers had become more precious to her than her own children. Each flower had begun to lose its blooms as the crisp fall air was creeping in.

My name day would mark the beginning of the harvest, typically an event that would be filled with excitement and feasts. Mother would be in mourning as she would watch each petal fall until winter claimed her last beautiful flower.

"Abstinence from worldly pleasures," I muttered. June flashed a puzzled expression.

"What was that?" She asked.

"That's what I heard makes a Saint. You know, no drinking, or gambling, or indulging, and especially no sex…"

June's face flashed red as she began nervously speeding up her pace. "Princess, you shouldn't be saying such things!"

I pursed my lips as I continued my personal contemplation. It couldn't just be abstinence that made a saint. Sacrifice, selflessness, a true, pure soul, all allowed the goddess's divine powers to manifest within myself. In my past life, I'd been forced to give up everything: wine, intimacy, my own desires to uphold this divine ideal. And where had it gotten me? Right back here.

Well, not this time.

The seasons wouldn't be the only thing changing. I would not become another withered rose in my mother's garden, falling to the dirt when the frost hit. No, not this time. I knew better, I knew more, I knew what was to become of me if I didn't grow thorns.

"Would you like me to leave so you can get dressed?" June asked, pulling out a dull blue gown and linen chemise. I stared at the muted fabrics with disdain. In my past life, my mother insisted that I not dress in excess as it could taint my purity. As I inspected the cheap woven fabric, I couldn't help but think even this dress was more extravagant than I had when I became a Saint. I shuddered at the thought of another scratchy linen robe touching my skin.

"Everything alright?" June inquired as she made her way to the door.

I saw it, just the flicker of memory, her past self in my mind, leaning against the laundry basin with her sleeves rolled up, chatting with the other maids. Back then, I'd overheard her complaining about how boring it was to serve a princess who wore the same lifeless dresses day in and day out. I hadn't been offended. I'd taken it as the price of humility. Now, I realize it was a missed opportunity.

"June, how would you feel about helping me dress from now on?" I asked.

A quizzical expression crossed her face "Is this a question, Princess?"

I sucked in a deep breath as I straightened my composure. I needed to be strong, I needed to be a commanding presence, and make my desires a reality.

"June," I said, turning from the window with a new sense of purpose. "I'd like you to buy me a new dress for tonight."

Her eyes lit up with the start of a smile. "New? I know Fedor's just got in some brown silks, if you're wanting something simple for the evening—"

"I'm going to need something a bit more *groundbreaking* than brown silk." I tilted my head slightly, watching her face as I chose my next words carefully. "Is this a task you'd be able to handle?"

June blinked once, then twice, before her face broke into pure, gleeful elation. "Princess, I can absolutely handle it. How much ground are we wanting to break here?"

I tried to summon the fashion of the time, combing my mind for something that would stand out, something the court would remember for weeks, not days. "Tell me," I said slowly, "Is Lady Laces still in business?"

June froze. For a second, I thought she'd faint. "Lady Laces?" she echoed, her voice hushed with reverence. "But their gowns are so... extravagant."

I smiled, letting a wry curve pull at the corner of my mouth. "Exactly. I want the flashiest, most absurdly lavish gown you think I can pull off. Jewels, corsetry, layers, everything. I plan to make a scene tonight."

June's jaw dropped. She blinked at me like I'd grown wings. "Are you sure? You aren't worried you'll attract the *wrong* kind of attention?"

I turned to her fully, placing both hands on her shoulders, my voice low and charged with a fire she had yet to see from me. "That's exactly the kind of attention I'm after, June."

Her brows shot up. I could see the questions forming in her head, but she didn't ask them. She didn't need to. I was already planning my next move. If the gods thought they could drop me into this world and expect me to follow the same script, they were sorely mistaken.

"I have some very specific plans for my future, starting today," I said softly.

June tilted her head, equal parts confused and amazed. "And what exactly are those plans, Princess?"

I leaned in, letting my voice drop into a conspiratorial whisper. "To leave every noble in that ballroom wondering when I became a girl worth whispering about."

June burst into delighted laughter, her eyes lit with excitement as she clutched the hem of her skirt. "Ooh, this is going to be fun."

I watched her skip from the room, then turned back to the mirror, steeling myself against what was to come.

Tonight, the game would begin. But first things first, I would do whatever I could to prevent my engagement to the Prince.

Chapter 2

W ith June off on her grand fashion quest, I decided it was time to indulge in something I hadn't tasted in what felt like a century, pleasure. Per my request, my private dining hall, typically quiet and austere, had been transformed into a banquet fit for a coronation.

Sunlight filtered through stained glass windows, painting the walls with kaleidoscopic hues as silver trays gleamed and porcelain plates steamed with freshly prepared delicacies. I had given the kitchens free rein; no limitations, no diet, no pious restrictions. Just opulence. The table sagged under the weight of it all.

A golden roasted duck, lacquered in apricot glaze, sat at the center like a crowned jewel, surrounded by a battalion of savory dishes: tender pork loin wrapped in herbs and garlic butter, roasted quail dressed in wine reduction, honeyed carrots with candied walnuts, and a whole baked trout resting atop a bed of fragrant wild rice and citrus slices. Bowls of velvety mashed potatoes were garnished with sprigs of rosemary and drizzled with cream. Fresh loaves of bread. Crusty, warm, and steaming, they were stacked beside ramekins of whipped butter, fig jam, and lavender honey.

However, it was the desserts that truly made my mouth water. A tower of pastries filled with spiced custard and glazed with rose-water icing stood like a sugary obelisk. There were lemon tarts with delicate sugar lattices, ruby-red cherry clafoutis, frosted short-cakes bursting with cream, and a shimmering bowl of spun sugar and violets so artful I hesitated to disturb it. And in the center of it all, the cake.

It was white, but far from plain. No, this was a cloud of vanilla sponge soaked in sweet milk and covered in whipped cream, petals of edible gold leaf pressed along the frosting. The scent alone near-ly brought tears to my eyes. The last time I tasted anything like this, I had been a bride-to-be. A Saint-in-waiting. A fool.

My stomach growled so loudly I feared it might echo through the corridor. By the time the staff finished arranging the final touches, silver cutlery, linen napkins embroidered with the royal crest, and fresh violets strewn across the table, I could feel the eyes of every maid and footman watching me from the shadows. They were confused, fascinated, maybe even horrified. Let them be.

I gripped my fork like a weapon, stabbed a chunk of pork, and took my first bite. The flavor exploded across my tongue, savory, smoky, tender beyond belief. I let out an involuntary moan and leaned back, closing my eyes. It wasn't just food. It was freedom. I had spent the last fifty years of my previous life surviving on stale bread, watery porridge, and cold soup. But this—this was life returning to my body one mouthful at a time.

I devoured a slice of duck next, its crispy skin crackling between my teeth, and chased it with a buttery potato and a generous spoonful of fig compote. I didn't care that I looked like a woman possessed. My mouth was full, my eyes watering, and I had never felt so alive.

I reached for the quail and sank my teeth into the leg like a starved beast. The juices ran down my chin, and I wiped them with the back of my hand, unbothered by decorum. And of course, it was at that exact moment I heard her voice.

"Are you... Alright?"

I froze. The quail leg dangled from my mouth, my hands glistening with the juices from my chin. Slowly, like a criminal caught mid-heist, I turned toward the door.

Standing there, her eyes wide as saucers and her freckled face flushed with confusion, was my sister.

"Margaret..." I breathed, rising to my feet.

She hovered in the doorway like she wasn't sure if she was allowed in. Her sage dress hung awkwardly from her shoulders, a hand-me-down that someone haphazardly altered for her. The resemblance between us was undeniable; those sharp chartreuse eyes, that curious, guarded expression. But the rest of her was all Father. Auburn curls, olive skin, patchy freckles, a jaw too serious for a girl of thirteen.

She had a quiet demeanor that held its own charm. Through no fault of her own, she looked like any ordinary girl; there was not a hint of royalty to her air. While our Mother spent our childhood grooming me to be the perfect bride, Margaret's own developments were tossed aside in favor of my own grandeur. With that, I was kept away from her as well, forced to only pay her an occasional glance as we would pass each other in the halls, or a courteous nod at the dinners we sometimes shared.

It wasn't until my tenth and final year in confinement that I was told of my sweet sister's fate. The Etherian empire had executed not just her but the entire Calbraxian royal court in a show of force. I had never gotten to say goodbye.

In that moment, her meek voice sounded like a raging boom in the overcrowded dining hall. There was so much I wanted to say to her, so many emotions that clung to me like a second skin.

"I was just absolutely famished." I finally mustered, plastering a convincing smile on my face. "Would you care to join me, Margaret?"

Her eyes widened as she took in the spread across the table. Her gaze fell upon a platter of sweet treats that were delicately decorated in stunning pastel shades.

"Are you sure?" Her soft voice cracked as she took another step into the room.

I smiled, gracefully gliding to her side and squeezing her hand tightly. "Of course, my dear, you can have whatever your heart wishes."

Margaret's eyes flashed with excitement as she shuffled to the seat across from me. She sat sturdy and tall in the massive leather chair that swallowed her. She didn't speak, just started at the beautiful spread in front of her, unsure where to begin.

"Please get my sister a plate, would you?" I asked, glaring down at the still vigilant staff.

As if they hadn't realized their own wandering eyes, they all snapped back to work. The chef left the hall, as a man I believed to be called Wilbur helped put together a dish for her.

I set my fork down and rested my chin on my hand, quietly studying the girl across from me. She matched my gaze for only a heartbeat before her eyes darted down to her undisturbed meal, cheeks warming as if she'd been caught stealing something.

"It's going to be quite the party tonight." I hummed, more to test the waters than start a conversation.

Her head snapped up. I knew I had attracted her attention.

"I'm sure it will be grand," Margaret mused, finally picking up her fork and waving it dangerously as she spoke.

"Dancing, music, all the food..." I slid a plate of fresh pastries her way. She eyed it, for only a second, but didn't touch them.

"I heard my Governess talking about it. She said the Prince of Etheria might show up."

I winced at the mention, forcing a pleasant smile. Beneath her skepticism, I could sense something deeper. Longing, fear, and the kind of loneliness I remembered all too well.

"Well, if the prince does show up, I'm sure he'll spare you a dance," I offered, gently.

She twirled her fork in her hands, lips pressed into a thin line. "No, I'm not allowed at the party." The words came out small, like she'd already fought this battle and lost.

"Why can't you?" I asked, leaning forward.

Margaret wrinkled her nose. "Because I'm too young, and the Queen says I must be presented formally at my own name day celebration before I'm allowed to attend such events."

The vulnerability in her eyes nudged something inside me, something buried beneath armor I'd worn for far too long. Gone were the days when I could afford to be cruel or distant simply because it was easier.

"Don't worry, Margaret," I said softly, setting my fork down. "You'll have your time. And when it comes, I promise I'll be there for you."

She blinked, surprised, her fork hovering uncertainly above her plate. "I don't mean to sound rude," she began, hesitating, "but why are you being so nice to me? I can't remember the last time you spoke more than ten words to me. And now suddenly..." she gestured to me, "this."

The question was gentle, but it hit like a blade sliding between ribs. My stomach twisted, and I regretted how impulsively I had eaten, even more how impulsively I had spoken. To me, it had been fifty years of distance and grief. To her, I was simply a sister who woke up one morning and began acting like a stranger wearing her face.

I inhaled slowly, trying to steady the trembling in my chest. "I—" My voice cracked, and I swallowed hard. "The truth is... I don't know how much time I have left in the palace. I'm of marrying age now, and the thought of leaving here—leaving *you*—without so much as a word..."

I cleared my throat, recomposing myself. "I thought if I distanced myself it would be easier to leave you. I thought being hardened meant being strong. But all I did was push everyone who cared about me away." I forced myself to meet her eyes. "I don't want to make that mistake with you. Not again. Not anymore."

Margaret watched me as if unsure whether to believe me. She was so young, so bright and full of life, and she had no reason to trust a sister who had always been an absence more than a presence. "You promise?"

"Cross my heart," I said with a smile. "And in the mean time, let's make a deal. After tonight's party, I'll tell you everything that happened. Every scandal, every dance, every terrible fashion choice."

"What do you want in return?" She demanded.

"I would like you to join me for dinner. Not just tomorrow but as long as I'm here in this palace. Deal?"

Margaret's brows crushed together, but despite her confusion I could sense the relief, as if she'd been offered shelter she could never ask for herself. "Really?"

"I swear it."

There was a beat of silence before a grin spread across her face. "You have a deal!" She exclaimed, leaning back with a satisfaction that felt foreign and heartbreakingly young. "But only if you promise you'll dance with the Prince if he arrives. I would die to hear the story."

For the first time in this second life, I felt a flicker of a changed fate. This time, I wouldn't take Margaret for granted. I would be the sister she deserved, the protector she needed.

She finally started on her plate, the knife screeched against the porcelain as she cut into a thick piece of quail. The shrill sent a shiver drawling down my spine.

"I promise Margaret."

"Your highness," we both jumped as Wilbur slunk back into the dining room. "Your presence is being requested by the Queen."

I stood and shared a glance with Margaret. She smiled and bowed her head as if telling me it was okay to leave her alone. I flashed her a smile.

"We will have a lot to catch up on tomorrow," I stated, a grin spread across her face as I started leaving the room.

"We most certainly will."

As I traversed the palace halls for the first time in my new life, I was struck by how breathtakingly beautiful everything was. The very walls seemed to glow beneath the sunlight pouring through stained glass windows, casting kaleidoscopic reflections onto the marble floors. Every gilded sconce, every ornamental pillar, every silk-draped window whispered of luxury, tradition, and the kind of power that once surrounded me like perfume.

I had walked these halls hundreds, no thousands, of times in my youth. But never like this. Never with the sharp ache of memory curling in my chest.

The last time I'd seen the palace, it had been in ruins. Smoke-stained walls, shattered windows, and blood on the stairs. The once shining chandeliers had been shattered, and tapestries that once bore the sigil of Calbraxia had hung torn and blackened by fire. The war had spared nothing. Not even the marble floors, which had cracked from cannon fire and echoed with the screams of the dying. Once freed from my tower, I got to witness it all. My kingdom, my home, was reduced to rubble while I was kept caged and forgotten.

But now, now it was like stepping into a dream half remembered. The polished floors reflected my footsteps like ripples on still water. Ornate portraits of ancestors I barely remembered lined the corridor, their regal expressions silently judging me as I passed. Velvet runners stretched across the floor in rich shades of cinnamon and emerald, muffling the quiet clack of my slippers. The scent of lavender and beeswax polish lingered in the air, familiar and comforting in a way that made my throat tighten.

My wing of the palace had always been far from my mother's by design, I now realized. As a girl, I used to think it was simply for privacy. Now, with the clarity of hindsight, I saw it for what it was: distance. Political, emotional, and intentional.

I turned a corner and paused, taking in the long stretch of hallway that led to the queen's chambers. The walls here were quieter, the bustle of servants fading behind me, replaced by a hush reserved for royalty. I had walked this path many times before, my steps careful, my dress smoothed just so. Out of the desire to impress a woman who rarely showed emotion beyond the gentle arch of a brow.

I used to rehearse conversations in my head, imagining how I might charm her, surprise her, maybe even make her laugh. But Queen Eleanor had always been reserved, elegant in her silences, measured in her praise. I never felt unloved, just distant from her, like a painting hung in a hallway I was meant to admire from afar.

Still, this was different. This time, I wasn't a child hoping for a kind word or subtle nod of approval. I was no longer the girl being shaped by her mother's expectations; I was a woman with memories far too heavy for a twenty-year-old heart. So I straightened my spine and stepped forward. I was here for a purpose. And no gilded memory could stop me now.

When I finally reached the queen's chambers, the door was open, sunlight streaming through the grand archway like an invitation laced with warning. Inside, everything was exactly as I remembered. No, *better* than I remembered.

The Queen's receiving room was an immaculate vision of elegance. White marble gleamed underfoot, veined with delicate silver lines that shimmered like starlight. Tall windows arched toward the ceiling, letting golden sunlight pour in and warm the pearl colored furnishings. The air smelled faintly of roses and old parchment, the scent of power, the scent of my mother.

Queen Eleanor sat at a delicate round table made of carved ivory, her posture as perfect as ever. A porcelain tea set, painted with blue irises and trimmed in gold, sat untouched before her. The spread of finger sandwiches was arranged so artfully that it looked more like a still-life painting than a meal.

She looked up, her expression unreadable, her face as composed as a statue.

"Silvia, dear," she said warmly as I stepped into the room. She picked up her cup of tea and gestured for me to sit. Her smile was genuine, her eyes soft with affection. "Happy name day. You look radiant today."

"Thank you, your Majesty," I replied, curtseying softly before taking my seat. The warmth in her tone rested my racing heart.

I couldn't remember the last time I had truly seen my mother, beyond the symbol of royalty. Her presence was just as regal as I remembered, wrapped in a soft lavender brocade that shimmered in the light streaming through the high, arched windows. Her raven hair was neatly swept back in her signature style, not a strand out of place. The air hung thick between us, triggering a strange ache of nostalgia deep in my chest.

For a moment, I wanted to step closer, to rest my head on her shoulder like I had when I was very young. But I didn't. We weren't that kind of mother and daughter. Not exactly. There had always been love between us, just not the kind that bloomed openly.

She poured me a cup of tea with effortless grace, her movements as refined as they had been in my childhood. "Tonight's celebration is going to be lovely," she said with a faint smile. "The musicians have been practicing since dawn, and I've had the garden lit with lanterns. It will be just as you deserve."

My fingers curled around the delicate teacup, letting the heat soak into my palms. I inhaled the calming scent of honey and lavender and forced a smile. "Thank you. That means a great deal to me."

For a moment, there was peace. The kind only tea and quiet could bring. But then I saw it; the subtle tension in her shoulders, the flicker of thought behind her gaze.

"Silvia," she said gently, "I received word this morning. The crown prince of Etheria has sent an envoy. He likely wishes to discuss a marriage proposal."

I lifted my cup again to mask my reaction. So it's begun. As I suspected, she didn't yet know that the prince himself wouldn't be coming. In her eyes, this was a diplomatic possibility, one full of hope, not certainty.

"So," she continued, voice light but careful, "They requested a private audience with me, they should arrive before your party.

The prince is a promising match. Educated, well-positioned, and decent, by all accounts. Plus, I hear the Etherian Delegation has been antsy to announce him as King since his Father's passing last year, but they refuse to do so without an engagement. This could mean great things for Calbraxia."

"I see," I said, placing the teacup back on its saucer with steady hands. "It's a lot to consider."

In my past life, I agreed to the opportunity right away, not that I had much choice. I had been groomed to say yes. This was what I had been bred for, as a woman. We were bargaining tools, meant to provide heirs and possibilities for the men. This time, I knew better. I hoped I would be able to trick my mother into realizing this as well.

She looked at me, searching my expression. "I know it's sudden. But it's an honor, Silvia. Truly. And one thing your father and I never dared to dream of for our daughters. This kind of union, it could secure peace for generations."

I nodded slowly. "I understand what it means for the kingdom, I do. But, Mother, I wonder, would it be wrong to hope for a little more time? To meet other suitors, perhaps? I've only been out in society for what, two years? I would like to make sure this is truly what's best, not just for Calbraxia, but for me as well."

Her brows drew together slightly, in concern. "You've always been thoughtful," she said, her voice soft. "But this kind of opportunity may not come twice. I would hate to see you wait and lose something that could be undeniably exceptional."

"Of course," I said gently. "I only ask for the chance to explore. To know my own heart before I give it away. Don't you think that's fair?"

There was a brief pause as she studied her teacup, her fingers tracing the rim in slow circles. "I do want you to be happy, Silvia," she said after a beat. "But happiness and duty don't always come hand in hand. Sometimes we make sacrifices, and in time, we grow to find joy in them."

"What if I never find that joy?" I asked, unintentionally letting the words slip.

She gracefully set her cup down, placing her hand on my own. "You will, even if it's a joy you create yourself."

I nodded, masking the growing tension in my chest. "I appreciate your honesty, Mother. And I promise, I'll be gracious tonight. But if the prince doesn't propose," I asked casually, "would I be free to consider other offers?"

Her gaze flicked up, slightly amused. "We have a quarter of the Etherian army camping in our garden. What makes you think he won't?"

I offered a small shrug, a smile tugging at my lips. "Just a thought. If this evening ends differently than expected, I'd like to know I still have options."

She chuckled under her breath. "We'll discuss it after the celebration. For now, go enjoy your afternoon. You've earned it."

"Thank you, Mother. For always thinking of me."

She gave me one of her rare, gentle smiles. "That's my girl. Tonight will be special, I can feel it."

She twisted her gaze elsewhere, out toward the garden where her prized roses bloomed in careful, symmetrical rows. The soft clink of her fingernail tracing the edge of her porcelain teacup filled the silence. That gesture, absentminded and measured, had always signaled the end of a conversation. Still, I remained seated for a beat longer, hoping that somewhere behind her calm exterior, my words had struck a nerve. That maybe, just maybe, she might think twice.

I stood and offered a final curtsy, then turned to leave her chambers, the weight of our exchange settling like a stone in my chest. But as I walked out of the room and stepped into the corridor, a strange thing happened. I didn't feel hopeless. Instead, my heart fluttered with something new. Something dangerous and exhilarating.

Hope.

Maybe she would hear me. Maybe she would take a moment to consider my future not just as a strategic asset, but as her daughter. Maybe, with a bit of gentle resistance, I could sway her.

But even if she didn't, I had no intention of surrendering. The queen may have held the illusion of control, but I had something she didn't: fifty years of hindsight, scars she'd never seen, and a heart that had once been ripped apart by the very future she now tried to shape again.

Not this time.

If she wanted a daughter who would sacrifice herself on an altar of diplomacy, she was fifty years too late. That version of me had died long ago, on a cold night, wearing a white dress, waiting for a wedding that would never come.

I stepped through the sun-drenched halls of the palace with a strange lightness in my chest. This time, I would not walk willingly into a gilded cage. I would run wild before they ever tried to lock the doors. I would find myself a husband, a suitable one, of my own choosing, before the prince could propose. Someone willing to take what the gods had kept locked away. Someone who would be willing to do what I had been too afraid to in my past life. It wouldn't be for love or for lust. This was for freedom.

Tonight, however, I would taste pleasure, scandal, and power; things the old Silvia had been too afraid to reach for.

Let the party begin.

Chapter 3

The ballroom glittered like a dream spun from gold and glass. Hundreds of candles danced in their chandeliers high above, their flames casting soft halos of light across every polished surface. Musicians played a lilting waltz from the raised gallery, their instruments weaving an elegant spell that hovered over the crowd like perfume. Crystal goblets clinked. Laughter echoed beneath the vaulted ceiling. Velvet and silk swept across marble floors in shades of ruby, sapphire, moonlight, and dusk.

And at the center of it all, me.

My name day celebration had drawn nobility from every corner of Calbraxia and beyond. Dukes and duchesses, lords and foreign envoys, all flocked like moths to the promise of politics, gossip, and a glimpse of a soft spoken princess who rarely debuted.

I stood poised at the top of the grand staircase, resplendent in the gown June had chosen for me. She had gone far beyond the expectations of a loyal maid. This was not simply a dress; it was a statement, a challenge, and perhaps even a scandal.

The deep green velvet clung to my figure with audacious confidence, catching the golden light in every fold and curve. Intricate satin ruffles trailed along my hips and fell like liquid over the steps, shifting in hues between emerald, moss, and brass as I moved. The bodice was scandalously low, scattered with pearls and tiny emeralds like drops of dew caught in a spring forest. And in my hair, loose curls pinned back with small golden flowers, June had tucked a single sprig of white alyssum. A symbol of truth. Of worth. Of defiance.

As I descended the staircase, the room fell momentarily silent, breath collectively drawn. Then the gasps came. Soft, sharp, followed by the rustle of bustles and murmurs behind jeweled fans. Whispers swirled like smoke, curling through every corner of the room.

The quiet caterpillar of Calbraxia had shed her chrysalis.

But I didn't falter. I let the weight of a hundred stares press against my skin like sunlight on armor and kept walking, my heels clicking like thunder on the marble.

I made my way to my mother's dais, where she sat like a statue carved from moonlight, her pale hands folded gracefully on her lap. Her expression was unreadable, her lips painted into a soft smile that never reached her eyes.

I curtsied low, the gown pooling around me like spilled ink, and looked up at her through my lashes with a smile far too wicked for a saint. Her gaze flicked over my dress, pausing at the neckline, and then she lifted her cup delicately to her lips.

The smile she returned to me was composed, polished, regal, but I caught the flicker of something else behind it. Uncertainty. Or perhaps amusement. She said nothing, but I could feel the quiet hum of a game being set in motion between us.

As I took my place beside her, the line of well-wishers began to form. One by one, nobles approached with shallow bows and flattering phrases, offering gifts and sickly sweet words of admiration. I met them all with practiced ease, but inside, my thoughts were sharper and more deliberate. Every suitor who crossed my path was silently evaluated for their possible usefulness. Could they help me escape the prince? Could they tempt fate?

And perhaps, just perhaps, could they undo me before the Etherian crown did?

After several minutes, I had begun to sense the ripple I'd created. The glances, the flushed cheeks, the hesitant smiles from men who had never dared look twice at the Princess of Calbraxia. I had been transformed into something else tonight: mysterious, desirable, untouchable yet inviting.

It was then that a baron approached me. Older, silver at the temples, his eyes sharp with experience and edged with mirth. He bowed with flair and offered his hand with a wink that made a few nearby matrons clutch their pearls.

"I would be honored, Princess," he said smoothly, "to claim your first dance. If you're not yet too dizzy from the crowd already."

I tilted my head, pretending to ponder it. I shot a glance at my mother, who softly pursed her lips in disapproval, then slipped my hand into his. "I suppose I can brave a turn."

As he led me to the center of the ballroom, all eyes followed. I couldn't hide my smile.

We spun around the floor. My dancing had never been my strong suit, and this being my first time dancing with a male partner, my movements were stiff. However, his polite conversation was easing the tension in my shoulders.

"You're quite the vision tonight, Princess Silvia," he said, his mustache twitching with amusement. "I daresay half the men here are already vying for your attention."

"And the other half?" I teased, flashing him a coy smile.

"Too intimidated to try."

I laughed, and to my own surprise, the sound that left me was light, genuine. Not forced, not calculated. The ballroom spun gently around me, and for one fleeting moment, I felt like a girl again, not a scheming Princess.

As the dance came to an end, I caught sight of my mother across the ballroom. Her gaze was a blade, sharp, steady, unrelenting. Her spine remained impossibly straight, her chin high, but her lips were drawn in a thin, unreadable line. When our eyes locked, she mouthed something with deliberate precision. I didn't need to hear it to know the word:

The Prince.

A jolt of dread crept up my spine, the sudden cold of reality crashing through my good mood. I turned on my heel before she could summon me and made a beeline for the refreshment table, my skirts sweeping behind me like a cape in flight.

I grabbed the nearest glass, a jewel-toned thing that looked far too pretty to taste decent, and downed it in two gulps. The burn hit the back of my throat like fire.

"Ack!" I coughed, face contorting in disgust.

"Not a fan of wine?" The baron chuckled.

"So that's what wine tastes like?" I muttered, snatching another glass.

I could feel it already, the warmth pooling in my stomach, a bloom of something light and fizzy in my head. I'd never tasted alcohol in my past life. The path of sainthood left no room for indulgence. But that life was gone now. And I had five decades of deprivation to make up for.

A young man approached, no older than I was, draped in a royal blue cape fastened with silver buttons shaped like stars. His eyes sparkled beneath a head of perfectly combed golden curls. He gave me a crooked grin and handed me another glass. I hesitated for half a breath before accepting it. The wine tasted sweeter this time, or maybe I was just too numb to notice the bitterness anymore.

"You seem to be enjoying all the party has to offer," he said, voice like cashmere, low and curling.

"Maybe not quite all of it," I replied, flashing a sly smile as I stole another glass from a passing tray. The server blinked at me but moved on without a word. I raised the rim to my lips with the grace of a princess and the recklessness of a drunk.

The warmth spread from my stomach to my fingertips. My tongue grew looser, my posture more relaxed. The cautious, quiet princess was gone. I flirted with anyone who dared approach, lords with perfectly polished boots, shy knights still smelling of steel and oil, even a sultry court musician who made his lute sing just for me. Every compliment sent a thrill through me. Every stolen glance felt like rebellion. I was intoxicated; in body, in spirit, in every sense that mattered.

I threw my head back laughing at some terrible joke a Marquess had made, and before I realized it, I was surrounded. Men were crowding around like moths drawn to something burning. Plates of sugared fruit and pastries were placed before me, hands eager to please. Every time I lifted an empty glass, another full one replaced it, like magic. I stopped counting after five.

My gaze occasionally shot to my mother, half to see if she had noticed the scene I created, half to ensure the proposal hadn't snuck under the radar. Luckily, she still sat alone, an observer of this careless new façade I was displaying.

My cheeks ached from smiling. My head swam. I danced until the soles of my feet throbbed and my curls fell loose around my face. A kind baron (whose name I didn't bother to learn) brought me a velvet-cushioned chair when my legs gave out, and I sank into it like a queen drunk on her own court.

I leaned back and tilted my head to the ceiling. The chandeliers above me sparkled like constellations I could pluck from the sky. The music slowed, then rose again, blurring into something that wrapped around my ears like chiffon.

I held up my glass. Empty. Again.

It was gone almost instantly, exchanged for another, the stem nestled between my fingers like it belonged there. Someone leaned in and said something, and I laughed, maybe too loudly. I didn't catch what they said. I didn't care.

There was a reason I had started drinking, I knew that, but it was fuzzy now, buried beneath layers of honeyed wine and silken words. I tried to reach for the thought, but it slipped further away with every sip.

All I knew in that moment was that I felt free. Unbound, alive, mine.

Then, I saw it. The familiar uniform that made my blood run cold. The crimson red velvet symbolized the color they spilled on the battlefield. The gilded tassels that embodied their wealth. The emblem of a shield showcasing their strength. Entering from a corner of the room was an Etherian guard.

And just like that, the world around me began to collapse.

The wine, which had dulled the edges of my thoughts all evening, now turned against me, blurring the lines between memory and reality. The cheerful music warped, souring into a discordant din in my ears. The laughter of courtiers twisted into screams, into battle cries. The clinking of goblets became the clang of swords, the whistle of arrows, the heavy thud of metal meeting flesh.

The ballroom flickered. And I was no longer in Calbraxia.

I was back on the battlefield, mud-caked, soaked in blood that wasn't mine, hands shaking as I clutched a broken shield. The stench of death and fire clung to my skin like a second cloak. I could hear the ragged, panicked breaths of soldiers around me, some younger than I was now.

Then...him.

I remembered the Etherian knight, young, draped in armor that clearly was too big for him. His eyes were wide with terror, locked on mine as a beam of divine light shot straight through his gut. It had punched through his armor like parchment, blood bubbling from his lips as he collapsed to his knees. He hadn't even screamed, just gasped, a wet, gurgling sound, like a fish pulled from the water. I'd watched him die. No, I *killed* him.

His body hit the dirt with a sound I could still hear in my dreams.

When I blinked, I was back in the ballroom. My chest began to seize. My breath came shallow, erratic, as if my lungs no longer remembered how to pull in air. The crowd, once warm and glittering, now felt like a cage. My heart pounded against my ribs, wild and primal. I clutched the arms of the chair, fingernails biting into the velvet, trying to ground myself. Trying to breathe. Trying to stay.

"Your Highness, are you alright?" someone asked near me. Their voice was muffled, distant, like it was coming from underwater.

"You look quite ill," another said.

"They're here..." I whispered, my voice too faint for anyone but myself. My eyes locked on the Etherian guard, and the memory of that boy dying in front of me wrapped its fingers around my throat. "They're here."

Panic churned in my gut like poison. I could feel it spreading through my limbs, making my fingers tremble and my knees weak. I raised a quivering hand to my face, wiping away the cold sweat that now dotted my brow and upper lip. My vision tunneled; too many lights, too many eyes, too much red.

"I need air," I muttered, barely coherent. My voice sounded foreign to my own ears.

A swarm of hands surrounded me, trying to help. Too many, too close.

"Do you need help, dear?" a concerned noblewoman asked, reaching for me.

"No," I rasped, shaking my head frantically. "No. Please, I need to go."

I scanned the room like a trapped animal, searching for an exit, any exit. The walls felt like they were closing in, and I couldn't get a full breath. My skirts tangled at my ankles as I stumbled forward, gripping the edge of a nearby table to steady myself.

I had to get out. Away from the guard, away from the music, away from the ghosts clawing their way out of my mind.

The party could go on. Let them dance, let them toast. But I had seen war. I had lived it. And no amount of wine or velvet could ever erase the blood that still lingered in my memory.

Hundreds of faces turned toward me, their laughter dimming into murmurs, then silence. A wave of heat surged to my face as panic prickled up my spine. The eyes that I was desperate for were now rebelling against me. I spotted a narrow gap between two tall noblemen and a fluttering line of courtiers, a path to the terrace doors, and darted for it, my skirts swishing furiously around my legs.

Voices called after me. Some with concern, others with idle curiosity. A few just wanted to gossip.

"Your Highness!"

"Princess, wait—"

I didn't stop. I couldn't stop.

Their voices, their reaching hands, all of it blurred into a haze. I shoved past shoulders, dodged flapping sleeves, and ignored the startled gasps and mutters. I saw lips forming questions. What's wrong? Is she ill? But the blood in my ears roared too loudly to hear the words.

And then, *thud.*

I collided with a pair of dancers spinning too close to my path. I stumbled, my heel catching on someone's shoe, and fell to one knee with a painful jolt. The sharp sound of tearing fabric split the air. I glanced down, mortified, to see a long, opulent piece of my velvet gown trailing behind me like a discarded curtain. Leaving my skin exposed just above my thigh.

June was going to kill me.

Heat bloomed under my skin, fury, embarrassment, desperation. I forced myself upright, brushing off helping hands as I tried to regain what little dignity I had left. All eyes were on me. Not as a princess. Not as a poised future queen. But as a trembling, wide-eyed girl, barely holding herself together.

I burst through the terrace doors.

The cool night air slammed into me like a slap, stinging my cheeks and drying the sweat clinging to my brow. I stumbled forward, bracing myself against the marble railing, gasping like I'd been drowning. My chest heaved with each ragged breath, but the tightness refused to release. I could still feel the eyes on me, still hear the phantom sounds of battle behind the music. My throat burned from the effort to keep the scream buried inside.

But then, I heard laughter. Drifting toward the terrace from inside. Bright. Silvery. Oblivious. No. They couldn't see me, not like this.

I spun on my heel and dashed down the wide terrace stairs, my hands lifting my tattered gown to keep from tripping again. Somewhere along the way, I tore off what was left of the ruined hem, letting the velvet fall like shed skin behind me. My new image lay crumpled on the terrace steps.

By the time I reached the garden's edge, I was shaking all over. I collapsed onto the cold stone bench tucked beneath a hedge, but it wasn't enough. I slid to the ground, curling into myself, arms wrapped tightly around my knees as I tried to contain the explosion that churned inside me.

I was unraveling, coming apart at the seams.

My pulse thundered in my ears. The weight of my dress felt suffocating, the bodice digging into my ribs like armor I could no longer bear. My nails dug into the fabric at my elbows as my entire body trembled with the force of keeping myself from screaming. I couldn't cry, not here, not now, but the urge burned in my chest like acid.

"Not now," I whispered as I rocked in place. "Please, not now."

But the images were back. The sound of that young soldier gasping for breath, the blood that soaked the earth, the cries that never left me.

I wanted to claw the memories out of my mind.

I wanted to disappear.

Instead, a voice rang through the night air, taking me by surprise. "You're breathing too fast."

T he voice was calm, steady, and unfamiliar. I turned, my vision swimming, to see a man stepping out of the shadows.

He was striking. So much so that for a moment, I forgot how to breathe again. His skin caught the moonlight in a way that made him appear otherworldly. He glowed of deep bronze and burnished gold, as if the sun had kissed him even in the dark. His hair was thick, and swept neatly back, a few strands curling rebelliously around his brow. A sweet sandy blonde that only comes from the heat of Etheria. But it was his eyes that stole the breath right from my lungs, warm honey, almost gilded, sharp as blades, but not cold. They watched me with a kind of steady curiosity, as if he knew I was on the brink of shattering.

He was tall, far taller than I was as he towered over me even if I were standing. My eyes instinctively dropped lower, taking note of his wide frame and tree trunk like arms. He wasn't just handsome, he was *strong*. It was then that I noticed the uniform he was dawning. The blood-red velvet clung to his powerful frame, trimmed with gold thread and bearing the unmistakable insignia of the Etherian elite confirmed my fears. The Prince had sent his men, and one was standing right in front of me.

My stomach churned, and I felt the beginnings of another dizzy spell. The red. *That* red. I could still see it staining the mud, soaking the ground, clinging to the bodies that never rose again.

I let out a soft whimper, but he didn't try to console me. He didn't crowd me, didn't speak. He simply crouched down in front of me, his movements fluid, graceful, impossibly controlled. His face was only inches from mine now, and I could feel the heat of him in the cool night air. He smelled of leather, pine, and something earthy like the faint scent of freshly picked sage.

"Focus on me," he said, voice low and smooth, the kind of sound that settles in the chest more than the ears. "Breathe in for four counts, hold for four, out for four." He took in a deep inhale, counting on his fingers before releasing. "Just like that. Can you do it?"

I nodded, blinking slowly, trying to match the measured rise and fall of his chest. I followed his rhythm like a lifeline, forcing air into my lungs, holding it there, then releasing it with a shudder. Again. Again.

"Focus on what you can, count each blade of grass you see in your head." He continued his breathing.

The panic slowly began to loosen its grip. The ground beneath me felt real again. Solid. My heartbeat settled from a frenzied gallop to a manageable pace. I let my shoulders drop and let go of the breath I'd been strangling inside me.

"Thank you," I whispered, my voice rough. "I-I don't know what that was. I think I almost exploded."

A soft chuckle rumbled from his chest. "If I didn't know any better I'd have thought you had just seen war."

He didn't know how right he was.

"Worse," I muttered, staring back at the palace. "A royal ball."

I looked up, blinking more from the haze of wine than tears now, and saw him still crouched, his warm smile disarming. His hand extended toward mine like an invitation. I hesitated only for a second before placing my fingers into his palm.

His grip was firm, anchoring me steadily to him as he lifted me effortlessly to my feet. The moment I stood, I felt the cool breeze brush against my now very exposed legs.

"Well, it looks like there *was* a battle." He noted dryly, motioning to the shredded velvet hanging unevenly around my thighs. "Your dress must have been a casualty?"

I glanced down at myself and cackled.

"Good riddance," I slurred, wobbling as I shot a kick towards the scattered remains of my gown. My foot caught air instead, and I tripped, again. This time, he caught me, one strong arm sliding around my waist, pulling me snug against him.

"Easy does it," he said softly.

That sent me into a fit of giggles. Something about his calmness only made my drunken state feel *funnier*, not more shameful. He didn't flinch as I laughed into his shoulder. His body was as hard as iron, but his grip was gentle, like he knew how easily he could break me.

His hands were massive, engulfing my waist. He shifted his hands up to my shoulders, his fingertips brushed against the bare skin above the velvet. My heart skipped. My thoughts spun faster than my head.

"What's your name?" I asked, breathless, still giggling, but the curiosity was genuine.

"Sagar," he replied, his voice still that same even, unshakable tone.

"And the getup, you know you're in the wrong kingdom right?"

I saw a smile crack across his face, fiendish and wicked. "Well, I'm the head knight of the Etherian army, I kind of have to dress the part."

The name fell like a dagger into my chest.

"Oh," I said, my mouth twisting with revulsion I didn't quite manage to hide. I scrunched my nose. "Head knight? Well. That's unfortunate. I best be going then—"

I pushed away, or tried to. My legs gave out beneath me again, wine and panic and adrenaline conspiring against me. I stumbled with a grunt, but before I could hit the ground, Sagar's arms wrapped around me and lifted me off my feet entirely. With what seemed like zero effort, he cradled me to his chest as if I weighed nothing.

"Let me go," I protested half-heartedly, pawing at his shoulder. "I can make it back to the party. I'm very good at walking. It's one of my top three skills."

He arched a brow, the corner of his lips quivering with amusement. Still, I didn't move. I felt warm. Safe. His arms were so strong, and the wine was screaming like a siren in my blood.

I pressed a hand to the velvet of his uniform, fingers sliding along his shoulder. It felt softer than I expected. My thumb grazed his skin just beneath the collar. Warm. Too warm. I blinked, and my fingers lingered longer than they should have, gently brushing his jaw.

"You're... suspiciously soft," I muttered, my words melting into a pout.

He huffed a laugh, low and private, the sound buzzing against my skin. "You're suspiciously drunk," he countered, shifting me slightly in his arms.

"I am not." I narrowed my eyes. "I just ate too much rich food."

He laughed again, and it rumbled through both of us this time. I didn't want to admit it, but it felt oddly nice, being held. Being seen. Even by someone I was supposed to hate.

Especially by someone I was supposed to hate.

"You can hardly stand on your own," he said, adjusting his grip as I half-squirmed, half-sank against him. "You're in no place to go anywhere."

"Let me down…" I groaned dramatically, my limbs going slack like yarn. My head lolled back with a sigh. "I don't want anything to do with Etheria now."

He let out a bellowing laugh, shaking my limp body along with it. "What, because I saved you?" he teased, one hand slipping behind my neck with careful ease, tilting me toward him until our faces were barely a breath apart.

The air caught in my throat, my heart threatening to burst straight out of my mouth. His scent was all-consuming and my eyes widened as my brain rapidly lost function. I felt a spark of heat and dizziness swirling around me. What was this feeling?

I did the only rational thing I could think of. I slapped my hands over my face and let out a muffled, "You're *so* close to me right now."

"Am I?" he asked, feigning innocent curiosity, clearly enjoying the way my face was combusting. "Let me bring you to your chaperone," he stated, breaking the spell with a casual flick of his brows and a glance toward the palace.

"I don't have one," I muttered, arms once again falling limp in defeat.

"That would explain how you got to this state," he sighed, shaking his head with disappointment. His gaze still locked on the palace which was still ablaze with candlelight and music. "I hope you know, you're causing me to leave some work unfinished."

He gave me a sideways grin, sharp and playful, the kind that could cause real trouble if not properly regulated. My stomach flipped as my heartbeat skidded out of control. Without thinking, I reached up and gently touched his nose with one uncoordinated finger.

"You're beautiful," I whispered, with the solemn gravity of a holy confession.

He groaned, less out of protest and more in resigned amusement, adjusting my weight in his arms again as he turned toward the darkened lawn. "Alright, that's it. We're going."

His feet started moving before I could protest. I watched as the palace lights began to shrink in the distance, the roars from the guests turning into soft hums with each step.

"Where are we going?" I asked, trying to crane my neck around him but nearly falling out of his arms in the process. "This isn't the way to the party. I want cake. There was cake. Someone said there'd be cake—"

"A lady without a chaperone," he interrupted, "unable to walk on her own, and in a very compromised state, shouldn't be left out wandering alone at night. I'm bringing you somewhere I know is safe."

He nodded toward the hill just beyond the palace gardens, where a faint orange glow flickered in the distance. "The Etherian knights have an encampment just over the ridge."

I followed his gaze, squinting toward the soft shimmer of firelight nestled in a sea of blood-red tents.

"A tent?" I asked.

"My tent." He corrected.

"*Your* tent?" I gasped, eyes widening in mock horror. "Alone?"

He glanced at me, one brow raised, clearly unimpressed but mildly amused.

"You're lucky I'm a man of duty."

"I'm lucky you're *pretty*," I said, letting my head rest against his shoulder with a theatrical sigh. "If you looked even slightly suspicious, I'd have thrown myself into the nearest bush."

"Oh, we're passing several," he replied, dry as sand. "Should I slow down?"

"Don't tempt me," I murmured, half-laughing, half-panicking. My stomach twisted with nerves at the thought of being alone with him, just us, in some private little canvas world.

"You're blushing again," he noted smugly.

"It's the moonlight," I lied, very poorly.

"Right," he said, that wicked smile creeping in again. "Definitely not because you're imagining something incredibly scandalous."

"I'm not!" I protested. "...Just theoretically scandalous."

He let out a warm chuckle, and I buried my face into his shoulder, groaning softly.

"I'm not ready for theoretical," I muttered, mostly to myself.

We continued the journey in silence, the only sound being his steady footsteps against the soft earth, each one sending a subtle jolt through me as he carried me effortlessly in his arms. The alcohol was starting to wear off, but the warmth of his chest against my side, and the memory of his strong fingers curled around my waist, kept me in a daze. This wasn't quite the plan I had started the night with, but I had to admit, he was painfully handsome, and so far, disarmingly kind.

"Well," I murmured, my voice muffled by the velvet of his uniform and my own tangle of hair, "are we almost there?"

"Close," he replied, his tone dry but warm. "You're a handful."

"Two, actually," I chirped with a grin, squeezing my hands around his biceps for emphasis. "But who's counting?"

"I could manage one."

Before I could question what he meant, he shifted me with surprising ease, suddenly hoisting me over his shoulder like a sack of flour. One large arm looped around my waist while the other swung free.

"Ahh!" I screeched, clawing at his coat until my knuckles glowed white in the moonlight. "What are you—?"

"See? One hand," he said smugly, waving the other behind him like he'd just won a prize.

A sudden gust of wind sent a rush of cold air beneath my dress, and I shrieked, squirming as the breeze danced up my thighs. "You proved your point! Put me back!"

He only laughed, a rich, delighted sound that shook me in such a way I feared he would drop me. Eventually, he shifted me back into his arms, cradling me once more. My face again burning hot from more than just the alcohol.

It was then that I noticed the tall flags rising up from the dark. Three massive banners stitched with the gold shield of the Etherian empire. They shimmered faintly in the torchlight like a cruel reminder of my past.

"Do I get the pleasure of knowing the name of the woman I'm carrying off into the night?" he asked casually, his tone teasing.

I shook my head, burying my face deeper into his shoulder.

He shrugged. "Alright, mystery maiden."

As we entered the encampment, the noise of Etherian soldiers greeted us, laughter, murmured conversations, the occasional clang of steel. They were relaxed, content, unaware that the very girl they were meant to deliver to the prince was now nestled secretly in the arms of their head knight.

Sagar approached a large crimson tent set slightly apart from the others. He ducked inside and held back the flap with surprising care, shielding me from the fabric as I was carried inside. I tried not to tense, but my limbs stiffened instinctively.

"Is this it?" I asked, too fast, too shaky. The moment felt far too real now. This was his tent. We were alone.

He set me down gently on a surprisingly soft cot, his hands lingering just a second longer than necessary at my waist.

As his hands slipped away, his body didn't move, hovering just inches from my own face for a reason I couldn't pinpoint.

"You'll be safe here for the night," he murmured, his voice low and kind. "I'll be sleeping elsewhere."

I blinked. "You... you're not staying?"

His eyes met mine, unreadable. "I'm not one to put a woman in a compromising position."

I let out a slow breath, my heart pounding painfully. I glanced around the room, its red hue made my head swim, or maybe I hadn't sobered up as much as I thought.

"No," I whispered. "I can't stay with the Etherian knights."

A low chuckle escaped his lips as he reached a hand and placed it on my cheek. "Then you might want to let go of me, dear." He whispered.

It was then that I realized his close proximity was my own doing. My hands were still clinging tightly around the back of his neck, fingers curled into the collar of his uniform like I was afraid to let go. I yelped softly and released him as if I'd been burned, recoiling with wide, embarrassed eyes.

He smiled at my reaction, an expression that softened the sharp edges of his face. His hand lingered on my cheek, only leaving as he brushed a thumb along the curve of my cheekbone.

He crossed the tent in a few strides, his presence dimming as he stepped into the corner where a small desk and trunk waited. I watched him open the trunk, rummaging desperately for something. I sat myself up, intrigued with his sudden determination.

"Aha!" he called triumphantly, his voice light and teasing as he rummaged. He glanced back over his shoulder with a boyish grin. "Don't worry, I'm just grabbing you some pants. I assume you'll be deeply missing the bottom half of your gown come sunrise."

"Good riddance," I muttered, my fingers brushing along the shredded velvet pooled around my thighs. The fabric was still soft, even if it looked like it had been mauled by a bear. A very clumsy, intoxicated bear. I sighed and picked absentmindedly at the torn edge, pretending I wasn't still flushed from his actions.

My hands moved slowly over the velvet, back and forth. A sharp sting suddenly pricked at my attention, and I frowned. Glancing down, I noticed angry red scrapes lining my palms and knees, souvenirs from my elegant tumble across the ballroom floor. I clenched my hands to hide the marks, but the throbbing ache pulsed in protest.

"Ow," I whispered, trying to sound more annoyed than vulnerable.

Before I could even think to hide them better, Sagar was kneeling beside me, a concerned furrow in his brow as he took my hands gently into his own. I hadn't even seen him cross the room. His fingers were warm, rough with calluses but tender in their grip. He held my palms up to the candlelight and studied them with more care than I'd expected from a man who wore a sword at his side.

"I've seen worse," he murmured, grabbing a bottle of clear liquid.

"What's that?" I asked, watching him pour it into a glass.

"Alcohol."

I grimaced, my head still swimming from earlier. "Please, no more—"

His laugh took me off guard, "It's not for drinking," He murmured, soaking a corner of cloth. "Hold still."

I tensed as he dabbed at the wounds on my hands. The sting was immediate and sharp, and I hissed through my teeth.

"Sorry," he said softly, glancing up at me. "This'll help, I promise."

The coolness followed quickly, and the pain began to ebb away. He focused intently on my hands, brows furrowed in concentration, and for a moment, I let myself study him freely. The flicker of the candlelight traced golden shadows across his face, softening the edges of his strong jaw and high cheekbones. His lashes were unfairly long, and his lips...

"Ouch," I hissed as he moved to my knee, the cloth soaked in alcohol brushing against the tender scrape, releasing me from my trance.

"I'm sorry," he murmured, his voice low, full of quiet concern. "Again..."

Each careful touch made my muscles twitch involuntarily, my leg instinctively trying to flinch away from the sting. A particularly sharp jolt sent my shin colliding with his chin.

"Now it's my turn to be sorry," I started with a breathless laugh, but the words died as Sagar's hand shot out, firm and unyielding.

He caught my thigh, pressing it gently but decisively to the bed. His fingers splayed across my skin, holding me there while his other hand continued its work. I froze, breath caught in my throat as his thumb swept over the sensitive curve just above my knee. The moment crackled, charged and taut. Electric with something I couldn't quite name.

My heart pounded loud enough to drown out everything else.

He didn't say a word, but his eyes flicked up to meet mine. Something passed between us. Something unspoken, raw, and real. My skin burned beneath his touch. No longer from pain. From awareness. From want.

Maybe it was the wine. Or maybe it was the knowledge that everything was already unraveling. But an idea popped into my head. Maybe I didn't have to marry a man I didn't love. Maybe I could lose the powers they were so desperate to protect before they ever had a chance to cage me.

"You know…" I whispered, my voice breaking before I could gather the thought fully. "you don't have to leave."

It came out too fast. Too honest. My stomach clenched the second the words escaped. *Idiot.* He froze for half a second. His eyes flicked up to meet mine. Then, he let out a warm, surprised laugh.

"Consider me old-fashioned," he said, resuming his gentle work. "I prefer the women I sleep with to be sober. Besides, I still don't even know your name."

I blinked. Oh, right. My name. The one he absolutely couldn't know. I opened my mouth, ready to blurt something, anything, and what came out was, "June."

He cocked an eyebrow. "June?"

"Yes," I said far too confidently. "Lady June. From… here."

His lips twitched with amusement, but he let it go. "Well, Lady June from here, you've had quite the evening."

"You don't say," I grumbled, sinking back against the pillow behind me. I didn't even remember lying down, it was as if the cot had grown beneath me. My limbs felt heavy. My chest, strangely light.

He finished by wrapping my palms in a soft bandage, then stood, smoothing his hands on his trousers. "You should sleep. It's safe here. I'll be outside if you need anything."

I didn't want him to leave. Not completely. Just a little longer, I wanted to stay in this moment, where everything felt suspended in something quiet and strange and unspoken.

I turned to look at him, my eyes heavy but clinging to the shape of him. "I expected the head of the Etherian army to be different."

He tilted his head. "What were you expecting?"

"Someone scarier," I mumbled through a yawn, grinning lazily. He snorted. "I'll work on it."

I felt the laugh buzz through my chest, but my eyelids were too heavy now to open again. The warmth of the cot, the soft ache in my hands, and the intoxicating scent of him wrapped around me like a lullaby.

"I'm not falling asleep," I said, though the words were barely a whisper.

"I'd be amazed if you didn't," he replied, his voice a low murmur near the tent flap. "Goodnight, Lady June."

I wanted to say something clever. Or charming. Or maybe just try "stay" again. But sleep was already pulling me under like a tide I couldn't fight. As my eyes finally gave in to my brain's demands, I couldn't help but find myself thinking about the fact that he didn't even try to kiss me.

Why was I so disappointed?

Chapter 5

I woke up with the worst headache I'd had in both lifetimes. The dim light filtering through the tent felt like daggers, and every sound from the rustle of the canvas to the faint chirping of birds was an assault on my senses.

My mouth was dry as parchment, and my stomach churned like a stormy sea. Never again, I vowed, though I knew it would be a lie.

As I sat up slowly, I took in my surroundings. The events of the previous night were a blur, but the Etherian red-and-gold decor of the tent jogged a few fuzzy memories. Sagar, the kind knight with warm eyes, and even warmer hands...

You don't have to leave.

"Did I really say all of that?" I groaned, burying my face in my hands. How had I managed to get into this position?

I ran my fingers across the soft fur that had been covering me, which must have been a gift from Sagar after I fell asleep. Wrapping myself tighter for a second, I realized he had kept his promise and left me in the tent all alone.

I stood on the cold dirt floor, stretching my feet and admiring the blisters from the dancing the night before. An unexpected casualty of the night must have been my shoes, as even with a deep search, I couldn't find the little heels June had so precariously picked out for me anywhere in the little tent.

I dropped the fur back onto the mattress, feeling the chilled breeze brush on my thighs as I remembered the other casualty of the night. Glancing over, I saw the black linen pants that were neatly folded on top of a deep wooden chest; I hated to admit but he was right, I did miss the bottom half of my dress.

A weird, warm feeling filled me as I held the pants close to my heart. Something so small, so insignificant, and he thought about it to keep my dignity. I felt like I needed to do something kind for him as well.

I spotted a piece of parchment and a quill on a nearby table. I grasped it and pondered what I should write. I had so many thoughts weighing me down in that moment, and an endless supply of poetic words to profess my feelings towards the evening that had ended in such a disarray. My hands shook as I scribbled:

Thank you.

— Lady June

Simple, direct, and hopefully enough to cover whatever embarrassment I'd caused. I placed it on the cot and, after ensuring the coast was clear, slipped out of the tent.

Luckily, it was a very foggy early morning. The dew stuck to the grass, like tiny jewels clinging desperately to a velvet robe. I trudged through the muddy earth, chilling my bare feet. The soft grass cushioned my walk for my aching toes.

A chill had crept into the air, subtle but insistent, the kind that whispered of summer's end and autumn's quiet claim. The leaves hadn't turned yet, but the wind carried that dry, crisp bite that made everything feel sharper. Cleaner. Like the world was pausing to exhale before the decay.

I shivered, tucking my hands into my sleeves before bringing them to my mouth. My breath fogged against my fingers, warm and fleeting, barely enough to chase away the cold. The ache in my joints and the sting of the breeze had me yearning for the one comfort that hadn't failed me yet.

A hot bath. A steaming, scalding bath that would wrap around me thicker than the fog and steal the last remnants of the chill from my bones. I could already imagine it: the way the heat would ease into my skin, how the steam would loosen the knots in my shoulders. Maybe I could wash away the warmth that flushed me from him.

I tapped up the steps to my wing, narrowly avoiding the frantic morning staff trying to erase all evidence of debauchery from the night before.

By the time I reached my chambers, my head was pounding, and my legs had gone completely numb. I barely had time to collapse onto my bed before June burst in, her usual cheery demeanor doing nothing to improve my mood.

"Princess!" she exclaimed, rushing to my side. "Where have you been? Everyone's been looking for you! The queen is beside herself! She summoned you to the throne room at once."

I groaned, dragging a pillow over my face. "Tell her I died. It'll save us both some trouble."

June yanked the pillow away. "There's no time for jokes! We have to get you ready."

I sighed, my bath would have to wait.

I allowed her to fuss over me, dabbing my face with a warm cloth and releasing the tangled mess that my hair had become overnight. She gently picked each of the flowers out that she had placed just the night before as she grimaced at the scuffs and scrapes I had acquired.

June had tied my hair off and out of my face into a neat braid and dressed me in one of my plain dresses. I didn't argue about the boring look today, as I assumed my Mother would have some choice words over my attire from the night before. Within minutes, I was presentable, or as presentable as someone could be while nursing the aftereffects of a wine-fueled evening.

As I made my way to the throne room, I could hear whispers amongst the staff. All had known I disappeared in the night, but seemingly, none knew where I had run off to. How utterly salacious it must have been, the Crown Princess disappearing without a trace from her own party. Especially after making such a scene.

I held my breath as I stood in front of the large oak doors. Somehow, I dreaded what lay beyond them, but I knew it would be a liberating experience. June placed her hand on my shoulder.

"Don't worry, Princess," she comforted. "She's probably just a little worried about how the events of last night make you look to the court."

I sighed. "Yeah, really helping me feel better, June."

She smiled and gently patted my back. "I'll meet you back in your chambers."

The throne room was as imposing as ever, its high ceilings and intricate carvings designed to make anyone standing before the throne feel small. Queen Eleanor sat perched on her gilded seat, her expression a mix of frustration and concern.

Next to the Queen sat a larger empty chair, the throne where my father once sat when he was still alive. Through the years, many advisors had tried to persuade my mother to remove the haunting reminder of such an imposing force, but she refused. It was heartbreaking, her grief still hanging over her even after all of this time.

"Silvia," my mother's voice cut through the still air like a blade. Clipped, regal, and sharp with disapproval. "I'm glad to see you in better spirits this morning."

"Yes, the party was lovely, your Majesty, I may have had a little *too* good of a time."

"So I saw." She scoffed. "You left your own party without a word. Do you have any idea how that looks?"

I bowed my head, letting my posture slump just enough to signal contrition without surrender. "I wasn't feeling well, Mother. I didn't want to cause a scene."

Her eyes narrowed. "And yet, somehow, you leaving *did* cause a scene. You tore your gown on the dance floor, and you were seen stumbling, laughing, drawing attention from half the court, men and women alike. And then you vanished. Your ladies couldn't find you this morning. Where were you?"

I pressed my lips together, carefully weighing my lie. "I ended up sleeping in the library," I said softly, weaving the falsehood as delicately as embroidery. "I had a bit too much wine. I embarrassed myself and just... wanted to wait out the party guests. I must have fallen asleep on one of the sofas."

She let out a breath, her features softening, just a little. Her fingers came to rest on her temple, her polished nails tapping gently as she sighed.

"I'm just glad you're alright," she murmured, though her calm was short-lived. "The Prince never arrived at the party," she admitted. "And the Etherian delegation never came to speak with me last night."

My head snapped up, my breath caught somewhere between relief and dread. For one glorious second, I thought maybe my night of chaos had bought me more than embarrassment; it had bought me time.

"Maybe...maybe they want to rescind their proposal," I offered, just a little too quickly. My tone, too light. Hopeful.

Her expression darkened like a storm gathering. "Do you realize what you've jeopardized?" she asked sharply. "You think this is some game? That your behavior does not reflect on this entire kingdom? That you can drink, parade around half-dressed, and somehow scare off a diplomatic union with the strongest kingdom on the continent?"

I bit the inside of my cheek and kept my expression neutral. "I apologize."

Her eyes studied mine, trying to determine if I meant it. I didn't. Not truly. But her gaze softened anyway. She wanted to believe me. That was something.

"I've sent an invitation directly to the crown prince," she continued, her voice lower now. "To apologize. Formally. If we're lucky, we can salvage this arrangement."

My stomach twisted. "Mother," I said carefully, "surely after last night there are other options to consider."

"I understand your reluctance, Silvia, but if there's to be a proposal, we have to accept it. There's no choice. This is not just about you, it never was."

My jaw clenched as the truth of that settled over me like chains. My life, my body, my future, all just part of the kingdom's bargaining table. My rebellion was a ripple. She was trying to keep the whole ocean from crashing.

"Maybe he got cold feet," I tried again, this time letting the bitterness bleed through. "Maybe he saw my antics at the party and realized he doesn't want me. Why should I be punished for that?"

Queen Eleanor's face tightened. "This isn't punishment. It's responsibility."

"But to whom?" I demanded, rising and kneeling beside her. My hands came to rest on her knee, her silk gown cool beneath my palms. "Mother, please. Don't keep me on a shelf waiting for a proposal that might not even come. I'm not just a prize to be claimed when convenient."

She stared down at me, the steel in her eyes trembling, but not breaking.

"You think I want this for you?" she asked quietly. "You think I enjoy watching my daughter thrown to the court like bait? If there were another path, I would take it. But we are royalty, Silvia. This is what we were raised for."

Her hand moved to mine, gripping it tightly. Her rings dug into my skin, little spikes of pain keeping me in the moment. But I didn't flinch.

"I see you," she said, her voice cracking ever so slightly. "I see the fire in you, it burned inside of me too once. I know it feels like I'm trying to snuff it out. But I'm trying to protect it. To protect you. We are surrounded by wolves, and I'm trying to keep them from realizing you're just a sheep."

I blinked hard, surprised by the tremor in her voice. A silence stretched between us, filled with things neither of us dared say aloud.

"You looked beautiful last night. The gown you chose to greet him was superb." She said softly. "This had nothing to do with not knowing him, did it? You're afraid you're not enough, that he will reject you."

I felt the inspiration strike me.

"Yes, mother," I turned my face away, releasing a fake sob. "What if he sees me and thinks i'm too plain? What if he decides to rescind his proposal? Whatever will I do with myself then?" She raised my hand to her lips, twisting my face back to hers.

"My dear, he would be a fool to reject a beauty of your caliber." She studied me for a long moment, her gaze softening as each silent second passed. "You have one year," she said, finally. "If you can find a suitable husband by then, I won't force you to marry the prince."

I let out a silent cry of rejoice. "Thank you, Mother."

She placed her hand on my cheek and gently stroked her finger. "But if you fail, or the Prince proposes, you will fulfill your duty to this family and this kingdom, and you will marry the man of my choosing."

I felt an immediate lump rise in my throat and swallowed it down as I solemnly nodded. "I will agree, mother."

She smiled and removed her hand from my cheek, gently scratching the skin with her ring. "That's all then."

I stood and bowed to both the Queen and the empty chair beside her before I turned and walked the long, solemn track back out the double doors.

As I left the throne room, my thoughts whirled like a spinning top. My mother was trying. I could see it in the way she rubbed her temples, how her voice stayed calm even when her words carried the weight of the crown. She didn't want to trap me into a marriage. She just believed with her whole heart, that it was the only way to protect our kingdom and me.

Still, her last words echoed with quiet finality. There was a chance, a sliver of hope. If I could find someone equal—no, *better* than the Prince, I could secure my own freedom.

I had to move quickly. I needed a plan. A distraction. A suitor. Someone of status, charming, and manageable. Someone I could court fast enough to complicate Etheria's plans.

My brain was already plotting a strategy. I chuckled as I thought of June, she would love this, she'd treat our shopping as a military operation, matching fabrics to personalities, gowns to targets. Did she know anything about attracting a man? Even through two lifetimes, I had no experience with love. Let alone the intricacies of courting.

I froze mid-step, the thought catching me off guard. I might actually have to try seduction.

The word alone sent a jolt of panic down my spine. Seduction...*me*? A terrifying prospect. I understood the logistics of love-making well enough, how could I not, after fifty years of life, war, and whispered gossip from the knights? But it wasn't the act itself that unnerved me. It was everything leading up to it. The looks, the subtle touches, the games of glances and half-spoken promises. That fragile dance of intimacy felt more foreign to me than any battlefield ever had.

I shook my head quickly, willing the heat from my face and trying to reset. One step at a time, Silvia. No need to think that far ahead yet. Focus on finding a man first. Worry about the rest later.

Lost in thoughts of poorly executed seduction and an even more poorly thought-out plan, I turned a corner and slammed directly into a wall of warmth and muscle.

No, not a wall. A man. A very solid, very real man whose chest was now pressed firmly against my face.

"Oof!" I stumbled back a step. His hands shot out to steady me, large and warm, gripping my arms with just enough strength to keep me from toppling.

I looked up, startled by the sudden closeness of our bodies, only to see an equally surprised face. It was the same one that was haunting me all day, stuck in my mind as if he had secretly made his encampment there instead of over the hill.

Sagar.

"June," he said smoothly, his mouth pulling into a rakish grin. "You seem to have a talent for showing up exactly when I'm thinking about you."

My stomach flipped violently. I offered a tight smile, trying not to drown in how effortlessly his voice wrapped around my faux name. "Sir Sagar. I—what are you doing here?" I asked, breathless, fumbling with the hem of my sleeve like it might save me from melting.

"I have a job to do, remember?" His tone was teasing, but his eyes, his eyes were entirely too aware. Too focused.

I forced a laugh. "Of course. Messenger boy. Very important work."

"You know, I could be serving my kingdom in plenty of ways. Playing messenger boy isn't exactly my idea."

"Were you successful?" I asked quickly, needing to reroute the conversation before it betrayed me. "In delivering, I mean."

"Unfortunately I was too preoccupied last night to meet with the Queen," He shot me a quick wink before a thought caused his grin to fade, the line of his jaw tensing ever so slightly. "My knights and I will remain here until the Queen produces the princess for me."

So he wanted the princess present for the proposal? This was different from my first life.

Relief flooded me, too fast and too loud in my ears. There was still time. Maybe if I could delay things further, I could have a chance to find a husband before they had the opportunity to propose.

"I see," I said, my voice a little too breezy as I took a step back. "Well, best of luck with that."

I turned to flee, but his voice caught me mid-step.

"Wait."

I froze.

He moved forward again, this time with that infuriating sense of ease, like he had all the time in the world and none of it would be wasted on anyone but me.

"What are *you* doing in the palace?" he asked, cocking his head, something amused—but suspicious—lurking beneath his words. "I thought you were just a mere party guest?"

My stomach dropped.

I bit my lip, my mind scrambling. The truth was out of the question, and the lies were getting harder to keep track of. His gaze bore into me, sharp and too clever. I could feel my heart hammering against my ribs like it was trying to run ahead of me.

Then, recklessly, I stepped closer, too close. Close enough to smell the faint hint of smoke clinging to his coat.

"To be honest..." I whispered, rising on my toes just slightly, enough to speak into his ear. "I'm the lady's maid to the Princess."

He drew back, blinking at me. His eyes scanned my face, then drifted downward in a not-quite-subtle once-over. I was suddenly very grateful I hadn't changed into anything more ostentatious that morning. My dress was simple, unadorned, forgettable, perfectly maid-like.

"But last night you were..." He held his hands to his sides in the shape of a gown. I nodded nervously.

"I wanted a night of fun, so truth be told, I stole one of my lady's gowns and enjoyed myself. Unfortunately, I learned that too much fun can be a bad thing. That's how I ended up outside."

"I knew something was off about you," he said slowly, his eyes narrowing, lips twitching. "You were far more fun than any noble I know. Although you are *very* confident for a maid..."

"Don't you know?" I said, letting my smile return, teasing. "Confidence is the only currency in a palace. Especially when you're invisible."

His brow lifted. "And here I thought it was secrets."

"Those, too," I replied, then dropped a mock curtsy. "Which reminds me, I hope we can keep everything that transpired just the two of us?"

He chuckled. "Your secret is safe with me. I must admit, I find the idea of a maid masquerading as a noblewoman rather charming. Tell me, June, is deception a common hobby of yours?"

I crossed my arms, hoping to salvage some dignity. "I assure you, Sir Sagar, I had my reasons, no matter how inconsequential it may seem."

"I'm sure you do."

We continued our walk down the hall, the echo of our footsteps bouncing softly against the marble walls. The palace felt emptier in the morning light, less grand, more cold space. Still, Sagar's presence at my side made it feel strangely alive.

"Don't you have anything better to do?" I asked, glancing sideways at him.

He smirked, hands tucked behind his back. "To be honest, yes. However, I'm in desperate need of entertainment while I await the elusive princess. And it turns out the palace has no shortage of distractions."

"I'm sure the knights are thrilled," I muttered dryly.

"Oh, I'm not talking about the knights." He tilted his head, brushing a single strand of hair from my cheek. "At least I know if I ever need my bed warmed again, you're just a stone's throw away."

His touch sent a current racing through my veins, but I forced a laugh, more air than humor. "I hope your patience doesn't run thin." I tried to sound distant, but the words came out soft.

"Patience is a virtue I've mastered," he murmured, stepping closer. "Though I admit, meeting someone as intriguing as you makes the wait far more enjoyable."

I took a step back. I needed to put space between us. My heart was doing dangerous things.

"You're quite the charmer, Sir Sagar," I said, my voice steadier now. "But I doubt you'll find what you're looking for here."

"On the contrary," he mused, eyes glittering. "I've already found something worth my attention."

"Do you enjoy getting a rise out of me?" I demanded, narrowing my eyes.

He leaned down, his grin infuriatingly perfect. "Is it working?"

"Only on the bile in my stomach."

He laughed, full and easy, and the sound was too warm. Too familiar. I hated how I liked it.

"Maybe I'm just trying to get on your good side so you'll produce the princess for me." He laughed, picking up his pace slightly, leaving his face unreadable.

"Oh, that's what this is?" I laughed, trotting to keep up. "Well, you just earned yourself an extra week of her hiding."

He froze, stopping in the middle of the hallway. I screeched to a halt, spinning to face him, staring him down directly.

"That's not fair. The longer it takes to see her, the longer I have to stay here."

My smile faded. Somehow, his words struck a chord with me.

In my first life, my engagement lasted one year, to get everything ready. I had time, was I being cruel by forcing others to live with my lies?

"Maybe I was hoping for that," I muttered, beginning my walk again.

We continued in silence for a while, the sounds of our steps and the light chatter of staff clinging to the awkward air between us. I glanced up, only for a second, just to notice his eyes were curiously latched to me, studying.

I looked away, forcing myself to focus on the hall ahead, not the way his eyes seemed to see too much.

"Do you like working for the Prince?" I asked, breaking the ineffable quiet.

Sagar thought for a moment, with no sudden witty response, which surprised me.

"The Prince is... complicated," he said finally. "He's got a heavy burden, and he hides it badly. But he's kind, when he wants to be."

His voice had lost its usual teasing edge. For just a second, he seemed like someone else. Someone I could have—no. No, that wasn't an option. He was still part of Etheria. Still, the enemy of my future, no matter how soft his eyes looked in the sunlight. Besides, how could he possibly compete with a prince? Mother would never approve.

"Do you like working for the Princess?" He asked, amusement returning to his voice.

"The Princess is..."

"Complicated?"

I shot him a glare. There was no way he could know the truth, who I really was.

"This is where I leave you, Sir Sagar," I said, trying to shake the strange warmth from my voice. "And for the record, I've heard the Crown Prince is a cruel scoundrel. My sources are fairly reliable."

He raised an eyebrow, clearly amused. "I'll take that under advisement."

I turned on my heel and climbed the staircase without looking back.

"And also for the record," I whispered under my breath, "I have no intentions of returning to Etheria."

Once inside my chambers, I slammed the door softly behind me and collapsed into my bed. The linens still smelled like lavender, a scent too peaceful for how tangled my thoughts had become.

There was no denying it, I was in trouble.

Not just because the Crown Prince might still propose, or because the Queen had already made up her mind. But because someone like Sagar, someone who shouldn't matter, had started to matter to me.

I groaned, flipping onto my back and pressing my palms against my eyes. I needed to get ahead of this. If the Etherian proposal couldn't be stopped directly, I would need a better distraction. One that could pull attention elsewhere, toward someone else. Someone suitable.

The door creaked open. June entered, her face immediately scrunching at the sight of the velvet massacre lying on the floor. She crossed her arms, her eyes flicking from the gown to me.

"Well," she said. "Do I even want to ask?"

"Probably not," I mumbled. I sat up, brushing hair from my face. "But I'll tell you anyway."

She bent down to examine the torn seams, muttering something about how fashion was wasted on the wealthy.

"I have good news and bad news," I said, watching her carefully.

She arched a brow. "Start with the bad."

"I need to find a husband."

June blinked. "Oh, is that all?"

I nodded. "Before the Etherians get restless. Which is soon."

She groaned dramatically and sank into the chair by my bed. "And the good news?"

I grinned, stretching out like a cat across my comforter. "You get to help me pick out an entirely new wardrobe."

June lit up, clapping her hands together.

"Oh, thank the stars," she beamed. "Because this..." she held up the shredded gown like a dead animal, "was a war crime."

We both laughed, and for a moment, the weight of everything lifted. But even as I smiled, I felt the pressure rising again.

The game had begun.

And I needed to win.

Chapter 6

The day had passed in a blur of fine silks, glittering stones, and more corset fittings than I had ever endured in my life. I lost count of how many shops June dragged me into, each more luxurious, over-perfumed, and absurdly expensive than the last. She had declared with divine certainty that retail therapy was "the only antidote to humiliation," and that we were not shopping for clothes, but for armor.

"We are not dressing for charm, Your Highness," June had said, hands on her hips as she assessed me like a canvas. "We are dressing to ensnare. To conquer. To remind men their hearts are fragile little things, and you—" she jabbed a jeweled hairpin toward me, "are not."

Somehow, her analogy had won me over. By mid-morning, I had tried on no fewer than sixteen gowns, including one in a shade of periwinkle so luminous it made me feel like a moonbeam. We bought it, of course.

By noon, I was sipping honeyed wine while June ruthlessly negotiated a discount on an embroidered cloak lined with fox fur, as though we were stocking a battalion for a winter campaign.

By late afternoon, I owned an entirely new wardrobe, a box of imported perfumes with scandalous names like Kiss of Dagger and Velvet Sin, and at least a dozen hairpins shaped like butterflies, swords, stars, and one rather ferocious-looking lion.

"This," June declared as we loaded up the carriage with our victories, "is what war preparation looks like. You're going to woo half the eligible nobility in the realm, and I—" she patted her bonnet smugly, "am going to manage your conquests like a general."

"You're ridiculous," I laughed, though I was grateful. For a few hours, I hadn't thought about Sagar or the Queen or the ghost of a proposal that hung above me like a blade. The anxiety hadn't vanished, but it had been muffled by silk, scent, and strategy.

We returned to the palace at dusk, the sky painted in streaks of apricot and violet. Maids trailed behind us, arms trembling under the weight of boxes, and I could hear whispers echoing through the marble halls.

We looked powerful, triumphant. But more than anything, we looked ridiculous.

Hearing the commotion, Margaret came slinking down the stairs to greet us. She tried her best to hide her amusement, but her fluorescent green eyes—wide as saucers—defied her.

"What did you do?" she gasped, staring at the mountain of parcels like a child staring at their gifts on their name day.

"I decided I needed a little... change," I said, striking a pose and flashing her a wink. "If we're going to be treated like royalty, we might as well dress like royalty."

"You are royalty," she mused, holding up a pair of embroidered gloves. "All you're missing are the crown jewels."

"Funny you should say that." I reached into a small velvet pouch and withdrew a hairpin I'd chosen just for her, a delicate golden sword encrusted with tiny emeralds. Its hilt curled into the shape of a stag head, our family crest.

Margaret paused, setting the gloves down and shifting her gaze between me, and the jewels.

"For you, my dear," I said, motioning for her to come closer.

She hesitated, but only for a moment. When she stepped my way, I gently gathered a piece of her soft auburn hair, twisting it back and sliding the pin in place.

"I had always dreamed of a grander life when I was a child, I would hate for you to follow the same path as me."

She glanced over at a shining silver saucer, catching a glimpse of her reflection. She softly reached her hand to her head, straightening her spine as she took in the vision.

"I look like a princess...." She whispered.

"Well, you *are* Princess Margaret," I reminded her, running a hand over her curls. "But you're going to be the kind of princess who writes her own rules."

Her smile softened as she leaned against me, warm and familiar. I kissed the top of her head and hugged her tightly.

"Besides," I said, straightening, "I have a promise to keep. And dinner should be ready by now."

Dinner with Margaret was a welcome balm to the frayed nerves I hadn't even realized I was carrying. The two of us had tucked ourselves into the cozy sitting room off the eastern balcony where the servants had set a smaller table just for us. Here, the fire crackled gently, and the air smelled faintly of rosemary and spiced wine.

I filled her plate with soft rolls and honeyed carrots as she leaned forward eagerly. I'm sure she would never admit it—at least not to me—but I swore her body hummed with anticipation.

"Tell me everything," she implored, elbows already on the table like she knew I wouldn't scold her. "I've read about parties, but how was it in real life?"

I regaled the tale of my name day party with the drama and flair she deserved, leaving out only the darkest details that even I wasn't ready to revisit. Her eyes widened at every turn, the glittering ballroom, the ornate gowns, the swell of music that filled the air like magic.

She gasped when I told her about my dance with the Baron, letting a chuckle slip as I described his overconfident grin and the way I curtsied without ever breaking eye contact.

"You had everyone watching you?" she asked, voice full of awe.

I smiled and took a sip of wine. "My dear Margaret, the room might as well have revolved around me."

She shot a grin back at me, digging into her meal. Margaret finally began to relax, peppering me with questions as she delicately stuffed each carrot into her mouth, savoring each bite. How did I choose my gown? What did the Queen say? Did anyone get jealous? But it wasn't until I mentioned the knight, the beautiful one who had found me in the gardens, that she froze mid-bite, her fork dangling from her fingers.

"So you just… talked to him? A real knight?" She tucked a loose curl behind her ear, eyes bright but wary, like she was testing how much she was allowed to be curious.

I smirked. "Yes. A real one. Armor, sword, horse, the whole thing. Although I never got to meet the horse..."

She blinked at me, then slowly let out a breath that was half-awe, half-laughter. "I've never met a knight. The Queen says they're all loud and rowdy. But he didn't sound like that."

There was a quiet, almost shy hopefulness in her voice. Not the boldness of gossip, more like someone peeking into a story she wasn't sure she was allowed to hear.

"Well," I said, nudging my plate aside, "he certainly wasn't quiet. But he was... kind."

Her eyes flicked to me, uncertain. "And you liked that?"

There was no teasing edge, just honest curiosity. Like she was still trying to figure out if kindness was something I gave freely, or something I expected in return.

I reached across the table and tapped her wrist lightly. "Your ears are far too young for knightly business."

She rolled her eyes, but there was a small smile tugging at her lips.

"I'm not a baby," she muttered, poking at her fruit. "I'm thirteen."

"Which is precisely why I must protect you," I teased. "Besides, it's not like I plan on seeing him again. I must focus on finding a husband, one worthy of wearing our crown."

There was a beat of silence. One that settled in the space between us like fog. I had spoken the truth, I had no plans of seeing Sagar again, not on purpose anyway. However, I hadn't meant for my voice to sound so tired, so disappointed.

"You don't... sound like you want to," she said softly.

The honesty of it made me pause. She wasn't prying, she was noticing.

I looked at her, at the way she fiddled with the hem of her sleeve, pretending to stare at her food.

"It's complicated," I admitted. "Sometimes the things we're told to want aren't the things we actually want."

Margaret's brows knitted. A thirteen-year-old trying to solve a puzzle much larger than she was. "Oh."

She chewed on that thought more carefully than she had her meal.

Then, almost reluctantly, she offered, "Well, I think the prince would still be very sensible."

I laughed and tapped the tip of her nose. "Then someday, you may take that advice for yourself. But for now, it's bedtime."

She nodded reluctantly, a thought straying at the tip of her tongue. She drug her feet only because she was tired, not because she wanted to be difficult. When I helped her up, she hesitated.

"I... don't want to be alone again," she murmured. The words came out soft, like she was afraid saying them too clearly might make them disappear.

My chest tightened. "Alright," I muttered gently, taking her hand. "Come to my room while we get ready. But then you sleep in your own bed. Deal?"

She nodded, relief loosening her shoulders. We walked arm in arm through the hallway. Her head rested briefly against me, her yawn echoing faintly off the marble floors. It was quiet, companionable.

Her eyes widened when we entered my chamber. "It's so warm," she whispered, stepping toward the sofa by the fire.

"You act as though you've never been here," I teased.

Her gaze didn't falter. "I haven't," she said simply, irises following the flames.

The realization hit me like cold water. Of course she hadn't. This room had belonged to the saint, not the sister.

I wrapped an arm around her shoulders, pulling her closer. "Well, you're welcome here now," I murmured. "Anytime."

She leaned into me a little, unsure but hopeful. "Really?"

"Really."

The two of us were interrupted as June waltzed in, parading a light white cotton dress, motioning for Margaret to make her way over. Margaret rolled her eyes, but did as she was commanded.

As June helped her, Margaret peeked over the fabric barrier like a child peering out from a doorway.

"So…" she began, cautious. "If you don't want to marry the prince, then who will you choose?" Her tone wasn't greedy for gossip, just curious, a little nervous, like someone who didn't want to overstep.

June twisted towards me, ears perked as if trying to listen

I grinned and reached for my own nightdress. "Oh, I haven't decided. But the last baron was very charming."

Margaret cruched her nose. "I know that's a lie."

June laughed patting Margaret on the head. "She's learning fast, that one."

Margaret shot June a tiny glare but didn't argue.

"We're not searching for just a husband," June declared, arms crossed like a general. "We're finding a future king. We have to pick the finest stock of the realm."

Margaret blinked. "…Like buying horses?"

"Exactly," June replied without missing a beat.

I nearly choked on my laughter. "Don't encourage her. She's thirteen."

"She's observant," June countered. "We'll have her trained before her debut."

The word made my stomach churn. Trained. That's all we were. Two porcelain dolls, perfectly trained to be good brides to future kings. Despite my horror, Margaret straightened a little at that, preening just the tiniest bit.

June turned to me. "And you, my lady, have letters to write."

"Letters?" I questioned. "Why do I need to write letters?"

"I mean, I could write them for you," She grinned. "But truly if you're looking for love, it should be personal. We'll start with an easy number. Five prospects to begin."

"Five?" I echoed.

She shrugged. "A girl needs options."

I looked down at Margaret, who had taken my hand again, clutching it like it was the only thing keeping her tethered to this world. Her smile was radiant, and her belief in me felt like a lifeline. For a moment, something bloomed quietly in my chest. Maybe courage. Maybe love. Maybe both.

I grinned, squeezing her hand. "Alright," I said. "Let the hunt begin."

June returned the smile, then turned to Margaret with a soft, guiding hand. "And while you handle that," she said, her tone gently teasing, "I'm taking this one to bed before she falls asleep on her feet."

I could see the edges of fatigue wearing on June, after all of our shopping escapades. Her eyes drooped despite the stubborn set of her mouth.

"You've done more than enough today," I told her, pressing her shoulder with a gentle firmness. "Go. Bring Margaret to her room and don't let me see you until after midday tomorrow."

She looked at me like she wanted to argue, but the yawn she bit back betrayed her. With a nod, she slipped away, leaving behind a quiet that I didn't realize would feel so loud.

They left together, June's arm curled around Margaret's shoulder as the girl leaned into her with a sleepy sigh. I watched them disappear down the corridor, the sound of their soft laughter fading with each step.

I turned back toward the bed. June hadn't stayed to help me change, and honestly, I didn't need her to. My fingers moved slowly but steadily as I unpinned the last pieces of my clothing, slipping into the cotton nightgown that hung beside my dresser. It was cool against my skin, comforting in its simplicity. I moved to the mirror and began to undo the braid myself, unwinding the strands one by one until my hair fell freely over my shoulders.

There was something tender about it, this act of care, done by my own hand. I had spent my entire past life taking care of myself, and it made me appreciate all June had done for me in our short time together in this life.

I eyed the parchment that June had left behind, and instead opted that it was a task that could wait until morning, as a deep yawn overtook me. June was off until midday, so I would have plenty of time to complete her request of five letters with no issue.

Instead, I opted to curl into my bed, the silk sheets a familiar embrace, but comfort eluded me. Sleep hovered just beyond reach, a cruel specter taunting the edges of my consciousness. My body was exhausted, my limbs heavy, my eyes sore, but my mind refused to quiet. Thoughts jabbed at me like thorns, sharp and unrelenting, and I tossed beneath the covers as if I could physically shake them off.

Could I find a husband in one year?

The question circled like a vulture, swooping lower each time I tried to push it away. One year. One year to find a partner—no, not a partner, a husband. One who met not only my standards, but hers. The Queen. She would be the final authority on who was "suitable" enough to share my crown, and I knew better than to believe she would be easily impressed.

It didn't matter if I found someone who made my heart flutter or who whispered poetry into my ear at midnight. If he didn't wear the right crest on his ring or speak with the practiced elegance of the old courts, he wouldn't be permitted within a hundred feet of the throne.

I didn't know how long I lay there, minutes or hours, it all blurred together. But the moon still hung high and indifferent in the blackened sky. Silver light streaked across the floor like spilled milk, and my frustration finally boiled over into a groan as I kicked off the sheets and swung my legs over the side of the bed.

The floor was cool against my feet as I crossed to the window, pulling the heavy curtain aside. The world outside was quiet, cloaked in the kind of stillness that only came with deep night. From the western gardens, the faint glow of fire caught my eye, the Etherian encampment, distant yet somehow still far too close. Their tents flickered like fireflies against the darkness, alive with a foreign warmth.

And I felt it again. That pull.

My heart tightened in my chest, aching for something I couldn't name. Part of me wanted to go there, just for a moment to see him, to remind myself that he was real and not some illusion conjured by moonlight and wine. Sagar. His name echoed too easily in my mind, dangerous in its simplicity. I thought of his grin, his voice, the way he looked at me like I was a riddle he wanted to solve.

But that was foolish.

I gripped the windowsill and stared harder at the camp, as if I could will the longing away.

I said it aloud, firm and cold as iron. "No."

I didn't need him. I didn't need distractions, didn't need fleeting comfort or pretty eyes that promised nothing substantial. I needed clarity. Control. A place to think without the world demanding something of me.

I remembered the natural hot spring that lay dormant in the woods just beyond the west garden. It had always been a place of solace for me, tucked away from duty and decorum. As a teenager, I'd slipped out to it during particularly grueling lessons, claiming illness or migraines when really, I just needed a place to breathe.

Tonight, it called to me again.

Slipping from the palace was easy enough. It was late, and the staff had long since retired, their energies spent managing the chaos of the day. The halls were silent save for the echo of my bare footsteps and the occasional creak of ancient stone cooling from the day's sun. I slipped through a side door that led straight to the garden, shuddering as a breeze blew through my nightgown, wishing I had grabbed a cloak before giving into my desires. From there, it was just a short walk through the tall hedges and out toward the line of trees where the earth began to slope downward.

The woods were hushed, blanketed in velvet night. A few owls stirred overhead, their haunting calls echoing between the trunks. My steps barely made a sound on the soft dirt path, now overgrown from disuse. But my feet remembered the way, guided more by instinct than sight.

Tucked between a quiet grove of trees, surrounded by smooth pale stones, the spring lay untouched, like a secret I had buried long ago. Steam curled up in delicate wisps, catching the silver glow of the moon and twisting into the night air like incense from a sacred flame. The water itself shimmered like liquid silver, so still it seemed painted onto the earth.

I approached with caution, my heart beating a little faster as if the spring might reject me after all these years. But it welcomed me, unchanged, undemanding. I stood at its edge, letting the familiar sound of softly lapping water pull the last bit of tension from my shoulders.

I undressed slowly, almost ceremoniously, the cool night air kissing every inch of exposed skin. My body, pale and glowing under the moonlight, felt unburdened here, free from eyes that judged or wanted or expected. This was mine. This moment, this water, this fleeting slice of peace.

I dipped my toes in first and hissed quietly, the heat stinging after the chill of the air. But I didn't hesitate for long. I slid into the spring with practiced ease, letting the warmth rise up my legs, across my back, down my arms until I was enveloped in its embrace.

A soft sigh slipped from my lips, unbidden. "Finally," I exclaimed. "I get my bath."

I tilted my head back and let it rest against the smooth stone edge, staring up at the stars peeking through the branches. My breath slowed, chest rising and falling in sync with the gentle ripples around me.

For a moment—just one blessed moment—my racing thoughts quieted. The voices of doubt, the pressure, the ghost of Sagar's grin, the tangled hope and fear of the search for a husband ahead, all faded into steam.

But only for a moment.

How did one even begin to court someone? What qualities should I prioritize? Handsomeness? Wealth? A complete lack of ties to the Etherian empire? I let out a bitter breath through my nose and sank deeper into the spring, the warm water enveloping me like a protective shroud. I held my breath and stared into the clear blue depths as if answers might be floating there, hidden among the shadows and moonlight.

But they didn't come.

I pressed my fingers to my lips, remembering how they had curled into a smile earlier that evening. With Margaret. With June. I wanted this, didn't I? To shape something real before they could shape me into something I wouldn't recognize.

I stared into the water, at the shimmer of my own reflection fractured by the ripples. My face looked calm, almost ethereal, bathed in the silver light, but I knew the truth that stirred beneath.

I wasn't calm. I was terrified.

But at least here, alone and surrounded by warmth, I could admit it. I could let the fear bloom in my chest without having to hide it behind smiles or sarcasm. Maybe that was enough for tonight.

With one last breath, I slid deeper into the spring, submerging myself fully. The water roared in my ears, washing away the last of the world's noise.

When I surfaced, I gasped quietly, breaking the natural silence that had surrounded me. The soft lull of the wind blowing through the trees quickly covered my breath. I turned in the water, staring into the trees, letting a hum escape my lips as I began to rinse my hair.

A soft sound froze me in my tracks. I stopped humming, trying to gauge if it was an animal or just the night playing tricks on me. A faint rustle escaped the brush. A break in the rhythm of the wind. My heart leapt into my throat as I waited. Silence. Too much silence. The kind that screamed Something is watching.

I didn't dare call out.

Instead, I backed slowly into the darkest corner of the spring, my movements calculated, silent. I pressed myself into the shadowed edge, where the overhanging rocks and trees cloaked me from the moonlight. My breath was shallow and quick, my arms wrapped tightly around my chest, squeezing so hard it hurt. The coolness of the rock against my back was the only thing grounding me.

Then I saw them.

A group of ten, maybe more, burly figures stumbling through the underbrush. Their laughter was rough, guttural, and far too loud for a night so quiet. They wore no uniform. Their clothes were patched and bloodstained, their faces hidden beneath hoods and travel-worn cloaks. Thugs. Mercenaries, perhaps. Or worse.

My stomach sank. No one knew about the spring but me and the royal household. No guards, no escort. Just me, the water, and the sharp edge of my helplessness.

Stay quiet, stay invisible, the voice inside me whispered. I did as I was told.

The men were rowdy, tossing bottles back and forth, boasting about spoils and raids. I counted their swords. Counted the spaces between them. No weapons on me. No magic. No escape. My heartbeat was a war drum in my ears.

"What do we have here?" one drawled, his voice twisted with amusement. He bent down and picked something off the ground. My nightgown. He let it dangle from the tip of his sword like a delicate, captured flag.

Shit.

"Looks like we may have ourselves a little mermaid," he chuckled darkly, lifting his gaze.

We locked eyes.

Double shit.

His grin twisted into something cruel, something hungry. My breath caught as the others turned to look where he pointed. I saw it in their faces, the shift from amusement to predation. Like wolves sniffing out a wounded fawn.

Another man caught the gown midair as it was tossed.

"A mermaid? She won't be needing this then," he jeered. I heard the sound of tearing fabric. My only garment, ripped in half, then again. Mockery. Power. Cruelty.

"Mermaid? More like fish," another sneered, waving the torn fabric like a banner.

"I don't know if she knows how to swim," a third rasped. "Maybe one of us should get in and help her."

Laughter erupted from the group. Vile, ugly laughter.

My heart hammered against my ribcage like a bird desperate to escape its prison. My mind screamed for a way out, but there was nowhere to run. I thought of calling out to the gods once. But it was the goddess left me in this life; she forced me into this horrific situation, with no way to escape. I squeezed my hands together beneath the water, praying with a fury I hadn't felt in years.

Goddess Leticia, if I ever get power again, I will take my time in making you suffer for what these men do to me.

The water rippled around me as I heard the heavy splash of someone entering the spring.

I swear it, not just on this life, but on my past and all future lives. You and all the gods will pay for forsaking me like this. For abandoning your most loyal servant when she needed you most.

"Praying won't help you, girly," came a sneer from the shadows.

I pressed myself tighter against the rock, my fingers white with pressure. I drew in a sharp, unsteady breath. My lips parted.

"Help!" I screamed.

He laughed, his voice filled with cruelty. "Screaming won't help you..."

Again, I sucked in a deep breath and shrieked, so loud my lungs stung. "Please! Anyone!"

Just as the thug reached out, the rough pads of his fingers only inches from my face, a sharp whistle sliced through the air. A heartbeat later, a sickening thud echoed across the water as an arrow embedded itself deep into his chest. His eyes widened in shock. He tried to speak, but only a choked sound escaped before his body crumpled into the spring with a splash.

Panic erupted among the others.

From the shadows, like ghosts emerging from the mist, a group of knights surged forward, blades drawn, armor gleaming in the moonlight. Their precision was terrifying, no hesitation, no mercy.

I recognized the familiar crimson of their uniforms, the same ones that had haunted me just the night before, now were my saviors.

"Help!" I choked, my voice losing its edge.

The knight holding the bow turned towards me, our eyes locking. Even in the dark, even behind his gilded helmet, I recognized those soft golden eyes; there was no mistaking them.

His bow was still raised, his expression unreadable save for the storm now brewing in his gaze. His jaw was clenched so tightly I could see the muscle twitch in his cheek. The deadly calm in his stance did nothing to mask the fury burning beneath his skin.

Everything inside me stilled. My breath, my fear, even the shame of my vulnerability. All of it paused under the weight of his stare. His eyes dropped for a fraction of a second, as if realizing just how bare I was beneath the water. He saw me, all of me. And in that one second, the sheer depth of his rage magnified, like the very thought of harm coming to me ripped something loose inside him.

"Drop your weapons and surrender," he ordered, his voice a low thunderclap. It cracked across the clearing like a whip, final, unforgiving, and laced with a barely leashed wrath that threatened to detonate.

The thugs faltered, hard, some tossed their weapons into the dirt, others turned and ran like cowards. Only their leader remained, eyes wild, fists clenched.

Sagar stepped forward, drawing his bow with a groan that sounded like a death sentence. Moonlight glinted off the arrow's tip as he closed the distance.

"A bow? We're close range, boy, what are you going to do with that?" The thug asked.

Sagar paused, just for a moment, his eyes drifting down to the man's feet, where the shredded remains of my nightgown lay in the mud like a broken flag.

His nostrils flared. A growl escaped his lips that sent a shiver down my spine. "Would you like to find out?"

The man froze. Whatever arrogance he'd had was gone. Without another word, he turned tail and bolted into the trees.

"After them!" Sagar barked, and the knights obeyed instantly, vanishing into the undergrowth with the efficiency of trained predators.

But Sagar didn't move.

He stood there, as still as a marble carving, his bow strung, his breath steady. His back to me. A sentinel. A storm waiting to pass.

"Are you hurt?" he asked, softer now, but still tense, as if I said yes, blood would be spilled.

"No," I croaked, only then realizing how tightly I'd been clenching my teeth. My body trembled from the aftermath of fear.

"Good," he murmured, exhaling. A low chuckle escaped him, unexpected and rough. He pulled his helmet off, letting it tumble to the soft earth. "You know, we really have to stop meeting like this."

There was a flicker of levity in his voice, but he still didn't look at me. Instead, his hands busied themselves with the clasp at his shoulder, loosening the velvet cloak that had clung to his armor like a shadow. He shrugged it off, letting it hang in his hand.

"Put this on," he commanded gently, holding the fabric behind him.

I moved slowly, my body aching with every step as I emerged from the spring. The cool air stung my bare skin, now steaming and raw from the heat of the water. I snatched the cloak from his hand, carefully appraising his gaze. His eyes never once shifted in my direction.

The cloak was still warm from his body. It smelled of leather, pine, and the faintest trace of something darker. I wrapped it around myself and held it close, breathing him in.

"Are you decent?" he asked.

I turned toward him, my lips parting in surprise. His back was still turned, but I noticed now the tips of his ears, glowing red with heat. A flush. He was embarrassed.

"Yes," I said softly. "I'm okay now."

He finally turned. The expression on his face was not what I expected. Not simply relief. It was conflict. A tight pull at his brow, a flicker in his eyes like he was battling something inside himself. He took a slow step forward and bent slightly, eyes never leaving mine, as though he was afraid I might disappear.

His hands found my shoulders, firm but gentle, and the contact sent a shock through me. The warmth of his palms seeped through the velvet and into my skin.

"What are you doing here?" he asked, his voice low, rough, possessive.

I frowned, lips pursed. "I always come to the springs. Usually during the day, but I needed to clear my head."

There was something different about my voice. Honest. Unfiltered. Maybe it was the trauma, maybe the spring's warmth still clinging to me. Maybe just him.

"By yourself?" His hands tightened on my arms. "No chaperone? No escort? Nothing?"

His tone was scolding, but underneath it was something far more primal. A possessiveness that made my skin heat beneath the cloak.

A cool breeze swept between the two of us, the scent of fall stinging in the air. I shivered, pulling the cloak tighter. I was suddenly aware of just how exposed I was, how vulnerable to him.

"We could discuss the pedantics of modern society," I teased through chattering teeth. "Or, you can get me somewhere warm."

Chapter 7

Sagar had once again carried me back to the Etherian encampment. His grip was strong but careful, as if he knew the weight of what had occured that night and the subtle storm that had brewing inside me for longer.

The silence of the night air was thick and suffocating. I wanted to crawl out of my skin, to run back to the palace and pretend none of this had happened. But the ache in my limbs and the cold air kissing my exposed legs reminded me that escape wasn't an option. Not yet.

"So..." I said, my voice breaking the tension like a stone tossed into still water. "A bow and arrow? Didn't have that on my list."

He glanced down at me, brow lifting with a hint of amusement. "Oh? And what list is that?"

"I just figured you for a sword kind of knight," I said, shrugging weakly. "You have the build for it."

Sagar's lips curled into a grin, slow, wicked, knowing.

Damn it. I walked right into that.

"You've been thinking about my build?"

I groaned, leaning back slightly in his arms to avoid his gaze. "Don't flatter yourself. I've been thinking about a lot of things. Mostly how I somehow keep ending up in your arms, and whether the gods are punishing me for my drunken crimes."

"Drunken crimes?" he echoed with a smirk.

"You were there. I practically threw myself at you."

"Hardly a crime," he murmured.

I rolled my eyes. "Maybe tonight was penance."

His smile faltered. He let out a breath, heavier this time. "I don't believe in divine punishment. Not for something like that. But those men—there's no justifying what they were going to do. No excuse."

The laughter drained from my face. A pit opened in my stomach, bile rising to the back of my throat. The night had taken a darker turn than I was ready to face again.

"I'm sorry," he said quietly, his voice softer now, gentler. "I didn't mean to bring it up again. I just—this is the second time I've swept you out of danger. It's starting to feel like fate."

"Fate?" I scoffed, trying to smile past the tension. "Fate is for fairytales. Could you imagine it? Me, the tragic damsel in distress, saved by the incredibly handsome knight?"

"So now I'm incredibly handsome?" he teased, voice low and warm.

"Minor details," I said, as we reached the outskirts of the camp.

Without breaking stride, he pulled the edge of his cloak up and gently draped the hood over my head. His fingers lingered near my cheek for just a second too long.

"Here," he said, voice dipping low again. "You've already become a bit of a legend among the Etherian guard. No need to give them another story tonight."

When we reached his tent, he stooped low to bring me through the canvas flap, then gently set me down on the narrow cot. He didn't speak as he reached for the thick black fur that lay draped across the foot of the bed and tucked it around me, making sure every inch of me was warm.

I pulled the hide closer, burrowing into its warmth, inhaling the familiar scent of pine and leather—his scent. It wrapped around me like a tether, grounding me, keeping me from spiraling into the memory of what had nearly happened in the springs. The tent around me was quiet, the dim light casting soft shadows along the canvas, but the echo of fear still pulsed beneath my skin, raw and unrelenting.

"I'll be just outside," Sagar murmured.

"Wait!" I shrieked. He froze. His eyes locked onto mine, widening as he caught the panic written plain across my face.

"Where are you going?" I whispered, barely able to push the words past the lump in my throat.

His expression softened instantly. He placed a hand on my shoulder, squeezing gently. "Don't worry," he said, his voice a soothing balm. "I'm just going to speak to one of the knights. I want to make sure everything's been taken care of."

Taken care of. Meaning: he wanted to make sure they were dead. All of them.

I nodded, forcing any objections to halt, watching as he disappeared through the tent flap with a quiet rustle. The moment he was gone, the warmth fled with him.

I pushed myself upright, dragging the hide around my shoulders like a shield and creeping closer to the flap. Just enough to hear.

"They caught nine," a voice said, clipped and tense. "One's still out there."

Silence.

Then Sagar again, his voice a low growl. "She was alone. No guards. No weapons. She could've died."

The words punched through me harder than any blow. It wasn't just fury in his voice; it was something deeper. Guilt. Protectiveness. Something that vibrated inside my chest like a drumbeat.

The tent shifted again, and he stepped back in, his boots silent on the worn ground. When he saw me standing, his brow furrowed.

"You need to warm up," he said with a soft chuckle, clearly trying to lighten the mood. "Let me get you some clothes."

"There's one still out there," I blurted, the panic rising again, thick in my throat. "He could come back."

Sagar crossed the space in a single stride. He placed his hands on my shoulders, gently guiding me back down to the cot. His gaze met mine, steady and unwavering.

"They won't get close again," he said firmly. "I promise. We won't let them."

He pressed a small stack of neatly folded clothes into my hands. "These should fit."

I looked at the bundle, then back at him. My fingers tightened around the fabric, but it wasn't the chill I feared; it was the memory. The helplessness. The what-ifs.

Sagar knelt in front of me again, one hand still on my shoulder. "You're safe now," he said quietly. "I'm here."

I nodded and, without a word, slipped the clothes under the fur, as if they were fragile treasures. My fingers lingered on the fabric, worn linen, a bit rough but freshly washed.

For a moment, neither of us spoke. The quiet stretched between us like a drawn bowstring, tight with the weight of what hadn't been said. Only the low hum of the campfire outside reached us, flickering shadows dancing across the canvas.

"You know if you keep getting in trouble, I'm not going to have any clothes left," Sagar teased, pulling away from me as he stood.

Normally, I would have laughed, but after the adrenaline had worn off, I was just worried.

He smiled awkwardly, turning towards the exit. "I'll step outside to give you some privacy."

"No," I said quickly, before I could second-guess myself. I felt a warm pulse beneath my hand, realizing I had inexplicably grabbed his wrist. My voice cracked slightly, the tightness in my chest squeezing like a vice. I hated how weak I sounded. "Can you stay?"

"Stay? But—"

"Just...turn around." I shifted my gaze away from him, heat sweltering to my cheeks.

It wasn't that I wanted him there. The thought of being alone again, in that moment, filled me with a sick dread. I glanced up at him, hoping he could sense my thoughts, read into my desperation.

His brows twitched, an almost imperceptible reaction, but he didn't question it. He turned and walked to the far end of the tent, folding his arms. His back was straight, but his shoulders weren't as relaxed as they tried to seem.

I stood slowly, letting the fur and cloak drop from my body with a soft thud. His spine straightened slightly at the sound. He didn't move, didn't glance, but the tension that pulsed in the space between us became unbearable, as though he felt me behind him, bare and exposed in ways that went far deeper than skin.

I pulled the oversized tunic over my head, the fabric brushing against my skin with a cool, weightless touch. Though Sagar had insisted it would fit, I was practically drowning in the garment. The hem skimmed the tops of my thighs, fluttering just above the curve of my knees like a curtain in a soft breeze.

I caught my reflection in the corner of a dented brass basin. The sight made me pause. I looked small in it, unarmored, undone. Yet somehow, wrapped in his clothes, I felt safer than I had all day.

I smoothed my hands over the front, biting my lip. Could I really get away with wearing just the tunic? Probably not. But for a moment, the idea warmed me. It felt intimate. Like I was borrowing a part of him to keep the nightmares away.

A beat passed. I heard Sagar clear his throat, shifting his weight uncomfortably while still facing away from me. Something inside me tightened, nervous, grateful, tired.

I took a steadying breath and said, almost too softly, "Thank you."

His head tilted, just enough that I knew he'd heard me. "I'm just fulfilling my duty," he replied, but something about his voice was different. Gentler. Less sure.

I didn't believe for a moment that he would treat anyone else the way he treated me.

"Still," I murmured, pressing the wool pants tightly to my chest. "Your duty is to serve Etheria, yet you saved a stranger in the woods of Calbraxia."

I walked behind him and gently placed a hand on his back. "Why?"

He turned at the touch, his eyes piercing mine with a warmth in his gaze that suggested I knew the answer already. His lips quivered into the faintest of smiles, and I felt my embarrassment deepen. I cursed myself for not putting the pants on before I started this conversation.

"My duty is to protect the people, doesn't matter where they're from," he said, his tone measured, almost formal. Then, softer, he added, "But tonight, my duty was to protect you."

A lump formed in my throat. The walls I so carefully built around myself wavered. I tried to will my voice steady. "You don't even know me."

His lips spun into a half-smile, as if he found my words amusing but also tragic. "Does it matter?"

I dropped my gaze, suddenly feeling exposed beneath the weight of his earnest stare. My emotions were still raw, strung too tight, and his quiet attention only made the cracks in my composure more visible. I turned away, pretending to be busy myself with the fraying edge of the sleeve, but the truth was simpler: I needed a moment. Just one breath to gather the unraveling threads of myself before I fell apart again.

"So... why a bow?" I asked, breaking the silence without turning back to face him.

He blinked, caught off guard. "I'm sorry?"

"A bow," I repeated, "You never told me why you use one. You're very good with it. I mean, you took out that man in the water like it was nothing. Clean shot. I didn't even hear it until it hit."

"Swords rely on strength," he declared, crossing his arms over his chest, clearly enjoying this. "Anyone can swing one if they're angry enough. But a bow?" He tilted his head slightly, that glimmer of pride never quite leaving his eyes. "A bow takes patience. Stillness. Control. Only someone with restraint is any good with it."

I arched a brow, folding my arms as well. "Is that your way of bragging?"

"It's not bragging if it's true," he quipped with a wink.

I rolled my eyes, but the corner of my mouth twitched. "Good to know."

He took a step closer, just enough for me to feel the warmth radiating from him again. "You've seen the worst of what I can do," he said softly, the humor dimming in his voice, replaced by something more thoughtful. "Do you still think the head of the Etherian knights isn't 'scary'?"

"I've seen worse," I muttered, turning away from him to hide my flush. "Much worse…"

My eye caught a small leather-bound book lying next to his cot, its spine cracked and worn with age. I edged closer and reached for it, brushing my fingers over the cover. It smelled of old parchment and something sweeter, something that stirred a forgotten ache in my chest, something that reminded me faintly of home, warm hearths, whispered stories before bed, the feeling of being safe and wanted.

"You read *The Tales of Alderin?*" I asked, my voice lighter, almost incredulous. I turned back to him, holding the book delicately as if it might crumble between my fingers.

I had remembered the tale instantly, the story woven into my earliest memories. A fierce female adventurer, Lysra, who braved a broken world in search of the spring of eternal life, only to find herself falling for her elf companion along the way. A love that was as healing as the waters she sought. It wasn't a well-known book by any means, boys detested the romantic subplot, but it held a sacred place in my heart, a reminder of innocence and dreams long before duty had replaced them.

Sagar's mouth lifted into a full, genuine smile that softened every sharp line of his face. "You know it?"

"I grew up on it," I said, almost longingly, as I opened the cover. The pages were heavy with use, the corners worn, and along the margins were scrawled careful notes in a tidy hand, his hand. I traced one of the lines lightly. "My governess used to read it to me every night when I was little."

He crossed the room toward me in three slow, deliberate steps, like he wasn't sure if he was allowed to share this part of himself and yet couldn't resist. A glimmer of shared memory brightened his expression. "Alderin was my escape," he admitted, voice dipping low, almost like he was confessing a sin. "Before I was taught swords and strategy, my mother gave it to me."

Something tender, almost painful, tightened in my chest.

"Your mother has good taste," I said, offering him a smile, hoping to ease the sudden heaviness between us.

"She did," he corrected gently, the word heavy with loss. His gaze dropped for a moment, and when it rose again, it was clearer somehow, stripped of its usual guardedness. "She died when I was little."

I pressed the book tighter to my chest, wishing I could take the ache from his voice. Wishing I could say something that mattered.

But Sagar found a way to turn the sadness into something lighter. "She used to pretend she was Arvera, the old maid; she would make this crazy sounding voice as she read it to me."

A laugh managed to bubble out of me, unbidden but pure. "I used to pretend I was Lysra," I said, tapping the book, grasping for a thread of common ground between us. "Fierce and fearless."

He chuckled, a low, rich sound that sent an unexpected warmth coiling through my chest. "I always wanted to be Caelen. Brave, stubborn, reckless."

"You *are* stubborn," I teased before I could stop myself, then froze, half-horrified by my own boldness.

But he only laughed harder, the sound crinkling the corners of his eyes. "I'll take that as a compliment."

A comfortable silence settled between us, the kind that didn't demand to be filled. It was a fragile, precious thing, and I clung to it like a lifeline.

Sagar glanced at the window where the night wind stirred the curtains, then back at me. "Would you..." he hesitated, almost shy. "Would you like to read a chapter together?"

I hesitated, my hand tightening around the book's spine. Sharing something so personal, so simple, felt far more intimate than the touches we had traded in stolen moments. It terrified me, and yet, it thrilled me, too.

Slowly, I nodded.

He sat on the edge of the bed and patted the spot beside him, looking more boyish than fearsome. I approached cautiously, heart thudding in my ears, and sat down, careful to keep a respectful distance between us.

He opened the book between us, the leather creaking softly as the worn pages fell open. His shoulder brushed mine, a touch so slight it could have been accidental, yet it seared into my skin all the same. He leaned in, close enough that the faint scent of stale wine clinging to him wrapped around me, pulling me into his orbit.

His voice was steady and low, each word from the story falling between us like a spell. As he read, the world outside faded away. For a moment, it was just him, me, and a memory we had both clung to in our separate, lonely childhoods.

I caught myself watching him more than listening. The way his lips shaped the words. The slight furrow of his brow when he stumbled over a difficult phrase. The flicker of something vulnerable in his eyes.

Before I could stop myself, the question slipped out. "What was she like?"

A look of surprise crossed Sagar's face, as if the thought of speaking her name aloud had never occurred to him. I instantly regretted asking, the words hanging heavy between us.

"Sorry," I blurted, my cheeks burning. "I didn't mean to pry—"

"No!" he said quickly, almost too quickly. His voice cracked slightly on the word. "No, don't worry. It's just that nobody's ever asked me about my mother."

"Nobody?" I repeated, my voice a whisper.

He chuckled under his breath, but there was no humor in it. He gently closed the book and placed it on his lap, tracing a thumb absentmindedly along the worn edge. "I grew up in the royal knight's guard. We're taught at a young age to leave all our family behind. Leave emotions at the door. Our soul is to belong to the crown, our bodies to Etheria. It's like…"

"Like you have to leave all worldly pleasures behind?" I finished for him, the words slipping from my mouth before I could think better of it. My eyes searched his face, desperate for some sign that he understood the ache those words left in my own heart.

A surprised look crossed his face, his lips parting slightly, and for a moment, I could feel my heart leap painfully against my ribs. I said too much. I always said too much. I should have built walls between us, high and unscalable.

And yet, the thought that there was another soul who understood—*truly* understood—what it meant to sacrifice your own happiness, your own dreams, for duty, made me want to lean into him. It made me reckless.

I wanted to know him, all of him. I wanted him to peel back every layer he kept hidden from the world. I wanted him to think of me as something more. More than a distraction, more than some damsel in distress; I wanted him to think of me as a friend.

The air between us grew thick, heavy with unspoken desires and forbidden thoughts. The only sound was the rasp of our breathing, mingling in the stillness of the tent. My nerves shook, trembling through me like a storm barely contained. Someone he could bare his very soul to.

I lifted my hand toward him, aching to touch the strong line of his jaw, the soft curve of his mouth, to confirm he was real, that this connection wasn't just some cruel dream. But at the last moment, I hesitated.

No.

The word rang through my mind like a bell, freezing my absent-minded movement.

I let my hand fall back to my side, curling my fingers into fists. I had to find a husband. I had to protect my future. I couldn't lose myself in a man who had no status, no name to offer me, no power to protect me from Etheria.

But even as I tried to reason with myself, his hand found my cheek.

His touch was feather-light, but it ignited every nerve ending in my body. I gasped softly, unable to mask the sound, and his thumb brushed a strand of damp hair from my face with a tenderness that undid me.

His eyes searched mine, and I could see the war waging within him, too. He wasn't immune to this feeling, this dangerous, beautiful pull between us.

"My apologies, June," he whispered, his voice hoarse with something I couldn't name. "Your princess must miss you. Let me walk you back to the palace."

His fingers lingered against my skin for a moment longer than they should have, a silent admission, a silent goodbye, before he pulled away and stood. Crossing the small space, he held the tent flap open for me, the chilly night wind rushing in around him.

Only then did I remember the bundle of dark fabric still clutched awkwardly beneath my arm, and the sharp bite of the night air against my bare thighs.

"I-I should probably put on pants first," I muttered, my voice embarrassingly small.

Sagar's eyes widened, and he quickly turned his back to me, ears burning red with a blush that was somehow devastatingly endearing.

Biting back a nervous laugh, I scurried to slip into the borrowed pants, fumbling with the ties as I struggled to will my racing heart into stillness.

I was shocked to see the cusp of dawn as we exited the tent, making our way silently through the garden. The air still stung with smoke from the fires of the camp the night before, and a chill blew down the ill-fitting linen that hung limp off my frame.

I was taken aback when a chuckle broke through the peaceful silence of the night air, light and warm like a ripple across a still pond.

"I think it's the first time we've walked together where I'm not carrying you," Sagar said, turning to me with a wicked smile, the teasing glint in his eyes making me forget how to breathe for a brief moment.

"Not true," I retorted, rolling my eyes even as a reluctant smile tugged at my lips. "Just this morning, we managed to walk perfectly fine side by side without any incidents."

"Ah, but there you are mistaken," he said, the mischievous flash in his eyes deepening. "If it weren't for me catching you, you would have toppled over yourself entirely. The Queen would have had to send her servants to scrape you off the marble."

I felt the heat rush to my cheeks, the memory of my clumsy stumble burning brighter with his teasing. "I wouldn't have stumbled if someone hadn't been sneaking about the palace like a shadow," I muttered, my voice full of mock indignation. "Besides, what were you even doing lurking about?"

"I was supposed to meet with the Queen," he said casually, and my heart seized in my chest at the mention of my mother.

"But," he continued, a slow, knowing smile curling his lips, "I found myself... preoccupied."

I shot him a wary glance, a nervous flutter sparking inside me, and forced a smile that I quickly smothered back into the safety of a neutral expression. "Well," I said coolly, "I hope you can complete your mission quickly and return to Etheria."

"You seem very hopeful," he said, tilting his head, amusement dancing in his voice.

We reached the looming silhouette of the palace, hints of morning sun gleamed on the stone walls. Sagar escorted me to the discreet back door of the west wing, the servants' entrance, hidden from the grand eyes of the court.

We stood for a moment, silence hanging above us with some sort of unspoken shroud. Was I waiting for something? Was I waiting for him?

"I must be going," I said, reaching for the door handle. But before I could touch the cold metal, warmth enveloped my hand, his hand, rough and steady, catching mine.

I froze.

Sagar stepped closer, his presence wrapping around me like the dawn air. Without a word, he lifted my hand to his lips, pressing a kiss against my knuckles so lightly that I wondered if I had imagined it. The world seemed to still, the only sound the frantic pounding of my heart in my ears.

He dropped my hand gently, his fingers lingering for just a second longer than necessary.

"Be careful, Lady June," he murmured, his voice low and unbearably tender.

The way he spoke my false name made my heart stumble over itself. I turned quickly, slipping through the door and into the quiet corridor beyond, but I could still feel his gaze on my back, steady, reassuring, and so dangerously real.

I hurried to my chambers, closing the door softly behind me as if afraid to disturb the fragile spell he had cast over me. Pressing a hand to my chest, I tried to steady my breathing, but it was no use.

Whatever this thing was between us, this magnetic pull, this aching need, it was dangerous.

Sagar was just a knight. Kind, yes. Charming beyond reason. But not a prince. Not a match my mother would ever deem suitable. And worse still, he was Etherian. The very kingdom I had sworn to distance myself from. I was determined to forge my own path, to seize a future dictated by my will, not by some foolish feelings, however powerful they were.

And yet, as I slipped into bed and stared up at the dark ceiling, I could still feel the ghost of his lips against my skin.

No matter how tightly I closed my eyes, no matter how firmly I told myself that I was overthinking it, Sagar lingered in my mind, a stubborn, smoldering spark I could not quite extinguish.

Chapter 8

June stood over me with a comb in one hand and a determined gleam in her eye, as if she were preparing me for battle rather than a simple afternoon tea.

"Hold still," she said, tugging gently at a knot in my hair. "You need to make an impression."

I groaned, letting her continue her battle without protest. Apparently, I had success with a potential suitor; some Lord from the western province had written back, hoping to share some tea. June leapt at the chance, considering it a perfect opportunity to test my skills.

"I don't even know why he's interested," I muttered, scowling at my reflection. "I made a complete fool of myself at my name day celebration."

It had been a week since the party, and more importantly, since I had seen Sagar. The more distance I kept between us, the more I could focus on this husband hunt.

June laughed, the sound light and teasing. "Lord Ronan thought your clumsy stroll across the dance floor was charming."

I groaned and buried my face in my hands. "I'm sure it had nothing to do with the fact that my thighs were completely exposed."

June tugged my hands away and smiled warmly. "Maybe you're overthinking all of this. Maybe someone finally sees you for who you are."

That thought—that terrifying, dangerous thought—lodged itself deep inside me. I wasn't sure if it comforted or terrified me more.

By the time June finished, I hardly recognized the girl in the mirror. My hair had been coaxed into soft, tumbling waves pinned delicately with pearl combs, and I wore a pale blue gown, simple yet elegant, cinched at the waist with a silver sash. I looked effortless. As if I belonged to this world of courtship and romance.

"You've outdone yourself." I beamed, twirling in the reflection.

"Why, thank you," She smiled, grabbing at my wrist. "But you're the one who's bringing my visions to life."

I stopped, turning to June and squeezing her hands in return. "June, I just want to thank you for all you've done for me. You don't know how much you've helped me feel alive again."

She paused for a moment, letting my words soak in as she tried to hold in tears.

"Go," she choked out, pressing a hand to my shoulder and giving me a gentle push toward the door. "Just try to enjoy yourself."

I had left the fine details of date planning to June, who set us up a table in my Mother's rose garden. It was cool with late afternoon sun, the air heady with the scent of blooms, nearing their end. The frost would be near, but it was a rare fall day that seemed warm enough to be outside.

I spotted a man in a navy blue coat already waiting by the tea table. Lord Ronan's face lit up as he saw me approach. He was handsome, disarmingly so, with warm brown eyes and dark hair that fell artfully across his forehead. He stood when I approached, bowing low before offering me a chair.

"Princess," Lord Ronan said with a roguish grin, "you look radiant."

I laughed, feeling the knots in my stomach loosen. Maybe June was right. Maybe I could enjoy this. Maybe it didn't have to be complicated.

"Lord Ronan," I said with a curtsey, "I should say the same."

I sat down, picking up the empty porcelain tea cup. It was cool in my hands, and I found myself absentmindedly tracing the rim with my finger. Lord Ronan grinned at me, glancing around the garden as though searching for something.

"Would you like tea?" he asked finally.

"I would love some!" I beamed, holding the cup out eagerly.

He rose from his chair, peering around once more with a furrowed brow. "Strange, I can't seem to find any servants."

My face fell slightly as I placed the cup back down. "Oh, yes, I thought it would be nice if it were just the two of us. So we could get to know each other."

His expression shifted from confusion to amusement in an instant, a playful light sparking in his eyes. "Oh, how bold of you Princess. Alone surrounded by such beauty? We could get into some awful trouble."

"Perhaps that was the plan." I grinned, picking up the ornate teapot and carefully pouring the steaming liquid into my cup. "Besides, I prefer pouring my own anyways."

He chuckled, a warm, pleasant sound, and hastily poured his own cup. I lifted mine to my lips, inhaling the sweet, earthy aroma of chamomile, letting it soothe me. At the same time, I reached out and plucked a delicate pastry from the towering tray between us.

For a few moments, we sipped quietly, the soft rustle of the rose bushes and the distant chirp of birds filling the air.

"Lord Ronan," I said, finally breaking the silence, "do you like the tea?"

He beamed at me, his smile brilliant, the deep dimples in his cheeks flashing. "Oh yes, the tea is lovely," he said, setting down his cup with exaggerated care before resting his chin atop folded hands. "But I think I enjoy the company even more."

A flush crept up my neck, but I fought to keep my expression neutral, playful.

"I have to ask," I began, swirling the tea gently in my cup, "what was it about me that intrigued you enough to join me today?"

He leaned back slightly, a thoughtful look crossing his face. "At your name day celebration, I couldn't help but notice you dancing with Baron Iverson. You were *remarkable*."

I cocked my head to the side, skepticism coloring my smile. "My dancing? I'm hardly the lightest on my feet," I confessed with a soft laugh.

"You underestimate yourself," he said earnestly, the intensity of his gaze catching me off guard. "The way you moved, you looked free. Like the world had faded away, and you were simply alive. I found myself wishing I could have had a dance with you."

I laughed again, this time more openly, a bright sound that felt like it chased away the lingering stress in my chest. The way he said it was so sincere, almost boyish, it was hard not to be charmed.

"Well then," I said impulsively, standing and holding out my hand, "how about you get that chance now?"

Lord Ronan's face lit up, and without hesitation, he stood and took my hand gently in his. His fingers were warm, steady, and he guided me a few steps away from the table into a small clearing between the rosebushes. The scent of the blooms seemed to swirl around us.

There was no music save the soft whisper of the wind, but he placed one hand carefully at my waist and took my other hand in his, bowing slightly. "May I have this dance, Your Highness?"

"You may," I said, laughing softly as he spun me into a slow, graceful twirl.

We moved in slow circles under the warmth of the sun, the marble pathways and flowering archways of the garden a dreamy backdrop. His steps were confident, his hands firm around my waist.

"You really are a superb dancer," he said after a moment, his voice low and warm.

"You're just saying that because you don't want me to step on your toes," I teased, my voice breathless from both the dance and the way his gaze lingered a moment too long.

He grinned, pulling me ever so slightly closer. "Even if I did, I imagine you'd forgive me."

"Forgiveness is not something given lightly," I mused, arching a brow.

"No?" he asked, dipping me gently, his grip sure and steady. "Then perhaps I'll have to earn it."

As he pulled me back upright, his forehead nearly brushed mine. For one heart-stopping moment, it felt as though the world shrank down to the two of us, and nothing else existed but the scent of dying flowers, the soft whisper of silk against silk, and the quickening of my heart.

We wandered deeper into the maze of roses, their heavy heads brushing against our arms like curious onlookers. The petals left faint trails of fragrance in the cooling evening air. Lord Ronan launched into a story about a girl he had once courted in his youth, a girl who, he assured me with a wink, was not nearly as graceful on her feet as I was.

I laughed politely, my heart lighter than it had been in days. Maybe he wasn't the perfect match, but he was kind and earnest. Maybe, just maybe, I could find someone like him to share my life with, someone who wasn't Sagar.

But as soon as I thought his name, it was like he carved a space into my mind. Why was it that no matter how charming Lord Ronan was, no matter how sweet his compliments, my thoughts strayed elsewhere?

I didn't need to think about Sagar. Not his roguish, perfectly imperfect smile. Not his beautiful, heart-stopping gaze that seemed to see straight through me. Not the memory of how his fingers had lingered against my cheek in the tent, sending tremors through me.

I shook my head as if physically casting the thoughts out.

Focus, Silvia. Focus on the man in front of you.

"Are you alright?" Lord Ronan's voice cut through my haze.

"Oh! Yes, I'm perfectly—" I began brightly, but my voice faltered as my eyes caught a familiar figure through a break in the hedges.

There, in the garden, as if my thoughts had willed him into existence, or some cruel cosmic joke. Sagar stood only a few yards away. He was casually speaking to someone I couldn't quite see. His posture was relaxed, confident, the lazy curve of his smile lighting up his face in a way that twisted something in my chest. He looked like he belonged here, among the roses and marble.

Panic fluttered up, a frantic butterfly caught in a net.

"Is something wrong?" Lord Ronan asked, following my gaze.

Without thinking, I dropped to the ground, crouching behind the rosebushes like a wounded animal.

"Princess?" Ronan blurted, far too loudly for my comfort.

I watched in silent horror as Sagar's head tilted sharply, his ears catching the noise like a predator hearing the rustle of prey.

Before he could say any more, I grabbed a handful of Lord Ronan's elegant coat and yanked him down into the dirt beside me.

"Shhh!" I hissed. The roses scraped against my arms, but I barely noticed. "Do you want him to come over here?"

Lord Ronan looked both bewildered and highly entertained. "Who? The Etherian?"

"Yes!" I whisper-yelled, shooting him a glare. "Keep your voice down."

He stifled a chuckle, pressing a hand over his mouth like an overgrown schoolboy caught misbehaving.

I ignored him, heart hammering against my ribs. I peeked between the heavy rose blooms, searching the path where Sagar had been, only to come up empty.

A knot of dread twisted low in my gut. Maybe he hadn't seen me. Maybe I still had a chance to escape.

"You know," a warm, far-too-familiar voice said from right behind me, "I've never considered viewing the roses from the dirt. How's the view?"

I jumped, knocking into Lord Ronan and nearly sending both of us sprawling into the bushes. I spun around on my knees to find Sagar standing over us, arms folded across his broad chest, one brow cocked in amusement.

The sunlight caught the silver threads woven into his dark tunic, making him look even more like a villain straight from a romance novel.

"Sir Sagar," I said, pitching my voice into the lightest, most airy tone I could manage, "what a... *pleasant* surprise."

His eyes gleamed with silent laughter as he tilted his head, studying me. "I didn't expect to find you lurking in the shrubbery today."

"I wasn't lurking," I said, scrambling awkwardly to my feet and brushing off my skirts. I offered a hand to Lord Ronan, who took it with a smirk.

"Of course," Sagar said, flashing a grin that made my stomach dip dangerously. "You were simply communing with nature."

I glared at him, feeling my face heat.

Lord Ronan cleared his throat, stepping protectively beside me. "We were simply enjoying a private stroll," he said, a note of irritation coloring his voice. "We weren't aware the garden was occupied."

Sagar's smile sharpened slightly, a predator scenting blood.

"Ah, forgive me," he drawled, his voice lazy and low. "I wouldn't want to intrude on anything *private*."

There was an edge beneath his politeness, a simmering undercurrent of something territorial that made a lump rise painfully in my throat. His gaze slid to me, lingering just a moment too long to be considered proper.

I needed to steer this back under control before either man said something that would unravel my carefully woven lies.

"I feel as though I'm deserving of a break every once in a while. Don't you?" I said lightly, forcing a bright, detached smile onto my lips.

Sagar chuckled, a sound that vibrated low in his chest. His eyes flicked meaningfully to Lord Ronan.

"Perhaps," he said, the grin tugging at his mouth entirely wicked, "although I don't know if I would quite care to be considered just a break."

I stiffened. The words were innocent enough on the surface, but the way he said them, low, intimate, was anything but. He knew exactly what he was doing.

"I beg your pardon?" Lord Ronan demanded, stepping forward, his voice taking on an edge of indignation.

Without thinking, I caught his arm, squeezing tightly, silently begging him not to escalate this. I could feel the tension thrumming under his sleeve, the way his muscles coiled as if ready for a fight.

Sagar's gaze darted down to where I held Ronan, and something unreadable flickered across his features before he masked it behind a lazy smile. He shifted his weight, all easy arrogance.

"My apologies," he said, his tone mockingly contrite. "I was merely meeting with the Queen. I was unaware there were others out here enjoying themselves." His lips curved wickedly around the last two words.

"The Queen?" I blurted, my voice cracking slightly. "So then your mission was successful?"

Sagar grimaced, his easy demeanor faltering for the briefest moment.

"Not quite," he admitted, watching me closely. "I need to give my message to the Princess. Directly."

With deliberate slowness, he turned his head back to Lord Ronan, his smile turning wolfish.

"So, it seems," he said smoothly, "I'll be staying in the palace for quite a while."

Lord Ronan's brows drew together, his confusion clear. He glanced at me, searching for some kind of explanation. I returned a stiff, hollow smile, praying he wouldn't dig any deeper.

"Sir Sagar," Ronan said tightly, straightening to his full height, "This has been... enlightening. But perhaps you would allow the Lady and me to finish our tea in peace?"

"Ah," Sagar said, feigning sudden understanding. "How foolish of me." He stepped forward, and before I could retreat, his hand slid over mine.

"My lady," he murmured, bowing low.

And then, before I could react, he pressed his lips to my knuckles, a slow, lingering kiss that seared heat up my arm and into my chest. His thumb brushed against my skin, deliberate, before he let me go.

I froze, torn between yanking my hand back and pretending it hadn't affected me at all.

Sagar straightened, his eyes locked on mine, a silent challenge burning in their depths. Without another word, he turned and sauntered off toward the palace, his silhouette quickly swallowed by the shadows of the garden.

Only when he was completely out of sight did I let out the breath I was holding.

"I apologize for that," I said quickly, smoothing my skirts with shaking fingers. "He's rather bold, that one."

Lord Ronan didn't smile. His mouth was pressed into a thin, grim line, his brows low over his eyes as he watched me carefully.

"Bold is one word for it," he muttered, before suddenly grabbing my hand. His grip was firm, but not unkind. "He was utterly indecent towards you, Princess. Why would you let him?"

I stiffened. "I think he just enjoys getting a rise out of me," I said quickly, glancing away. "Truly, I barely know the man. I only met him at my name day party, the same as you."

Ronan let go of my hand abruptly, as if burned. I turned to face him fully, heart pounding in my throat.

"It's strange," he said, voice low and heavy, "you say that, but..."

"But what?" I demanded, fear creeping into my voice despite myself.

"Perhaps," he said slowly, watching me with an expression I couldn't quite read, "you and I are looking for different things."

The words struck deeper than I wanted to admit.

"I assure you," I said stiffly, the world tilting slightly under my feet, "I am perfectly committed to—"

"To what?" he interrupted, softer now. "To lie in the rosebushes to avoid a man you claim to barely know?"

I opened my mouth, searching for an argument, a defense, anything, but nothing came out.

"I could handle many things in a courtship, Princess," He muttered, his voice low and honest. "But I could never marry a woman who's mind is preoccupied with another."

"You're *severely* mistaken," I argued.

"Am I?"

The silence that fell between us was heavy, almost suffocating.

Finally, with every inch of dignity I could muster, I gathered my skirts and forced a brittle smile onto my lips. "Thank you for the lovely tea, Lord Ronan. Now, please excuse me."

Before he could say another word, I turned and fled down the winding garden path, a newfound chill in the air biting against my flushed cheeks, the scent of decaying roses clinging to my dress like a memory I could not shake.

I found myself alone, hidden by the hedges. I dropped to my knees, tarnishing the once beautiful blue of the dress. I dug my fingers into the dirt, letting the cool ground keep me together without success.

The tears melted on my cheeks as I let out all the emotions that had built up over the day. I couldn't accept this failure, but for now, I could wallow in it.

How foolish. How utterly, painfully foolish I was.

 Chapter 9

Weeks had passed since my first foray into the brutal arena that was the courting world, weeks since Sagar had so thoroughly humiliated me that I still woke up some mornings swearing I could hear his laughter echoing through the halls. Not that I had much time to dwell on it. No, my days were now consumed by a new kind of misery: the exhausting, soul-sucking campaign to secure myself a husband.

To say it was going poorly would have been a kindness.

Every glance in the mirror caught me off guard now. Somewhere along the way, I had transformed into a glossier, shinier version of myself, a glittering peacock desperate to catch a wandering eye. My wardrobe had exploded into a dazzling collection of extravagant dresses, many of which teetered precariously on the edge of propriety. Necklines plunged. Sleeves billowed. Embroidery slithered across my skirts like vines trying to trap me in place.

Every morning when June dressed me, she squealed with the sort of glee normally reserved for children unwrapping presents.

"Ooh, today the sapphire silk!" she'd trill, brandishing yet another gown that probably cost more than what it took to feed a small village.

It wasn't just the gowns. There were jewels now. Earrings that dangled like chandeliers, ornate necklaces so heavy they left red indentations on my collarbone, hairpins sharp enough to be considered weaponry. I was dolled up daily like a prize show dog, paraded before lords, barons, and minor viscounts who barely remembered my name by dessert.

It was exhilarating, in a way. But also disheartening. Sometimes I would catch a glimpse of myself in the mirror and worry if this charade actually worked, would it be with someone who actually cared about me? Or someone who cared about my looks?

Some days, the absurdity reached new heights. During one particularly ill-fated outing with a duke from the southern provinces, I found myself trapped, literally, inside my carriage. The elaborate butterfly pins in my hair had snagged the satin seat so thoroughly that it took three maids and an entire cup of animal fat to set me free. The duke watched the entire ordeal unfold with a kind of horrified fascination, then muttered something about "ill omens" and never saw me again.

Despite the endless parade of jewels, silks, and catastrophes, every man I courted seemed to drift away after only a few meetings. It didn't matter how charming I was, how witty my conversation, how painstakingly I learned their hobbies. In fact, I spent an entire afternoon pretending to be fascinated by falconry. Inevitably, they would find some excuse, urgent business back home, ailing mothers, sudden bouts of existential dread, and slip away, never to return.

By now, I was convinced I was cursed, or worse, that the men were terrified. And not of me.

Whispers had begun slithering through the kingdom, that the crown prince of Etheria himself had me in his sights. He had never formally proposed, never even acknowledged the rumors. But word spread quickly in court, and fear traveled even faster. No one wanted to be the fool who crossed him.

One evening, after a painfully uneventful date that left me more exhausted than enchanted, June stood behind me, muttering under her breath as she wrestled another tangle of pearls from my hair. Each tug of the comb felt less like grooming and more like she was trying to mend pants far beyond their wear.

"Hold still," she scolded softly when I flinched.

"I *am* holding still," I sighed. "My scalp is just trying to flee the scene."

June snorted, working her fingers through a snarl with exaggerated patience. "These suitors of yours," she said, giving the comb a deliberate jerk, "should be legally required to pay a hair-maintenance tax."

June huffed again, stepping back to glare at the mess of silk and strands. "You know," she said finally, tone edging into that familiar teasing she used whenever she was about to say something ridiculous, "I'm beginning to think this would all just be easier if you decided to marry the prince."

I let out a sound somewhere between a groan and a laugh, then threw myself backward onto the bed like a tragic heroine awaiting her doom. "That," I declared dramatically, "would be giving in to my mother's will. And I would rather die in a heap of tulle and broken hairpins than give her the satisfaction."

June sighed, plopping down beside me with a bounce that nearly sent a few of the hairpins flying. "I'm just thinking," she said, stretching out her legs, "you wouldn't be stuck jumping through all these hoops. All these awful teas, walks, and charity balls with men you clearly can't stand."

I stared at the ceiling, feeling the weight of it all press down on me. "It's not about ease, June. It's about choice. About taking control of my fate and finding someone who will accept this." I turned my head to look at her, and for a moment, all the humor slipped from my face. "I don't just want to marry a man who tolerates me. I want to seduce a man, June. I want to make him so deliriously in love with me that he will give me my own freedom."

June blinked at me, startled. Then, slowly, a grin spread across her face like mischief blooming in springtime. "Well, here I was thinking you were looking for love. Seduction, is it? Why didn't you say so sooner?"

I lifted my head, suspicion prickling. "Why? Do you have experience?"

June burst into laughter, clutching her stomach. "Truthfully? No. However," she dropped her voice to a theatrical whisper, leaning in close, "I know a secret."

I narrowed my eyes. "What kind of secret?"

"There's a book," she whispered, eyes gleaming like she was handing me a treasure map.

I arched an eyebrow. "A book? What's it about?"

"Seduction. Pure and unfiltered. It's practically a manual. All the tricks and whispers and glances you'll ever need to have men falling at your feet."

I stared at her, half horrified, half intrigued. "And you're just telling me about this now?"

June shrugged, utterly unrepentant. "I thought you were aiming to fall in love with someone, not have someone fall for you. Different skill set entirely."

I sat up, peeling off the gaudy brocade gown that still clung to me like a suffocating net. "Where exactly does this legendary book reside? Hidden away in some seedy back-alley bookshop?"

"Oh no," June said, hopping up to help unbutton the more complicated fastenings. "It's right here in the palace library. You just have to know where to look. Find the second hall of histories, behind the treaties with the southern provinces. It's called *A Winter's Eve*."

"*A Winter's Eve*," I repeated skeptically, slipping into one of my old, comfortable cotton dresses. "Sounds... intellectually enriching." My voice dripped with sarcasm, but a thrill of curiosity ran down my spine.

"Trust me, it's well sought out amongst the staff who can read." June leapt forward, cupping my chin in her hands like she was about to knight me. "I promise after reading it, you'll feel *inspired*."

I rolled my eyes and flung a pillow at her, but she danced out of reach with a gleeful laugh, darting from the room.

Left alone among a battlefield of discarded gowns and hairpins, I sat for a moment, letting the quiet settle around me. A smile tugged at the corners of my lips despite myself.

Maybe it was time to stop playing the perfect princess. Maybe it was time to get a little wicked.

After all, the proper path had gotten me nowhere.

I slipped through the palace halls like a common criminal, my plain blue dress brushing softly against the stone floors. June had insisted the stain near the hem made me look "positively unremarkable," and for once, I was grateful for it. The less attention, the better.

The palace library loomed ahead, grand and cavernous. Columns stretched into the vaulted ceiling, each one painted with sweeping murals of scholars, muses, and solemn philosophers. Even the architecture itself seemed to judge me as I crept through its hallowed halls.

I tucked my chin low, avoiding the wary glances from a pair of archivists hunched over a crumbling scroll, and made for the Hall of Histories, keeping my steps light and unassuming.

My fingers brushed the spines of ancient tomes, trailing dust and the scent of old paper. I searched for the title June had whispered like a secret, the book that had transformed the lives of the serving girls of the palace.

Finally, tucked between two weighty treatises on economic reform, I found it: a small, battered volume whose title was so scratched and faded it was nearly invisible.

A Winter's Eve.

Before second-guessing myself, I snatched it free and retreated deeper into the library, weaving through the maze of towering shelves until I found a secluded alcove nestled behind a bookcase close enough to the fireplace that I could feel the heat brush my face. I dropped into a worn velvet chair, tossing the book with a soft thud to the oak table in front of me. I cracked the cover open with the piety of someone about to commit a great and terrible sin.

At first, I wasn't impressed.

The story unfolded slowly: a humble milkmaid named Eve, wide-eyed and hardworking, caught the attention of a brooding, widowed Duke. They exchanged lingering glances. There were fields of wildflowers. Moonlit strolls. Entire paragraphs devoted to the color of Eve's skirts.

I flipped a page with a sigh. It was clear to me why the servants felt such a connection to this book. It was the serving girls' dream. Falling for a handsome Duke, being plucked from the life of hard work.

I found myself wondering, was this the secret to seduction? Floral metaphors and chaste sighs?

But then, I found the passage.

"Eve," the Duke groaned, his voice low and roughened by hunger not entirely of the earthly variety. His body bathed in moonlight, he pressed against her, his breath hot against her throat.

Her protests were weak things, crumbling under the heat of his touch. "We mustn't," Eve whispered, yet her body betrayed her, arching into him as his hands roamed lower, claiming the curves hidden by her simple gown.

His fingers slipped the straps from her shoulders with aching slowness, exposing skin that gleamed like milk under the stars. The Duke's mouth followed the path of his hands, tracing a reverent trail down her trembling body.

I blinked hard, my mouth suddenly dry.

I should close the book. I should.

Instead, my trembling fingers turned the page.

Eve gasped as his hands cupped her bare breasts, thumbs stroking until her knees buckled. Her moans were a melody, each one coaxing a fiercer response from him.

"You are mine, Eve," he growled against her skin, and with a single rough tug, her bodice fell away completely. His mouth closed over her nipple, sending shockwaves through her quivering frame.

Helpless to resist, she grasped at him, her hand sliding down to where he strained against his breeches, gently pulling out his thick—

"Eeek!" I squealed, clapping the book shut so fast I nearly trapped my fingers in the pages.

I darted a frantic look around, half-convinced that the archivists had summoned the Royal Guard to have me escorted out for indecency.

But no one was there. The library was unearthly silent.

My heart thundered painfully in my chest as I pressed a hand against my burning cheek.

This...*this* was what June thought would help me court a husband? I felt more likely to faint in the presence of a man than seduce one after that.

Still, curiosity gnawed at me. My body tingled strangely, a sensation I had never quite experienced before.

Surely it couldn't get worse, I reasoned. Perhaps there were some subtle lessons hidden in the later chapters, once they finished whatever it was they were about to do in the moonlit garden.

I bit my lip as I cracked the book open again, flipping forward.

His hands slipped lower still, lifting her skirts as Eve whimpered, torn between scandal and need. The cool night air kissed her bare thighs as the Duke's fingers found her most secret place, stroking with maddening tenderness—

For a second, despite my better judgment, I couldn't help but imagine the Duke with the same deep skin and soft eyes as Sagar, sending an entirely new sensation spiraling through my body.

My heart leapt painfully as I continued reading, unable to stop myself.

In the scene where the Duke and Eve were finally, breathlessly, tangled together, I could hardly hold back a shudder. I was finally understanding what June meant by "inspiration".

In my mind, it wasn't the Duke, it was Him.

Sagar, whispering "Silvia" against my throat, his warm breath against my ear, his hands tracing dangerous, devastating paths along my skin.

But I couldn't have that, not even in my wildest fantasy.

With a strangled noise, I slammed the book shut again, harder this time. I cursed myself silently.

It was then that I realized I wasn't alone at the table.

Sitting directly across from me, lounging like he owned the entire library, was Sagar, an amused smirk tugging at his lips as he flipped through a book.

Maybe it was a coincidence, maybe he didn't recognize me.

"Light reading, Lady June?" he drawled.

Damn.

My heart plummeted to my stomach. I very nearly died of sheer embarrassment on the spot. But he didn't know, he *couldn't* know what had been running through my mind.

"How long have you been there?" I hissed, sitting bolt upright and clutching the book like a shield between us.

"Long enough," he said, his honey eyes flickering to me with far too much wicked amusement.

I forced myself to straighten my spine, willing dignity back into my body.

"Are you stalking me?" I shot back, desperate to regain control.

"This is the library. People come here to read." His lips twitched as he snapped his book shut. "You just happen to be fascinating to watch." His gaze flicked deliberately to the book still clutched in my hands. "Especially your choice of material."

I tightened my grip. "You don't know *anything* about my choice of material."

"Oh, I think I know plenty," he said, leaning back, completely at ease while I squirmed.

No matter how hard I tried, I couldn't seem to will the flush from my face.

It was infuriating how he managed to undo me with just a look, while I couldn't even ruffle his stupid, smug hair.

"It's... research," I said weakly, sliding the book onto the table between us as though it burned my hands.

"Research?" he repeated, clearly delighted.

Without asking, he tugged the book toward himself and flipped it open.

"I see." He raised a single brow as his eyes scanned the page. "So you're interested in a Duke's 'throbbing member'?"

I dropped my forehead onto the table with a loud thunk. I kept it there. It was the only place where the world couldn't see the sheer mortification radiating off of me like a bonfire.

"I'm looking for a husband," I muttered into the wood, lifting my eyes just enough to glare at him. "My—um—friend recommended it to me as reference material."

"Huh, that would explain all of the parties, I suppose," Sagar mused, lazily flipping through the pages of *A Winter's Eve* as though he hadn't just caught me red-handed.

I straightened myself up, smoothing my skirts with deliberate precision. "You *have* been stalking me!"

He didn't look up, only turned another page, his mouth quirking in amusement. "Not stalking, just observing," he muttered, finally lifting his gaze. "I don't know if I've met a maid allowed to roam freely in the Queen's rose garden."

The moment our eyes locked, my heart gave a traitorous leap. I could feel the heat rising under my skin, my body betraying me in ways that infuriated me.

I needed to think fast.

"Why else do you think I was trying to hide?" I snapped, folding my arms in front of me like a shield.

"So it wasn't because you were embarrassed to be seen with Lord Ronan?"

I let an exasperated chuckle escape my lips. "Sagar, I have a plan for my future. A very specific plan. Unfortunately, that plan involves finding myself in the same situation as Eve here."

He arched a brow, lounging in his seat as though he had all the time in the world. "Looking for a distraction?" he asked smoothly. "Or a duke to 'slip himself into your slick—'?"

"Ahhh! No more!" I shouted, practically knocking the book from his hands. "Why do author's insist on using *that* term?"

He chuckled. "I assume the same reason maids eat this kind of stuff up. They relish in the idea of a rich man falling for them and sweeping them off their feet. Is that what you're looking for?"

"I'm looking for my freedom," I snapped, the words sharper than I intended.

A heavy silence fell between us. For a moment, it felt like the entire library stilled, the dust motes in the beams of light, the slow ticking of the ancient clock, even the air itself. He studied me intently, as if trying to see straight through to my very soul.

Finally, a low chuckle rumbled from his chest. It was a sound that sent an involuntary shiver down my spine.

"Well," he said, sliding the book back toward me with a single lazy finger, "if you ever find yourself wanting a distraction, you know where to find me."

I stiffened, not trusting myself to answer. There was something dangerous in his smile, something that promised trouble and temptations I couldn't afford.

His eyes flashed with something rakish as he leaned in, close enough that the heat of his breath hummed against my neck. He was far too close for comfort, yet I found myself leaning in closer.

"Gotcha," he whispered, his voice a low, amused murmur that sent a shiver straight down my spine.

Before I could stop myself, I swung the book at him. The worn leather met his cheek with a soft but deeply satisfying clap.

Sagar straightened, blinking at me, one hand flying up to rub at the faint red mark I had left. There was a stunned pause, just long enough for me to feel a flicker of regret before a low chuckle escaped him, rich and thoroughly unrepentant.

"I'm usually quicker than that," he mused, pleasure curling at the edge of his lips.

I smirked, tilting my head as I let my gaze flick lazily over him. "I'm sure you're told that quite a lot."

His mouth parted slightly, as if he had the perfect retort waiting, but I spun on my heel before he could get it out, savoring the brief victory.

I had taken exactly two steps before his voice followed me, laced with something far too smug.

"Really an unfortunate recommendation, however," he called out, freezing me in place. "Eve never marries the Duke. She dies from the lung."

I whirled back around. "What!"

My voice carried far too loudly through the library, startling a pair of archivists at the far end of the room.

I hesitated, mortified at my outburst, but the betrayal sank too deep. I stormed back to his side, flipping frantically through the book as though sheer willpower could rewrite its cruel ending.

"How could they do that to her?" I whispered fiercely, scanning the pages. "She gave him everything, and he just lets her die?"

Sagar exhaled, slow and easy, as if amused by my devastation. Then, with a deliberate stretch, he rose to his full height, arms lifting lazily above his head, muscles flexing under the taut fabric of his tunic.

I tried not to notice. I failed miserably.

"Unfortunately," he murmured, his voice dipping into something almost gentle, "Not all stories get happy endings."

I clutched the book tighter, feeling a strange and unexpected sting in my chest, not just for Eve, but for something else. Something unspoken.

Not all stories get happy endings.

Not for Eve.

And perhaps, not for me either. A lump formed in my throat. I swallowed it down.

Sagar's gaze lingered on me, something unreadable flickering behind the teasing smirk. For a fleeting moment, the playful mask slipped, and there was something raw beneath it, something real.

But then, like a well-rehearsed act, his expression shifted. The mischief returned, sharp and knowing.

"Be careful with that book, Lady June," he said, his voice smooth as silk. "Otherwise, you may get some ideas."

His fingers trailed lightly along the edge of the table as he turned, a featherlight touch that should have been nothing.

It meant everything.

I stood there, rooted to the spot, my breath caught somewhere between indignation and something I dared not name.

Ideas, indeed.

He was the worst idea I could possibly have. And yet, as I watched him disappear down the marble corridor without so much as a backward glance, I already knew.

Some part of me was dangerously tempted to chase after him anyway.

Chapter 10

I rambled toward my bedchamber, the words from A Winter's Eve still rattling around in my skull like marbles in a tin. The feelings it stirred in me, confusion, heat, and want, clung to my skin like summer sweat. I needed to talk to someone. Someone who wouldn't laugh. Someone who wouldn't smirk like Sagar. But mostly, I needed air.

Luckily, I found June just outside the servant quarters, sleeves rolled to her elbows, her whole body engaged in a merciless battle to get the dust out of a rug.

"June!" I called, hurrying over, the book still tucked tightly under my arm.

She looked up, her face brightening as her eyes locked on my own. "You finished it already?" she grinned, tossing me a second rug whip. "Come on. Let's take out some frustrations."

I grinned back and snatched the whip, ready to imitate her. I smacked the rug with the kind of force I hoped would be cathartic and was instantly disappointed when barely a puff of dust escaped.

June barked a laugh, her swings rhythmic and powerful, each one sending clouds into the air.

"You've got the party at Viscountess Malina's manor tonight, don't forget," she said between strikes.

I groaned, letting the whip hang limp in my hand. "Another party?"

She glanced over with a teasing smirk. "You're the only noblewoman I know who sees a party as punishment."

"They are!" I exclaimed, giving the rug another feeble whack. "They're loud, crowded, everyone talks in circles, and nobody really talks to me. They just bow or hover. I get maybe a few feeble glances from men, but nobody wants to talk to me!"

I gave the rug another swing, this time with so much momentum I lost my balance and nearly toppled into it.

June burst out laughing. "You're hopeless," she said, catching me before I completely lost my footing. "Don't worry. Tonight we'll make sure you shine. I'm thinking the navy blue dupioni with the white roses."

I nodded vaguely, the name of the gown conjuring no real memory. She probably already had the shoes, hairpins, and earrings laid out, and was just biding her time before she got to play sculptor with my body again.

"Besides," she added with a grin, pausing to stretch her back, "maybe you'll get to put what you learned from your little education to good use."

I snorted and collapsed onto the grass, legs out, whip tossed aside.

"I'm thinking about giving up on the husband hunt," I admitted. "Mother's deal be damned."

June flopped down beside me with a grateful sigh, letting her braid fall over her shoulder. I watched the sky, clear and brilliant, every blade of grass brushing my arms like it was trying to remind me I was still here, still breathing, still me.

She glanced at me sideways, then let out a low whistle. "Why are you so desperate for a husband with a title anyway? You could have any man in the kingdom if you just asked. Hell, you could probably take two."

I didn't answer. The truth, it wasn't safe to speak it. Not even here, surrounded by clear air and someone I could trust.

I groaned, flopping over dramatically, and grabbed the whip again. "I'm not desperate," I muttered. "I'm just... trying to survive."

"You sound miserable."

"Because I am miserable!" I burst, snapping upright again. "All these parties, these men with oily smiles and titles I can't keep straight. The pressure, my mother's ridiculous deadlines, it's too much. I can't even breathe without someone trying to sell me off or measure my worth like cattle."

June blinked, taken aback.

I was pacing now, whip clenched in my hands, hair wild from the wind and my flustered steps, eyes surely glowing with the fire of too many unspoken truths. Something in me had cracked. Snapped like a thread pulled too tight over too many years.

I turned to June, words trembling on the edge of my lips. Not clever ones. Not rehearsed. Just raw, ugly, true. All the pressure, the performances, the expectations, I wanted it gone. I wanted this threat of fate exterminated.

The answer was so clear, laid out in front of me as it had been this entire time. Marriage? Who needed that? Losing my powers was so easy, even a dimwit like Eve could do it. I didn't need all this pageantry, this rebellion, this precarious dance.

I gripped the whip tighter, turning to the rug like it had offended me personally, and let all the fury and confusion and impossible longing fly through my arm. Maybe it was seventy years of pent-up rage, maybe it was the weight of all the recent stress, or maybe it was whatever emotions that decrepit book surged in me. My whip whistled through the air, the smack echoed as a thick cloud of dust billowed into the air.

"I just need to fuck someone!" I shouted.

June sprang up as though I'd set fire to the grass, her eyes as wide as saucers. "Gods above!" she hissed, glancing wildly around as if a priest or my mother might leap out from behind a tree.

The world stood still for a moment, just the whisper of wind brushing past the linens strung on the lines, birds suddenly too quiet, the echo of my outburst still hanging in the air like a stubborn cloud on an otherwise sunny day.

I stood frozen in place, chest heaving. "I didn't mean to say it," I muttered, then frowned, correcting myself, "No, actually, I did mean it. Every word."

"Hush, hush, hush!" June rushed to me, grabbing my arm like she could physically shove the words back down my throat.

"It's true, though," I insisted, a strange, giddy lightness spreading through me. I felt free. "I don't even need to get married! I could just find someone to—"

June slapped a hand over my mouth so fast my next word came out as a muffled grunt. I squawked into her palm in protest until she froze and lifted her other hand.

She pointed.

Just to the left of us, between two swaying sheets on the laundry line, stood a figure.

I turned my head slowly. Dread slithered down my spine like ice water.

There, standing still as stone, was Sagar.

He wasn't smirking. He wasn't smug. His face was unreadable, caught somewhere between curiosity and caution, like a man who had accidentally wandered into someone else's confession.

He blinked once. Then his gaze dropped, just slightly, to the whip in my hand—to June's hand covering my mouth—to the stunned horror written all over my face.

My cheeks flamed so hot I thought they might spontaneously combust.

June's hand fell away. No words would save me now.

Sagar said nothing, just nodded once, almost politely, before stepping past the edge of the line and vanishing behind a row of drying sheets.

I stared after him, heart pounding, stomach twisting. Of course, it was him. Had he heard everything? Of course, he had.

The silence stretched. I could barely breathe.

"Well," June said finally, voice strangled with the effort of not laughing. "Seems like you might already have someone in mind."

"June!" I shrieked, throwing the whip at her, but she was already stumbling back, howling with laughter, her face red with the effort of keeping it in.

"Come on," June said, brushing the dust from her skirt. "Let's continue this conversation inside. You're going to be late for the party, and I'm not letting you go out there looking like a wind-blown lunatic."

I helped her carry in the rugs, still mildly dazed from my very public declaration of sexual frustration. The sunlight filtered through the tall windows of my bedchamber, casting long gold stripes across the floor as June set to work transforming me from scandalized wreck to polished princess.

She squeezed me into the blue dupioni dress I could barely recall ever purchasing. But as the fabric settled against my skin, I couldn't deny how breathtaking it was. Hundreds of tiny white silk roses clustered along the ruffles, each thorn picked out in fine golden thread. The whole thing shimmered like moonlight on deep water.

"I don't even remember choosing this one," I murmured, smoothing the skirt.

"I did," June said, with a little huff of pride. "I saw one just like it in the window of Madame Levior's shop and knew you would look breathtaking. Of course this one's not the *real* thing, but it's close enough."

I smiled softly. "You really do know me better than I know myself sometimes."

"Obviously," she replied, tugging a final ribbon tight. "Now, hold still."

She adorned my hair next, hands working with the grace of a sculptor. Matching silk roses were pinned with precision, curling around the crown of my head, allowing a few ringlets to fall freely against my cheeks.

When she stepped back to admire her work, her eyes gleamed.

"My masterpiece!" she declared, and I laughed as she crowned the entire ensemble with an ornate gold and sapphire necklace that sat heavy and regal at my throat.

I turned to the mirror and hardly recognized the girl staring back. For a moment, I saw someone who might belong at one of these parties. Someone who might be wanted. Even chosen.

"I wish they could see me the way you do," I whispered.

June met my eyes in the mirror. "They don't deserve to."

There was a quiet honesty in her voice that made me pause. I reached out and took her hand. I couldn't help but think that maybe, if June had been born to the privilege I had, she would have made everyone fall for her so easily.

"So..." She started, sprawling herself across the chair by the fire. "How do you know, sir Sagar?" She asked.

"He's saved me...once or twice." I turned to her, confused by her casualty with his name. "How do *you* know Sagar?"

She chuckled, staring at the flames. "A few weeks ago," she said, her voice low, "He showed up at my bedchamber in the middle of the night."

My heart stopped. "What?"

June laughed at the look on my face. "Not like that—well, he may have thought it was like that. I was surprised by a knock, only to see him standing there, silent, as if he was waiting for me."

My mouth went dry. "What did you do?"

"I asked him what the hell he was doing waking me up," she said flatly. "He looked almost disappointed. Said something about being mistaken and walked off. No apology. Just vanished. Creepy little encounter, if you ask me."

I stared at her, confused, horrified, and oddly intrigued. "You think he was looking for...?"

"No clue," June shrugged. "But he's handsome, I'll give him that. Too pretty, too smooth. There's something dangerous about men who know they're beautiful. You chose well, Silvia."

I swallowed. "He's not...He's not mine, June. I'm sure he has no interest—"

She raised a brow. "You shouted that you needed to fuck someone while holding a whip. Right in front of him."

I buried my face in my hands. "Goddess Leticia, if you're merciful, you'll kill me right now."

June chuckled and stood, brushing invisible lint off her skirt. "Too late. You've got a party to survive."

She grabbed a deep navy cloak from the wardrobe and draped it gently over my shoulders.

"There's a chill tonight, Princess," she murmured, fastening the clasp beneath my chin with care. "Please, stay warm."

I turned to her, my chest aching with something I couldn't name.

"Thank you, June."

"For the dress?"

"For all of it. For you."

She only smiled. "Go. Before I try to come up with some excuse for you to stay home."

With one last glance in the mirror, I turned and slipped out into the quiet halls of the palace.

The silence hit me at once, unnatural, almost deferential. For a place usually humming with gossip and the soft patter of servants' footsteps, it now felt like it was holding its breath. Maybe I'd just been too distracted lately, too tangled in silk gowns and failed flirtations, to notice the way the stillness clung to the marble walls like dust.

The grand staircase stretched out before me, golden light pouring from the chandeliers like honey. And there, as if summoned from the depths of my most inconvenient thoughts, stood Sagar.

He lounged on the balustrade, one arm resting on the stone rail, his posture relaxed, but his eyes sharp. That damnable smirk curved across his lips like a challenge.

"Finally," he drawled. "Your princess let you off the leash? And looking like that?"

I narrowed my eyes. "Gods, don't you sleep?"

"I'll sleep when I'm dead," he said with a grin, hopping down the last step to land beside me. His shoulder brushed mine, too casually. "So, what high-society circus are you gracing tonight?"

"Viscountess Malina is throwing a ball," I muttered. "For her cat..."

"For her cat?" he finished, amusement flickering in his voice. "And you *want* to go to that?"

My eyes rolled before I could stop them. "It's ridiculous, I know. But I don't have a choice."

He tilted his head, studying me. "Ah. The glamorous quest for a suitable husband. How noble."

I groaned. "Don't start."

"What?" he asked, faux innocence in every syllable. "Isn't this all part of your plan? Find a man. Flash a little smile, maybe something more. Get ravished under a gilded ceiling and married by next week?"

"Shut up, Sagar," I snapped, turning to face him full-on. "Why do you care? Go stalk someone else for once."

The air between us shifted, cracked like glass under tension. His smirk faltered for a heartbeat, replaced by something quieter. He took a step back, jaw tightening ever so slightly.

"It just doesn't seem like you," he said, voice lower now. "You're not someone who tricks rich men into falling into your bed."

My breath caught.

"...What did you say?" I whispered.

He didn't flinch. "That's what this is about, isn't it?" His hand hovered near mine, close enough that I could feel the heat radiating from his skin. "But something tells me this isn't what you want."

Before I could think, before I could reason, my hand lashed out, sharp and fast and connected with his cheek in a sharp, echoing slap.

The silence that followed was deafening.

His head jerked slightly from the impact, and for one long, horrified moment, we both froze. My hand trembled, still suspended in the air. He lifted his own, gently pressing it to the reddening mark across his cheek.

"I deserved that." He muttered, letting his hand fall back to his side.

When our eyes met, there was no smugness in his gaze. Just surprise. And behind it hurt.

"I—" My voice broke. "I didn't mean—"

His fingers brushed my own, but his gaze didn't falter. The warmth in his hand sent a fire through me, one I knew I wouldn't be able to control.

"I have to go," I whispered, throat tight. I pulled my hand from his grasp like it burned.

But then he did something I didn't expect.

He bowed slightly, taking my hand once more, this time slowly, and brought it to his lips. The kiss was feather-light, reverent. His gaze never left mine.

"Take care, Lady June," he murmured.

I didn't wait for another word. My feet moved before I could think, carrying me down the corridor and away from him. Away from the moment I hadn't meant to create. My heart pounded against my ribs like it wanted to burst free.

I had a party to attend. I had a future to secure. I had no business letting him unravel me like this.

And yet, even as I stepped into the waiting carriage, I could still feel the ghost of his lips on my skin, continuing to haunt me like a shadow.

"Miss?" the driver called from the front. "Are you ready?"

"Oh! Yes, let's go now." My voice cracked slightly, but I didn't think he noticed.

The carriage jolted forward with a creak of wheels and a clatter of hooves. I sank into the plush velvet seat, heart still pounding, skin still burning. I pressed a hand over my chest as if I could steady the rhythm, calm the storm he had stirred inside me.

Why did he have to look at me like that? Why did it feel like he saw something I hadn't even admitted to myself yet?

I leaned my head back and shut my eyes, willing the thoughts away. This wasn't the time. I had a mission tonight: to charm, to smile, to pretend I wasn't unraveling.

But the silence inside the carriage left too much room for thought.

The tears came suddenly, hot, traitorous things that slid down my cheeks before I could stop them. I wiped at them furiously with the back of my hand.

Stop it. You're fine. Pull yourself together.

I turned my gaze to the window, watching the world blur by in streaks of shadow and silver. The forest hemmed in around the road like silent sentries. The stars overhead blinked cold and distant, their light indifferent to whatever mess I had made of myself.

At least the Viscountess's manor wasn't far. Close enough that I could make a graceful exit should I need to, assuming I didn't start weeping at the punch bowl.

The carriage rocked gently along the uneven path, the faint creak of wood mingling with the thrum of hooves. Just as I allowed myself to believe I might regain control, the driver's voice broke through the stillness.

"Hang on, Miss!"

The urgency in his tone snapped me upright. I pressed my face to the window and squinted through the dark.

A man stood in the road ahead, a torch burning in his hand. He was cloaked and hooded, his features indistinct, but something about him struck me as wrong. He wasn't waving for help or stepping aside.

He was waiting.

The horses whinnied in protest as the driver tugged the reins. The carriage screeched to a halt, throwing me forward. My shoulder slammed into the door.

"What's going on?" I called out, but before the words could fully leave my lips, the door beside me burst open.

A rough hand seized my wrist.

"Hey!" I shrieked, kicking, clawing, twisting. But another hand clamped down on my arm and yanked me out into the night.

Cold air rushed into my lungs as I hit the ground. I tried to scramble, to find footing, but a thick, scratchy rag pressed over my mouth. The scent was chemical, sickly sweet and sharp, like rotting flowers and bitter wine.

I screamed, or tried to. It came out muffled, weak.

My limbs thrashed wildly, but they no longer felt like mine. My fingers tingled, my knees buckled. I blinked, desperate to stay awake.

The torchlight blurred, then doubled.

I caught a glimpse of the driver slumped in his seat. A figure moved past me, muttering something I couldn't understand.

My eyelids fluttered. I turned my head, gasping for one final breath, one last protest.

But it never came.

The last thing I saw was the sky, stars wheeling overhead in their ancient silence.

Then...nothing.

Chapter 11

I awoke to the gnawing soreness of my body pressed against cold stone and the bite of ropes chafing my wrists. My head throbbed, my mouth was dry, and gagged with coarse fabric that left a bitter taste on my tongue.

My heart thundered in my chest, fast and frantic, as though it were trying to break free from my ribs. My eyes flew open, darting across the dim space, taking in jagged shapes and flickering shadows. The air was thick with the smell of damp earth and mildew, a cold, fungal staleness that clung to the back of my throat. I gagged.

Panic rose like a tide, cresting with dizzying force.

The tower.

No, no, it couldn't be. It wasn't time yet, this wasn't the Prince's doing, this isn't right.

But my body didn't understand reason. My lungs tightened. My fingers clawed at the bindings, shaking, fumbling. The coarse rope chafed against my wrists as I thrashed, every knot a cruel chaff for my former hopes of freedom. My breath came in fast, sharp gasps, too quick, too shallow. I was suffocating.

The walls felt closer now. Too close. They were pressing in, narrowing. I couldn't move. Couldn't think. My skin crawled with the phantom sensation of cold tower stone, of chains that no longer held me but whose memory still gripped like iron.

"I'm not...I'm not in the tower...I'm not—" My voice cracked as the words muffled from my gagged mouth, disjointed and desperate.

I screamed. Raw, hoarse, and useless.

No one answered.

I bent forward, yanking at the rope with my teeth, trying to bite the knot apart. The coarse fibers scraped my lips, drawing blood. My teeth ached, jaw trembling from the effort. Still, the knot held firm.

Tears blurred my vision. My pulse pounded in my ears like war drums.

It was happening again. I was trapped here, alone. Forgotten. Just like before.

A sob tore from my throat, my whole body shook as I pressed my forehead to the ground, trying to pull myself together, trying to remember anything beyond the storm of fear.

My head snapped up as something in the distance pulled me from my despair. Voices. Low and muffled. Not the cold silence of the tower.

The lantern above me flickered, casting a dim golden glow that caught on a cracked clay pitcher. In the corner sat a worn woolen blanket on the floor. A broom was leaning against the doorframe.

Small, insignificant things, but too human, too mundane to belong to the cursed, sterile tower I had once called home.

I wasn't in the tower. This was somewhere else.

But I was still a prisoner.

I sucked in a breath, deep and shaking, and then another. I clenched my fists against the rope and squeezed my eyes shut. The panic didn't vanish, but it dulled enough for clarity to pierce through the fog.

I may not have been in the tower's clutches, but whoever had brought me here, they knew what they were doing. This wasn't their first kidnapping. Unfortunately for them, they may not have known, but this wasn't my first time being kidnapped, and I wasn't about to let whoever this was get away with it.

The door creaked open with a slow, theatrical groan, and the lantern's light caught on the silhouette of a man, tall, broad-shouldered, and wearing a grin that chilled me to the marrow. Recognition struck like a dagger to the gut.

One of the men from the hot spring. One of the cowards who had run when the Etherian Army slaughtered the rest. The one that got away.

He sauntered into the room with slow, calculated ease, dragging a splintered chair behind him. The scrape of wood on stone made my teeth clench. He set it down in front of me and sat, legs splayed, arms resting on his knees as if he was here for a casual chat.

"Well, well," he said, voice slick with amusement. "Had I known it was the princess at the hot spring. We wouldn't have taken so long with you."

"Mmmf!" I yelled, biting down on the cloth still wedged in my mouth.

He laughed, placing his dirty finger on my chin, tugging me forward.

"We can just call this payback for last time." His smile sharpened. "Your dog of a knight made quite the mess of my men."

My eyes narrowed, burrowing hatred burning bright within them. The gag muffled the curses I tried to hurl his way.

He leaned in, close enough for me to smell the stench of sweat, leather, and stale ale. "But revenge," he whispered, "will taste better when it's slow. When it seeps under the skin. Your knight will get to feel every inch of what he did to us…"

He let his words hang in the air like smoke before straightening with a mock sigh. "Now, now, don't look at me like that. I'm not going to hurt you. Not yet."

My pulse thundered in my ears. I felt the walls pressing inward again, that creeping helplessness trying to reclaim me. What could he want with me? What could I offer him? Then it hit me, there was only one thing I could offer him in this moment, one bargaining chip I hadn't considered. Desperation shaped into resolve.

I let my shoulders sag. Let my eyes soften. I shifted just slightly, enough to ease the gag from the corner of my mouth. His gaze flicked to the movement, and I saw curiosity spark in his eyes.

With a low chuckle, he leaned forward and slipped the gag down.

I gasped in a breath, coughed against the dryness in my throat, then forced my voice into a whisper. "Y-you don't have to do this," I said, breathy and trembling, like a deer in a trap. "You don't have to hurt me. I can give you something better."

His brow lifted, his smile curling at the edges with a mixture of suspicion and delight.

"Oh?" he said. "Do tell, little Princess."

I leaned closer, lowering my lashes. "I can give you what you want. All of me. Willingly." I choked the words out as if they were acid on my tongue. "You can have what you wanted at the hot spring, if you'll let me go."

For a heartbeat, the room held still. His smile faltered, just slightly, and his eyes studied my face, maybe even lingered at my lips. My heart pounded with hope. Maybe he was the kind of brute who thought with his cock. Maybe this would buy me time. A chance to escape.

He leaned forward again, closer than before, and this time the humor in his face turned razor-sharp.

"I know exactly what you're doing, Princess," he said, voice low and almost pitying. "Tsk. Trying to seduce your way out like a tavern girl. Clever. But see…" He placed one rough hand under my chin and lifted it, forcing me to look directly into his eyes. "You're worth more untouched, aren't you? That's what makes you valuable."

His fingers left my skin like the brush of a spider's leg. I recoiled inwardly, bile rising in my throat.

"You think I grabbed you for a quick fuck?" he sneered. "Please. I'm here to make money. And men will pay kingdoms for a pure little princess, especially if they think they're the ones who get to ruin her."

I froze, disgust turning to something deeper. He wasn't trying to hurt me because he wanted power; he was trying not to, because he wanted profit. I wasn't a prisoner. I was a commodity.

He stood slowly, brushing off his trousers as if my presence left him dirty. "You know, perhaps I'll keep you even longer. What is it? Five? Ten years until your powers develop?"

My breath caught, and he noticed the fear flash in my eyes.

"Men will pay pennies to fuck the princess, but they will pay thousands for power. All I have to do is wait."

"You monster," I spat, my voice low and trembling.

"Yes, well, that's what your kingdom made me." He muttered, turning away from me. There was a strange sense of sadness in his voice, as if he was speaking to himself, not his tied-up prisoner.

"Anyways, if you behave, I'll untie you."

"And if I don't?"

"Then get comfy princess," he said, pausing in the doorway with a glance over his shoulder, his tone suddenly light and mocking, "It'll be a long ten years."

The door slammed behind him with a heavy, metallic thud that reverberated through the stone, my own personal death knell. I flinched, then slumped sideways against the frigid wall, my pulse wild and erratic.

I couldn't tell if I was sitting or sinking, if the floor beneath me was truly solid or just another illusion waiting to fall apart. The air around me thickened, pressing down on my chest like invisible hands. I was back in the ballroom again, surrounded by chattering mouths and judgmental eyes. Back in the tower, walls closing in, silence louder than screams. Back in every moment where I had no say, no choice.

A jagged sob ripped from my throat, raw and involuntary.

I curled inward, arms trembling against the ropes that bit into my wrists. My fingers were ice. My gown clung damply to my skin, offering no protection from the biting chill of the stone floor. I couldn't even feel my toes anymore.

Then, through the roar of panic in my head, his voice echoed. "In through the nose, out through the mouth. Focus on what you can."

Sagar's words in the garden the night of my name day party, words that had begun to creep into my mind more and more each day. I pictured his face, his sweet tawny eyes, as I followed suit.

I squeezed my eyes shut and inhaled deeply, dragging in a lungful of stale, musty air. I held it for four seconds, then exhaled slowly. Steam curled in the air in front of me, twisting like a ghostly ribbon. I did it again. And again.

"In through the nose, out through the mouth."

I blinked back the tears and let my eyes scan the room. There had to be something, *anything*, that could help me.

The room was sparse. A single lantern flickered in the far corner, hanging crookedly from an iron bracket bolted into the stone. The floor was uneven, cracked in places. Water pooled in the edges, glinting with a slow drip from the ceiling. The smell of mildew was stronger near the far wall, an old storage cellar, maybe?

I shifted my weight slowly toward one side of the room. My movement was limited, but I could wiggle-shuffle on my knees. Every scrape of my gown against the stone was loud in the silence.

Near the wall, I spotted it. A rusted nail. Barely the size of my finger, sticking out of a fallen beam. I didn't know if it would cut the rope, but it was something.

Focus on what you can.

I set my jaw and pressed forward, dragging myself toward that splinter of salvation. I reached my arms out, stretching just shy of the nail before the rope caught my wrists, sending me tumbling to the cold stone floor.

That's when I noticed my cloak was gone. They'd stripped me down to my party gown and tossed me onto a slab of frozen stone like I was meat in a cellar. I didn't know how long I'd been out, but the cold had already seeped deep into my bones.

"Hey!" I croaked, voice hoarse and cracking. "I'm freezing!"

Laughter erupted from the other side of the wall. Harsh and guttural. A pack of wolves entertained by the suffering of the lamb.

The sound of fire, of wood crackling, flames licking the air, slithered through the cracks. I imagined them out there, warming their hands, drinking, feasting. My limbs ached just thinking of the heat, of the cloak they must have tossed casually by the hearth.

"Hey!" I shouted louder, fury overriding fear. "I know you can hear me!"

The laughter dulled into a murmur, as if I had become a passing amusement, something to be forgotten once the wine flowed again.

Then came a crash. A jarring, splintering noise shattered the silence, followed by another uproar of laughter. Something sloshed beneath the door, liquid, dark, and shimmering. Ale maybe, or worse. I didn't care to know. It crept toward me in a slow, oily wave, soaking into the hem of my gown.

I slumped back against the pillar I was tied to, the last dregs of strength draining from my spine. Despair settled into me like rot. It clawed deeper than the cold, deeper than the ropes. It made my body feel heavier, my breath shallower.

My head lolled to the side, eyes drifting toward the ceiling, keeping my gaze moving to avoid slipping under completely. I wasn't searching for a way to escape anymore; I was searching for a way out.

If I could bite down hard enough on the gag, maybe I could choke. Or if I loosened the ropes just enough, perhaps I could loop one around my neck and lean forward hard enough to make it count. Would they stop me? Would they even notice?

Would it be better to end it here? To die on my own terms, not theirs? To avoid becoming some twisted weapon in a political play?

Then I remembered the lantern, flickering so sweetly in the corner, if I could knock it over, tip it just right with enough force from the pillar, the dry timber of the cellar would catch. I could start a fire, enough to catch their attention and maybe escape in the chaos. I could burn this place down, possibly with me in it. A firestorm. A holy martyrdom for a woman who was tired of being a pawn in everyone else's games.

It was worth a shot.

I slid towards the pillar, slamming my feet against it with such force that if they hadn't been numb from the cold, I would feel each bruise developing. The lantern jumped and the spark of hope inside of me flared.

I kicked once, pausing to listen to the thugs, hoping they wouldn't hear my commotion and try to stop me. An echo of laughter told me I was safe.

Another round of kicks.

This time, silence.

I stared at the door, listening for anything besides the crackle of embers from the fire. No more laughter. No idle chatter. No crude jokes echoing through the cracks in the door. Just silence.

That's when I heard it. A scream. No, shouts. At first, only one. Then another. And then, chaos. The clash of steel. The thud of boots. The unmistakable cry of a man being impaled.

War.

"Help!" I gasped, my voice hoarse and cracking as I twisted back in place. "Help me! I'm in here!"

The door burst open. The same thug who had mocked me before slipped inside, slamming the door shut behind him. His face was pale, lips bloodied, eyes wide with fear. The scent of iron wafted off him, thick and foul.

"I'm in—!" I started to shout.

He lunged toward me and clapped a bloody hand over my mouth.

"Shut up if you want to live, bitch!" he hissed, breath coming in ragged pants.

His hand stank of sweat, dirt, and fresh blood. I gagged, the metallic tang of it hitting my tongue. My mind spun, but through the terror, a new light was kindling, bright and sharp.

He's scared.

I scanned his face, the trembling in his jaw, the sweat gleaming along his hairline. He wasn't in control anymore. Someone was coming.

A crash exploded just outside the door, this one louder, heavier. The man gripping me stiffened, his knuckles white around the handle of his knife. I didn't need to see who was coming. There was only one man who could cause such chaos. I knew. It was him.

Panic flooded the thug's face. He cut one of the ropes binding me and yanked me to my feet, dragging me like a shield toward the corner where the lantern burned low. The small blade trembled in his grasp, but he pressed it close to my throat anyway.

Screams echoed through the halls beyond. Not drunken shouts this time, but real, raw, dying screams. Each one made the man flinch as though he felt the death in them seep through the stone.

A metallic clang rattled the door. Something, or someone, had slammed into it from the other side.

"Let me in! Please, boss!" came a voice, panicked and wild. A shadow rattled the door, hammering it with a weapon. Then, a wet crack and a gurgled screech. Silence.

A moment later, the door burst open.

Something skidded across the floor with a grotesque series of thumps, a body. It tumbled like a sack of meat, limbs bent wrong, blood smearing the stones beneath it. It hit the pillar where I'd once been bound and slumped into a heap of torn leather, broken bone, and silence.

I could hear my captor's breathing, shallow, rapid. He dragged me tighter against him, the knife trembling at my neck. I could feel his sweat drip onto my shoulder. His false confidence had fully evaporated.

"Who's there?" he rasped, trying to sound menacing, but his voice cracked on the last word.

From the darkness, the soft, steady sound of boots striking stone grew louder.

Sagar stepped into the flickering lantern light, his coat drenched with blood, some of it his, most of it not. His bow was drawn, an arrow already knocked, held with deadly ease. His eyes didn't scan the room. They found me, locked on with a burning ferocity that made my knees go weak.

He looked like a god of war, like wrath carved in flesh.

The thug yanked me back tighter and pressed the blade harder against my neck. "Stay back!" he screamed, panic cracking through the façade. "I'll mangle the bitch!"

Sagar didn't blink. Didn't lower his bow. His voice was cold enough to freeze the firelight.

"Let. her. go."

The man's laugh was high and desperate. "She's more use to me alive," he said, dragging me closer as a meat shield, "but I'll slit her throat if I have to."

Sagar's lips curled, slow and dangerous. "You won't get the chance."

Something about the way he said it made me shiver.

I caught his gaze again, just for a second. It was like standing on the edge of a cliff and realizing the man across from you would dive without hesitation just to keep you from falling. I turned slightly, enough for him to see the glint in my eyes.

Now.

I sank my teeth into the thug's filthy hand with everything I had. My jaw locked down with savage force until something tore. Hot, thick blood gushed into my mouth. He shrieked and jerked back, flinging me to the ground.

I slammed against the stone with a breath-stealing thud, my shoulder screaming in protest. Still bound, I rolled as far as I could to get out of the way. I didn't even have to look up.

A snap.

The arrow struck home, dead center into the thug's shoulder. Within seconds, another to the thigh. He shrieked again and crumpled to his knees, the blade clattering uselessly to the floor.

Sagar didn't hesitate. He crossed the room in a blur and dropped to his knees beside me. His hands, bloody, calloused, and shaking, reached for me as if to make sure I was real.

He brushed the hair from my face, cutting my bindings with a swift flick of his dagger.

"You okay?" he asked, voice thick with adrenaline.

I blinked up at him, dazed. "I bit him."

"I saw," he said, a ghost of a smile breaking through his fury. "Remind me never to piss you off."

I coughed a breath, half laugh, half sob. "We really have to stop meeting like this. If we keep going, I'll be dead before the first snowfall."

As soon as my hands were free, I brought them to my mouth, wiping away the vile mixture of blood, spit, and dirt that clung to my lips. My fingers shook as they passed over my skin, smearing more than cleaning. I glanced down, deep red stains bloomed across the front of my gown, dribbling down my chest and onto my neck like war paint.

"Ugh, perfect," I muttered, brushing at the filth with the back of my hand.

Behind me, steel rasped against leather.

I turned to see Sagar standing tall, bow drawn back so casually it almost seemed an afterthought, except the arrow pointed straight at the thug's throat. The man cowered, half-slumped against the wall, blood from his mangled hand pooling beneath him.

"Hold on!" I called, hurrying to Sagar's side with as much grace as someone covered in grime could manage.

He didn't take his eyes off the thug. "Do you want him alive?" he asked evenly, voice all calm calculation.

The thug whimpered and tried to shrink further into the stone. "You don't want to kill me," he said, breath ragged. "I wasn't even the one who *wanted* to kidnap her!"

I bent down, plucking the dagger from the floor, the same blade that had been pressed to my throat only minutes ago. Now I held it in steady hands, the weight familiar and strangely comforting. I pressed the point against the thug's skin, just hard enough to make him wince.

"Who?" I asked. The word came out low, cold. I was even surprised by myself.

His eyes darted between me and Sagar. "A Woman," he stammered. "She paid us. Said we could sell her, said she was a holy weapon. Worth a fortune."

Panic twisted in my gut. Had the Prince set this up? Had he sensed my doubt, my wavering resolve, and decided to punish me for it?

The thug caught the change in my expression. He smiled through cracked lips, smug even in his blood-soaked misery.

"You don't know the half of it," he hissed. "They want her. You're both in over your heads. I can help! If you give me a chance, I can help you prin—"

I didn't let him finish. Without hesitation, I drove the dagger into his throat.

The motion was swift, practiced. Final.

He gasped, eyes wide with disbelief, gurgling on his last words as blood bubbled at his lips. His body convulsed once... twice... then stilled. His eyes fixed on nothing, though his mouth still moved in a breathless whisper: "Your... majesty..."

Sagar stood beside me, unmoving. His eyes slowly shifted from the corpse to my face, his expression unreadable. When he finally spoke, it was with a dry kind of respect. "I take it that's a no," he said, calmly re-sheathing his arrow.

I exhaled, trying not to collapse under the weight of what I'd just done.

"You really thought I'd let him finish that monologue?" I murmured, more to myself than him.

"To be honest," he stepped closer, brushing a piece of hair from my cheek. "I didn't think you had that in you."

I looked up at him, something between a smile and a snarl forming on my face. "This isn't the first time you've underestimated me."

His mouth twitched, amusement tugging at the corner of his lips. "Fair enough."

He took my hand again, his fingers wrapping around mine, warm and steady. The contrast sent a jolt through me. Only now did I realize how truly frozen I'd become. Not just my hands, but deep inside, in the hollows of my bones. The adrenaline that had kept me upright was draining, leaving me empty and aching.

"How did you find me?" I asked, surprised by how steady my voice sounded given the chaos still ringing in my head.

Sagar didn't even blink. "I followed you," he said, as though it were the most natural thing in the world. "I've been following you for a while now. To a few parties, actually."

I yanked my hand from his, instantly regretting the loss of heat. "Why would you do that?" The words came out more sharply than intended, but I didn't retract them.

He rubbed the back of his neck and glanced away, a flicker of guilt passing over his face. "You've been acting different. Distant. I just wanted to make sure you were okay."

A strange feeling twisted in my chest. A kind of crawling discomfort, like realizing someone had been reading a diary you thought was hidden. Just how much had he seen? How much had he understood?

I glanced up at him again. He looked earnest now, soft, almost sheepish. His eyes were wide, almost apologetic. Like a dog that had chased you too far and now wasn't sure if it would be welcomed or kicked.

"June," he began softly, the nickname catching me off guard. "I'm sorry I lied. I—"

"If you don't mind," I interrupted, voice flat, but not cruel. I stepped past him, brushing against his shoulder as I moved toward the door. "I'd rather not have this conversation *here* of all places. Let's go."

Outside, the night air bit through my silk gown like a dagger. The wind howled around the crumbling farmhouse, slicing straight up my skirts. I flinched as the chill clawed up my spine. My body, already taxed, shivered uncontrollably.

"Here," Sagar said behind me.

I felt the soft weight of velvet settle on my shoulders. His cloak. Still warm from his body. I paused under the gesture, overwhelmed by the familiar scent of pine and leather, the undeniable comfort of it. I didn't thank him. But I didn't shrug it off either.

For a few long moments, neither of us spoke. The only sound was the wind whistling through the broken shutters and the faint creak of an approaching carriage.

The carriage wasn't one I recognized, plain and unmarked, but clearly expensive. Not a royal escort, but not the kind of ride anyone could just flag down on the road. Sagar opened the door and extended a hand to help me in, his expression unreadable.

I looked at his hand, then back at his face. And stepped past him again, grabbing the frame of the door to hoist myself up. The movement was awkward, graceless, my tired limbs struggling. I didn't care.

Sagar leapt in behind me, landing smoothly across from where I collapsed onto the padded seat.

"What are you doing?" I asked, pulling the cloak tighter around me as the carriage lurched forward.

"If you think I'm leaving you alone after that, you've taken a harder hit to the head than I thought." A sly smile slid onto his face. "Besides, I have some questions."

Chapter 12

The carriage rattled along the uneven road back to the palace, each bump jolting through my bones, making it harder to forget how recently I'd been trussed up like an animal. The silence between us was palpable, the kind that pressed down like fog, thick with unspoken words and half-formed thoughts.

My fingers twisted nervously in my lap, playing with the edges of Sagar's velvet cloak. Eventually, I shrugged it off and folded it neatly beside me, even though I still craved its warmth. I needed to feel like myself again, or at least whatever fractured version of myself remained after tonight.

The memory of the blood-soaked floor clung to me, but stranger still was the man sitting across from me. Sagar hadn't said a word since we left the farmhouse where I had been held captive. He stared out the window, jaw tight, brow furrowed with concentration. Like he was assembling a puzzle and didn't like the picture it was forming.

I watched him from under lowered lashes, uneasy. He looked like he wanted to speak but didn't know where to begin. That made two of us.

A bead of sweat rolled down my temple, and I lifted my hand to fan myself. The air inside the carriage had thickened. My skin prickled with heat, an odd contrast to the chill that had burrowed deep inside me earlier.

"Is it hot in here?" I asked, hoping to break the silence. "I feel like I'm burning up."

His head snapped toward me, eyes scanning my face as if seeing me clearly for the first time. Then, without a word, he leaned forward and reached out, placing the back of his hand on my face.

"What are you—?"

"You don't have a fever," he said, cutting me off gently, his fingers brushing my forehead. "Probably just your body temperature returning to normal after freezing in that barn. You shouldn't have taken the cloak off."

His hand lingered a second too long. It drifted from my forehead down to the curve of my cheek. His touch was careful, feather-light, but it sent a current through me nonetheless. Our eyes locked. I forgot the ache in my wrists, the blood on my gown, even my name for a moment.

He pulled back, returning to his seat with a suddenness that made me exhale.

"I don't think I thanked you yet," I said, my voice a little hoarse.

A smirk tugged at the corner of his mouth. "Whatever could you have to thank me for? I'm just fulfilling my duty, remember?"

I offered a half-smile, letting my gaze drop to my hands. My fingertips had returned to a healthy pink, no longer icy and blue.

I touched them to the cool glass of the carriage window, watching the fog bloom beneath them in soft bursts.

Sagar's voice came after a moment, soft, deliberate, but his expression remained carved from granite. "I have questions."

My hand slipped from the fogged window to my lap. "I'm tired," I muttered, already bracing for a fight. "Can the questions wait?"

"No." His reply was sharper than I expected, cracking the strange aura that had blossomed between us. "It's time for repayment. I saved your life, more than once now, so I think I've earned ten questions. And you have to answer each one honestly."

A scandalized gasp escaped my lips. "Ten? What kind of inflation is that?"

He leaned back, folding his arms with smug ease. "Seems like a bargain. Your life in exchange for a handful of answers."

"Oh no," I said firmly. "You get one. One question. That's it. Make it count."

He shrugged. "Fine. I'll just have the driver turn us around. I'm sure that cellar will be more inviting than the palace."

"Okay, okay, two," I snapped, eyes narrowing.

"Five."

"Three."

"Deal," he said far too quickly.

I slumped in my seat with a dramatic sigh. "Alright then. Get on with it."

Sagar leaned forward slightly, his tone shifting to something low and coaxing. "First question," he said, voice almost a purr. "Who are you?"

I blinked, confused. "I told you already. My name is June."

His eyes locked on mine like twin blades. "I told you these had to be honest answers," he said, his voice laced with quiet danger. He reached out, guiding my chin up with a single finger. "And that, my dear, was a lie."

My throat tightened. "Okay," I breathed, eyes flicking away. "My name is Silvia."

He chuckled, low and maddeningly satisfied, dropping his hand. "Nice to finally meet you, Silvia, but that was not my question. I didn't ask your name. I asked who you are."

"That's not fair!" I snapped, fists curling in my lap. "I *am* Silvia."

"Your name is Silvia," he said, a smile tugging at his lips. "But who *are* you?"

I groaned and threw my head back against the seat. "Fine," I muttered, drawing in a breath as if I could inhale courage. "My name is Silvia Stephan, and I'm the Princess of Calbraxia. Are you happy now?"

The carriage gave a soft rattle as silence fell again. Sagar stared at me for a long moment, unreadable. His eyes were soaking in every inch of me, leaving me feeling exposed. Then his lips quirked into a slow, smug grin. "Very. You're braver than I thought."

I narrowed my eyes. "What's that supposed to mean?"

He leaned in, eyes glinting with mischief. "You lied to the head knight of the Etherian army without a second thought. Either you're dangerously bold or wildly stupid."

"Or both," I muttered under my breath, letting my face fall to the floor.

Sagar gave a low laugh, then reached out again, this time more tenderly. His hand tilted my chin up, and he inched forward, close enough that I could feel the warmth of his breath. "I'm tempted," he said, voice like velvet, "to say that kind of betrayal deserves a punishment."

My heart skittered. "You're joking."

"Of course," he whispered, "I already knew you were the princess, for a while now."

My eyes widened, the blood draining from my face as I pulled away from him. "What?"

He laughed again, delighted by my shock. "Sweet Silvia," he said with exaggerated pity, leaning back smugly in his seat. "You seem to forget that there are portraits of you hanging in the palace halls. You didn't honestly think you were incognito, did you?"

I opened my mouth, then closed it again, struggling to find a retort. "W-when did you find out?"

"I started putting the pieces together after the hot springs," he said, fingers tapping idly against his knee. "I went looking for 'June.' Asked one of the maids where your room was. She took me to a girl who looked nothing like you, though she was equally confused, bless her heart."

I groaned, burying my face in my hands.

"But the real giveaway," he continued, clearly enjoying himself now, "was meeting the Queen. You two could pass as sisters." He leaned in again, softer this time. "But your eyes, the eyes of a Divinial. Hard to miss, once you know what to look for."

I couldn't tell what it was I was feeling. Shame? Embarrassment? Or maybe longing to close this distance between us. To do anything to make this moment stop and release this burning.

"Which leads me to my second question," Sagar said, his voice slicing cleanly through the thick quiet that had settled. I could feel his attention shift, like a hawk circling, ready to strike. "Why did you lie about who you are?"

My mouth went dry. Heat rose in my chest again, not from the carriage, but from a tide of panic I barely kept at bay. "Pass," I snapped. Too quick. Too defensive. It gave me away instantly.

"You don't get to say that," he countered, sharp and unwavering. "I get three questions. You gave your word. Answer truthfully, that was the deal."

I swallowed, pride sticking to the back of my throat like something bitter. Slowly, deliberately, I let the words out.

"Because if you found out who I really was, you'd be forced to complete your mission."

That admission landed like thunder between us. Sagar finally turned his full attention to me, his face tightening, not in anger, but in something close to alarm. Or disbelief.

"I'll be honest, Sagar," I continued, my voice quieter now, trembling at the edges. "I don't want to marry the Prince. No, I *can't* marry him."

His expression shuttered instantly, any hint of emotion vanishing behind a well-trained mask. "Marry the Prince?" he repeated, the words slow and cautious.

"Absolutely not!" I said, sharper this time, as if volume could drown the ache beneath it.

He tilted his head slightly, a furrow appearing between his brows. "Why not? I thought Princesses dreamed of marrying Princes. Besides, I thought you were looking for a man with a title."

I hesitated, but the flood had already started. "Because," I said, breath quickening, "I may not know everything about him, but I know enough. He doesn't want a wife, he wants a weapon. A tool. A puppet he can parade and control. Just like those men tonight. I'm a means to power. That's all I will be to him."

I paused, barely holding myself together. "That's why I've been going to all those awful parties. Meeting dukes and lords and sweaty counts who smell like cheese. I've been trying to find someone—*anyone* of high enough status to marry instead. I don't care about a title, personally, I just need to find someone good enough that I won't be forced to say yes. So I wouldn't have to be given away like some gilded prize. In my role, I don't always get to choose love, but I want to at least make my own choice."

The words spilled out in a tumble, louder than I meant, rawer than I expected. And for once, Sagar didn't smirk. He didn't grin or tease. He just watched me with unsettling stillness, as if trying to read beyond what I'd said, to peel back the layers I had so carefully been hiding behind.

"You and I are such similar creatures, Silvia," he murmured, almost too quietly to catch. But I heard him. And the weight of those words pressed into me like a bruise. "Fools who still believe in love, even when the world tells us not to. Even with the cages carved from our status."

I crossed my arms tightly over my chest, the motion more instinct than comfort. As if holding myself together might somehow keep him from seeing the truth, how much his words cracked something open in me.

"My mother made a deal," I said, my voice taut with restraint. "If I found someone suitable, she promised I wouldn't have to marry the Prince."

He laughed, bitter and sharp. "There is no suitable replacement. Not for her. If her goal is power, she'll settle for nothing less than a royal alliance." If his face didn't reveal his frustration, the bleached knuckles of his fists did.

"She trusts my judgment," I shot back, but even as the words left my lips, they felt brittle. Hollow.

He raised a brow. "Does she? Or is that just the illusion she dangled in front of you, just enough hope to keep you blind and busy?"

My stomach twisted. I hated how much sense he made. I hated that he could see through everything. My mother, my plan, me.

"You are infuriating," I hissed, turning away from him before my emotions could betray me.

"And you," he said, that maddening smirk slipping into his voice, "are beautiful when you're angry."

I whirled around. "Don't try to charm me into forgetting that you're impossible." I let out a breathy sigh. "A marriage is the only way out."

"Would marriage really free you?" He asked, the question seemingly more honest than he had intended. "Or just keep you shackled to someone new?"

"I don't care!" I cried, my voice breaking. "Even if it isn't perfect, it's something. It's a door, a way out of a life I didn't choose!"

He shifted closer, his voice low. Each slow, heady breath filled the air with his scent, like a perfume. "Is that really what you want? An arrangement? A title with a warm body next to you? No love. No trust. Just convenience?"

"And what would you know about love or trust?" I fired back, voice like a blade. "You're a knight, sworn to the crown, sworn to silence. What would you know about choosing someone with your heart?"

Something in his face flickered, hurt, maybe, or something deeper, something buried. And gods help me, I wanted to take the words back the second I saw it.

But it was too late.

He leaned in slowly, elbows resting on his knees, his face now close enough that I could see the glare of moonlight caught in his irises. "I know relationships shouldn't be based on lies, and you are still lying to me."

"I told you the truth!" I shot back, my voice cracking.

"Then why does your voice sound like a lie?" he asked calmly.

"I am not lying!"

"Then tell me," he said, his voice dropping, quiet and almost cruel in its softness. "What's the real reason you lied to me?"

I hesitated. The silence throbbed between us.

"I don't want to marry the Prince!" I shouted again, desperate, but it felt hollow now. Less like a declaration, more like a deflection.

"If that were true," he said, voice rising, "you'd simply decline an offer when it was made. You'd face the consequences and take the power back into your hands. But you didn't. You ran. You lied. So no, I don't believe you."

My heart thundered in my chest, certain he could hear it in the tight space. I cursed the closeness, eyeing for any escape. How fast were we going? Could I open the door and slip out with only minor injuries?

"Tell me," he said again, voice tight. "What is it you're really afraid of?"

And then, before I could stop myself, before I could reason or prepare, I blurted it out.

"If you completed your mission," I whispered, "you would have no reason to stay."

He stilled.

I didn't meet his gaze. I couldn't. I turned to the window, the glass suddenly far too cold beneath my fingertips.

"I didn't want you to leave." The admission came out barely above a whisper, but in the confined space of the carriage, it was impossible to miss.

"What?"

"I didn't want you to leave," I repeated, louder this time, steadier. "You've been one of the only constants I can rely on. Through all the lies, the pressure, the danger, you've been there, every time. I didn't want to—no, I *couldn't* lose you."

The air between us changed, electrified with something volatile. Not just tension, something deeper. Longing, maybe. Recognition. The truth I'd tried to bury even from myself was now exposed, naked and trembling in the silence.

I didn't look at him, but I could feel him. The way the space between us grew smaller, like the very gravity in the carriage had shifted. Sagar moved closer, his presence washing over me like a tide, inevitable, overwhelming.

"Tell me it's not one-sided," I whispered, the words catching in my throat like a prayer. "Tell me you've felt it too, this—this strange, impossible thread pulling us together. I've tried to ignore it. Gods, I *wanted* to ignore it. But I can't anymore."

I swallowed hard, my voice breaking as I spoke the next words. "If you walk away from me now, I don't know what I'll do. I don't think I can go back to being what I was before I met you."

His hand rose, cupping my cheek with a gentleness that startled me. The roughness of his palm contrasted with the softness of the moment, his thumb stroking a slow, reverent motion. My skin sparked under his touch, hypersensitive and aching for more.

"You won't lose me," he said, voice low and intimate, barely more than a breath. "Tell me to stay, and I'll stay."

Time suspended. I felt it all crashing down at once, fear, longing, the ache I'd buried beneath layers of pride and duty.

"Stay," I breathed, the word barely leaving my lips before he closed the space between us.

He didn't hesitate. Our lips met, tentative at first, barely a brush. The kiss was soft, uncertain, with an electric heaviness like the moment before lightning strikes. Slowly, his lips began crushing mine with a ferocity that left me weak. It wasn't gentle anymore; it was consuming. A storm. A promise. His mouth moved against mine with aching precision, coaxing, demanding, teaching.

My lips parted, deepening the kiss. His tongue swept into my mouth with a hunger that stole my breath. My gasp was swallowed by his mouth, my heart pounded so hard I feared it might burst. The heat bloomed in my lower belly, causing my hands to move of their own accord to clutch the front of his tunic, pulling him closer, needing more, needing all of him.

Then embarrassment surged through me, a sudden awareness of my inexperience. I tried to pull away, my body flushing with heat and panic. He held me tight, like I was something delicate and burning in his hands.

"No," he growled against my lips, his voice dark. "Don't run from this."

He drifted back to me as if I were the gravity keeping him grounded, pressing his mouth to mine, harder this time, deeper. The kiss was a claiming, his teeth grazing my lower lip before sucking it between his, dragging a ragged gasp from my chest. I melted beneath him, any resistance crumbling like ash in the wind.

"I've felt it," He whispered between ragged breaths. "Since the moment I saw you. That strange feeling that we were connected by something greater than this world, than the gods."

I placed a hand on his cheek, steadying myself in that moment. Nothing mattered now, not the world, not the Queen, not my responsibilities. In that moment, there was only desire, and it was thick and overwhelming.

"We shouldn't do this," I whispered, trying to convince myself.

Sagar pressed his forehead to my own, his eyes boring into mine. "Do you want to stop?"

I shook my head.

"That's not an answer," He growled. "I want to hear you say it."

"I don't want you to stop."

Before I could draw another breath, he was there, erasing the space between us like it had never existed. His lips crashed into mine, insistent, like a hunger he'd denied himself until now. The first sweep of his tongue against mine made the world tilt beneath me. Every sensation surged, fierce and unfamiliar, as his hands moved with slow purpose over my body.

His fingers traced the line of my collarbone, and a soft whimper escaped before I could swallow it. I trembled from the overwhelming ache he stirred in me.

Sagar pulled back just far enough to look at me. Really look at me. His pupils were blown wide, the amber flecks of his irises nearly eclipsed. His lips were red, parted, kiss-bruised and damp, his breath coming in short, ragged bursts.

"Gods, Silvia," he rasped, voice thick with awe. "You're... perfect."

Then his mouth was on me again, lower this time.

His lips grazed a slow, reverent path down the column of my throat, pausing to press a kiss to the place where my pulse thundered just beneath the skin. I could feel a smile crack across his face as he paused, absorbing my racing pulse.

"You're heart's beating so fast." He laughed, trailing lower, ignoring the flush that had taken over my face.

His mouth found the swell of my breasts, gently trailing kisses from one to the other, leaving a trail of fire in its wake. I arched into him with a helpless cry, my fingers tangling in his hair, holding him to me like I might shatter if he let go.

He held me like I was both sacred and dangerous, like he couldn't decide whether to worship me or burn with me.

He looked up at me, his lips curved in a soft, crooked smile. "You have no idea what you do to me," he said, stroking his tongue across his lips as if preparing for a meal.

My thighs clenched around nothing, desperate for friction. He must have felt it, because a wicked smirk curved his mouth as he moved lower, hitching my skirts up around my waist. I trembled, my body buzzing with need.

"Sagar..." I gasped, whispering his name like a prayer.

He knelt between my legs on the carriage floor, parting them with firm, sure hands. My soaked underthings were the only barrier between his mouth and the throbbing ache that had taken over every coherent thought.

"Tell me to stop," he said again, his voice thick and guttural. "And I will."

"I don't want you to stop," I whispered, breathless and shaking.

He kissed the inside of my thigh, slow and teasing, his stubble scraping my sensitive skin just enough to make me whimper. Then he peeled the last scrap of silk keeping him from me, baring me completely. The air was warm and grazing against the intimate skin between my thighs, but his breath was hotter, so much hotter.

His mouth finally found the place I ached for most.

The first stroke of his tongue was slow, torturously slow, drawing a gasp from my throat as heat curled low in my belly. He licked again, a languid sweep from base to tip, savoring me like I was his last indulgence. A low, guttural groan vibrated against my skin, making my thighs tremble. I cried out, hips instinctively jerking forward, but he gripped them hard, holding me in place with maddening control.

"Stay still," he murmured into me, voice wicked and velvet-soft. "Let me enjoy you."

Then he focused, his tongue found me and began circling it with precision, teasing me with a rhythm that felt designed to unravel me. My entire body lit up, every nerve stretched taut, every breath ragged and shallow.

My hands fumbled for stability, his shoulders, the edge of the cushion, the side of the carriage, anything to ground myself as wave after wave of white-hot pressure coiled tighter inside me.

"Oh gods…" I moaned, the word barely intelligible. "Please, please…"

His only response was to suck harder, his tongue flicking and pressing against the swollen, aching spot with such relentless perfection I thought I might scream. My thighs trembled around his head as my body spiraled closer to the edge. I could feel him smirk against me, the arrogant bastard, and the sound of his low laugh sent a new shiver of heat across my skin.

Suddenly, his arms wrapped tighter around my thighs, yanking me forward and holding me flush to his mouth. I let out a yelp, half-surprised, half-overwhelmed.

That was it.

My back arched, my cry echoing in the tight space of the carriage as pleasure consumed me. I bucked against him, legs shaking, fingers digging into his shoulders. My entire body pulsed and quaked, riding the waves as they crashed again and again, fierce and uncontrollable, raw and holy.

Still, he didn't stop.

Not until I was trembling, boneless, gasping for breath. My limbs were limp. My vision blurred. The air felt too thick in my lungs, my heart thundering inside my chest.

Then I heard myself-my own voice, barely a whisper. "More..."

He laughed softly, the sound dark and breathless. "Your first kiss and your first orgasm in the same night, and yet you're already begging for more?" He brushed his mouth up my inner thigh, pausing to kiss the damp skin. "Careful, princess. Greed is a sin."

He began to kiss his way back up my body, slower now, each touch of his lips leaving a trail of fire across me. When his mouth reached mine, he kissed deeply, letting me taste myself on his tongue. The kiss was wild and consuming, a mixture of hunger and need that left me dizzy all over again.

I threaded my fingers through his sandy hair, fisting the strands tight as I tugged his head back. He growled, low and rough, the sound vibrating against my chest, a beautiful mix of surprise and desire.

"I'm a princess," I whispered, my voice teasing and breathless. "I'm supposed to get what I want."

His lips curled into a slow, wicked grin, eyes glinting with something primal. "And what is it that you want, Princess?" he murmured, the title turning molten on his tongue.

For decades, I had needed nothing. Wanted nothing. But in this moment, I wanted everything.

I leaned in, my lips brushing his ear as I spoke, each word dripping with purpose. "I want you to show me exactly what I do to you."

Just as the warmth began to flood through me, spreading like fire through my limbs, the carriage lurched to a sudden stop. The spell shattered.

Sagar pulled away from me, his movements swift and composed, slipping my body gently back into something resembling propriety. My dress still bunched awkwardly around my waist, my hair askew, skin flushed and humming.

"I'm going to see what's going on," he muttered, already reaching for the carriage door.

"Wait!" My hand shot out, clutching his tunic with a desperate grip.

He paused instantly, reading the panic in my voice. His expression softened, softer than I'd ever seen, and he leaned forward, brushing a kiss just beneath my jaw, where my pulse still raced beneath the skin.

"Don't worry," he whispered, voice like velvet. "I'll be right outside. We'll finish what we started later. Oh, and Silvia..."

"Yes?"

A malicious grin spread across his face. "I still have one question left, don't forget that."

My body shuddered at the promise in his words, the heat between my thighs still aching for him as he slipped out into the cool night air.

Alone, I pulled the skirts of my dress back into place, smoothing trembling fingers over the fabric. My cheeks burned, and I pressed both palms to them, as if I could force the blush to recede. It was no use.

I touched my lips, still tingling, still swollen from his kiss. Gods. What was that?

That sensation, that warmth that once moved me only in prayer, in ritual, now surged through me from something entirely different. Not divine. Not sacred. Human.

It wasn't the Goddess who set my soul alight. It was him. And whatever we had just done—whatever we nearly became—I wanted it again.

A sudden gust of cold air tore me from my thoughts as the carriage door flew open, slamming against the side with a hollow bang.

"Sagar—!" I called, turning towards him with an anticipated grin.

But he wasn't there.

An unfamiliar knight stood there, backlit by torchlight. He was tall, armored, the Calbraxian crest emblazoned across his chest like a brand. His eyes were sharp, his posture rigid, one hand outstretched toward me.

"Your Highness," he said firmly.

I froze. Confusion and dread locked my limbs in place. My gaze drifted past him, past the open door.

We were at the palace gates. Dozens of guards flanked the path, swords at their sides, eyes trained on the carriage like it held something dangerous. At the head of them all stood a woman dressed in silver and shadow, her crown gleaming in the moonlight.

Queen Elanore, my mother.

Chapter 13

The Queen stood at the center of the palace steps, her spine straight, her hands folded in front of her, draped in velvet and moonlight. Grace and elegance clung to her as naturally as breath. Her face remained unreadable, stoic, regal, until I stepped from the carriage.

My heart pounded as I passed through the line of green-uniformed guards, their eyes locked ahead, disciplined and unmoving. Sagar stood at her side, still dusted with the heat of what we'd shared. He looked every bit the dutiful knight again. His expression was carefully neutral, hands clasped behind his back.

A thousand thoughts crashed through me.

Had she seen? Had one of the guards overheard something, glimpsed something? My stomach twisted. Had she sensed that I had nearly lost my powers in one reckless, fevered moment? My skin prickled with cold sweat.

As I inched closer, I noticed something strange across her face. Only, it wasn't anger or disappointment, it was relief. It radiated from her like a gentle fog. Her shoulders, usually drawn back like a bow, were relaxed. Her gaze, though sharp, wasn't accusing. There was no rage, no fury burning behind her eyes. Only calm.

My pace quickened, shifting from stiff caution into a quiet run, until I was nearly breathless before her.

"Your Majesty, I—" I dropped to my knees, my voice catching.

"Hush, my dear." She extended a gloved hand, palm soft, commanding. I rose slowly, blinking up at her in disbelief.

For a long, pregnant silence, she simply looked at me. Studied me. Her eyes roamed from my tangled hair to the bruises on my arms, to the faint tear along the edge of my gown. She said nothing about them. Instead, she turned to Sagar and placed a hand upon his shoulder, her expression warm and almost maternal.

"Great Sagar, Head of the Knights of Etheria," she announced with a voice that carried across the courtyard, clear and imperial. "On behalf of all Calbraxia, thank you for returning my daughter safely home."

The gathered soldiers responded in thunderous unison. "Thank you!"

Sagar gave a graceful bow, all nobility and poise, but I saw the flicker in his eyes, the flicker he saved only for me. He winked, so quickly no one else could have caught it.

"The pleasure was all mine," he said, his tone light but deferential. "I'm proud to serve the people of Calbraxia in whatever way I can."

The Queen turned her back on him momentarily, addressing the line of knights behind her with a scathing sweep of her gaze.

"You could all learn something from the Etherians," she declared, her voice hardening. "They accomplished in hours what our forces failed to do. With a fraction of the numbers."

A ripple of unease passed through the men. Some bowed their heads; others stiffened.

Then she turned back to Sagar, her tone softening once more. She stepped closer and lifted her hand, cradling his chin with deliberate intimacy.

"I hope you won't think poorly of us," she said with a small, knowing smile. "And I hope that once our great kingdoms are joined in marriage, we'll be fortunate enough to benefit from your wisdom."

My heart stopped. Marriage?

I turned sharply toward her, disbelief crashing over me like icy water.

Sagar hadn't proposed on behalf of the prince. He wouldn't, he couldn't, not after what happened between us. Not after that. I searched his face, hoping to find the same confusion there, but his expression had shuttered, his eyes unreadable once more.

My mother's voice broke the silence again.

"Silvia," she said gently. "Shake the hand of the man who saved you. And let us all take shelter from the cold. You'll catch ill out here."

Stunned, I stepped forward, my movements slow and detached, like I was walking through a dream. Sagar stood still, a marble statue of chivalry.

I extended my bare hand. "Thank you, Sir Sagar," I murmured, the words scraping their way out.

As Sagar took my hand in his, it felt alien.

There was no spark, no heat, only the cold pressure of formality. His grip, once so eager and hungry, was now distant, calculated. Like he was wearing armor again, not on his body but in his soul. The fingers that had once trembled on my skin now felt indifferent.

I couldn't look at him. If I did, I knew my composure would shatter. My lips trembled, my vision blurred, and I turned my face away, clutching the memory of him from less than an hour before, his mouth on mine, his breath catching my name. Had I imagined all of it?

"Come, Silvia," my mother called gently. "Let's clean you up, my little rose."

There was a thread of warmth in her tone, but I felt no comfort. Only the pang of guilt and grief tightened in my chest. I followed her into the palace, swallowed by its familiar grandeur. The golden halls, once magnificent, now pressed in on me. The chandeliers hung too heavy, the tapestries whispered secrets I didn't want to hear. Everything smelled of perfume and control.

The Queen walked with the precision of someone who always knew the next step in a dance. My steps, however, dragged with the weight of a future I hadn't chosen.

When we reached my chambers, a cluster of maids awaited us with downcast eyes and quiet readiness. The Queen gave a single nod, and I was swept into the adjoining bath without a word.

Steam rose from the water, but it failed to melt the chill in my bones. The maids worked quickly and wordlessly, hands scrubbing and rinsing in clinical repetition. I tried to dissociate, but I couldn't ignore what this was. Inspection. Confirmation. Surveillance dressed in civility.

Shame curdled in my gut. I stared into the water, but it offered no reflection.

When they were finished, I was draped in a silk robe, my skin pink and raw. But it wasn't the heat of the bath that left me aching; it was the hollow space Sagar had left in me. What we had shared had meant something. I knew it had. But why had he acted so cold? Had he really finalized the proposal with the Queen?

I stepped into my room to find my mother seated, composed as ever, her presence filling the chamber like smoke.

"Sit, Silvia," she said with a soft authority that left no room for refusal.

I sat on the edge of the bed, the silk of my robe clinging to my damp skin. She observed me, like a ruler evaluating a chess piece.

"You're unharmed. The thugs didn't...?" she asked, her tone clipped but careful.

"No, Your Majesty," I murmured.

Her brows furrowed slightly. "Please, in here, call me Mother." She clasped her hands around mine, her touch surprisingly warm, though I felt nothing. "I cannot express how relieved I am to have you back. When I heard you hadn't made it to the party, I sent the entire force out searching for you. I'm amazed that the knight found you so quickly."

The words were kind, but hollow. Perfumed air over a rotting truth.

Her hand moved to my back, stroking slowly. I inhaled, steadying myself, and dared to speak.

"Mother, what did you mean when you said, 'once our countries are joined by marriage'?" My voice was barely above a whisper. "The prince hasn't proposed, has he?"

She rose from the bed and walked to my vanity, picking up the silver-handled brush June used on me each morning. She began running it through my hair with practiced ease, detangling knots one by one.

"We don't always choose how fate finds us," she said softly, her fingers delicately weaving through my hair. "The gods guide with crooked hands."

A chill slid down my spine. "What does that mean?" I asked, voice tight.

She sighed, her touch pausing for a moment before resuming. "The Prince sent me an offer."

My breath caught. "An offer?" My fists clenched in my lap, every muscle suddenly on edge. "What kind of offer?"

"You don't need to worry, my rose," she said, tone too casual, too smooth, as though I were a child asking about monsters under the bed. "He hasn't proposed marriage, not directly. But he made it clear what he wants. And what he's willing to give in return."

The floor dropped from beneath me. "What does he want?" I asked, even though I already knew.

"A means to become king. He wants a princess," she said calmly, as if it were a line in a ledger. "In exchange for resources. He sends knights, food, protection, everything our people desperately need. And I give him a bride."

My mouth went dry. My stomach twisted so violently it felt like I might retch. The question clawed at my throat, one I didn't want to ask, but had to.

"Mother…" My voice cracked. "If you agreed to these terms, why would *I* not need to worry?"

She hesitated. That was the first sign that something was truly wrong. Her polished veneer faltered as she suddenly found something incredibly fascinating on the floor.

"You have to understand," she said at last, her voice barely above a whisper. "He has a contingent of knights camped outside our gates. I couldn't refuse him, not without risking everything."

"Tell me," I snapped. "If not me, then who?"

She straightened and let the brush fall gently to the vanity. Then she took my hand again, this time with force.

"For the safety of the kingdom," she said, her voice low and sharp, "and for your safety, I gave him my answer."

"Who?" I spat, voice shaking with rage.

She turned from me, her shoulders a statue of burden and resignation. "Your sister may not be the Prince's first choice," she said coldly, "but she was apparently good enough for him."

The world stopped.

"Margaret?" My voice cracked. "You're giving him Margaret?"

She didn't flinch. "You've made your desires clear. There were no other options."

My vision swam. The room bent and blurred, and the breath in my chest felt foreign. I imagined Margaret, sweet, smart Margaret, dressed in ivory and gold, a wedding veil trembling over her soft curls. I imagined her eyes wide and uncertain, her hands trembling as they were placed in a stranger's. I saw her locked away in some distant tower, like I had been in my past life.

"You would give him my sister?" I whispered, my voice a blade drawn clean from the scabbard. "After everything?"

"We are not safe here! You were just kidnapped! Gods know that our people are in need, and they've made it clear who they want to hold responsible tonight. We need Etheria's support, Silvia," my mother replied, her tone ironclad. "He wants a Stephan. A Divinial. A symbol of divine right. This is what it costs to keep the peace."

"She's a child!" I screamed, leaping to my feet as the chair clattered behind me.

"She's a *princess*," my mother snapped, her voice sharp as winter glass. "I was only twelve when I was sent to your father. You two have lived in freedom far longer than I ever did. You've both been spoiled by choice."

Her words hit like a slap, and yet I couldn't look away. Rage twisted in my chest. My memories twisted with it, memories from before, from then. Of stone walls. Of silence. Of prayers that went unanswered. The lonely nights and the war I struggled to survive.

The Crown Prince hadn't chosen me, not in this life. But if he was willing to wait a decade for my powers to develop, what difference would another seven years make for Margaret?

"She's only thirteen," I said, my voice breaking. "You can't send her. You can't let her endure what I—what they will expect of her."

My mother looked at me then. I didn't see a queen, nor a ruler, but a mother, one who had borne too many burdens, and passed them like heirlooms. A single tear traced a line down her powdered cheek.

"Do you think I want this, Silvia?" she asked, her voice barely more than a breath. "Do you think this was ever my dream for either of you? But I have no leverage. No time. He arrives tomorrow. I'll announce the proposal on her behalf before the evening banquet."

"Wait—" The word escaped me in a gasp, and I dropped to my knees. "This is my fault. I…I'll fix it."

She tilted her head, her eyes narrowing. "And how exactly do you intend to do that, my dear?"

I swallowed hard, the words burning my throat. "He wants a Stephan, a Divinial right? That's all? Then I'll do it. I'll marry the prince."

Silence fell like snow.

Her expression shifted, shocked, cautious. She walked to me and gently cupped my chin, her eyes searched my own for an answer, as if I would change my mind at any moment.

"You'll marry him?" she asked.

I nodded, my limbs trembling. "If it means sparing Margaret, yes. I'll do it."

She said nothing at first. Then, after a long, assessing pause, she gave a slow, regal nod. "Very well," she said. "If you are certain, truly certain, I will present him the offer when he arrives. If he finds you acceptable, I'll announce your engagement at tomorrow's banquet."

She leaned forward, pressing her lips to the top of my head. The gesture was tender, but I felt no warmth. Only a strange, resigned silence was creeping through my body like frostbite.

She released me then, the sound of her rustling skirts the only indication she was moving. I didn't look up. I couldn't.

"Rest well, Silvia," she said, pausing at the door. "Tomorrow is the beginning of your future."

I forced myself to lift my gaze. She gave me a smile, warm, kind, and yet hollow as an echo. Then she turned and left, the door clicking shut behind her.

The room was swallowed in silence. I stared at the polished wood, willing it to open again. When it didn't, I melted onto the floor, the cold stone pulling the last of my strength from me. I sprawled across the marble like a discarded gown, cheek pressed to the chill as my heartbeat pounded through my bones, a frantic drumbeat of a soul looking for escape.

But death wasn't an option this time. Not for me. Not now.

The Crown Prince didn't care if I lived or died. I wasn't special. I was a vessel, a means to an end. And if I died before we wed, he'd take Margaret in my place. He'd get his weapon, one way or another.

A knock at the window startled me.

I bolted upright, wiping my face with trembling fingers. Sagar's silhouette stood in the moonlight, his cloak dark against the glass. I stumbled to the window and unlatched it, letting him slip inside. The moment he saw my tear-streaked face, his expression darkened.

"What happened?" he asked, his voice rough with concern.

For a moment, I teetered on the edge. I wanted to tell him everything: the second life, the memories, the deal I had just made to save Margaret. I wanted to beg him to run away with me, to disappear into the mountains or across the sea, to start a quiet life where no one knew our names.

Instead, I grabbed his tunic, clinging to him like the dream he was. His face, so steady, so achingly beautiful, made the fantasy feel almost real.

He reached up and cupped my cheek, his thumb brushing a fresh tear from my skin. A smile flickered across his face, softening the lines of tension.

I couldn't speak. So instead, I kissed him.

It was desperate, searching, a silent scream into his mouth. He didn't hesitate; his arms wrapped around me like he'd been waiting for this moment forever. For a brief, stolen second, I let myself believe in it.

But then he pulled away, just far enough to search my face. His brows knit in concern, his lips still trembling from our kiss.

"While I do *love* what you're doing right now," he murmured. "Tell me what's wrong,"

I shook my head, my fingers trailing down the hard lines of his chest. "Not now," I whispered. "Please. Just stay with me."

"Silvia…" he started, but I kissed him again, deeper this time, more urgent. My hands moved without thought, pulling him closer, trying to erase the world with his warmth. For a while, he surrendered. Our lips collided in a tangle of need, our bodies falling onto the bed, a mess of limbs and heat and longing.

I wanted to lose myself in him.

I needed to.

Instead, his hands stilled mine, firm and gentle. He raised them above my head, holding them firmly in place. His mouth moved from my lips to my jaw, to my neck, and then paused.

"Silvia," he murmured, his breath warm against my skin. "Whatever it is, this isn't going to help. Talk to me. What's going on?"

I felt my lip quiver, the words caught somewhere between my throat and my ribs. I was too raw, too exposed to say what I truly wanted. And he knew it, his gaze stayed locked on mine, unwavering, until he glanced down.

Sometime during our fall to the mattress, my robe had slipped loose, just slightly. A sliver of freshly washed skin was exposed, stretching from my collarbone down to the gentle curve of my navel, the candlelight catching along the trail like it, too, was holding its breath.

His eyes stayed there, a glimpse of hunger and something I couldn't name burning in them. And then, when he realized, they snapped away just as fast.

"Shit," he muttered, instantly letting go of my hands and turning his back to me, jaw clenched. "I didn't mean...I didn't realize—"

"No," I said quietly, fingers fumbling to retie the sash at my waist. "It's okay." I paused, forcing a steady breath. "Tonight's just been a lot."

The words felt hollow against the weight of everything we weren't saying, what we had barely survived, what we both still wanted. My pulse still raced from the ache of vulnerability left in its wake.

His voice was strained when he finally replied. "Yeah. A whirlwind."

He didn't press. He just ran his fingers through my hair, slowly, tenderly, and I melted into the rhythm of it.

"Was it the carriage ride?" he finally asked quietly. "Did I push you too far?"

I shook my head and pulled myself closer to him, my hand tracing the shape of his arm beneath the soft fabric I had nearly torn from him minutes ago.

"You did nothing wrong," I said, my voice thick. "It's something that's been on my mind for longer than you'll ever know."

He chuckled, a sound that wrapped around me like a blanket, then pressed his lips to my forehead. He held me tighter, and for a fleeting second, the world stopped spinning.

"Sagar," I said, shifting so I could meet his eyes. "What would you do if you had to choose between me and the Crown Prince?"

His expression shifted, eyes narrowing, tension creeping into his shoulders.

"I'd never have to choose."

"But if you did," I pressed. "If following his orders meant hurting me. Would you do it?"

He sat up, pulling away slightly, and I immediately missed his warmth. There was something unreadable in his eyes now, something that made my chest ache.

"The Prince would never hurt you, Silvia," he said, his words dripping with certainty.

"You don't know that," I murmured, my voice so small I wasn't sure he heard me.

"I don't understand why you're so convinced he's trying to use you," he said, frustration flashing in his tone. "He's not the monster you think he is."

"And I don't understand why you're so loyal to him," I snapped. "Why else would he keep you here this long? He didn't send an entire army just to send a message, Sagar."

He stiffened. "You don't know him."

"Then tell me," I gestured to the glowing encampment outside the window. "Tell me why you're really here."

Silence fell again.

He turned to the window, staring into the darkness. His voice, when it came, was soft.

"I'm here for you," he said. "Those were my orders. We were sent to find you and deliver a message."

This was it, the proposal. Had he avoided speaking it out loud? Afraid whatever this thing between us would crack if he did?

"I know what the message is," I said, the admission scraping my throat raw.

He turned, surprised. "You do?"

I nodded. "Of course I do."

He looked at me like he wanted to believe I was wrong. Like he needed me to be wrong. I reached for him again, threading my fingers through his, guiding him closer.

"Sagar," I breathed. He followed willingly, settling beside me. He gently guided my head to the pillow, lying close enough that our noses nearly touched.

The moonlight bathed him in silver. He was a shadow etched in light, dangerous, loyal, beautiful. And mine. For now.

"I would never let anything happen to you," he whispered. The words shattered me.

The dam broke. The weight of the day crashed into me like a tidal wave. The pain. The helplessness. The decision. I began to cry. Silent, hot tears that ran down my cheeks like rivers. I didn't try to hide them this time.

He shifted toward me, his face softening with worry. Then he gathered me into his arms and pulled my head to his chest.

"It's been a long day," he whispered, stroking my hair. "You don't have to hold it in anymore."

I wept for Margaret, for my mother, for the past life that haunted me, and the future that loomed like a blade above my neck. I wept for the truth I couldn't speak, and the man beside me who might never understand.

Tomorrow, I would meet my fate.

Tomorrow, I would kneel before the prince who was the mastermind of my captivity.

"Please," I choked out, barely above a whisper. "Don't go."

He hesitated. "Tell me to stay," he whispered back.

"Stay," I said.

His eyes searched mine for a long moment before he nodded. "Alright."

He settled beside me, pulling the plush sheets above me and tucking me in. The warmth of his body and the steady rhythm of his heartbeat soothed me, and for the first time that night, I felt a semblance of peace.

My eyes felt heavy as I was swallowed in his embrace. I willed myself to remember everything about this moment. I needed to remember, for soon all I would have is the memory as I rotted in the tower. I inhaled, I would always remember the scent that followed him and enveloped me whole.

His warmth, Goddess, I would miss his warmth. No fire on this earth could warm me quite like his body. So sculpted but soft, he carried himself with such bravado, but with me, he was always kind. His charming convictions that somehow made me flush with every word he breathed. His touch that stayed with me like a shadow.

I unburrowed my face for a brief moment and forced my sleepy eyes open. I wanted him to know that I was thinking of him. As I gazed into his eyes, a soft whisper took control of me.

Tonight would be the last night he would hold me this way, and I wanted to dream of it forever.

Chapter 14

A veil of delicate lace framed my vision, and the sound of jubilant music filled the air. My feet moved on their own accord, gliding along an aisle lined with roses in full bloom. Nobles stood on either side, their faces indistinct, but their murmurs filled with awe. The gown I wore was heavy with jewels, and every step seemed to echo with finality.

At the end of the aisle stood the prince, his back to me. I felt sick. Today was the day we were to be wed. I continued along the aisle, my feet slowing as if I were traversing through sand. As I reached the end I turned to face him, the thick veil covering my face.

He turned slowly, and my heart caught in my throat. His face was not human; it was the head of a stag, its antlers adorned with gold and rubies. The seal of Calbraxia. The seal that adorned my father's tomb, and soon to be my own.

I tried to scream, but no sound came. My hands flew to my mouth only to find them bound, my body restrained. The weight of the bindings tightened as panic surged through me.

My vision blurred as I turned to the room of nobles.

Why won't any of you help me? I thought, trying to shake away from my restraints. My gaze shifted, and my audience applauded as the priest said the words "you may now kiss the bride."

Tears streamed past my cheeks as I twisted and tugged, trying to get out in any means possible. The stag made his way to me, slowly stalking me like a tiger hunting its prey. I fell to my knees and pulled with all my might.

"Till death do us part." The creature whispered in a foul, unearthly voice, leaning in closer and closer until our lips nearly touched. I squeezed my eyes shut in anticipation of what was going to follow.

I jolted awake with a gasp, my body drenched in cold sweat. My room was shrouded in the gray light of early dawn, the eerie silence broken only by my ragged breaths. My hands gripped the sheets tightly, my robe clung to my damp skin, and my hands trembled as I pushed the hair from my face. The dream was vivid and unsettling, like a half-remembered memory.

The room was quiet, save for the soft crackle of the dying fire. I reached out instinctively, but the space beside me was empty. Sagar had slipped away sometime during the night, leaving behind the faint scent I had so desperately clung to the night before.

I let my fingers linger there, tracing the shallow impression his body had left behind as if the pressure of my touch might call him back. But the sheet had already gone still. The ghost of him had gone stale.

A sharp, hollow ache bloomed in my chest. He left, he promised he would stay, but he left. I sank back into the mattress, my fingers still clenched around the blanket as my thoughts spiraled. Why would he break that promise?

My stomach twisted violently. There was only one reason I could think, one that made sense, and it filled me with dread. The Prince had arrived.

A fresh wave of panic crashed over me. I sat up again, suddenly feeling as if I couldn't breathe. The air felt heavier now, as though the entire palace had shifted during the night as if it knew he was here.

Before I could unravel further, the door creaked open. I jumped.

June entered, carrying a tray of tea and her usual air of delightful command. Her eyes swept over me in a glance that saw far too much. She didn't comment on the dark circles beneath my eyes or the tremor in my fingers as I pulled the blanket tighter around me.

"The Prince arrived! It's amazing, Silvia, there's already celebrations starting across the kingdom," she said calmly, setting the tray on the table. "Her Majesty insists you wear your finest. All the noble houses are already gathering for a grand welcome feast."

Her words hit me like a blow to the chest. So it was true.

I gave a small nod, numbness creeping through my limbs. June moved through the room with practiced grace, her hands already selecting the gown draped over a nearby stand. It was crimson, deep and rich like blood, embroidered with golden thread that glinted like flame in the early light. A nod to Etheria. A symbol of my loyalty.

I stared at it as she held it up, bile rising in my throat.

"How are you feeling today?" she asked gently, brushing my cheeks with a hint of rouge to disguise the pallor in my skin.

"I am managing," I replied quietly. It was the only words I could offer.

But I wasn't. I wasn't managing at all.

With Sagar gone, everything felt wrong, empty, brittle. I clung to the memory of his arms around me, of the warmth that had shielded me for one fragile night. But it was gone now. He was gone. And I was alone again, left to face the storm he had helped me forget.

June filled the silence with idle chatter, her voice a faint hum behind the roar in my ears. I could barely focus as she arranged my hair and fastened the heavy gown around me like armor.

Then the door burst open with a rush of color and noise.

"Silvia!" Margaret sang, bursting into the room with a flurry of ribbons and curls. "Did you hear? The Prince is here!"

Her voice rang like a bell through the chamber, sweet and shrill. I flinched. My sorrow must have flashed too plainly across my face because her smile faltered instantly.

"What's wrong?" she asked, voice dipping into concern.

I forced my expression into something passable, stretching the corners of my mouth upward. "Nothing, my dear," I lied, reaching out a hand and motioning her to sit beside me.

Margaret paused, eyes flickering between my hand and my stilled expression before making her way beside me. Her youth shimmered around her like sunlight on glass. She stared at me with wide, hesitant eyes, clearly itching to ask a thousand questions.

The difference between us was quite noticeable. She was still untouched by fear, still dreaming of princes and balls and reading fairy tales.

And I was preparing to meet the man who had once caged me in a solitary prison. The man who had chosen me, not for love, but for war.

"Do you know why he's come?" she asked, her voice tinged with amusement. "Is he here to propose? Are you going to marry him?" My hand twitched.

"Yes Margaret, I'm going to marry him."

Her face erupted with an explosion of glee, eyes shining like the sun breaking through storm clouds. Without warning, she threw her arms around my neck and tumbled into my lap, her laughter spilling into the quiet room like a songbird's tune.

"You did it!" she squealed, her voice bursting with excitement. "You've finally found your husband!"

She said it like a gift, as if I were being crowned with hope instead of shackled in duty. She didn't know. She couldn't. To her, this was the end to my months long battle she had been watching with weary eyes. This was supposed to be a happy moment, *I* should be happy. She didn't understand the weight of it, the sacrifice. What I was surrendering, who I was surrendering, for her.

My fists clenched in my lap, nails biting into the soft skin of my palm as I forced down the swell of rage. A scream coiled inside me, begging to escape. I wanted to tell her to go, to run, to never speak of this again. To understand that this wasn't joy, it was my personal demise dressed in a wedding veil.

But then I saw it.

The glint of a gold hairpin nestled in her curls. The one I had bought for when I started my ridiculous round of courting. It sparkled as she smiled, catching the sunlight like a tiny star.

The anger melted into something quieter. Something older. I remembered why I had agreed to marry the prince. Not for the Queen. Not for the people. For Margaret, and the childhood she still deserved to keep.

My hand relaxed, and a small, genuine smile found its way to my lips. I reached up and gently tucked a loose strand of hair behind her ear, careful not to dislodge the pin.

"Margaret," I said softly, "I'm a little too tired to horse around like this."

Her eyes widened, and guilt painted across her face as she quickly sat up and slid off my lap.

"I'm sorry, Silvia!" she said, her voice earnest. "I forgot about what happened last night." She reached for my hand, her fingers brushing mine with such tenderness it made my chest ache. "I'm just glad that handsome knight saved you."

The air in the room shifted.

June, who had been folding a silk sash across a nearby chair, stilled. Her eyes flicked toward us with a subtle sharpness, a flicker of something, curiosity, passing across her face.

My heart stuttered. I felt the blood drain from my cheeks.

I held Margaret's hand a little tighter, recomposing myself.

"Yes," I managed, my voice hushed. "I'm glad too."

June's gaze lingered on me a second too long. Then she cleared her throat and smoothed the front of her gown as if she hadn't heard anything unusual at all.

"My Princesses," she said, her tone clipped and formal. "It's time to go now. The court is waiting."

But there was something in her voice. A new edge. She was watching me closely now, adding pieces to a puzzle she hadn't realized were missing.

I swallowed hard and nodded, rising to my feet with the mechanical grace of someone donning armor. I pasted a smile onto my lips, pretty, polished, and entirely false as I extended a hand to Margaret.

"Ready to meet the Prince?" I asked, voice light as air.

Margaret beamed and took my hand eagerly, but I could still feel June's eyes on me.

My steps were slow and heavy as I forced my feet across the palace. Margaret stayed by my side, excitedly chatting about the man she had envisioned he would be. Tall, handsome, a regal aura falling around him. He would be young enough to marry me, but old enough to seem distinguished. He would be the pinnacle of Etheria, strong, bold, courageous.

She froze once we reached the outer doors of the throne room. The delight that filled the room now vanished.

"What's wrong?" I asked, turning her towards me.

"Silvia," She whimpered. "What if he's not a good person? What if he's not good enough for you?"

"Oh, my dear Margaret." I took her face in my hands and gazed into her soft eyes. "Truly, whatever he's like, I will find happiness. Be happy my sweet sister, you will find happiness one day too."

The lie may not have been as convincing as I had wanted, but it was enough to appease Margaret for the meantime. She wrapped her arms around my throat and squeezed tightly.

"He will be." She promised. "He will be perfect."

As we stepped into the throne room, a hush fell over the assembled nobles like a curtain drawn tight. The air was heavy, thick with perfume, sweat, and anticipation. Dresses rustled, fans flicked nervously, and the dull scrape of boots against marble echoed faintly as all eyes turned toward us.

Margaret squeezed my hand, her earlier excitement dimmed to solemn awe. At the far end of the room, atop the dais, stood our mother, poised and imperious, draped in royal blues and silver. Her eyes found mine, and in them, a flicker of hope burned far too brightly. It made my stomach churn.

We approached in measured steps, curtsying in unison before her. She nodded her approval, and we rose to stand at her side.

My gaze swept the chamber.

The sea of nobles, with their colorful brocades and polished jewels, was a blur. I searched for Etherian colors, the familiar blood red that had haunted me, but found nothing. No standard. No guards. No Prince. No Sagar.

The absence was louder than the crowd.

My fingers tightened together in front of me. Beneath my calm façade, I was trembling. I could feel it in my bones, the shifting of fate. I had never met the prince in my past life. I had always been a step behind the decisions made for me. But this time, I would face him. See him. And somehow, that made it worse.

A beat of silence rippled across the room as the heavy double doors creaked open.

Light poured in from the corridor beyond, golden and blinding. The nobles turned toward it, their faces cast into silhouettes, shadow puppets against marble and firelight.

The master of ceremonies stepped forward, his voice slicing through the stillness. "Announcing His Royal Highness, Prince Gerraint Petris of Etheria." He boomed.

The name alone brought a fresh chill to the air. I kept my eyes glued to the floor, hoping, praying that I wouldn't have to meet my former captor's gaze.

His footsteps were the only sound as he entered, slow and deliberate. Each step echoed with precision, as though choreographed to unnerve. I held my breath as I counted each step, calculating just how long I had until I was forced to see him, to speak to him, to breathe the same air as him.

The footsteps came to a sudden stop as I stared at the black leather shoes that now stood before me. My eyes followed the legs up before I finally saw his face.

He emerged from the halo of light, and for a moment, I thought I was seeing a ghost. He was young. Far younger than I had imagined. No older than I was, perhaps even a little younger. And beautiful, in the cold, unreachable way that marble statues are beautiful. He didn't look Etherian; his skin was pale, almost translucent, like fine porcelain kissed by moonlight. It made the dark cascade of his hair and the near black shadows around his eyes seem even more otherworldly.

His eyes arrested me. A deep, endless brown, so dark they almost looked black. They shimmered faintly beneath heavy lashes, unreadable. Unforgiving.

His features were strikingly familiar. It wasn't just that he resembled the paintings of royalty; it was something deeper. Something personal. A shadow of someone I had known.

His gaze locked with mine as he bowed with an effortless grace that felt more like performance than sincerity. "Princess Silvia," he said, his voice smooth, velvety, and disturbingly calm. "Pleasure to meet you after all this time."

I hadn't realized I'd been holding my breath until he said my name. I let the air release, stinging my lungs as I sucked in another. I traced the motion of his polished shoes up to the crimson tunic embroidered with gold. We were—gods help us—matching. Like two characters in some well-illustrated fairy tale.

Except this felt nothing like a storybook. It felt more like walking into the mouth of a dragon.

He extended his hand, and I placed mine in his, because there was no other choice. His fingers were cold, and his grip precise. He brought my knuckles to his lips with mechanical delicacy, his eyes never leaving mine.

He kissed them lightly. When he finally withdrew his hand, the ghost of the touch lingered, cold, impersonal. I could still feel the chill pressed into my skin, as though he had marked me with frost. It was a sensation I couldn't shake.

"Your Highness, may I present my daughter, Princess Silvia Stephan of Calbraxia," the Queen announced, her voice smooth and regal, commanding the full attention of the room.

"I'm honored," the prince said. But there was no true feeling in his voice, no warmth, no joy. Only something calculated, something deliberate, as if he were reading lines from a script he had memorized long ago and long since grown tired of performing.

"The honor is mine," I responded automatically, each word brittle and dry on my tongue. I dipped into a curtsy, suppressing the instinct to recoil.

As I rose, my eyes swept the gathered crowd, finally spotting him.

At the front of the Etherian guard, cloaked in the unmistakable scarlet of his station, stood Sagar. Even from this distance, he knocked the air from my lungs. His form, usually so familiar, now seemed miles away. His armor gleamed beneath the chandelier's golden light, his helmet obscuring all but his eyes. Those eyes, once warm and tender, were now distant. Clouded.

He looked at me. Only for a moment. Just long enough for my heart to shatter all over again. Then he turned, his gaze moving over the crowd with forced indifference, as if we were strangers.

My body remained still, poised, but inside I was splintering.

The Queen's voice sliced through the tension in the room. "We are forever grateful for the Etherian knights' assistance in returning my daughter safely."

"I'm sure it was his pleasure," the prince said, smiling faintly. But beneath the civility, there was something else, something razor-sharp. The words tasted like mockery, like he knew of my feelings. Like he knew what we had done.

I glanced at my mother. She was glowing, pride radiating from her like the sun. To her, this was the end of every sacrifice she had ever made. To me, this was the beginning.

And then her hand moved, pressing gently but firmly against the small of my back, nudging me forward.

"As a thank you," she said sweetly, "my daughter would like to ask you something."

A wave of dread surged through me. She wouldn't make me do this. Not here. Not like this.

But her smile was unwavering. Margaret stood dutifully at her side, a strange expression spreading across her face as her eyes swept from me to Gerraint. I wanted to scream.

My mouth felt dry. My limbs, wooden. "Your Highness," I began, my voice trembling beneath its practiced elegance. "I'm deeply appreciative of the efforts of your knights. They have been a great comfort to our kingdom over the past few months."

He bowed his head slightly, his dark eyes fixed on me. "Princess Silvia, I'm glad they could be of use to you." There it was again, that veiled edge.

I ignored it. I had to.

"As a proper thank you," I forced my voice to steady as I curled my nails into my palms, "I was hoping you would do me the honor of being the one to unite our great kingdoms."

The moment the words left my mouth, I felt hollow.

"Are you asking *me* to marry you, Princess?" He hummed, a strange smile creeping across his lips.

"Yes."

The room exploded into a murmur of hushed voices and susurrating silks. Whispers hissed like wind through the trees. I stared at the polished marble beneath my feet, as though it might crack open and swallow me whole.

There was no answer.

Silence spread, thick and oppressive. I could feel each second drag across my skin, a slow and excruciating death. My heartbeat thundered in my ears. Ten seconds. Twenty. Forty. Fifty.

Only then did I dare lift my eyes.

Gerraint hadn't moved. His eyes flicked toward his council, a silent exchange I couldn't interpret. And there among them, Sagar. His jaw was clenched, his fists rigid at his sides. He stared at the prince like a man on the edge of something violent. But he said nothing.

Then the prince turned back to me.

His eyes, those deep, dark pits, scanned me slowly, as if trying to determine exactly what kind of creature I was. His smile curled, more serpent than suitor.

"I'm surprised, Princess," he said, though his tone suggested he was anything but. "But, if it's what you want, I would be honored."

The room erupted into applause.

A hundred noble faces turned to me, smiling, nodding, approving. I stood frozen in the center of it all, a puppet suspended by golden strings, applauded for sealing my own fate.

I couldn't feel my hands anymore. I couldn't feel anything. Sagar had given his approval to this sham of an engagement. Why? Was he just fulfilling his duty? Did he know what the Prince had in store for me?

"What a wonderful surprise!" the Queen exclaimed, her voice ringing like bells across the marble chamber. "We are so delighted you would accept such a proposal. I'm positive Silvia will make you very happy."

I wanted to tear off my tiara and flee the room before the walls crushed me under their weight. I knew she didn't mean to wound me, not intentionally, but her joy, her triumph, felt like mockery. Every word felt like another blade twisting in my chest. Each one whispered the same thing, *You chose this.*

Not only had I lost, but I had also done so with my own voice, my own will. I had walked willingly into the cage and sealed the lock myself.

"To celebrate this union," she continued, radiant with pride, "we shall host a grand ball in two days' time."

The room erupted into fresh applause, louder this time, livelier. The air buzzed with excitement. Nobles clapped with flushed cheeks and wide smiles, their eyes gleaming with anticipation of the spectacle to come. None of them looked at me now, and that allowed my mask to falter.

I let my breath escape in a shaky rush and turned my head just enough to find him.

Sagar was still standing at attention, a pillar of red and gold among his men. But his eyes, his eyes were no longer the ones that had held me so gently just the night before. Now they burned. Not with anger. Not even sadness. Just absence, a deep, cold void.

Our gaze met for the briefest of moments, and I bit down hard on my lip, willing him to see the truth in my expression.

This isn't real. It's not what I want. It was never supposed to be like this.

But he turned away. Back to the men he had led, the kingdom he had served, and away from me.

"If you wouldn't mind our knights remaining on property while we plan," the prince remarked smoothly, gesturing to his knights as if he knew they would bend to his every whim. "I would like to help in any way that I can."

The Queen beamed. "Calbraxia is eternally in your debt, Your Highness." She placed a hand on his shoulder as if he were already family.

Prince Gerraint nodded once, then leaned down to whisper something into her ear.

Her smile faltered for the first time that day. The words seemed to sit on her shoulders like stones. Still, she nodded and took his offered hand.

"You are all dismissed. Enjoy the feast we prepared in the ballroom," she called to the crowd.

The nobles began to file out of the throne room, their laughter and conversation blooming into a garden of gossip and plans. I could already hear the whispered promises of velvet gowns and gilded invitations, of champagne fountains and flirtations in candlelight.

They left us behind, like debris in the aftermath of a celebration. The royalty. The knights. And the silence. It was worse than the noise had been.

The Queen turned toward the private chamber with the prince at her side. "The Prince and I have some important details to discuss," she said, almost softly now. "You are *all* dismissed.

The words barely registered. I couldn't look at her. My eyes remained glued to him. I couldn't look at anyone except Sagar.

He stood like stone, his cape cascading down his back, the very one that had so often wrapped around me like a second skin. I took a slow, trembling step toward him, reaching out instinctively, like a child in the dark.

I needed to explain. I needed him to understand that none of this meant I had stopped needing him. That I had done this for Margaret. For my kingdom. For something bigger than us.

"Men," he said, his voice loud and clipped. The word cracked through the stillness like a blade, and I froze mid-step. "I must go help advise the Prince."

Then he turned. He was only a foot away. Close enough to reach. Close enough to touch. But his eyes passed over me without a flicker of recognition. As though we were strangers. As though I was nothing.

"Sagar," I whispered, desperation curling into the edges of my voice.

His stride faltered, but only for a breath. Then he walked on, disappearing with the others into the corridor.

The ache inside me turned sharp and relentless. It clawed at my chest, burning its way through the pit of my stomach.

"Silvia!" Margaret's voice broke through, small and urgent. She wrapped her hands around mine with a gasp. "You're bleeding!"

I looked down. My hands were slick with blood, crimson blooming like roses in my palms. It dripped slowly onto the marble, painting delicate petals onto the pale stone. I hadn't even noticed how tightly I'd been clenching my fists.

The pain arrived late, sharp, but somehow distant. Like it belonged to someone else. I let a few tears fall. Just a few. Quick enough to wipe away before they became something permanent.

"Yes," I murmured, my voice hollow. "It looks that way."

"Come on," Margaret urged gently, tugging my arm. "Let's find June. She'll fix it."

She dragged me out of the throne room, marching me down the hall. I tuned out every word as she spoke of the party that was to come, hoping that maybe this would be her time to attend the festivities.

June would have a field day on another one of her last-minute shopping trips. I knew she would prepare me perfectly for the party.

But inside, I knew there was no preparing for what lay ahead.

Chapter 15

The morning sun streamed through the palace windows, gilding the dining room in a golden hush that belied the storm churning in my chest. Everything looked soft and peaceful; the way the light played against the crystal goblets, how the velvet drapes swayed with the spring breeze, but inside, I felt as though I were slowly unraveling.

I hadn't slept. The past night, I'd tossed and turned, my thoughts tangled hopelessly around Sagar; his silence, his retreating back, the way he hadn't looked at me once since the throne room. The weight of the engagement I hadn't truly consented to clung to me like wet wool, suffocating and inescapable. And no matter how desperately I tried to reach him, every path was blocked.

My newly appointed guards were as efficient as they were relentless. Wherever I turned, one was there, always with the same practiced bow, the same polite but firm reminder that "Her Highness's safety must be ensured." I could barely go to the bathroom without a shadow lurking just behind.

I'd tried writing a letter, just a few simple lines, nothing more. Something I hoped I could discreetly deliver. But the Prince kept Sagar tethered tightly at his side. Even the most loyal servants couldn't get near him without raising suspicion. And I was beginning to suspect that it was no accident.

The only ease to the slow erosion of my will was Margaret.

She had become a light in the gloom, her slow growing excitement for the upcoming ball bubbled over into every moment. Even though she may have tried to hide her interest, her small quips about gowns told me all I needed to know. She wanted to be apart of it this time, in any way possible. Her optimism gave me purpose, even if only for a little while.

This morning, we sat side by side at the long mahogany dining table, a modest breakfast arrayed before us. Most of it sat untouched. My appetite had vanished since the proposal, and no amount of coaxing from the kitchen staff could bring it back.

Margaret, on the other hand, was practically glowing.

"I wonder what the ballroom would look like draped in gold?" she asked, her eyes wide and shimmering like the dawn. "Do you think that's possible?"

I let out a soft chuckle, reaching to refill her tea. "We'll try. It's a bit last minute, but we're royalty, aren't we? If anyone can make impossible things happen overnight, it's us."

She beamed, leaning back in her chair with a dramatic sigh. "Silvia, isn't this just perfect?" she said, twirling a spoon in her fingers. "I've always dreamed of parties like this, and now I get to help plan one! I want everything to be perfect. All eyes in the kingdom will be on you."

A knot caught in my throat. I smiled, but it wavered just enough for me to feel it crack. I turned to my plate and poked absently at a slice of fruit, praying she wouldn't notice.

Of course, she did.

"You're not eating again," she said, her voice softening. "Is something wrong?"

"I'm fine, Margaret," I replied, schooling my voice into something calm and measured. "Just a little overwhelmed, is all."

"How could you be overwhelmed when we're having so much fun?" she said, though quickly her eyes soured as she said more than she meant to. "I mean, it's not every day we celebrate an engagement, especially not one for royalty."

Her words stung more than she could've known, and for a moment, I couldn't speak. She turned away from me, but her gaze drifted down, settling on the bandage wrapped tightly around my hand.

Her smile faded. A long silence stretched between us. "I hate seeing you hurt," she said at last, her voice small.

"It was an accident, Margaret. New jewelry didn't fit quite right," I lied, wrapping my voice in nonchalance I didn't feel.

She pursed her lips in thought, her auburn brows drawing together as she examined me with that unnerving perceptiveness children sometimes possess. Then her gaze flicked upward to my eyes, their glowing green catching the morning light like polished gems. For a moment, I wondered if she could see the truth hiding behind them.

"What do you think of Prince Gerraint?" she asked, so suddenly that my heart paused briefly.

My hand stilled mid-motion, frozen on the stem of my teacup. The purgatory I'd managed to retreat into was shattered, invaded by the very name I'd been trying not to think about. His face surged forward in my mind; those sculpted features, eyes that revealed nothing and yet knew everything. A face that haunted me now as vividly as the moment he'd walked away after whispering to my mother.

"He's..." I faltered, hunting for a word that wouldn't betray me.

"Scary?" she offered, voice light but gaze focused. Her fingers brushed the edge of the bandage on my hand, tracing the frayed edge with feather-light curiosity.

"Maybe," I admitted softly, my thoughts drifting back unbidden to Sagar. His face, not the prince's, filled my mind. His furrowed brow, his rigid jaw, the way his fingers had once so gently brushed mine. "Sometimes, people seem scary, but they're kind underneath. It's just hard to tell at first."

Margaret scrunched her nose, her expression doubtful. "Perhaps," she murmured, still fiddling with the edge of my bandage. "But something seems off about him. I can't quite place it, but he's—"

The door burst open with a jarring slam, cutting off her thought. We both jumped.

June stood in the doorway, breathless, her hair askew and cheeks flushed. She looked as though she'd sprinted across the entire palace. Behind her, two guards exchanged amused glances, clearly entertained by her undignified entrance.

"May I... sit?" she gasped.

I sprang to my feet without hesitation, guiding her to the nearest chair and pouring her a glass of water. She took it gratefully, drinking as if it were the sweetest wine.

June wiped her mouth, still recovering, and pulled something from her satchel. "The Queen...her Majesty, your mother...told me to give this to you."

She extended a thick envelope, sealed in gold wax bearing the royal crest. My stomach twisted as I accepted it. Even before I cracked the seal, I recognized my mother's handwriting, elegant and slanted, as if nothing in the world could ever shake her composure.

"My Mother? What were you doing with the—?"

My question was paused as I peeled open the wax and unfolded the parchment. Her words spilled out in ink as refined and cold as her voice.

My dearest daughter,

I know this road has not been easy, but you have done the kingdom a great service. For that, I and the people of Calbraxia are forever grateful. Someday, I will repay you for your sacrifice. In the meantime, accept this invitation as an act of good gesture.

I tilted the envelope, and a formal card slipped into my hand. My eyes scanned the heavy, embossed paper and stopped.

Princess Margaret Stephan

The name was written in delicate script across the line marked invitee. I blinked, stunned.

"What is it?" Margaret asked, her voice pitching up as she tried to peek over my shoulder.

I turned to her with a real smile for the first time in days and placed the invitation into her waiting hands.

"Looks like you'll be doing more than just helping *plan* the ball," I said, my voice rising in forced cheer.

She snatched the invitation from my hands, tearing at the seal with wild eyes as she read what I already knew.

"I get to go to the ball?" She whispered, her gaze whipping between me and June. "Is this real?"

I nodded. Margaret let out a little gasp.

"I get to go to the ball!"

June, who only moments ago had been breathless with fatigue, lit up with equal excitement. She jumped up and joined Margaret with a twirl of celebration.

I laughed, the sound coming out airy and brief. For that moment, I let myself celebrate, too. I let the joy in Margaret's eyes pull me out of my misery, just long enough to breathe. But then, like a shadow creeping across sunlight, I remembered what the ball truly was.

My engagement party.

I lifted the letter again, scanning the rest of the text. My eyes narrowed as they reached the final paragraph.

As for the party, to ensure there are no mishaps such as last time, I have personally arranged an appointment at Madame Levoir's atelier for today. Both my daughters must be dressed appropriately for the affair.

"Madame Levoir?" I echoed aloud, the name rattling something loose in my memory.

Instantly, June froze mid-spin, her attention snapping back to me like arrows loosed from taut bows.

"What about Madame Levoir?" She asked breathlessly, her eyes wide with anticipation, cheeks already flushed with the momentum of their dance.

I held up the letter, the Queen's golden seal still warm in my hand. "Apparently, Mother arranged an appointment at her atelier. For both of us."

Their reaction was immediate, squeals erupted from both of them as they launched into a fresh round of celebration. June swept Margaret into her arms and spun her in a dizzying circle, their laughter ringing off the high ceilings.

"Who is that?" I asked, blinking at their enthusiasm. The moment the words left my mouth, both of them stopped and turned to me in slack-jawed disbelief.

"Madame Levoir is the most sought-after dressmaker in the kingdom!" Margaret declared, as if I'd asked who the gods were.

"Not just this kingdom," June added with dramatic flair, "the entire continent. She's legendary. She tailors gowns that turn heads and hearts. Her designs are like spells, they reshape the body, draw out your best features, and hide even your worst secrets."

Her voice carried such piety, I half expected her to cross herself in devotion. I couldn't help but laugh, the sound light and genuine.

I reached across the table and took her hand, squeezing gently. "Would you come with us?" I asked softly. "I can't imagine choosing a gown worthy of this occasion without your help."

Her eyes widened, her hand flying to her chest as if I'd proposed marriage. "Your Highness," she whispered, visibly moved, "I would be honored."

I offered her a grateful smile, one not forced but sincere. For a moment, the unease in my chest quieted beneath the joy blooming around me. My eyes drifted back to the Queen's letter, its delicate handwriting now less like cold ink and more like a gesture of... dare I say, kindness?

Margaret clutched the invitation to her chest like a sacred artifact. "I get to leave the palace? Did this really come from mother?"

I nodded, letting her voice wash over me like sunlight. "Of course, she wants what's best for her girls—"

Just then, a folded slip of parchment slid from the envelope, fluttering to the ground at my feet. I bent to retrieve it, unfolding it with a strange sense of foreboding.

The handwriting was the same, but the words were not for June or Margaret.

P.S. Remember to remain on your best behavior. A new bride-to-be should be smiling.

The warmth in my chest drained. I stared at the message, my heart beating a little too fast. There was something calculated in the phrasing, a delicate balance between affection and expectation. A mother's reminder, or a Queen's warning?

The words chilled me, despite the fire flickering in the hearth nearby. With deliberate calm, I crumpled the note and tossed it into the flames. The paper blackened at the edges, curling into itself with a hiss before collapsing into ash.

I watched it burn, and with it, tried to will away the memory of Sagar's face. The weight of the carriage, his touch on my skin, the unspoken words between us, each flickered behind my eyes before disappearing like smoke.

I needed to let it go. All of it. Whatever flare of feeling remained for Sagar, I would bury it deep beneath jewels and smiles. Let it smolder into nothingness. If I didn't, my time in the tower would only be more difficult.

I rose to my feet, smoothing my skirts with practiced grace. When I turned back to June and Margaret, a warm, practiced smile spread across my lips.

"Well," I said, lifting my chin, "we can't keep a legend waiting, can we?"

The soft clatter of wooden wheels on cobblestone pulled me from my thoughts. As the carriage slowed before the unassuming store-front, I felt a wave of anxiety creeping over me.

"Look!" June cried, practically bouncing in her seat. "She's waiting for us!"

Indeed, Madame Levoir stood at the steps of her atelier, her figure poised with the elegance of a woman who understood the power of presentation. Her dark curls were wild, hanging past her shoulders in unruly ringlets. Her slate-gray gown cut in sharp angles that whispered of wealth and practice beyond her young years.

As our carriage came to a stop, she dipped into a graceful curtsey. "Your Highness," she greeted smoothly, her voice soft with the slightest hint of an accent I couldn't quite pinpoint. "You honor my humble atelier with your presence."

June was the first to leap from the carriage, unable to contain her excitement. "Madame, the honor is ours! I've dreamed of seeing your custom work in person."

The designer blinked, briefly caught off guard by the enthusiasm, but her surprise gave way to a measured smile. "And you must be Princess Margaret?"

"No, that would be our maid," Margaret called from inside. A knight reached out to assist her down, and she emerged with regal energy, even as her wide eyes roamed the windows of the shop like a child experiencing a festival for the first time.

Madame Levoir's gaze flickered over June, not unkindly but with a curiosity that lingered. Still, she accepted the flattery with a nod. "Well then, ladies, let's not waste daylight. Come in. It's getting far too chilly for introductions."

She ushered us inside with a gentle sweep of her arm, and the moment the door closed behind us, we were swept into a different world.

If her shop appeared modest from the outside, the interior was anything but. Bolts of fabric in every imaginable hue spilled over tables draped in velvet, gleaming dupioni, and chiffons as light as air. Silver thread shimmered beneath the glow of delicate glass chandeliers. Against one wall, a row of display cases glittered with jeweled brooches, tiaras, and ornaments finer than any I'd worn.

Margaret stood, mouth agape as her eyes glistened with wonder. "This...this is..." Her words dissolved as she darted toward the glass. "Can we get anything we want?"

"As long as it's tasteful," I chuckled gently, already knowing her imagination had no such boundaries. Still, her joy was a relief. For her, today was a dream.

Madame Levoir approached, her steps measured but not slow, confidence laced into every movement. Her dress was simple only in silhouette. Up close, embroidery of delicate cranes wove across the hem, so subtle I'd missed it at first glance.

"I received the Queen's note this morning," she said, holding a length of deep red brocade up to my chin. "She suggested scarlet for both of you. But..." Her head tilted, sharp eyes studying my complexion. "No. Red's too harsh on you. It would wear you, not the other way around."

I blinked, startled by the precision of her observation. Few ever told me something didn't suit me.

She smiled faintly, already drifting toward a different rack. "You need something with quiet power. You're not the kind to shout for attention, Your Highness, but when you walk into a room, you should not have to."

Her words struck me somewhere deeper than fashion. I exchanged a glance with June, who gave me a subtle nod of encouragement.

Margaret, meanwhile, was carefully eyeing a set of earrings shaped like falling stars. "If all I get is one night, I want it to count. I want to sparkle," she whispered, utterly enchanted.

Madame Levoir chuckled, returning with two new fabrics. One was a pale, icy pink with a satin sheen, the other a stormy blue-gray that seemed to shimmer as it caught the light. She held them up to each of us, her expression thoughtful.

"You're not keen on picking out your own fabrics, are you?" she asked.

An amused smile crossed my face. "No, not quite," I admitted.

"Green is her true color," June exclaimed, selecting a soft satin and holding it on the other side. Madame Levoir's face soured as she snatched the fabric from her hands.

"Green is obvious." She paced around me, placing a finger to her lips. "We could do a blue..."

"I think I like this one." Margaret cut in, holding up a length of sapphire silk. "Or maybe this?" She pointed to a pink taffeta.

I laughed softly, guiding her toward the fitting area. "You'll look stunning no matter what. We should get our measurements first and make Madame Levoir's life easier, don't you think?"

"I guess i'm just anxious," She admitted. "I just want to skip to the fun part of prancing around in something made just for me."

"In life, we don't always get to skip to the fun parts," I muttered, my heart aching.

June and Madame Levoir exchanged a glance before Madame gently placed her hand on Margaret's back.

"Come on, dove," She laughed. "Let's get the tough part over with."

As she walked away, I eyed her hands. They were worn with her work, stuck with needles, sliced with scissors. I could understand June's admiration at that moment. She earned her reputation because of the work and love she put into each garment she made. She truly created not just dresses, but masterpieces.

I let a sigh escape my lips as I sprawled on the sofa, awaiting my turn. June sat beside me, gently stroking my hair.

"You've been quiet since the engagement." She whispered, hoping Margaret wouldn't catch ear of our conversation. We both waited a moment as we could hear her chattering with Madame.

"There's been a lot on my mind, I guess."

"This wouldn't have to do with a certain knight now, would it?"

My breath hitched, and I shot up sharply. "How did you—?"

She smiled knowingly. "Women's intuition. You've been distracted since he arrived, then came the husband hunting, which was an absolute whirlwind."

June leaned in just a few inches from my face. "Besides, next time you decide to give an alias, you should probably choose someone other than your maid." My face flushed as I realized her implication.

"Oh Goddess," I groaned, burying my face in my palms. "I'm sorry, June. I never meant to drag you into this mess."

June let out a hearty, almost musical laugh as she leaned back against the plush cushions. "Please explain what exactly *this* is? Because from the outside, it looks like a very dramatic, very noble-level romantic catastrophe."

My mind spun. What was this? Was it a secret romance? A mistake? A fantasy I had clung to because I didn't want to face the reality of my engagement? My stomach twisted.

"I don't know," I admitted, my voice small. "Honestly, I have no idea what we are, or I guess were, if anything."

June pursed her lips thoughtfully. "So... does this mean he thought I was the princess?" She grinned. "Because that would be hilarious. If I had a copper for every time somebody thought I was royalty..."

I smiled, her lighthearted question easing some of the tension hanging over me. "No, he always feigned ignorance, but he apparently knew I was the princess the whole time."

"Huh," June chuckled. "I was wondering why every nobleman you met seemed to disappear from you like you'd grown a third eye. It makes sense now, I guess."

I blinked at her. "Wait, what?"

"Oh, I did some digging," she said casually, examining her nails like she hadn't just dropped a bomb. "After that whole dinner with Lord Marquette ended and he refused to see you again, I asked his head maid what had happened. She said he got a visit from—guess who—the head of the Etherian Knights himself."

My head snapped up. "He what?"

June sat up straighter, alarmed by my sudden shift in tone. "I think he may have *discouraged* a few of your more promising prospects. Told them that the Etherian Crown Prince had his eyes for you. Probably threatened to skewer them if they so much as looked at you the wrong way."

"That bastard!" I shouted, springing from the couch and beginning to pace like a caged animal. "He acts like I betrayed him, refusing to talk to me or, Gods forbid, even look at me because of my engagement. But the whole time he was out there sabotaging any chance I had of finding someone other than the Prince?"

The rumors that had flooded the kingdom suddenly made sense. Of course, the kingdom would assume the crown prince was proposing if his guard was sneaking around, intimidating any suitor who got in the way.

I threw my hands in the air, seething. "Unbelievable! I told him everything, I showed him everything in the carriage, and he dared to call me a liar?" My voice caught in my throat, and I froze mid-step, my hands raking across my face. "The carriage..."

June's brows lifted. "What about the carriage?"

I could feel my blood freezing as a new wave of mortification swept over me. My knees wobbled as I sank back onto the sofa. "We...Sagar and I..." My mouth went dry. I couldn't meet her eyes.

June scooted closer, eyes wide. "Wait. Wait. Wait." She grabbed my shoulders, shaking me gently but firmly. "Silvia. What happened in the carriage?"

I swallowed hard. My whole body felt like it was vibrating. I stared into her eyes, the same eyes that had always seen through me, even when I didn't want to be seen.

"Sagar and I..." I hesitated, a war waging inside me. Every part of me resisted speaking the truth, as if naming it out loud would make it more dangerous, more real. "We had... an *intimate* moment."

The last two words slipped out like a confession in a cathedral, barely louder than a breath.

June's eyes widened in horror. "A Winter's Eve..." she whispered dramatically. "Oh no. I did this to you."

I blinked. "What?"

She placed a hand over her heart. "I knew giving you that book would corrupt your pure little royal soul."

"June," I groaned, rubbing my temples. "No. That had nothing to do with it."

"Are you sure?" she asked with a suspicious squint. "Because you were blushing when you came back from the library that day and then when you yelled that you wanted to—"

"There was something between us even before that book, I swear." I interrupted, hoping to forget my embarrassment. The moment I said it, something lifted from me, a thick, heavy fog that had clung to my chest for weeks. I could breathe again.

June stared, letting the weight of my words settle. "How long has this... *thing* been going on?"

I hesitated.

"Since my Nameday," I admitted softly.

June gasped, then beamed. "I knew you didn't fall asleep in the library!"

She leapt forward, eyes gleaming, and I barely managed to slap a hand over her mouth before she shouted it to the heavens.

"Shh!" I hissed. "You want the entire kingdom to know?"

She shook her head vigorously under my hand, and I let go with a wary squint.

June gave me a sly look, wiggling her eyebrows. "Have you two...?" She made a scandalous gesture with her hands that nearly made me drop dead from embarrassment.

"No!" I yelped, slapping her hands away. "At least...I don't think so?"

June's brow furrowed. "Page two forty-seven," she said solemnly, invoking that infamous chapter. "Eve and the Duke on the balcony..."

"Definitely not!" I cut her off, mortified.

June let out a loud, relieved sigh, fanning herself as if she had narrowly avoided fainting. "Okay. Good. That chapter is a lot. And you'd never look me in the eye again if you'd done that."

I managed a tired laugh, pressing my hand to my forehead. "You're insufferable."

Her teasing melted into something softer. "You've been carrying this alone?" she asked gently.

I nodded, finally letting myself be vulnerable. "I didn't know what to do, June. I feel like I'm stuck between duty and..." I stopped, swallowing hard. "And something I'm afraid to put a name to."

She reached across the cushion, placing a hand on my arm. "You don't have to carry it alone anymore. You have me, and you can always tell me anything."

The simple truth of it hit harder than I expected. My throat tightened, but the tears didn't fall. There was relief now, warm, slow, and honest. June wasn't just my maid or companion. She was my confidante. The first person truly let into the hidden world Sagar and I had built in glances, arguments, and quiet moments no one else had seen.

"I've tried to reach him," I whispered. "I've tried every chance to see him, but—" I glanced toward the window where my new knights were laughing by the carriage. "They're not exactly... subtle."

June followed my gaze and scoffed. "Subtlety isn't their strong suit."

I smiled faintly. "He's been avoiding me, or maybe keeping his distance on purpose. I don't know."

She opened her mouth to respond, but the studio curtain flew open before she could.

"I'm all done here." Margaret smiled, walking next to June and latching onto her arm. "Madame Levior agreed to make me an entire new wardrobe."

I glanced back toward Madame Levoir, who stood with a bolt of pale lilac velvet draped over her arms. Her expression was an artful blend of mild exasperation and reluctant fondness, the look of a woman whose patience had been tested and somehow passed.

"She hasn't stopped praising me since we began," she said, nodding toward Margaret, who was now twirling in front of a mirror with a feathered headband perched precariously on her brow. "I don't think the Princess needs to continue wearing hand-me-downs."

I smirked. "No, she certainly doesn't."

She gave me a measured look. "Your turn now, Your Highness. Step up before I stupidly decide she needs an entire opera costume."

As I rose, June's voice cut in from behind me, light and mischievous. "You know my favorite part in A Winter's Eve?" she said, causing me to freeze halfway to the pedestal. "The masquerade scene. When Eve and the Duke dance together in secret, and no one knows it's her."

I turned slowly toward her, one brow raised, lips quirking with intrigue.

"I think that's my favorite part too," I said, voice low with implication.

Our eyes met across the room, and a grin curled at the corners of June's mouth. She was always better at saying the things I couldn't.

"A masquerade?" Margaret asked. "I've read about those. They always sound so grand."

"I think a masquerade would be delightful, exactly what would make this party entertaining," I said, reaching out to tuck a lock of hair behind her ear. "We'll contact the party planner the moment we return home. It will be the grandest ball the kingdom has seen this season."

Margaret flashed a wicked smile before dashing off to the far side of the studio, already chattering about mask designs and how her dress would need to shimmer like the stars. Madame Levoir wisely stepped out of her path as she darted toward the accessory cases like a magpie hunting glitter.

"Madame Levoir!" June called out, her voice rich with mischief and a strange sort of pride. "Make it gold. Gold is Silvia's color."

I blinked, taken aback, but not by her accuracy. By the way she said it. Like it meant something. Like she knew me, truly knew me, down to the colors that made me shine.

Madame Levoir smiled. "I couldn't agree more."

For the first time in what felt like weeks, something warm and fierce stirred inside me. Hope. Determination. A fire that refused to die out.

I was going to see Sagar at that ball. I was going to tell him everything about my engagement, about the choices I never truly wanted to make, and about the way I still thought of the moment in the carriage every time my fingers brushed my skin.

Madame Levoir approached, eyeing me with curiosity as I stepped up into the fitting room.

"I'm sorry, Madame," I said softly, but with new resolve strengthening my voice. "But I'm going to need two dresses for tomorrow night."

Chapter 16

The grand hall of the palace had been transformed into a world pulled straight from the pages of fantasy. Gilded columns framed the vast space, each wrapped with enchanted ivy that shimmered faintly under the soft glow of the golden lanterns.

Above us, three massive crystal chandeliers dripped with jewels, casting flecks of gold and silver across the marble floor like starlight scattered in a dream. The scent of blooming night jasmine floated through the air, mingling with the warm notes of spiced wine and honeyed pastries. Music from a hidden orchestra drifted through the room like smoke, the rhythm beckoning masked guests into a waltz of shadow and light.

Everywhere I looked, there were masks, some simple, some impossibly ornate, made of porcelain, lace, velvet, or feathers, glittering with gems or gold. It was a world of illusions and secrets, a place where names and titles meant little and eyes did all the speaking.

At the top of the grand staircase, Margaret and I paused.

A hush rippled through the crowd like the sweep of a curtain.

We descended in tandem, golden twins blazing beneath the chandeliers. Our gowns, identical in cut but unique in detail, shimmered with layers of silk and chiffon that seemed to ripple like sunlight on water. Mine was embroidered with fine golden thread in patterns that resembled flames curling up from the hem, while Margaret's had delicate beading that twinkled with every movement.

Our masks, crafted by Madame Levoir herself, were breathtaking. Mine was a soft gold with sculpted wings that arched subtly around the edges, while Margaret's was adorned with a miniature golden laurel crown, nestled perfectly against her auburn curls.

She clutched my arm, practically vibrating with nerves. "Silvia, it's just like the books I've read," she whispered, her voice filled with awe. "Everybody is looking at us."

I smiled despite myself, warmed by her wonder. "As they should. It's your first ball, Margaret. Make sure you remember every second."

"I will," she whispered, as if afraid the moment might shatter if she spoke too loudly.

As we reached the base of the staircase, the Queen awaited us like a figure from a painting, elegant and composed. She was resplendent in a deep sapphire gown, understated yet regal.

Margaret's arm tightened around mine. I felt it before I saw it, the way her fingers curled as if she might disappear if she let go. Her gaze dropped immediately to the marble floor, shoulders pulling inward. I waited for her to speak, for the rehearsed introduction she had practiced all afternoon.

She didn't.

Her mouth opened, then closed again. A soundless attempt. Her eyes flicked up once, met our mother's cool stare, and dropped just as quickly. She stood frozen at my side, a child caught in a spotlight with nowhere to run.

"Your Majesty," I said at last, dipping into a low curtsey and gently drawing Margaret down with me.

The Queen's lips curved into an unreadable smile. She reached out and brushed a finger against Margaret's cheek, her touch light, assessing.

"You look beautiful, little Princess."

Margaret flinched before she caught herself. "Thank you," she murmured, voice barely above a whisper as she stepped obediently to her mother's side. "Madame Levoir is a miracle worker."

"So I see." The Queen's attention shifted to me, her gaze lingering on the gold mask that concealed my face. "And what, exactly, are you meant to be?"

"A phoenix," I answered.

"Hm." Her eyes traced my silhouette. "Gold would not have been my first choice." Then, after a brief pause, "But you are both stunning."

She looked to me then, an earnest, fleeting look that softened her otherwise impenetrable façade.

But even my Mother's earnest compliments couldn't drown out the tightness building in my chest. Standing beside the Queen meant standing on display. I wouldn't be permitted to wander the floor unless I was dismissed, like a bird in a very attractive, very golden cage.

Margaret, sensing the danger of silence, straightened abruptly. "They've outdone themselves, Your Majesty," she said quickly, sweeping a nervous hand toward the grand hall. "The flowers, the lights, it's like a dream. We should send the servants something. A gift. Something grand. Don't you think?"

Her words came too fast, eager and careful all at once, like she was trying to fill the space before it swallowed her whole.

The Queen tilted her head, approval flickering in her eyes. "You are very kind, young Margaret. Yes, we shall."

Margaret exhaled softly, relief loosening her shoulders, but only for a moment.

Across the room, I spotted June. She stood near the orchestra in a striking forest green gown, her mask an elaborate design of ivy and silver. When her gaze found mine, she gave the subtlest of nods. The signal.

Tonight would not end in silence.

"Why is everyone wearing masks?" the Queen asked, arching a brow as her gaze swept the room. "Was there a change in the planning?"

Margaret and I exchanged a panicked glance.

Before the Queen could question any further, the herald's voice rang out, his announcement slicing through the music like a blade.

"Announcing the arrival of His Royal Highness, Prince Gerraint Petris, Crown Prince of Etheria!"

The room hushed, a sea of glittering masks turning as one toward the great entrance.

And then he appeared. Prince Gerraint strode into the ballroom with the unmistakable presence of a man born into command.

Even amidst the decadence, he stood apart, tall and imposing, his presence carving a path through the crowd without a word. His mask was a work of ruthless beauty: gold filigree shaped into a stag's crown, the antlers arcing high and proud, tipped with deep crimson rubies that glimmered like blood caught in moonlight. Beneath his black velvet cloak, his suit gleamed a deep, regal red, the color of Etheria, the color of power, and the color of warning.

The haunting dream I'd had days before surged back with sudden clarity. Was this what it had been pointing to? Was it a warning? Or a test?

Gasps and whispered speculation rippled through the ballroom like wind through a wheat field. All eyes turned toward the Etherian prince, unsure whether to admire or fear.

Behind him, the royal guard followed in perfect formation, dressed in finely tailored black. They were shadows to his flame. But my eyes were not on the prince.

They were searching for the one person I needed at this party, the one person that mattered. He appeared at the edge of the formation, Sagar.

Not dressed in the traditional deep crimson of Etherian steel, but in something darker, sleek obsidian threads with the faintest glint of scarlet embroidery down the collar and cuffs. His mask was simpler than Gerraint's, but no less striking: matte black, shaped like a hawk in mid-flight, its wings sweeping across his temples.

He hadn't seen me yet. Or perhaps he had, and was pretending otherwise.

Either way, my breath choked in my throat.

He looked devastating. More than that, he looked untouchable.

Before I could unravel the thought, a voice cut cleanly through the air like the edge of a blade.

"Princess Silvia." The prince's tone was polished, practiced, and undeniably commanding.

I turned to face him. His approach was smooth, a calculated blend of grace and dominance. His hand rested briefly against his chest in greeting before he turned to the Queen, bowing with sharp elegance.

"Your Majesty," he said. "Might I be granted the honor of a dance with your daughter?"

The Queen gave a small, pleased smile, dipping her head in approval. "Of course, Your Highness. It would be our honor."

The prince turned toward me, extending a leather-gloved hand. His expression beneath the mask was unreadable, but his gaze was sharp and curious, as if he were already trying to peel me open.

"May I have this dance?" he asked.

Every instinct screamed at me to run. To search the crowd for Sagar, to pull him from the shadows and demand answers. But I couldn't. Not yet.

I hesitated for only a heartbeat before placing my hand in his.

Prince Gerraint's grip was firm, cool through his gloves. He guided me forward with the ease of a man used to the world stepping aside for him. The crowd parted before us like the sea before a god. A haunting waltz began to swell, the melody dark and elegant, pulling us toward the center of the ballroom as if it, too, obeyed his will.

A thousand eyes tracked our every move, but the only pair I searched for was missing.

We slipped into the dance seamlessly. The prince moved with the grace of a man far beyond his years. His dance was a perfect display of courtly grace honed from years of rehearsals, battles, and negotiations. I matched his steps with equal polish, but while his control came from mastery, mine came from survival.

The silence between us was suffocating in its civility, thick with meaning neither of us dared to utter aloud.

"I've been meaning to speak with you," he said finally, his voice like velvet drawn over a blade.

I lifted an eyebrow. "What did you mean to say?"

"That I wish to know my future wife more intimately," he replied without hesitation. "We've exchanged only a few words. And yet you proposed marriage to me. I would like to know why."

I inhaled slowly. The word wife struck like ice against my ribs.

"I suppose diplomacy leaves little time for pleasantries."

He tilted his head, his gold-antlered mask catching the light in eerie glints. "Indeed. But I make time for the things I find important." He leaned close, his breath grazing my ear. "And I would think one's future would be one of them."

My gaze flicked over his shoulder, searching, pleading even, for the one face I longed to see. And then I spotted him.

Sagar had appeared at the edge of the dance floor, carved in stillness, like a soldier watching a battlefield he could not enter. His hawk-like mask revealed just enough of his eyes for me to know they were on me.

I gasped, a pulse of heat blooming in my chest. The kind only he could summon.

Our eyes locked, and the music seemed to drop away for a moment; only the beat of my heart and the weight of his stare existed. My entire body hummed with unspoken words, with promises and regrets.

I wondered, did he feel it too?

"You move with confidence," Gerraint said, drawing me back with a graceful turn. His voice was gentler now, almost amused. "I had expected you to be more guarded."

I forced myself to look at him. "I've spent my life being watched. You learn to walk a certain way when every step is a performance."

He laughed softly, a deep, resonant sound. "That, Princess, we have in common." His hand slid a fraction lower on my back, just enough to make my jaw tighten.

With a dancer's ease, he pulled me into a low dip. I caught a glimpse of Sagar once more, his expression unchanged, but his hands now clenched at his sides.

When Gerraint drew me back up, his voice dropped lower. "Tell me, do you believe in fate, Princess Silvia?"

I stared at him for a moment.

"I believe," I said, tone cool and deliberate, "That fate likes to wear a mask."

A slow smile curved his lips. "How about prophecies?"

I shot him a quizzical glance, but before I could ask any further, the music ended, and the room erupted into polite applause. I stepped back and began to curtsy, already angling to disappear into the crowd, the punch table calling to me.

But the prince's hand caught mine. "One more dance?"

There was something in his voice, pleasant on the surface, but edged beneath. A request spoken like a command.

"Your Highness, two dances are highly innapro—"

His grip tightened just slightly, shutting down any argument I had.

I shot a glance toward my mother, silently begging for reprieve. Instead, she nodded, and the musicians struck up again.

Gerraint wasted no time. He pulled me close, closer this time. The polite distance of courtly dance vanished in a single breath. His hand slid to the small of my back, warm and possessive, while the other gripped mine with a confidence that bordered on claim. We spun into the next waltz not as acquaintances nor allies, but as actors in a performance laced with power.

The music surged, a darker melody now, as if the strings themselves sensed the shift in the air. Every step carried the weight of the lies I had told, the truths I could not speak, and the one pair of eyes I could still feel burning across the ballroom.

"I must admit," Gerraint murmured, voice low and intimate, his breath brushing my ear like a secret. "Your letters came as quite a surprise."

I faltered, just for a heartbeat. "Letters?"

He paused slightly in his step, just enough to confirm he hadn't misspoken. His brow furrowed beneath the golden curve of his antlered mask, his eyes briefly uncertain.

"Sagar told you why we're here, didn't he?"

The mention of his name snapped my focus back into place. I blinked once, then slipped a smile into my voice. "Sagar?" I repeated airily. "I hardly know who you're speaking of."

"Funny," Gerraint said, and the smile that curled across his face was sharp as a dagger, gleaming with mischief and something darker. "That's not what he told me."

My cheeks burned, both humiliation and confusion fighting for dominance.

What did you tell him, Sagar?

"Oh! Sagar," I said, forcing a breathy laugh, "The knight who saved me. Of course. He didn't have to tell me why you're here. I already knew."

Gerraint pulled back just enough to look me in the eyes, his grin stretching wider. "Excellent, I hadn't intended on coming myself, but when Sagar told me everything that happened, well...I hope you understand this is all for the best."

The best. For whom?

I swallowed hard, forcing my voice to steady. "I do wish to know what he spoke of me."

Gerraint's eyes gleamed as he studied my face. "Don't worry, Princess. Sagar spoke very highly of you. He said you are unlike anyone he's ever known."

A jolt ran through me. My head turned instinctively to the corner of the room where I had last seen him. And there he stood. Still, silent, watching us like a hawk tracking its prey, only his gaze wasn't on me. It was locked on Gerraint.

What are you thinking, Sagar? What game have you dragged me into?

"If I may speak freely, Your Highness," I said softly, my eyes still fixed on Sagar, "*he* is truly unlike anyone I have ever known."

Gerraint laughed. It was not cruel, but it was cold, an elegant chill that spread through the space between us, as if winter itself had taken root in his voice.

"I wonder what Sagar will think of that," he replied, though his tone carried the subtle weight of warning. "Although I'm certain he'll be charmed to know the future queen of Etheria has a sense of humor."

The music tapered off, a final lingering note echoing as the room burst once more into applause. I offered a graceful bow, my skin prickling with tension, my chest aching with the need to break away.

"Two songs may carry implication," I said lightly, pulling my hand from his, "but three would be scandalous."

Gerraint leaned in once more, the heat of his breath brushing my ear.

"Don't worry, Your Highness," he murmured, a touch more softly this time. "I hadn't planned on occupying any more of your time."

There was something almost apologetic beneath the bravado. A flicker of restraint, maybe even self-awareness. For a moment, the sharp edges of his presence dulled, revealing a glimpse of the man behind the crown. It caught me off guard.

I met his eyes and offered a small, careful smile as I dipped into a curtsy. "Your company has been *enlightening*."

He took my hand again, but this time with less show and more grace, leading me away from the center of the ballroom. As we neared my mother, I slowed my steps.

"Actually, Your Highness," I said, affecting a lighter tone, "I find myself terribly thirsty. Might we visit the refreshment table?"

He blinked at me, surprised, maybe even amused, but nodded. "Of course."

The buzz of conversation grew louder as we stepped through the crowd. I could feel eyes on us still, speculation brewing behind painted masks and jeweled veils.

By the table, I accepted a glass of punch and kept my posture relaxed, though my every movement was deliberate. I knew my mother was watching, her gaze flashing to me between her pleasant exchanges with nobles. Her subtle nods reminded me: Smile. Behave. Be perfect.

This was exactly what I had planned: keep her happy, so later I can make an escape without argument. I let out a chuckle, perhaps too loud, too fake, and pressed my hand against Gerraint.

My mother's smile deepened, turning to my sister and continuing some conversation, I'm sure was about the party.

Gerraint, to his credit, didn't press. He took a glass of wine and leaned one elbow on the table, suddenly looking less like a prince and more like a boy who had been caught somewhere between roles.

"You know Prince Gerraint," I started, grabbing my own glass of wine. "I don't mean to speak out of line, but you seem awfully young to be accepting proposals."

A grimace tugged at his lips. "I believe you're only a year older than I am, Princess." He paused for a long sip. "Besides, it's been a year since my father's death and the people can't have a King without a Queen."

"I imagine Etheria is quite different from here," I said, coaxing conversation. I needed to understand him, whether for diplomacy or self-preservation, I wasn't yet sure.

He gave a short chuckle, swirling the wine in his glass. "Very. The capital is warm, especially in summer but the mountains in the north cradle the city like an old friend. The sky there, it's bluer than anywhere else I've been. And the air smells of pine and iron and fire. The further south you go, there's a vast ocean surrounded by beaches."

He surprised me again with the quiet fondness in his voice, his features softening with the memory.

"There are markets in the lower cities that stretch for miles," he continued. "Spices from the East, glass from the south ports, pelts, books, weapons, anything you can imagine. And in the spring, the lavender fields bloom along the southern pass. The whole valley turns violet."

I sipped slowly, studying him. "I didn't think lavender grew in Etheria."

He looked momentarily caught, then smiled sheepishly. "Well... it doesn't. Not naturally. I brought some from the mountains where I summered. Had it replanted in the southern estates. Reminded my mother of her homeland in the north."

I gently emptied my cup, making sure to be obvious about filling another. "From the north? As in Calbraxia?"

"No." He took a deeper drink of his wine. "Somewhere in the midlands, she hated summers in Etheria, claimed they were too hot for my health. But now, I can't imagine being anywhere else." His mouth curved upward, though the smile didn't reach his eyes.

He leaned just slightly closer, brushing his fingers along the rim of his glass. "But don't worry, Princess. You'll get to see it all for yourself soon."

The words hung in the air like a promise, or maybe a warning.

"Thank you, Your Highness," I replied coolly, the warmth in my chest quickly smothered by the reminder of what his intentions truly were.

He inclined his head, his expression unreadable again. The regal, composed mask of the prince slid back into place.

"If you'll excuse me," he said, downing the rest of his one in one swift movement, "I think I'll get some air. Too many secrets in this room, you can never truly know who to trust in a place like this."

"Of course, let me take that for you." I offered, grabbing his empty glass from his hands.

He turned with practiced grace, disappearing into the crowd flanked by silent guards. As I stood there, my gaze drifted instinctively to the far side of the room.

My moment had finally arrived.

Across the ballroom, June stood near the edge like a sentinel, her eyes catching mine with a flicker of urgency. She nodded once. My heart quickened. This was it. No more waiting, no more stolen glances from across the room. It was time to act.

I wove my way through the shifting tide of dancers and courtiers, Prince Gerraint's empty wine glass still tightly grasped in my hand. The residual warmth of his touch clung to it, but my mind was already leagues away.

"Mother," I said, affecting a woozy smile as I approached her side. "I believe I may have had too much to drink... again."

Her eyes flicked to the goblet, then to the doorway where the prince had just disappeared.

"The Prince has taken his leave," I added softly, then leaned in, lowering my voice to a whisper meant only for her. "May I retire to my room? We wouldn't want another embarrassment like my name day, would we?"

A muscle in her jaw twitched ever so slightly, and I saw the memory flash behind her eyes. She scanned my face, searching for a reason to keep me, and found only weary innocence.

After a long moment, she sighed and waved her hand. "Very well. Have June walk you. The knights are busy ensuring the safety of the guests, and I'll not have you wandering alone."

"Of course." I dipped my head dutifully.

I turned toward Margaret, who looked half-asleep already, her head drooping slightly against the high back of her seat. I bent to kiss her cheek, letting my hand linger over hers. For a moment, I envied her peace. Then I stepped away, catching June just as she appeared at the ballroom doors.

"We only have a few minutes," she whispered urgently, looping her arm through mine. "Everything's ready."

We hurried into the corridor just beyond the golden double doors, the music and laughter of the ballroom muffled behind us. The moment the doors shut, the world shifted. The quiet here was intimate, electrified by the danger of discovery.

Without ceremony, June dropped a satchel to the ground and began frantically working at the laces of my gown.

"June! Wait—hey!" I hissed, trying to keep my balance as she attacked the fastenings with near-feral precision.

"We need to be quick," she snapped. "Who knows if someone followed you!"

Silk and beads slithered to the floor as she stripped me down, and in moments I was stepping into something else entirely, something darker, sleeker. The black dress clung like moonlight on water, molded to my body in a way I'd never allowed before. I barely recognized myself. I wasn't Princess Silvia now, I was a stranger, a shadow, a woman with purpose.

The gown whispered around my legs as I turned to the mirror hanging in the dim corridor. I stared at the reflection, breathless.

The plunging bodice emphasized every curve, drawing attention to the power of my form, not just the beauty. While the entire structure was held up by a single thick, ropy choker. Madame Levioir had outdone herself.

Then came the wig-golden, riotous curls that tumbled over my shoulders. June fastened it with expert hands.

"I hate how good this looks on you," she muttered, smirking. "You're going to break hearts tonight."

"For only a moment," I said, barely recognizing the voice that came out of me.

June added the finishing touch: a sleek, black velvet mask that hugged my cheekbones and disguised the familiar lines of my face. A thin organza covered each eye hole, thin enough to see out of, but it would hide the peridot irises that would easily give me away. As she smoothed long gloves up my arms, she stepped back and tilted her head, admiring her work.

"You look like a Goddess," she said softly, eyes wide with pride. "No one will know you."

I dabbed a bit of rouge on my lips, checking my reflection one last time. I looked dangerous. I looked free.

"What if someone checks on me?" I asked, not taking my eyes off the mirror.

June shrugged with a mischievous grin. "I'll be playing the part of Sleeping Beauty tonight. We're close enough in size, and in the dark, no one will know."

I reached out and caught her arm before she could slip away. "Thank you," I said, my voice thick with gratitude.

She squeezed my fingers. "Remember what I'm doing for you. You'll get me back someday. But for now, go find him."

And just like that, I turned and stepped back into the sea of masks and chandeliers.

Chapter 17

To my astonishment, no one seemed to notice my disappearance from the party. Dancers still spun wildly across the floor, raucous laughter continued to erupt from opposite corners, and kisses were stolen in the shadows. The guests became more comfortable as the night and the liquor flowed on. My absence had left no ripple.

Even in my new attire, nobody seemed to pay me mind as I entered the room. I was just another shadow, another faceless guest cloaked in satin and secrets. But I moved with purpose now. I wasn't hiding, I was hunting.

And then I saw him.

Sagar.

He stood just beyond the glittering swirl of dancers, near a towering marble column crowned with ivy and candlelight. Removed, watchful as he always was. His tall, imposing figure cast a long shadow in the flickering light. Arms crossed, jaw tight. His gaze swept the room with military precision, and more than once, I saw it flick back to where I had stood beside the queen. He was looking for me.

A sharp ache twisted in my chest. Had he watched me the entire night? Had he been watching me since my proposal?

I moved through the crowd like smoke, my gown gliding along the floor as if it were darkness taking form. The mask hid my face, but the fire in my chest betrayed me. My heart drummed against my ribs, louder than the violins, faster than the waltz. Each step drew me nearer to the edge of reason and him.

He didn't see me approach. His eyes were fixed on the dancers, but there was something brittle in his stillness. Tension clung to him like mist, silent, but thick.

I stopped at his side, close enough to breathe him in. That familiar scent struck me like a spell. My fingers twitched with the urge to reach for him. To just touch him. Anchor myself. But I let my hand fall.

Coward.

My pulse ached. The moment I had longed for was here, and still, I couldn't speak. Suddenly, I knew how Margaret had felt earlier in the evening.

Unable to bear the closeness, I turned and slipped away toward the refreshment table, through a blur of dancers and revelers. I needed a moment, a breath, anything to regain my courage.

I reached for a glass of wine, the crystal chilled against my glove, and tried to steady the war raging inside me. But peace was not mine to have.

"A copper for your thoughts, beautiful?" a voice slurred behind me.

I turned slowly, now aware that I was surrounded. Four men stood clustered near the table, their eyes raking over me with thinly veiled interest. Predatory amusement painted their faces. One leaned closer, far too close.

"Not sure you could afford it," I said, voice cool, guarded.

They laughed, loud and vulgar. One reached out and brushed his fingers along my exposed bicep.

"You're feisty," he said with a grin that made my skin crawl. "I like that."

I flicked my eyes back to where Sagar had stood. Empty.

"Shit," I whispered under my breath, scanning the room frantically. Where had he gone?

"Such a foul mouth for a lovely little thing," the first man scoffed.

I felt eyes from across the room turning toward the commotion. The queen. The guards. I couldn't afford this. Not now.

"Excuse me," I said politely, already stepping away. But a hand caught my wrist, firm and insistent.

"Come now," he said, tugging me toward him. "Just one dance with Lord Armine, what do you say?"

I froze. Though my mask hid the disgust twisting my face, my voice was sharp and unmistakably real. "Absolutely not. Now, if you'll unhand me—"

But he didn't. Instead, he yanked me closer, pressing me to his chest. The scent of wine on his breath turned my stomach. I felt the tension of watching eyes, the edge of scandal threatening to burst. I couldn't afford to fail, not now, not when I was so close.

"Let me go," I hissed, gripping my wine glass so tightly my knuckles practically tore the seams of my gloves.

He laughed, bold now, dragging me toward the dance floor. "Just one. You'll enjoy it, I promise."

The orchestra surged behind us, but all I could hear was my pulse screaming.

"I believe she said to let her go." The voice struck like a blade.

Deep. Steady. Unmistakable.

My breath caught in my throat as I turned just slightly, just enough to see him.

Sagar towered above us, a storm cloaked in black and steel. Even with the mask obscuring half his face, his presence was undeniable. His voice had quieted the air around us, a storm ready to strike. And when he stepped forward, placing a single hand on my shoulder, I nearly collapsed into it.

The touch was nothing, just the brush of his fingers to my bare skin, and yet it unraveled me. His eyes, visible through the dark slits of his mask, were locked on Lord Armine with blistering precision. Cold. Controlled. Dangerous.

"This lady is spoken for," Sagar said, his voice low, calm, cold, and coiled with warning. There was no need to raise it. The menace in his tone did all the work.

The drunken noble blinked, his bravado crumbling beneath the force of Sagar's gaze. With a scoff and a muttered curse, he released my wrist and stumbled away with his companions in search of easier prey.

I turned to Sagar, pulse still racing, though not entirely from fear. The chandelier above cast its golden light across his black uniform, catching the gleam of maroon threading and faintly outlining the disciplined curve of his shoulders. He looked every inch the knight: imposing, unreadable, devastating.

Gods, I wanted to tear the mask from his face. I wanted to see the truth in his eyes, to hear my name on his lips, to feel—

"T-thank you," I said breathlessly, barely trusting my voice.

He gave me a polite, almost distant smile, bowing with military precision. "My pleasure, my lady."

He turned to leave, already slipping back into the shadows where he belonged. No. Not yet.

"Wait!" The word escaped sharper than I intended, and he paused mid-step. I smoothed the tremor from my voice. "May I at least know who my savior is?"

He tilted his head, just slightly. "I'm just a simple partygoer," he said smoothly, though the words tasted like a lie even as he spoke them.

"You lie," I said it plainly, amusement dancing behind the veil of my mask.

That caught him. He turned, the barest flicker of something, confusion or perhaps curiosity, passing through his expression. "I beg your pardon?"

"You're lying," I repeated, stepping closer, letting the warmth of my wine-stained breath hang between us.

"S-Sagar." He muttered, his eyes shifting between me and the empty chair still next to my mother.

"I asked who you are, not what your name is."

His gaze, razor sharp, settled fully on mine now. The flicker deepened, and I could almost see the wheels turning behind that mask. His body was still, but tension rippled beneath the surface.

"And who might you be, to see such truths in me?"

I gave a theatrical curtsy, my voice sugar-sweet. "Lady June, at your service."

He studied me then, longer, closer. His fingers reached out, catching my gloved hand with the same precision he used when wielding his bow. His touch was steady, familiar. The calluses on his palm brushed against mine.

"Lady June," he repeated slowly, his voice dipping. "You've always been terrible at subterfuge, Silvia."

Heat bloomed across my cheeks, but I refused to look away. "Perhaps I've had a good reason to practice."

His mouth twitched into his regular smirk briefly, there and gone again. "Have you?"

"You know," I said, leaning in, my words barely more than a breath, "you lied to the Princess of Calbraxia with nary a thought of the consequences. I can't help but think that deserves... *punishment*."

"Oh?" His hand slipped, bold and confident, to the small of my back. He drew me in with practiced ease, until there was barely a breath between us. "And what punishment does Lady June suggest?"

My heartbeat roared in my ears. All around us, the party carried on, laughter, music, footsteps, but none of it touched us. The world narrowed to the space between his lips and mine.

"I haven't decided yet," I whispered, leaning closer until only he could hear me. "But perhaps tonight, You and I could take a carriage ride and come up with something together."

His fingers flexed subtly against my back, his breath faltering for a heartbeat. I could feel the shift in him; something warm and dangerous blooming just beneath the surface.

"Dance with me," he said suddenly, voice low, but edged with urgency. There was something raw in his tone, something that took me by surprise.

"Sagar, no," I hissed, instinctively pulling back. My eyes darted around the room. "If anyone recognizes me—"

"They won't." His hand tightened just slightly. "If I didn't recognize you at first, nobody will."

Before I could protest further, he swept me into the air, drawing me into the center of the ballroom just as the orchestra shifted into a waltz. A few guests glanced over, but none lingered. Just another masked pair among many.

The music curled around us, lush and golden, and I found myself moving before I could think. He led with quiet confidence, his hand warm at the small of my back, the other cradling mine in a firm, sure grip. Our feet fell into perfect rhythm, as though we'd danced this same waltz a hundred times in secret.

"You're playing a dangerous game," he murmured, his breath fanning against my temple as he spun me gently beneath the chandelier's glittering light.

"And you're not?" I whispered back with a breathy laugh, letting the mask of coyness slip just for a moment.

I caught myself. This wasn't just another stolen moment. I had come back for a reason. This was my only chance to set things right, to bridge the silence that had stretched like a chasm between us since that fateful day. I pulled in a breath and steadied my voice.

"Sagar, I have to talk to you." My tone shifted. "I know you must have questions. I owe you answers."

His jaw clenched, just briefly. The mask couldn't hide the flicker of conflict in his expression. He spun me once, the motion sweeping my gown around us in a slow, silken arc. When he pulled me back to him, we were closer than before, his hand splayed against my spine.

"You're here now, with me," he said softly. "I have no questions."

His voice was soothing, seductive, velvety, but it sank through my defenses too easily. I couldn't let him dismiss this so easily.

"Well, I have questions," I countered, a little breathless. "If you knew who I was, why didn't you say anything? Why let me go on pretending?"

He laughed, the sound low and warm in his chest. "The same reason you didn't tell me who you were." He tilted his head, eyes dancing with mischief. "Besides, you were far too entertaining to give up that quickly."

My cheeks burned. "You're insufferable," I muttered, though my heart betrayed me with every thunderous beat.

He grinned. "You say that now. But just a moment ago, you were inviting me on a midnight carriage ride. Which is it, my lady?"

"Sagar," I said, quieter now. "You can't keep being this sweet when I'm trying to stay serious. You do things to me..."

His brow lifted slightly, his grin twisting into something wicked. "Oh?" he breathed. "Do tell me exactly what I do to you. I want to know every feeling. Spare no detail."

"Right now?" I rolled my eyes, trying to hold onto the last threads of composure. "You're irritating me."

"Good," he said, with maddening satisfaction. "You know how that makes me feel."

Before I could reply, he spun me one last time. And as I came back into his arms, he dipped slightly, pressing a quick, forbidden kiss just below the line of my collarbone. My breath faltered, my body flooded with warmth. I clung to him, trembling from the inside out.

"Gods," I whispered. "You're dangerous."

His voice ghosted against my skin. "And yet you keep coming back."

"And you..." I choked out, voice trembling as the truth cracked through my chest. "You left me."

His smile dropped instantly. The warmth vanished from his face, replaced by something sharper. Guilt, maybe. Or something worse.

"The other night," I continued, the words tumbling before I could stop them, "I woke up and you were gone. No word. No note. Nothing. And since then, you've been avoiding me."

"Avoiding you?" he echoed, incredulous. His hand at my waist tensed, almost imperceptibly. "I've been trying to protect you, Silvia."

I faltered in the next step of the waltz, and he steadied me as if it were nothing. But to me, it was everything.

"Protect me?" I asked, my voice tight. "From what?"

He didn't answer. But his eyes, burning through the mask, spoke volumes. Frustration. Fear. Pain.

"I can't tell you," he said finally, the words brittle, almost broken.

The orchestra rose into the final swell of the waltz, wrapping around us like thunder and rain.

"Why not?" I demanded, barely keeping my voice from shaking.

"It's... complicated."

I scoffed. "It's because of the engagement, isn't it?"

His grip tightened instantly, just enough for me to feel the weight behind it. "No," he whispered, the word barely brushing past his lips. "I want to tell you everything. But not here. Not now."

I wanted to scream. To shout. But the words died in my throat. The music ended, and the moment slipped from us like sand through fingers. Sagar stepped back, bowing slightly.

"Excuse me," he said, his voice flat.

He turned and strode toward the terrace, vanishing into the shadows beyond the open doors. For a second, I couldn't move. Panic flared in my chest. I couldn't lose him again, not like this.

I followed, the night air biting at my skin as I stepped outside. The laughter and warmth of the ballroom disappeared behind me.

He stood at the edge of the terrace, hands braced on the marble railing, staring out into the darkness like it held the answer to some question he couldn't bring himself to ask.

"You're not leaving me again, not without answers," I said, louder than I intended. Firmer than I felt.

He laughed without humor, his back still facing me. "Then we're going to be outside for a long time."

"I can wait." I snapped, sliding next to him. His body heat radiated next to me. "I'm used to waiting."

He sighed, turning to me, his gaze piercing into mine. "Silvia, I can't tell you."

"Is it the Prince?" I fired back. "Is he the one ordering you?"

His shoulders tensed, jaw clenched tight. "Ordering me? Ordering me to what exactly? Silvia, you just have to trust me with this—"

"Trust you?" I laughed, bitter and sharp. "Why should I trust you? You don't answer any questions I have."

He turned, his eyes thunderclouds behind the mask. "There are things in this world you don't understand."

"Then explain them!" I snapped. "I'm not a child. Stop treating me like I'm too delicate to know the truth."

He looked away, into the moonlit gardens, as if the stars might give him the words. I stepped forward and caught his hand.

"Let's start with what *you* don't understand," I said softly.

His hand gripped mine, tight and trembling. "The Prince," he said. The word landed like a blow. "After everything, after all we've been through, you proposed to him. Why?"

I froze. My mouth opened, but the answer caught in my throat.

"It's... complicated," I said.

He let out a cold laugh, ripping off his mask to meet me face-to-face. His eyes were raw, furious. "And yet when I say that, you act like it's some kind of betrayal."

"Sagar, it's not what it seems," I said quickly.

"Then what is it, Silvia?" His voice cracked with something deeper than anger. "Why did you choose him?"

My voice broke. "Do you think I wanted this? Do you think I had a choice?"

"There's always a choice!" he shouted, stepping toward me. "Whatever it was, you could have refused. You *should* have refused."

"You don't understand," I snapped. "I'm not doing this for love. He wants a Stephan, he wants my bloodline, a Divinial. If I refuse, he'll turn to my sister next. He'll take her. He'll take everything."

"You're assuming!" Sagar's voice cracked with frustration as he ran a hand through his hair. "You're building your entire argument on fear and conjecture. You don't know him."

"And you think I should wait around and find out?" I spat, my voice rising with fury. "My people have been used before, sacrificed piece by piece for power. I won't be the fool who lets it happen again."

His expression hardened. "The only one playing games here is you. *You're* the one who proposed to *him*. You invited him to the palace. I thought—" his voice broke slightly, "I thought you were different. The only woman in this godsforsaken world who didn't care about power or status. Who felt the same things I did. And yet here you are, proving me wrong."

The words landed like a blow to the chest.

"You think that little of me?" I whispered. "You, who stood in front of me and demanded honesty, judging me when I only told you half-truths. How hypocritical, you lied. You've been lying."

His jaw twitched, but he didn't respond. And that silence ignited something white-hot inside me.

"I didn't *want* to propose," I hissed, stepping forward. "I didn't *want* any of this. I've been clawing for air, looking for any way out of this mess. You know this better than anyone; you squashed any chance I had of being with someone besides the Crown Prince, and all the while, I thought I could trust you. You, who kept preaching truth while hiding behind a mask thicker than mine!"

"What do you mean?" He asked.

I scoffed, twisting my gaze away from him. "You sabotaged every chance I had, every suitor who showed interest, I know you did."

His brows drew in, shame flickering across his features, but I didn't stop.

"You forced this union between me and the prince. And for what? Because you're ashamed of what happened between us? That night in the carriage? You disappear like it meant nothing, and then dare to look at me like I'm the liar?"

His face faltered. "I didn't mean—"

"No, you never do," I snapped. "But you keep doing it anyway. You look at me like I'm the dangerous one, like I'm some scheming princess using people to climb higher. And all this time, you've been the one keeping secrets."

He was silent, but I could see the storm building in his eyes.

"I was ashamed," he finally said, voice raw. "I didn't know how to face you after that night. What we did—what *I* did that night in the carriage, I didn't know what to say. I told myself it was a mistake—"

"I'm not ashamed," I cut in, my voice trembling but firm. "That night meant more to me than I can even put into words. I've spent every waking moment since then reliving it, wondering what I did wrong. Wondering why you punished me with silence after giving me something so... real."

He turned away, shoulders tense. "It shouldn't be real."

"Well, it was! For me!" My voice cracked. "You left me burning for you and vanished without a word. You made me believe I was just another burden you had to carry. And now, you stand here and act like I'm the one who's made everything impossible."

His fists clenched at his sides. The tension between us was suffocating, a thick stormcloud brewing just on the horizon. Then, without warning, he surged forward.

His hand reached up and tore the mask from my face, the delicate fabric hitting the floor with a soft, final sound. He stared at me like he was seeing me for the first time, like he'd finally let himself look.

"You want the truth?" he rasped. "Fine."

He stepped closer, so close I could feel the heat radiate from him. My heartbeat faltered for a second as I held my breath.

"The truth is, I did scare off all of your suitors, not because I wanted you to have the prince, but because none were worthy of you. They didn't care about you, not really. I saw you trying to twist yourself into someone else just to fit them. And I—gods help me—I didn't want you with anyone who couldn't appreciate you the way you are."

"Why would you do that?" I whimpered, my hands trembling. The storm had arrived.

"I thought it would be obvious. Silvia, I've thought about you every damn day since I've met you. Every moment. Your touch. Your kiss. The sounds you made when I tasted you." He swallowed hard, eyes blazing. "Every time I've seen you, I've wanted to finish what we never got to that night in the carriage. And now, no matter how much I try to convince myself I should push you away, let you go, I can't. I don't want to."

His words struck deep into the ache I hadn't dared name, into the hollow he'd left behind. I blinked, heart thudding against my ribs. "Why?" I whispered, the fire in my voice faltering, softening. "Why can't you?"

The silence that followed felt like an eternity. The music inside faded into a distant hum, replaced by the sound of our ragged breaths and the thunder of our hearts pounding against fragile ribs.

The cold night air wrapped around us, sharp and unforgiving, but neither of us noticed. We stood locked in place, eyes fixed, searching each other for a reason, any reason, to end this madness before it began again.

"You haunt me, Silvia. Mind, body, and soul. Seeing you with him, with anyone else... It's destroying me."

Before I could second-guess it, before either of us could find a reason to walk away, I moved. I launched myself into him, crashing into the space that had grown too wide, too empty, too cruel. My lips found him with feverish desperation.

The kiss was fire, pure, consuming, and reckless. It wasn't soft or patient. It was the kind of kiss born from too many sleepless nights and too many unshed tears. His mouth claimed mine in a frenzy of longing and frustration, his hands threading through my hair, gripping, anchoring, needing. I opened for him like I'd been waiting to do for years, allowing him to devour every ounce of defiance I had left.

I gasped as he backed me against the stone terrace wall, the chill of it a shocking contrast to the heat of his body pressed tightly against mine. His hands roamed down, firm against my spine, splaying domineeringly across my hips as if trying to memorize the exact shape of me. I tangled my fingers in the fabric at his shoulders, tugging him closer, needing him impossibly nearer.

He pressed into me, all heat and muscle and barely restrained need, his thigh sliding between mine. The friction stole the breath from my lungs.

I moaned softly into his mouth, and he grinned in response, breaking the kiss only to trail hot, open-mouthed kisses down my jaw, to my neck, to the hollow of my throat. Each one felt like it would brand me, like he was marking every place he touched.

I bit his lower lip in retaliation, in challenge, and he groaned low in his throat, the sound vibrating through me. He responded with a sudden urgency, his tongue sweeping past my lips, tasting, teasing, demanding more. I gave it. I gave everything.

When we finally pulled apart, our mouths wet and breathless, we hovered there, foreheads pressed together, chests heaving. Our breaths curled into the cold air between us like smoke from a fire barely under control.

"If that's how you feel," I whispered, my voice trembling from the force of it all. "I-I want to be yours. Completely."

His hands gripped my waist tighter, and his eyes darkened with some feral hunger. A slow, wicked smile spread across his face as he leaned in, brushing his nose against mine. "You're so delicate, Princess," he murmured, voice low and molten. "I fear I may break you."

His words made my knees weaken, heat blooming in places I dared not name. My body ached for him, not just with desire, but with trust, with surrender. I reached up and cupped his face, letting my fingers graze along the stubble of his jaw. I leaned in, my lips hovering over the shell of his ear.

"I don't want you to be gentle," I whispered, my voice barely more than a breath. "I want you to ruin me."

His entire body tensed, the air between us clapping like thunder. I felt the growl rumble from his chest before he let it out in a low, dangerous chuckle. His hands slid up my back and then down again, slower this time, more deliberate, until they settled on the backs of my thighs.

"It'll be my pleasure..."

Chapter 18

The library was still and quiet, the muffled sounds of the distant ball barely creeping past the thick oak doors. It was as if the whole world had faded away, leaving only us in this timeless, dimly lit sanctuary.

The air stilled in my lungs as Sagar led me inside, his hand lingering on mine long after the door clicked shut behind us. That small contact buzzed through me like a sword strike in slow motion.

The flickering fireplace painted long, dancing shadows across the walls, casting an almost sacred glow over the worn leather bindings and towering shelves. The scent of old parchment, candle wax, and something unspoken hung in the air, something wild and forbidden.

"Looks like we have the place to ourselves," Sagar said, his voice a low, devilish rumble that made my face burn. He turned toward me, his eyes locking onto mine with such heat I half-expected the books to catch fire.

"Perfect," I murmured, though I wasn't sure if I meant it or if the word just fell out of my mouth because my brain had stopped functioning properly the moment he looked at me like that.

He stepped closer, brushing my cheek with the backs of his fingers with a maddeningly slow motion. Every stroke sent molten sparks down my spine.

"Are you certain about this?" he asked, voice rough, like it took every shred of his restraint just to ask the question instead of pinning me to the nearest bookcase.

My heart was racing so fast I half expected it to leap out of my chest and confess everything on its own. "I've never been more certain," I whispered, breathless, my voice shaking with need and nerves and anticipation.

Without warning, he pulled me to him, capturing my lips with his. The kiss was soft at first. Just a graze. Like he was giving me a chance to run. I didn't.

I surged forward, fingers threading into his thick, tousled hair, pulling him deeper into me. That was all the permission he needed. His hands explored, firm against my back, then sliding lower, curving proprietarily over the swell of my hips.

We stumbled backward into a shelf, the books rattling in protest. "Shhh," he murmured against my lips, laughing. "The library is judging us."

"Let it," I breathed, tugging his jacket off his shoulders. "It's overdue for a scandal."

He growled in amusement, hands now roaming more boldly, tracing every inch of me like he was trying to memorize it. The room felt too warm suddenly, the air thick with want. I found myself trapped between the bookshelf and him, his hand slipping between my thighs, sending a delicious jolt up through my body.

"Sagar," I gasped, arching against him.

"Say that again," he groaned, burying his face in my neck. "Gods, I've missed hearing you say my name like that."

"Sagar," I whispered again, slower this time, dragging my fingers down his chest until he hissed through his teeth.

He leaned in and captured my mouth with his, a kiss that stole the air from my lungs. There was no hesitation this time, no faltering step. Just heat. Urgency. Tongues tangling with abandon. Teeth grazing lips.

This felt nothing like the carriage. That night had been hesitant, tender, and uncertain. But now? Now, I wasn't some fragile princess he was afraid to shatter. I was fire, and he intended to burn with me.

His hands glided up my thighs, worshipful and confident, before pausing at my waist, grounding us in the moment. He continued his exploration, making his way up to my throat. He touched it with reverence, fingers brushing the sensitive skin as if feeling the echo of my racing pulse. Slowly, they drifted back lower.

His palm cupped the swell of my breast, thumb brushing the fabric until he found the peak beneath. My nipple tightened instantly, trapped between his fingers. I gasped, back arching as heat spiraled through me.

"I can't believe I get to see your pleasured face again," he whispered, his breath hot against my cheek. "Every night I've been picturing it, wondering how you would react if I touched and tasted your soft, sensitive spots again."

His lips curled into a smile while he watched me squirm, as if the sight of my unraveling undid him more than anything else.

His fingers grew restless, tugging at my bodice, searching for skin with growing impatience. His mouth returned to mine, this time deeper, darker. His tongue coaxed mine into a slow, sensual dance. His other hand gripped my waist, holding me steady as we pressed impossibly closer.

I moaned into the kiss, only for him to pull away abruptly, taking my breath with him. My lungs burned, chest heaving.

Then, without warning, one hand tangled in my hair, ripping the blonde wig from my head in one swift, almost savage motion. My long raven curls cascaded over my shoulders, down my back, a dark curtain catching firelight.

"There you are," he murmured, eyes wide with something like awe. "Gods, I hated that thing."

His lips trailed from the corner of my mouth to my jaw, then lower, tracing the line of my neck with soft, deliberate kisses. When he reached my collarbone, his teeth grazed my skin, just enough to make my pulse skip.

"Sagar," I whispered, needing more, needing him.

He looked up, lips swollen, gaze searing. "Silvia," he murmured, voice low and teasing, like he already knew I'd melt if he said my name again.

Then, suddenly, his arms were beneath me, lifting me like I weighed nothing. I let out a surprised laugh that dissolved into a moan as he kissed me mid-motion, carrying me deeper into the library, to the same spot I had found myself indulging in A Winter's Eve. The irony wasn't lost on either of us.

He paused just long enough to glance around, then nudged a stack of books off a nearby table with a smirk. "Oops," he said, clearly not sorry. "Guess we'll have to make use of the space."

I let out a breathless laugh, the word barely audible. "Sacrilege," I muttered, though I hardly meant it.

Sagar swiftly lifted me to the table, silk pooling around my thighs like spilled ink, the polished wood cool against the backs of my legs. He stood between my knees, his hands braced on either side of me, eyes gleaming with something primal and hungry.

But he didn't move.

"Do you have any idea what you do to me?" he asked, his voice hushed, frayed with a raw honesty I rarely heard from him. It wasn't a line, not this time. There was a plea in it. A quiet confession.

The question hung between us, heavier than the silence surrounding the library's ancient tomes.

"Perhaps," I murmured, teasing, the faintest smile playing at my lips. "But... you could always show me."

His lips twitched into a wicked smirk, eyes flickering with dark promise as his hands slid up to the neckline of my gown. There was a pause, one heartbeat, and then a sharp rip sliced through the air. My bodice gave way beneath his fingers, satin and lace parting with an almost ceremonial violence. The cool air hit my skin, chased by the heat of his gaze.

A gasp burst from me, startled, breathless. I found my arms instinctively flying to cover my bare chest. Sagar caught them before I could do so, pulling them above my head.

He stood above me, silent, eyes drinking me in with a hunger so intense it made my skin flush. I shifted, growing self-conscious beneath his gaze. "Is everything alright?" I asked, biting my lip, my voice far smaller than I intended.

"No, I want to see you, all of you."

My breath quickened, then it turned to a laugh, husky with disbelief. "June's going to kill you," I said, imagining my maid's scandalized shriek at the ripped masterpiece.

"She'll have to stand in line," he murmured, hands bold as they cupped my breasts, thumbs brushing teasing circles over the sensitive peaks. "But it's worth it."

His lips returned to my throat, tasting the skin with slow, indulgent kisses. My body arched under the gentle worship, each kiss a spark feeding the flame that now roared inside me. Down, he traced the path of my desire: collarbone, sternum, the underside of my breast. And lower still.

He knelt before me like a knight about to pray. Except there were no prayers on his lips, only sin.

His palms gripped my thighs with restrained urgency, thumbs stroking the tender flesh as his gaze flicked upward. "I need you to spread your legs," he said, reverent and ravenous all at once.

The sheer hunger in his voice sent a bolt of heat straight through my core. Embarrassment tingled along my spine, but it couldn't hold a candle to the anticipation curling in my belly.

I nodded, biting my lip, and slowly let my knees fall open.

His mouth descended, lips brushing the inside of my thigh first, then peppering kisses upward. Each touch was maddening, a promise left unfulfilled. When he reached the center of me, I gasped an involuntary sound that echoed faintly through the cavernous library.

He paused only to chuckle, the sound low and smug. "That," he murmured, brushing the same spot again with a flick of his tongue, "was gorgeous."

I bucked under him as he returned, his tongue moving with deliberate, devastating precision. Every flick, every press, every swirl sent waves crashing through me. I was lost in it, completely undone. Nothing else existed. Not the ball, not the crown, not the engagement. Just this heat. Just this sensation. Just him.

The moans that spilled from me were wild, uncontrolled, primal things. My fingers clutched at the table edge, the wood digging into my palms as I trembled beneath his touch.

My eyes fluttered open in a daze as he paused. "Sagar?" I breathed, glancing down.

He looked up, mouth glistening, eyes lit with dark fire. "Silvia," he said, voice like gravel and honey, "don't hold back. I want to hear every filthy, gorgeous sound you make. I want anyone passing those doors to know what I'm doing to you."

The sheer audacity of it, combined with the low growl of his voice, sent a violent jolt of arousal through me. I moaned again, louder, my legs twitching as if to obey on instinct.

A surge of need ripped through me, and before I could talk myself out of it, I sat up and reached for him, threading my fingers into his hair and pulling him up to meet my lips. I kissed him fiercely, tasting myself on his tongue, claiming him as mine.

He blinked in surprise, eyes blown wide as I broke the kiss and cupped his jaw.

"Sagar..." My voice trembled with nerves and boldness all at once. "I want to do something for you."

The tension shifted, still electric, still charged, but laced now with something softer. His expression changed, flickers of emotion crossing his face too quickly to name.

"You already are," he said.

I shook my head, brushing my thumb across his lower lip. "No," I said, more firmly now. "Tell me your fantasy. Let me ruin you."

His pupils darkened. He exhaled a laugh, breathless and stunned, like I'd just knocked the wind out of him.

"Gods help me, Silvia," he muttered, his voice low and feral like a man watching his last bit of self-control slip through his fingers. "You're going to be the death of me."

His thumb traced the shape of my mouth, soft and devoutly, like he was trying to memorize the curve of my lips. I leaned into the touch, letting myself melt into it.

But then he stepped away.

The energy shift was palpable. I watched, spellbound, as slowly, deliberately, he slipped off his coat and rolled up his sleeves just past his elbows. The veins along his forearms flexed with each careful fold, the movement unhurried, he was savoring the way he was unraveling me.

When he turned back to me, something had changed in his eyes. There was a flicker of mischief, yes, but beneath that shimmered a much darker hunger. He slammed his hands down on the table on either side of me, the sound sharp in the quiet. I gasped, falling back instinctively. His body hovered above mine, casting me in his shadow, caging me in.

"Do you remember that book you were reading the last time we were in here?" he asked, his voice gossamer-wrapped steel.

I blinked, caught off guard. "A Winter's Eve?"

His grin curled into something wicked. "That's the one." He dipped lower, his mouth barely grazing my ear. "Did you think about me when you read it?" he whispered, each word laced with intimate cruelty.

My breath stuttered. That damn book. My hands flew to my face as my cheeks flamed. "What? No!"

"Oh, you liar," he laughed, dark and amused, pulling my hands away from my face with maddening gentleness. "You absolutely did. I can see it."

My heartbeat thundered in my chest as my legs wrapped instinctively around his waist. I pulled him closer, needing to feel him again. "Stop teasing me and keep going," I demanded, surprising even myself with the edge in my voice.

He drew back with an arched brow. "You said you wanted to do something for me, right?"

I nodded, still breathless, the air thick with the scent of my arousal.

Sagar turned toward the shelves, his fingers skimming across the spines like he knew them by heart. He pulled the novel free and held it between us. A Winter's Eve. My mouth went dry.

"I want you to find the passage," he said as he laid it down beside me, "the one that made you think of me."

I stared at the book like it might bite me, remembering the words that had sent such a flush through my body before.

"I want you to read it."

I scrunched my nose in confusion. "That's it?"

He grinned, slowly descending back to his knees. "Out loud, please."

My hands trembled slightly as I opened the familiar cover, the pages practically turning themselves. I found the line, of course, I had known where it was. But before I could speak, a sharp, unexpected sting lit up my skin. I gasped, looking down. Sagar had just bitten the inside of my thigh.

He wasn't even looking at me, his expression uncharacteristically shy, like he was embarrassed by his own boldness. His mouth ghosted over the bite, pressing a slow, apologetic kiss to soothe the sting.

"Now?" I asked, voice hoarse and small, clutching the book like armor.

"Yes," he murmured, his lips grazing the tender skin. His breath was hot, his gaze darker than I'd ever seen it. "Read it to me."

My hands trembled as I opened the book. The pages fluttered like the wings of a bird desperate to escape, and maybe I was just as frantic, caught somewhere between shame and desire, fantasy and reality. The words blurred for a moment until I forced myself to focus.

"Eve sensed the danger of her moves, the way her pulse quickened each time his fingers brushed hers. The Duke hovered behind her, his breath teasing the shell of her ear. 'May I?' he whispered, unrelenting. 'I will not take unless you ask me to.'"

I paused, lips parting to speak again, but instead, a gasp escaped me as Sagar's fingers found the peak of my arousal. His touch was slow, subservient, circling the delicate flesh with practiced intent. My back arched off the table, a strangled sound fleeing my lips as pleasure shocked through me like lightning.

The book nearly fell from my hands.

He looked up at me from between my legs, his face glowing with restraint and hunger. "Keep reading," he ordered, voice thick with control. "You said you'd do something for me."

I swallowed hard, suppressing the moan tangled in my throat. I forced my gaze back to the page, the words now taking on a devastating new intimacy.

"'Yes,' she breathed. The word escaped before she could stop it. And the Duke—"

His fingers moved again, circling and squeezing, causing me to cry out.

"—The Duke didn't hesitate. He parted her gently, carefully, and then filled her until she forgot her name."

Sagar's fingers slid inside me with unbearable ease, stretching and filling me in a way that made me tremble. My thighs clenched around him, but he held steady, pausing just long enough to make me ache before pulling back again.

"Her fingers clawed at the velvet desk as her body writhed against him, lost in the rhythm of what they had become."

The book trembled in my grip as his touch deepened. His pace matched the mounting tension in the words, each thrust of his fingers perfectly timed to strip me of dignity and leave only sensation.

"His mouth found the pulse in her neck. He whispered filth and poetry into her skin, urging her to fall apart for him..."

His fingers thrust deeper, curling inside me with an intimacy that felt sacred. He moved with purpose, stroking the place that turned thought into noise. My body bowed toward him, seeking more, needing it.

"...And she did, over and over again, until her voice was no longer her own."

His tongue swirled across my clit as his fingers continued to piston inside of me. I let out a yelp; it was too much, but it was perfect.

"Sagar—" I choked out, barely able to breathe, let alone speak. My body arched toward his hand, desperate, frantic.

He pressed his forehead against my thigh, his free hand gripping my hip tightly to hold me in place. "That's not in the book."

"I can't read any more," I gasped, panic and pleasure crashing into one. "I-I think—"

He smiled, that wicked, knowing grin, and didn't let up. "Good," he said. "I want you to, Princess."

The warmth that had been simmering inside me erupted into a full blaze. It curled up my spine, down my legs, and between my thighs until I could no longer contain it. I shattered, violently and beautifully, a cry tearing from my throat that echoed through the vast stone chamber. My hands fell open. The book tumbled from my grasp and hit the floor with a hollow thud, irrelevant now.

The words on the page vanished. All I could feel was him.

My whole body tensed, my voice a string of breathless, obscene cries echoing off the stone walls. The world narrowed to the crashing waves inside me. My skin burned. My vision blurred. He kissed my knee softly, obediently, as I came down, his fingers slowing but not leaving me just yet.

"Sagar," I gasped, my voice laced with newfound confidence, "take off your clothes."

He hesitated, his brows furrowing. "Silvia—"

"I'm not going to ask again," I said, my tone soft but insistent. The words carried a weight that made his resistance crumble.

With a quiet, resigned sigh, he began to unbutton his shirt. Panic clutched my lungs with each undone clasp, every slow reveal of his skin drawing me deeper into something that felt impossibly raw. Firelight danced across the contours of his torso, shadows carving out the shape of him, broad chest, defined muscles, the hollow beneath his ribs where his breath deepened.

That's when I noticed them.

Soft, reddish-brown ridges marred the perfection. Scars, faint and gleaming, scattered across his chest like constellations. I reached out without thinking, the tip of my finger brushing one near his collarbone.

He flinched.

A breath trembled from my lips as the weight of it sank in. These weren't just marks. They were memories. Wounds that had once bled now faded into silence. Pain and survival written across his skin.

In a strange, almost shameful way, I felt envious. His scars were proof that he had lived through something, that he had endured, bled, fought, and come out the other side. They marked him with stories I hadn't been there for, pain I couldn't touch.

My own battle scars were buried in my past life, left behind on the corpse of the saint I used to be. Here, in this new world, I was untouched, unburdened in body, though not in soul. My skin remained smooth, flawless, unmarred by the past, and yet that made me feel more fragile, not less. As though my suffering had been erased, invalidated by the absence of proof. No one could see what I had lost. No one could trace my pain with their fingers. And standing here next to him, broken open and beautiful, I felt like a ghost trying to touch something solid.

I didn't speak. Instead, I gently guided him down to the furs by the fire, his body yielding to my touch like it had been waiting. He lay there, exposed and beautiful, and I moved over him, worshipping each scar with my lips, tracing their paths with admiration. My kisses whispered a vow into every mark.

I want you.

My mouth trailed lower, across the firm plane of his abdomen, down to a long, jagged scar that slanted just above his pelvis. I paused. My lips hovered. Then I kissed it, slow and unhurried. He groaned, one hand burying itself in my hair, the other tightening into the rug beneath him.

"Silvia," he warned, voice thick, strained. "If you keep going... I won't be able to stop."

I met his gaze, my eyes dark and steady. "Good," I said softly. "My turn to punish you, remember?"

His breath trembled the moment my hand slipped beneath the waistband of his trousers. The heat of him met my palm like a brand, pulsing, alive, eager. My fingers curled around him, drawing a shudder from his chest.

He was already impossibly hard, thick, and heavy, twitching with anticipation. I freed him slowly, savoring the weight of him in my hand, watching his face as his brows furrowed and his mouth parted. His expression teetered between awe and panic, as if he still couldn't quite believe this was real.

He was big. Bigger than anyone had warned me. The crown of him glistened with the first hints of his desire, a single drop catching the light like dew on a blade. I stared, perhaps a moment too long, speechless at the raw vulnerability of it. His yearning made him beautiful.

Sagar reached up, brushing a loose strand of hair behind my ear, his fingers trembling slightly. His palm lingered at my cheek, warm and tender. "Silvia," he murmured, voice hoarse with restraint. "If it's too much, I—"

But I didn't let him finish. I silenced his worry with the soft press of my lips against his skin, then slid him into my mouth, slowly, longingly. He gasped, his entire body going rigid as his hands flew to the table behind him, gripping the edge like a lifeline. His hips jerked, unbidden, as a whimper escaped him, unfiltered and raw.

I found myself loving the sound, him bending and breaking beneath me.

I took my time, learning the shape of him with my tongue, adjusting to the stretch and heat. I could feel every twitch, every tremble as I hollowed my cheeks and moved in slow, deliberate strokes. Sagar's breathing fractured above me, ragged and shallow, his head tilting back as if the sensation overwhelmed him.

As I grew bolder, his reactions rewarded me. Every broken sound, every whispered curse of my name pushed me further.

"Gods, Silvia," he groaned, his voice breaking. "You're unbelievable."

His fingers slid into my hair, holding as if it were the only thing keeping him from shattering. As if I were the only real thing left in his world. And for a moment, maybe I was.

I loved it. The control and the vulnerability braided together, the intimacy of knowing I was the one guiding us, holding the fragile balance of both our fates in my hands. A new flame of desire stirred inside me, urging me on, and I moved faster, more sure.

A look of panic flickered on his face briefly, and I knew this was uncharted territory for us both. It only deepened what passed between us. His retention unraveled piece by piece until he cried out, his whole body trembling as he surrendered to the feeling and spilled into me, his climax rough and affectionate all at once.

I sat back, wiping my mouth with the back of my hand, and smiled, a slow, wicked curl of satisfaction. The heat that filled me was overwhelming. My senses grew fuzzy as I crawled up to Sagar's face. There was only one thing on my mind.

"That was fun," I said simply. "But I want more."

He stared at me, chest still heaving, golden eyes burning now with something darker. "More?" he echoed, voice hoarse. "Silvia... I don't know how much more I can give you."

I trailed my fingers down his chest, back to where his cock twitched in anticipation, already stirring again under my touch.

"You'll give me everything," I whispered.

He growled low in his throat and surged up, pulling me into his arms with sudden strength. "You can have whatever you want," he said, voice thick with devotion and hunger. "Just remember, when it's my turn, I won't be gentle."

Our lips met again, fiery, consuming, like the last spark from a fire ready to ignite. His mouth tasted of want and something unspoken, something deeper. My hands roamed his bare skin, memorizing every line, every scar, every shiver under my fingertips. It felt as though our bodies would melt into each other, as though the space between us was no longer permitted to exist.

With a smooth, instinctive motion, he flipped me gently onto my back, settling above me. His hips pressed into mine in a slow grind that made me gasp, the thin barrier between us the only thing stopping him from claiming me fully. I flinched from the overwhelming nearness of what we were about to do. His eyes searched mine, uncertain for the briefest moment, but I wrapped my arms around him, guiding him closer.

"Sagar," I whispered, breathless. "I want—"

But the words never had a chance to finish.

The heavy creak of the library door broke the moment like glass underfoot. We froze, our bodies still tangled together, our breath suspended in our throats. The crackling fire, once warm and inviting, now felt accusing.

Sagar reacted instantly, rolling off of me and pulling me beneath a table with him. He threw his coat over my body, shielding me from view as my pulse thundered in my ears.

"Sagar," I whispered, heart racing.

He silenced me with a finger pressed gently to my lips. His expression was calm, calculated, but his jaw was tight with tension.

A cloaked figure slipped into the room, their footsteps muffled but purposeful. We watched in breathless silence as they moved to the fireplace, pulling something from beneath their cloak. The item, a sealed envelope or scroll, I couldn't tell, was tossed into the flames without a word.

The figure didn't linger. They turned sharply, disappearing as swiftly as they'd come, the door slamming shut behind them with a finality that sent a chill down my spine.

As soon as the intruder was gone, Sagar sprang into action. He grabbed the fire poker, working quickly to retrieve the burning remnants. Ash and blackened parchment clung to the metal as he sifted through it, trying to salvage whatever he could. I watched, still beneath the table, as his eyes flicked over the scorched fragments before tucking them into his pocket.

His face was unreadable, a mask of calculation over something deeper.

"What was that about?" I asked, finally crawling out from beneath the table. My voice was shaky, still laced with the rawness of what had almost happened and what had just interrupted us.

"I'll tell you later," he muttered, brushing a hand through his hair before stepping toward me. His fingers tucked a loose curl behind my ear, a tenderness that contrasted sharply with the storm brewing in his eyes.

He pulled me close, pressing his lips to my temple. "I'm sorry," he whispered. "The moment's gone."

It had. And yet, part of me still ached for it.

"You should go back to your room," he said softly. "I need to take care of this. Tonight."

I searched his face, trying to read the thoughts he wouldn't say aloud. The walls between us hadn't come crashing down, not yet. There were still secrets behind those eyes, even after everything we had risked for each other in the last hour.

Still dazed, I nodded. "Alright."

He gave me a small smile as he reached down and plucked my torn gown from the floor. The satin slipped between his fingers like water. The smile on his lips twisted into something rueful.

"We may need to do something about this," he said, chuckling.

I laughed too, though it came out thin and tired. He helped me into the gown, carefully slipping it over my head before wrapping his coat around me again, securing it at my shoulders like a cloak. His fingers lingered just a moment too long, as if he didn't want to let go.

He kissed my forehead, slow and deliberate. "Stay safe, sweet Silvia," he murmured.

I reached for the door but paused with my hand on the handle. "You're not leaving with me?"

He shook his head. "I will. But not yet. I don't want us to get caught. It'll raise fewer suspicions if we go separately."

I nodded. It made sense, but it didn't ease the ache in my chest.

As I stepped out into the corridor, I turned back one last time.

Sagar stood motionless, staring into the fireplace where the last embers still glowed. The firelight flickered across his face, dancing shadows and sorrow over his features. He looked powerful. Haunted. Alone.

The image stayed with me all the way back to my chambers, and well into the night, long after the warmth of his touch had faded from my skin.

Chapter 19

I woke with a groan, my body protesting the contorted way I'd slept on the cursed excuse of a sofa. Every joint in my back cracked in defiance as I sat up, the light from the window far too bright for my liking. The memories from the previous night surfaced in scattered fragments, heat, breathless kisses, the flicker of firelight on skin, the ache of almost. My cheeks flushed before I could stop them.

Had that all really happened?

I blinked hard, trying to compose myself. Returning to my chambers after the encounter had felt like walking through fog. I'd opened the door to find June sprawled across my bed, blissfully unaware of the turmoil unraveling inside of me. Rather than disturb her and possibly face a barrage of questions I wasn't ready to answer, I had surrendered to the lumpy sofa. My neck was now exacting revenge.

The door creaked open, and in marched June, bright-eyed and practically glowing with energy. Her eyes immediately swept over me, taking in my tangled hair, wrinkled nightdress, and the undeniable bags under my eyes.

"Well, good morning, Princess," she sang, flopping onto the bed with the grace of a falling cat. "You look like you had a restful night."

I gave her a pointed look, rubbing my temples. "I believe the plan was for you to stay in my bed until I came back, not sleep in it."

June shrugged, pulling the covers over her as if they belonged to her by divine right. "I was just doing my duty," she replied smugly. "What if someone had checked on you during the night? It would've been very suspicious if your bed looked untouched."

"And it wasn't at all suspicious that you were drooling on my pillow?" I shot back, crawling beside her despite myself. Her presence was oddly comforting, like a buffer against the storm still swirling in my chest.

June rolled to face me, her blonde curls bouncing against the pillow. Her eyes locked with mine, suddenly serious. "So?" she whispered, voice low and urgent. "How did it go?"

I buried my face in the pillow, groaning. "It was... something," I muttered.

June's brows shot up. "Something? That's the best you've got?" She gave me a theatrical gasp. "You didn't just talk about books, did you?"

"Well," I mumbled, my voice muffled by cotton. "We did read a little..."

"Did you confess your love? Kiss passionately under moonlight? Swear a blood oath and run off together?" she asked, hoping to get any information she could.

I peeked at her from under the pillow. "No," I said again, quieter this time, but the weight in my voice made her pause.

June frowned thoughtfully, propping herself up on her elbows. "Huh. That's odd. I was certain he would be impervious to your charms."

I laughed despite myself, then let her pull me up from the bed with a huff of exertion. She began rummaging through my wardrobe and pulled out a soft yellow day dress. I reached for it, but she was already peeling my nightdress over my head with expert efficiency.

She froze mid-motion, eyes narrowing.

"What is this?" she asked, a gleeful spark in her voice.

I blinked. "What is what?"

June's smirk spread like wildfire as she stepped closer. "Well, I see what you meant by 'something'."

Dread bloomed in my chest. I dashed to the mirror.

There it was. A perfect, unmistakable bruise, deep violet, artfully placed right on the inside of my thigh. My jaw dropped.

I swiped at it like it was a stray ink mark. "Oh gods. No, no, no. That wasn't supposed to stay."

June burst out laughing. "That's not just staying. That's making a statement."

My hands flew to my legs, my mortification complete. "It's nothing."

"Nothing?" She leaned in, looping an arm around my shoulders while pinching my cheek with exaggerated affection. "That's nothing, and I'm the Goddess Leticia herself."

I glared at her half-heartedly, cheeks burning hot enough to melt steel. "June."

"Yes, Princess?" she said sweetly.

I crossed my arms, huffing. "Don't make me throw you out of my chambers."

"You wouldn't dare. Not after I helped cover for your scandalous library tryst."

"I haven't even told you anything yet!"

"Exactly," she said, plopping onto the chair and crossing her legs like she had all the time in the world. "So, start talking. I want details, metaphors, and a dramatic retelling. I'll settle for vague longing and strategically censored euphemisms if you're shy."

I stared at her, at a complete loss for words, and for a moment, I thought I might just combust.

I hesitated, unsure where to begin. "It's... complicated," I said finally, the words barely audible over the thrum of emotion in my chest. "I don't even know how to describe it."

June's teasing melted away. She reached over and gave my arm a warm, reassuring squeeze. "Alright. You don't have to tell me anything you don't want to. But let's get you ready for the day first, hmm? One battle at a time."

Only then did I become acutely aware of the cool air brushing across my skin. June had dressed me a hundred times before, but today my body felt foreign, more exposed. Every inch still hummed with sensitivity. Tender, marked, remembered. I couldn't help but wonder if Sagar had left more on me than that bruise.

June tossed a soft chemise over my shoulders with practiced ease and spun me toward the vanity, pulling out the brush. We slipped into a long, stilted silence, the kind that crackled with unsaid things. As she combed through my tangled hair, I winced more than once.

"He really made a mess of you," she muttered, tugging at a stubborn knot.

"June," I said suddenly, perhaps a little too loudly.

She jumped, startled, and the brush went flying from her hand. It hit the wall with a thunk and skittered across the floor in defeat.

"Gods, you startled me," she muttered, standing to retrieve it. "What is it, Silvia?"

I hesitated again. The words were fragile, still forming. "I can't put a word to it, but... there's this feeling I get when I'm with Sagar. It's like something takes over me. It's overwhelming and confusing and..." My voice dropped. "It scares me."

June sat beside me again, her eyes soft but alert. She rested her chin on one hand, the other still gripping the brush loosely. "How do you feel about him?" she asked carefully. "Because it sounds like you could be falling in love."

My heart leapt with an anxious flutter that made my stomach twist.

Love?

The word felt too big. Too bright. Too dangerous.

I had never been in love before, not like that. Not even in my past life. Saints were taught that desire was a distraction, a detour from divinity. Love was sacred only in theory, distant and untouchable. To crave someone, to want them like this, it had never even occurred to me that I could.

"What does it feel like?" I asked the question coming out raw and honest. "To fall in love. Or what does it feel like to you?"

June leaned back in her seat, her gaze drifting upward, a wistful softness settling in her expression. "Love, for me, feels like watching someone in a quiet moment and realizing you'd memorize every part of them if you could," she said gently. "It's noticing the way their fingers move when they work, the way they hum under their breath when they think no one's listening. How they command a room without ever raising their voice." Her lips curled into a faint smile, one that didn't quite reach her eyes. "It's not loud or dramatic, it's this quiet kind of awe. Like every little thing they do becomes sacred, just because it's them."

She paused, her voice lowering. "And maybe it's not returned. Maybe it never could be. But you'd still do anything to protect that brilliance, to be near it. Because even admiring them from afar feels like a kind of privilege."

I took that in slowly, her words rippling through me like wind across water. "That doesn't sound like what I'm feeling at all," I admitted, frowning. "It's not calm or quiet. It's fire and confusion. It's as if my entire body is inching towards a blaze that I know will kill me."

"Sounds like the start of something, though," she said with a small grin. "Not all love starts soft. Some of it explodes first."

I sighed. "Maybe I'm just enjoying myself. Or maybe I'm too broken to know the difference."

"You're not broken," June said firmly, tucking a strand of hair behind my ear. "You're just new to this. And thinking about him this much? It means something, even if you don't have the name for it yet."

Before I could answer, she clapped her hands together with renewed mischief. "Now, enough emotional excavation. You need something special today."

"I don't know if that's a good idea..." I began cautiously.

June was already halfway across the room, flinging open my wardrobe with the determination of a woman on a quest. "You're not dressing for him," she said over her shoulder. "You're dressing for you. But if he happens to see what he's missing..." She paused, then turned with a wicked grin. "All the better."

"Are you trying to torture him?" I queried, placing my chin on the chair.

"After what he did to your dress last night? Yes, of course I am."

She emerged with a bundle of sheer peridot organza, holding it up like a prize trophy.

"For breakfast?" I asked, eyebrows raised.

"Not just for breakfast," she said, already motioning for me to lift my arms. "I have a feeling when he sees you in this, it'll stir something up." She gave me a devilish wink. "I want him in absolute agony."

She slid the dress over my head, carefully arranging the ruffles and fastening the corset with expert speed. The fabric hugged me like it had been sewn with whispered sins. The neckline plunged with a confidence I didn't yet possess, ruffles guiding the eye in ways that felt dangerous and thrilling.

By the time she stepped back, I hardly recognized the woman staring back at me in the mirror.

"I don't know if I can pull this off," I whispered, tugging at the hem. My reflection looked powerful, feminine, and alive. Yet I wasn't sure I belonged in it.

June spun me gently to face her, hands on my shoulders. "Silvia," she said with adoration. "Look at you, you can and you will."

As I turned to the side, catching my reflection once more, I couldn't deny the allure of the look. The bright green of the dress made my eyes gleam like polished gemstones, the organza shimmering with every subtle movement. It clung to me in ways I wasn't used to, but instead of feeling exposed, I felt undeniable. I didn't just feel beautiful, I felt dangerous. Alive.

A wicked smile curled across my lips. "A rightful punishment indeed."

Twirling slightly as I left the room, I let myself bask in the confidence that bloomed in my chest like spring after a brutal winter. All

I had to do was survive breakfast with Margaret, surely a stream of dramatic retellings of the ball, before I could go searching for Sagar. Part of me hoped I wouldn't have to look far.

Just as my hand reached for the handle to the dining room, I froze. A deep, amused laugh trickled through the heavy wooden door, followed by the unmistakable high-pitched giggle of my sister. My stomach twisted. Someone was already with her, and I had a sinking suspicion I knew who it was.

I shoved the door open with more force than intended. Margaret jumped slightly but quickly recovered, standing to greet me. "Wow, Silvia you look stunning." She whispered. "Look who decided to join us for breakfast."

My eyes flicked toward the table, and sure enough, there he was. Prince Gerraint, seated like he belonged there, his sharp eyes catching the light like polished amber. And behind him, standing by the window as stiff and still as a shadow carved in stone, was Sagar.

A wave of nausea and dread crept up my spine, tangling with something else far more dangerous: desire.

"That's... wonderful," I stammered, forcing a polite smile.

"I hope I'm not an intrusion," the Prince said with a falsely modest smile, the corners of his mouth too sharp, too knowing.

"Of course not," I said, my voice smooth as I offered a shallow curtsey. "We're honored."

I glanced briefly, intentionally, at Sagar. For a heartbeat, his eyes flicked to mine. Just a flicker. But it was enough. The flush that lit up his ears was unmistakable.

June was correct, he was in agony.

"You look absolutely exquisite today," Gerraint added, his gaze dragging across me far longer than it should have. "Is there a specific occasion? Or perhaps you knew of my intrusion and just wanted to dazzle me."

"I was thinking of making a round in the library later, actually," I said breezily, taking my seat.

A small, strangled sound came from Sagar's direction, a muffled cough or maybe a choked laugh. Either way, it earned him a few curious glances from around the table. I hid my smile behind my teacup.

"Margaret," I said quickly, eager to redirect the room's attention. "How did you enjoy the ball last night?"

A longing smile crossed her face as she stared down into her own cup. "It was magical, truly everything I've ever dreamed." While her expression remained soft, her eyes lit up like a lantern. "You left before the best part. There was this mysterious woman in a black dress, no one knew who she was, but she danced like a shadow across the floor. She managed to slip away before midnight like a ghost before I could ever catch her name..."

I glanced at Sagar again, and this time his gaze met mine with something volatile behind it, hunger. I forced myself to look away, feigning interest in Margaret's fantastical retelling.

I couldn't help sneaking another look at the Prince. He seemed thoroughly entertained by Margaret's vivid descriptions, laughing at her dramatics like he genuinely found her amusing. But then, his gaze slid to me.

I felt it before I saw it: heavy, calculated, intense.

His deep eyes locked onto mine, clouded with something I couldn't quite read.

I looked away, a flicker of unease worming its way into my gut. I turned to Sagar for a distraction, but he wouldn't meet my eyes. He was stone again.

Eventually, I let myself return the Prince's stare, hoping to at least level the playing field. He smiled, slow and chilling, before calmly returning to the meal on his plate.

My appetite had vanished.

Just as Margaret opened her mouth to launch into another saga, the Prince rose to his feet.

"Your tales have been as ravishing as this meal, dear Margaret," he said warmly. "You are wise far beyond your young years. However, I was hoping I might steal your sister for a brief word. If that would be alright?"

Margaret's smile faltered, but she remained composed. "Of course Prince Gerraint." She stood, making her way to me. "Silvia, I hope we can talk more later?"

"Of course, my dear," I said, brushing her fiery curls behind her ear fondly.

She leaned in close, just enough that only I could hear her as she whispered. "You were right by the way, the Prince isn't scary, when you get to know him."

Before I could respond she shuffled quickly from the room, humming to herself. The door closed with a solid, echoing thud. It left me alone with the Prince and the imposing presence of the knights, one of which I was possibly in love if not had a very complicated relationship with.

"You seem to be out of tea, Princess," Gerraint said smoothly, his voice dipped in honey. I glanced down at my empty cup, as he'd no doubt already noticed.

"That's quite alright," I replied evenly, forcing my features into calm neutrality. "I prefer refilling myself—"

"Nonsense," he said with a smile that didn't quite reach his eyes. He turned slowly like a cat choosing which mouse to toy with. His gaze landed purposefully on the one man who had remained perfectly still.

"Sagar," he said, each syllable slow and deliberate. "Would you kindly refill the Princess's cup?"

Sagar didn't move at first. I saw the faint flicker in his jaw, the way his hands remained clenched behind his back. Then, with the grace of a soldier obeying a command he loathed, he stepped forward.

Each stride dripped with coercion. Controlled, quiet, but brimming with restrained force.

He reached for the teapot.

Our hands met, just barely, as I handed the porcelain cup to him. The touch was brief, no more than a brush of skin on skin, but the jolt that surged through me was immediate and undeniable. Like a spark catching dry kindling.

My gaze snapped to his.

His eyes, usually so steady, so guarded, flashed with something raw. Something that seared. It wasn't just anger. It wasn't just desire. It was the ache of things left unsaid, of things that never should have happened and yet did.

"Oh! That's right, you two have met before, haven't you?" he asked, far too casually. He leaned forward, resting his chin atop interlaced fingers, watching me with barely veiled amusement.

"Yes," I said carefully. "He saved me. From the kidnappers." My eyes flicked to Sagar again, but he didn't return the glance. "He was a great comfort to me that night."

The Prince nodded slowly, as though savoring each word. "Is that so?" he murmured. Then, sharper: "So the two of you are... close?"

The question sliced through the air. I froze.

"Pardon?" I managed at last, my voice thinner than I liked.

Gerraint's smile widened.

At that moment, Sagar's voice cut in quietly, a lifeline tossed into rough waters. "Your tea, Your Highness."

I startled slightly as he placed the cup before me. The briefest touch again, this time so light it might have been imagined, but it steadied me. I looked up to him, hoping for a glance, but he didn't look at me. Instead, he gently slipped a beige envelope on my lap.

I glanced down at the crimson seal that gave it weight, slipping it deeper under the table, away from view.

Sagar bowed swiftly and returned to his post without a sound.

The Prince's eyes followed him, then returned to me. "I would like a moment alone with my betrothed," he said coolly, lifting a hand and gesturing toward the door.

The knights—Sagar included—obeyed instantly, walking out without hesitation. The door shut behind them with a final, echoing click that seemed to reverberate through my bones.

I sat frozen in place, the envelope clutched between my fingers, still radiating with his warmth. Gerraint moved slowly, with the casual arrogance of someone who always got what he wanted. He didn't walk, he prowled, gliding across the room until he stood beside me.

He pulled the chair next to mine with a deliberate scrape and lowered himself into it, his presence swallowing the space between us in a creeping fog.

Without asking, he lifted my chin to meet his gaze. I flinched, just slightly, but didn't pull away. His grip was warm and firm, too intimate for a conversation I hadn't agreed to have.

"Have you thought about what I said last night?" His voice was low, voile wrapped around a dagger. He spoke slowly, as if expecting every word to root itself in my skin.

I searched his eyes, but there was no softness behind them, only calculation.

My stomach twisted into knots. I'd forgotten. His words from the night before had been cryptic, unsettling, but they'd been swallowed by the chaos that had followed.

"I haven't had much time," I admitted softly. A half-truth. I hadn't dared to think about it. Not after Sagar. Not after what I'd felt.

A single bead of sweat trickled it's way down to my chin, landing on his finger. He grinned fiendishly.

"You should," he murmured. "These are important matters, Silvia. Matters of fate. But you of all people should know this."

I couldn't breathe as the air grew impossibly tight between us. I didn't know what he meant. And worse, I had the awful sense that he knew more than he was letting on.

I forced a tight smile and nodded. "Yes, Your Highness. I will."

Before I could pull away from his touch, his hand left my skin. He turned away from me and adjusted his coat.

"I best be on my way," he said lightly, brushing invisible dust from his sleeve. "Please forgive the short intrusion."

"Y-yes," I stammered, rising far too quickly. "Thank you for keeping my sister company."

I dropped into a practiced curtsy, holding it just long enough for my heart to stop hammering. When I rose, he was already halfway to the door.

But then he stopped. His hand rested on the handle, his back still to me.

"Oh, Princess?" he called over his shoulder.

My head snapped up. "Yes?"

He turned just enough for me to see the gleam in his eyes. "I spoke to the Queen yesterday. About the wedding..."

I schooled my expression into something soft and pleasant. "I imagine there's much to plan. Are you going to return home in the meantime?"

His voice sliced through my thoughts. "Oh, no. After a rather long chat with the Queen, I think it best that you stay within my sights. I wouldn't dream of returning home without my betrothed." He smiled as if offering a gift. "The ceremony will be next week."

The world tilted beneath my feet.

"Next week?" I echoed, barely able to form the words. "But..."

He nodded, clearly pleased with himself. "I know it's sudden, but trust me, it's for the best." With a final, gallant smile, he opened the door and left me with a final, foreboding word before disappearing through it. "Think about what I've said, Silvia."

I stood there, rooted in place, the sound of the latch clicking shut behind him echoing in my ears like the toll of a bell.

One week.

Panic gripped me by the throat. In my past life, I had time. I had space. Now it was collapsing, my future closing in around me like a cage.

The teacup slipped from my hands and shattered against the floor, shards scattering like glass raindrops.

I didn't move. I couldn't.

My knees gave out, but the numbness had already taken over. I hit the floor hard, but the pain didn't register. Only the sound of my heartbeat roared in my ears. Only the weight of those two words.

June burst through the doors, collecting me off of the floor and pulling me into her arms. "Silvia, are you okay?" She asked, forcing my eyes to meet hers. "Who do I have to hurt? Don't worry, I'll make it painful."

"One week, I only have one week." I muttered as tears blurred the contours of her face.

"I know, I heard. I came here as soon as I—" She picked up the tawny envelope Sagar had placed in my lap. It must have fallen when I collapsed. "What's this?"

I took the heavy envelope from her hands, gently inspecting every corner. "Sagar gave it to me."

"What do you think it says?" June asked lightly, but I didn't answer.

I broke the seal. The scent of parchment and lavender oil rose faintly from the folds. His handwriting was sharp, deliberate, almost like a sword on paper, but the words within were anything but cold.

Silvia,

WE LEFT THINGS UNFINISHED LAST NIGHT. THAT WASN'T MY INTENTION, BUT I THINK YOU ALREADY KNOW THAT. YOU KNOW HOW I HATE TO LEAVE UNFINISHED BUSINESS.

THERE ARE THINGS ~~I WANT TO TELL YOU~~ I NEED TO TELL YOU. BUT I CAN'T, NOT HERE, NOT WITH SO MANY WATCHING, WAITING, LISTENING. YOU CAN NEVER TRULY KNOW WHO TO TRUST IN A PLACE LIKE THIS. YOU DESERVE HONESTY, AND THE ONLY WAY I CAN GIVE IT TO YOU IS IN PRIVATE.

COME TO THE HOT SPRING TONIGHT. MIDNIGHT. ALONE. I'LL BE WAITING.

—SAGAR

I read it twice, then a third time, trying to calm the tremble in my fingers. The words blurred slightly at the edges.

But questions screamed beneath the quiet: What does he want to tell me? Why now? Why like this?

Behind me, June practically vibrated with excitement. "A midnight meeting at the hot spring? Silvia, this is the most romantic thing I've ever heard! It's like something out of a ballad! 'A Heated Encounter,' or, ooh, 'Steam and Secrets.' I could write it."

I turned sharply. "Were you reading over my shoulder?"

June gave an unapologetic shrug, spinning a shattered piece of teacup between her fingers. "I mean, you can't expect me not to peek. I'm only human."

"You're a menace," I muttered, stuffing the letter into my pocket before she could commit it to memory.

She grinned. "I'm *your* menace."

I rolled my eyes, but a reluctant smile tugged at the corner of my mouth. I turned away before she could see it, pretending to look out the window to what remained of the gardens. Winter was finally here, and nearly all the leaves had fled with the warmth of summer. Still, the words pulsed behind my ribs like a second heartbeat: unfinished business.

My thoughts drifted, unbidden, to that first night back in this life. The night I'd sworn to take control of my fate by any means necessary. I'd been steel then, sharp, clear, unflinching.

Somewhere along the line, that resolve had dulled. Not anymore, I still had one way out of this fate, one I had only briefly considered but pushed deep within me. But now, Sagar was spoon-feeding me the perfect opportunity.

I straightened, catching a glimpse of myself in a polished silver vase. My reflection stared back, wilder now, more worn but with a spark in her eyes. That spark could start a fire.

If I were going to marry the Prince in a week, then I would not give him the weapon he was waiting for. If my body, my choice, my power meant anything in this world, I would wield it myself.

It was time to seduce Sagar, to finish this business once and for all.

I stood at the edge of the hot spring, my breath forming fragile ghosts in the crisp night air. The moon hung low and luminous, its silver light spilling across the snow-dusted landscape like spilled milk over a tablecloth. The world was far too quiet, and yet the air buzzed with a kind of anxious electricity, as if even the stars knew what I was about to do.

Snowflakes drifted lazily from the sky, dancing in the breeze before vanishing into the warm mist rising from the spring. I blew one off my glove, watching it melt before it could land. It felt like a metaphor I didn't want to think about.

I pulled my cloak tighter around my shoulders, the rich velvet doing little to calm the anxious chill brewing beneath my skin. My heart was racing beneath the sheer nightdress June had insisted I wear, her voice still echoing in my head.

"You'll take his breath away," she'd said while fastening the clasp with mischievous glee. "Along with a few other things."

At the time, I'd managed a half-mortified, half-exhilarated laugh. Now, alone in the silence of the trees, I wasn't sure what I felt. Courage had seemed so easy in the daylight. But under the moon, everything felt more vulnerable. *I* felt more vulnerable.

The icy air prickled across my skin like a warning. For a moment, I questioned everything: my reasons, my readiness, my control. I had wanted this. Needed this. But the truth was, I wasn't just looking to change my fate tonight, I wanted him.

The minutes dragged, each second winding my nerves tighter. I crouched beside the water, letting the heat of the spring curl against my fingertips. The steam swirled around me, thick and fragrant with pine and something mineral.

The world was still, eerily so, and in that stillness, every creeping thought in my head got louder.

What if he didn't come? What if he did, and everything between us shattered the moment it became real?

The sound of snow shifting behind me made me jump to my feet, my heart catapulting into my throat. I turned sharply.

Sagar emerged from the darkness like a phantom out of myth; silent and strong, except he was undeniably real. Moonlight carved sharp silver lines across his face, highlighting cheekbones and jaw like they'd been shaped by the hands of a god.

He wasn't wearing his armor tonight. No uniform. No bow slung across his shoulder, no layers of leather or hardened duty to weigh him down. Just a loose linen tunic and worn trousers. I swallowed hard, choking the breath back into my lungs. There was something disarmingly human about him in that moment, so painfully reachable. He didn't look like the kingdom's most feared knight. Not like a weapon trained to follow orders. He looked like someone

I might've met at a market stall or a midsummer bonfire in a life where my crown didn't exist.

And gods, I was already drunk off of him.

"You made it," he said, jogging toward me. The light caught the sweat beading on his brow, glistening even in the crisp night air. "How did you get away from the palace?"

I grinned, lifting my chin. "I climbed out a window."

His eyes widened, caught between disbelief and awe. "You didn't."

"I did."

I rose onto the balls of my feet, trying to match his height, smug now, proud of myself. "You think you're the only one who knows how to sneak around the palace?"

As I shifted, the edge of my cloak slipped from my shoulder, just a little, just enough. Sagar's gaze caught the motion, and without a word, he stepped in, his fingers brushing lightly against my arm as he pulled the velvet back into place.

"Silvia," he began, voice low, almost scolding, "fix your cloak or you'll catch a—"

The words died in his throat.

His eyes had dropped, just briefly, catching a glimpse of the sheer fabric beneath. His jaw tensed. The corner of his mouth twitched, betraying the flicker of something unspoken, something hungry. Not quite a smirk. Not quite innocent.

I felt the heat rise to my cheeks like fire through kindling. "Sorry," I mumbled, fumbling to pull the cloak back over myself.

"Don't." His voice was low, roughened by something that wasn't cold. He took a step forward, closing the distance between us. "Never be sorry for this," he said, his voice softer now, gentler. His hands came up to cradle my face, fingers brushing lightly along my jaw, my cheekbones, like I was made of something fragile and sacred. His thumbs stroked the apples of my cheeks, chasing away the cold.

His breath brushed my skin, as if placing a warm kiss on my collarbone.

"You are…" he whispered, his voice raw, unfinished. He shook his head slowly, his eyes sweeping over my face like he was trying to memorize every detail before it was taken from him. "You're devastating."

My heart gave a painful, traitorous leap. I didn't speak. I only took his hand in mine, letting its heat burn into my memory. I brushed my thumb across his knuckles, tracing the calluses he'd earned protecting a kingdom that didn't deserve him. I wanted to melt into that warmth, to disappear into it, to never have to move again.

But time was not a luxury I possessed, not anymore. Not with the wedding looming like a guillotine overhead.

We both opened our mouths at the same time, our words colliding midair and tangling into nothing. We paused, laughing softly, awkwardly. I turned my face away, suddenly unable to look at him. His hand lingered on my cheek, trailing a slow, hesitant line as if torn between comforting me and pulling away.

"What's wrong?" he asked, his voice dipped in concern. He turned me gently back to face him.

I swallowed. "Sagar, tonight, you said there was something you needed to tell me, right?"

His silence hit harder than a yes. His eyes darted to the ground, then back to mine, as though the truth he carried was too heavy for words. I reached out, lacing my fingers through his.

"I need to know…" I whispered. "Will it make me think of you any differently than I do right now?"

He hesitated. I could see the war in him, duty versus desire, truth versus tenderness. Then, finally, he nodded.

"Yes," he said carefully, his voice no louder than the wind. "Silvia, I have to tell you the truth."

He drew in a breath, steeling himself. But I stepped closer before he could say another word. My finger pressed gently to his lips.

"Wait," I said, my voice breaking on the word. "I don't want to know. Not yet. If it's going to change anything between us, let it wait. Just for tonight."

He looked stunned. Conflicted. As if the truth in his chest was burning to get out, but not as badly as he wanted to hold me.

"But—"

I didn't give him time to argue. I stepped back slowly and let the cloak fall from my shoulders. It dropped in a soft whisper of velvet, forgotten in the snow. The nightdress clung to my skin, translucent beneath the moonlight. My curves, my body, my vulnerability, everything about me was on display, and yet, I didn't feel afraid.

Sagar's eyes darkened, his jaw tightening as if it took everything in him not to reach for me.

"Not fair," he breathed, voice thick with tension, with want, with restraint. "You are..."

"Yours," I finished for him, my voice shaking but steady. "I don't want the prince to have me, any part of me. Not my hand, not my name, not my body."

"Silvia..." Sagar whispered, like the name itself was sacred.

I leaned up and kissed him, fast, needy, decisive. It was messy and desperate, more emotion than precision, and for a moment, he didn't respond. His lips stayed still, his muscles tense beneath my hands.

Then, as if my desperation finally got through, he gave in.

His arms came around me in a sudden rush, pulling me close, kissing me back with so much intensity it stole the air from my lungs. The warmth of him flooded through me, melting every shard of hesitation, every drop of fear.

I pulled away, breaking the link between us. His expression softened, no longer the sharp edge of desire, but something deeper. His fingers brushed a loose strand of hair behind my ear, lingering as they trailed down to cup my jaw.

"You say the word," he said. "You tell me you want me, and I am yours. No hesitation. No restraint."

"No interruptions." I joked, leaning close enough that my lips brushed against the curve of his ear.

With trembling fingers, I slipped the delicate straps of the nightdress from my shoulders. The fabric slid down my body, pooling soundlessly at my feet. The cold air bit at my bare skin, but the way he looked at me like I was art, like I was salvation, was more than enough to keep me warm.

I stepped toward him, bare beneath the moonlight. No longer a pawn, no longer a princess promised to a stranger. Just a woman choosing her own damn fate.

Sagar met me halfway, his fingers grazing my arms with feather-light touch before trailing down to my waist. He leaned in close, his breath warm against my temple.

I could feel his breath stutter as I whispered, "I want you."

I wrapped my arms around his neck, standing on tiptoe as I kissed him. My breath caught in my throat when I felt him press against me, already hot, solid, ready. The heat that had flickered in my chest now surged into a wildfire.

Sagar's heart hammered against mine, a frantic rhythm that strangely calmed my nerves, confirming his unease mirrored my own. Pressed so tightly together, the boundaries between us blurred, and even the pulse I felt seemed indistinguishable as his or mine.

His arms locked around my waist, and before I could catch my breath, he lifted me into the air with effortless strength. I giggled as my legs wrapped instinctively around his hips, my body arching into his. His mouth crashed back into mine, urgent and wild, as our tongues tangled in rhythm.

Sagar groaned against my lips, the sound low and raw, as he ground his hips into mine. Sparks erupted wherever our bodies met, and I let out a shaky moan as pleasure bloomed through me, electric and all-consuming.

He broke the kiss, panting, lips parted. His mouth found the line of my jaw, then the sensitive hollow of my throat, where he placed a string of hot, open-mouthed kisses that made my toes curl.

I could feel Sagar's pulse against me, throbbing uncontrollably with each new noise that escaped my lips. The sensation was unbearable, and I couldn't hold back anymore.

"Tell me you want me." I growled, raking my fingers through his locks.

"Please," he whimpered, his voice so low and aching it sent shivers down my spine. "I need you, Silvia."

Something shifted inside me at his words, something tender and fierce all at once. To see him like this, begging for me, lit a fire beneath my skin I didn't know existed. I leaned in, gently catching his bottom lip between my teeth.

"Then take me," I breathed.

Without a word, he turned and carried me toward a wide, flat stone at the edge of the spring. He laid my cloak across it first. Gently, he placed me down, shielding me from the cold.

I lay back against the cloak, exposed in every sense of the word. He stood above me, his eyes scanning the length of me, as if committing me to memory. But there was only wonder in his gaze.

I didn't flinch. I didn't hide. I wanted him to see me. All of me.

He knelt beside me, and the world fell away. His hand moved to my torso, brushing down my center in a slow, agonizing trail. His touch was tender, curious, almost worshipful. Each pass of his fingers across my skin sent a tremor through me, and yet I couldn't bring myself to close my eyes. I didn't want to miss the look in his.

Sagar's devilish grin, a familiar mask of playful mischief, wavered, revealing a fleeting glimpse of vulnerability beneath. A softer, more unguarded emotion flickered in his eyes, momentarily eclipsing his usual confident swagger. The air crackled with anticipation as he lowered his head, his dark gaze fixed on me. The barest brush of his lips against the sensitive curve of my breast sent a shiver through me.

A playful flick of his tongue teased my already erect nipple, a sensation that sparked a sudden heat within me. He swirled his tongue over the stiff bud before gripping it between his teeth, a sweet, sharp pressure that made me gasp softly, the unexpected intensity sending a wave of sensation through my body.

He laughed before fighting me with a delicious tug, relishing in my reaction, savoring the way I cursed his name under my breath.

A gentle warmth emanated from his touch as his hand moved in slow, deliberate circles on my thigh, the friction creating a pleasant tingling sensation. The movement became more intimate, a silent question in its descent, until his fingertips delicately pressed against my most sensitive spot, testing the burgeoning heat that throbbed with increasing intensity between my legs.

A moan escaped my lips, an involuntary response to the escalating desire. My hand shot out, instinctively grasping his wrist to halt his exploration, my eyes snapping down to meet his with a mixture of surprise and a sudden wave of vulnerability.

His gaze flickered upwards, a startled expression clouding his features, as if he hadn't anticipated my reaction or the depth of the emotions swirling within me. The air crackled with unspoken tension, the intimacy of the moment hanging heavy between us.

"Is something wrong?" He asked, a flash of worry clouding his eyes.

I brought his hand to my lips and kissed his fingers softly, teasingly, before looking up through my lashes. "I said, I want *you*," I murmured, the words trembling against his skin. My gaze dropped to the rigid line between us. "I expect to get what I want tonight. Before any possible interruption."

For a moment, he froze, his expression shifting into something unlike anything I'd seen from him before. Fear. The cocky knight was gone, replaced by a man undone.

He stood without a word, slowly slipping off his clothes and letting them fall away. The moonlight painted silver against the hard lines of his body, highlighting every scar, every shadow. For a single moment, I just looked at him. His frame was powerful, yes, but there was something deeply human in the way he stood there, naked and silent in the snow.

I sat up, taking in the map of discolorations across his chest. I reached forward, trailing a finger over the raised skin. "You're beautiful," I whispered, and meant it.

He moved toward me slowly, as if any movement would ruin the moment. "We'll take it slow, okay?" he said softly. "If anything feels wrong, you tell me. I'll stop. I swear."

I nodded, unable to find words. My hand found his cheek, and I guided him closer, my trembling fingers brushing along the edge of his jaw. He leaned in, and for a moment, we just stayed like that, our foreheads touching, breaths tangled.

Sagar eased me back onto the cloak-draped stone, his hands guiding my thighs apart. My heart pounded as his body pressed against mine. My hand slid down, gently grasping at his thick appendage. It sat sturdy in my hands, still stiff for me.

I trembled at the thought of taking him; it was bigger than I remembered. Being so close to finality filled me with anxiety.

I began to softly stroke his shaft as his body trembled beneath my touch. His hand stopped my movement. I glanced towards him in surprise.

"Silvia," He muttered. "If you keep doing that, I won't last long."

A laugh caught in my throat, half nerves, half thrill, as he shifted forward, dragging the tip of his cock against me in maddening strokes, coating himself in my arousal. I gasped, heat flooding my body like wildfire.

We locked eyes. Just one look and everything that needed to be said passed between us.

He slipped inside me slowly, carefully, the stretch intense but somehow right. A soft cry escaped my lips, and he froze.

"Are you okay?" he asked, voice taut with restraint.

I nodded, barely able to speak, and kissed his thumb in reassurance.

The sensation was unlike anything I had ever known, something sacred and scorching all at once. It felt as if something buried deep inside me was suddenly bursting forth, like a bowstring being tightly pulled back before releasing a bolt of pleasure.

"I'm okay," I breathed. "I didn't say you could stop."

He let out a chuckle as he moved again, each slow thrust unwinding a knot of tension buried deep inside me. My body arched into him, begging for more. Each time I took him inside me, he would drive himself deeper, his movements growing stronger.

I was no longer Silvia, the dutiful princess, the sacred Saint, or the manipulated pawn. I was just me. Entirely, finally, me. The power that haunted me in my past life and hung above me like a cloud in this one would no longer define me.

Sagar moved with care, his hips rocking slowly, building a rhythm that sent waves of warmth surging through me. His length, soaked in my juices, viciously stroked and stimulated my clit every time he slid in and out.

Soft groans spilled from his lips, matching the sounds tearing from my throat. His hands anchored me as his pace quickened. Lewd, wet slaps echoed throughout the night.

"I can't believe I get to see your pleasured face again." He purred, his voice a thick velvet.

I cried out, louder this time, no longer shy about the sounds spilling from my mouth. It was raw. Messy. Perfect.

"Sagar, don't stop," I begged, my voice a broken whisper. "I want you to devastate me."

His rhythm deepened, becoming more urgent, every thrust sent lightning through my veins. My hands explored his body, feeling the heat building in unbearable waves. The moment crackled with something larger than us, some energy I didn't understand but welcomed with open arms.

Power, emotion, ecstasy, all fused until I couldn't tell where I ended and he began. I was light, fire, thunder. I felt myself slipping into something I couldn't control, something vast and terrifying and freeing all at once.

Guided by instinct, I pushed against his chest and flipped him onto his back. He let out a startled laugh, but the hunger in his eyes only grew as I straddled him and slowly, confidently, sank onto him again. I let out a breathless cry as I took him again, the stretch only leaving me wanting more.

I leaned forward, hands on his chest, hair falling around us like a curtain. "Do you want me to keep going?" I asked.

Sagar's surprised expression was everything I relished. He throbbed with delight as I shifted my hips. He nodded.

"I want you to beg for it."

He pulsed inside of me, gasping. "Silvia Stephan, I will give you my life if you keep going."

I let a chuckle escape me, quickly transforming into a moan as I began rocking. His hands found my hips, but this time, he let me lead. I found a rhythm, riding the wave between pain and pleasure, past and future.

"Fuck, Silvia." He whispered.

His head tilted back, jaw clenched, lip caught between his teeth. I watched him unravel beneath me, the power of it sparking something fierce and wild inside me. A devilish grin tugged at my lips as I moved faster, chasing the momentum that surged through my veins like fire.

This freedom, this control, it was intoxicating. For the first time in so long, I wasn't performing or obeying or sacrificing. I was living. I was feeling.

And gods, was it great to feel. The presence of his length, the way he filled me up, the way he stretched me. I wanted more—no, I *needed* more. My inner muscles clenched around him, pleading for the pleasure I longed for.

"Wait! Silvia!" Sagar's voice cracked with tension, but I didn't stop. I couldn't. I was too far gone, and some part of me didn't want to let go of this new, heady sensation.

"I'm going to—" he gasped, but the words dissolved as his body arched beneath me, going rigid with release.

A rush of warmth filled me, and I stilled, straddling him in the aftermath, heart hammering as the world held its breath. The snow continued falling, the silent audience to our chaos. Only the gentle bubbling of the spring and our mingled breaths broke the silence.

My voice was quieter than I expected when I finally spoke. "Are... are you okay?"

Sagar groaned and covered his face with both hands, clearly mortified.

"I'm sorry," he muttered, voice muffled. "I didn't mean to—"

"You didn't mean to what?" I asked, trying to keep the sharp edge out of my tone. A hint of sour disappointment curled in my chest before I could stop it.

He lowered his hands, revealing a face flushed crimson with embarrassment. "I didn't mean to finish that fast," he admitted. "I wanted to make it last. For you."

The corner of my mouth twitched into a sly smile. I crawled closer, pressing a kiss to his burning cheek before cupping it in my hand and squeezing playfully.

"You're adorable when you're flustered," I teased.

His hands tightened possessively around my waist, sending a shiver down my spine despite the heat still hanging between us. Before I could fully register his intent, he playfully tossed me into the hot spring.

The air around me instantly filled with a fragrant steam, carrying the subtle scent of sulfur and earth. A surprised yelp escaped my lips as the initial shock of the warm embrace registered, and I sputtered, pushing my hair from my eyes as I popped my head up from the swirling milky water of the secluded spring.

"Hey!" I shouted, wiping the water from my face. "Uncalled for!"

Sagar laughed and joined me with a splash, sliding in behind me and pulling me back against his chest. His arms wrapped around my waist. His fingers traced idle shapes along my spine, slow and deliberate, as though he were trying to memorize every breath of me.

The heat wrapped around me like a blanket, melting the leftover tension from my limbs and cooling the ache of desire that had driven me moments ago. I sighed, letting the water soothe my skin and my racing mind.

"What came over you tonight?" he asked, his voice low, with hints of surprise.

I tilted my head, resting it against his chest. "I don't know," I said truthfully. "But for once, it felt like I wasn't being pushed or pulled by anyone else. I chose this. I chose you. I felt like I changed something in myself." I rung a strand of hair between my fingers, suddenly struck with a wave of embarrassment. "Was it bad?"

"No! Gods, no." He reassured, his face burning with more than just the heat of the water. "In fact, I think I liked it more when you were in control."

I smiled, touched in a place words couldn't reach. I looked up into his face, studying the golden flecks in his eyes.

"What was it you wanted to tell me earlier?" I asked gently.

He hesitated, just long enough for me to know it wasn't something trivial, then shook his head with a quiet smile. "Tomorrow," he said. "Tonight was for us."

I nodded, the answer satisfying in a way I didn't expect. Whatever came tomorrow, it could wait. This moment in his arms, his warmth, the quiet hum of the night, was enough...for now.

"Sagar," I murmured, lifting myself slightly so my lips brushed the shell of his ear. "You know, we could always go again. Try to beat our record."

A rakish grin spread across his face, mischief returning to his gaze as he turned toward me. "Oh really now?" he said, pulling me closer, his hands cradling my face like I was something precious. "You think I'm ready already?"

I reached my hand below the water, gently caressing his already stiff cock in my hands. I could feel it twitch as his eyes turned hazy. My grin widened.

"Feels like you might be," I whispered, trailing kisses down his chest.

The night was far from over.

Chapter 21

I awoke to the pale light of dawn slipping through the seams of Sagar's tent, soft and golden as it kissed the rumpled fabric above us. The warmth beside me was steady, his body half beneath mine, our limbs tangled in a lazy sprawl beneath the thin blankets. The air was cool, but pressed against his bare skin, I was wrapped in a heat that went far deeper than flesh.

For a moment, I let myself breathe him in, filling me in a way that felt both new and achingly familiar. My head rose and fell with the steady rhythm of his breathing, the peace of it tugging at something fragile in my chest. A dull ache radiated from deep within me, reminding me that the events from the night before weren't just a dream: his hands, his voice, the look in his eyes when I'd taken control. My cheeks flushed scarlet, and I bit my lip to keep the small, giddy sound from escaping.

I couldn't remember when we'd stumbled back here, wrapped in each other's arms, or if we'd even bothered with proper clothes at all. But I was glad the night had never truly ended. This morning felt different, heightened. As if the world itself had shifted.

The smells around me were sharper: the earth beneath the tent, the leather of his armor somewhere nearby, the faint, fading spice of sweat and skin. My body was humming, alive with sensation.

My fingers moved without thought, tracing slow, methodical patterns across Sagar's chest. His skin was warm and lightly freckled, the muscle beneath taut and soft all at once. The blanket slid with my movement, revealing more of his golden skin, dappled in the morning light like a living statue.

Heat flared across my face and down my throat as I instinctively tugged the blanket up, covering myself. We had shared so much in the shadowed silence of night, but in the sharp honesty of morning light, I felt exposed, almost raw in a way I hadn't prepared for.

The sudden motion stirred him. Sagar's arms tightened reflexively around me as I realized in horror he was already awake. Not just awake, but already watching me.

A slow grin curled his lips. "Good morning," he murmured, his voice low and scratchy from sleep.

I opened my mouth, then closed it again, unsure what to say. I must have looked utterly flustered because his grin only widened.

"You're adorable when you're embarrassed," he teased, eyes dancing.

I groaned, burying my face against his shoulder. "Stop teasing me," I mumbled, though my voice lacked any true bite.

He laughed, the sound rumbling through his chest and into mine. His arms wrapped tighter around my waist, anchoring me to him. "I can't help it," he whispered, nuzzling against my temple. "You're irresistible when you blush."

His lips found mine, unhurried and soft, coaxing me back into the warmth I felt the night before. I inhaled sharply as his hand slid down the curve of my spine, resting at the small of my back. His fingers splayed wide, as if to claim me as his own.

The moment radiated with potential. My body ached to respond, to close the distance between us again. But I turned my head slightly, breaking the kiss.

"We shouldn't. Not again," I said, barely above a whisper. My heart fluttered with uncertainty even as I spoke the words. The truth was, I wasn't sure if it was the act itself I was hesitant about, or what it meant. What might it change?

Sagar's brow furrowed slightly, but he didn't pull away. Instead, he exhaled a soft breath, and a tender smile curved his lips. "As you wish, Princess."

He kissed my forehead, gentler this time, then brushed a loose strand of hair behind my ear. His touch lingered. "But you can't blame me for trying."

I chuckled, sinking back into him as the tent filled with the scent of morning: crisp snow, ash from a dying fire, and the lingering spice of Sagar's skin. His eyes found mine, and something soft passed between us. His fingers slid up, brushing lightly along my shoulder blades, igniting a shiver that rippled deep through me. I trembled from the memory of how those hands had worshiped me hours ago.

"I should get back to the palace," I whispered, forcing my thoughts into order.

His expression twisted, the softness melting into a scowl. One arm wrapped around my back in protest, tugging me down against his chest with sudden force. I gasped, startled by the intensity of his grip-and by the low growl of need buried in his throat.

"I think you should stay by my side," he murmured, his lips grazing the hollow of my collarbone. "Specifically in my tent. All day."

The temptation in his voice was a knife drawn slowly over silk. I laughed, half-heartedly, trying to defuse the pull I felt. "Sagar, I don't know if you've noticed, but the full palace is in the middle of wedding planning. I think someone might notice if the bride vanishes."

He sighed and let me go reluctantly, his hand slipping from my back. The sudden loss of his warmth sent a chill across my skin, like a phantom frostbite. I wrapped the blanket tighter around myself, but it couldn't quite dull the ache he left behind.

"Wedding planning?" he muttered, bitterness seeping into his voice. "Now? You'll have plenty of time to plan back in Etheria."

The words landed like a slap. I turned sharply to face him, my tone tightening. "Back in Etheria?" I echoed, incredulous. "The wedding is happening here, Sagar. Next week."

His gaze sharpened, lips parting in disbelief. "What?"

"You didn't know?" I asked, watching the confusion gather behind his eyes like a storm cloud. "Your prince insisted the ceremony be moved up. Next week, I'll be the wife to the ruler of your country."

My voice cracked, raw and uneven. I hated how the words tasted, hated the cold finality of them.

Sagar sat up in bed, the muscles in his body tensing as if bracing for a blow. His eyes clouded with something darker than confusion, something bordering on panic. "What are you talking about?" he asked, his voice low, brittle. "The plan was to bring you back to Etheria first—"

"Plan?" I cut in, heart lurching. I pulled the blanket tighter, like it could shield me from the sudden shift in atmosphere. "What plan, Sagar?"

He blinked, as if realizing too late what he'd said. "I didn't mean that," he said quickly, his jaw tightening.

"No," I said, my spine straightening. "Don't do that. Don't backtrack now. What exactly was supposed to happen? Does it have anything to do with what you were going to tell me last night?"

Sagar's mouth opened, then shut again. Guilt flashed across his face, too fast to hide, too honest to ignore. He ran a hand through his hair, clearly grasping for the right words.

My pulse thundered in my ears. The intimacy of the morning was gone now, replaced by a jagged tension that cut through the air like shattered glass. I felt exposed, not just physically, but emotionally, like he'd stripped away a layer I hadn't meant to reveal.

"After everything, you still won't tell me?" My voice trembled, half fury, half betrayal.

Sagar sat up, letting his hand drop from his hair. "Silvia, you have to trust me," he said urgently. "The Prince doesn't want to hurt you."

I shot out of bed, the thin blanket wrapped haphazardly around me, clinging to dignity where I could. I began tearing through the tent, desperate for my clothes, for armor, for anything to separate myself from this unraveling vulnerability.

"I thought I could trust you," I muttered, venom lacing my words. "But clearly, I was wrong."

"Silvia, please." Sagar stood and reached for me, placing a hand on my shoulder.

I jerked away like his touch burned. "How do you know he won't hurt me? How do you know I'm not just some pawn in whatever twisted game he's playing?"

His features hardened, and for once, the glint of charm vanished from his eyes. He stepped in front of me, forcing me to face him. "Because the prince and I are two ends of the same sword," he said, voice steady. "One is the hilt, steady and guiding. The other is the blade, sharp, swift, and silent. We don't make each other's decisions. We execute them. That's all."

I frowned, the words slicing deeper than I expected. "And which one are you?"

His lips curled into a faint, ironic smile, but he didn't answer.

"Sagar," I whispered. "Tell me the truth. Was last night...was any of it real? Or was that part of your plan, too?"

His eyes locked onto mine, intense and unreadable. "Silvia," he said slowly, "if I were part of something nefarious, do you really think I would've done what we did last night?"

The blood in my cheeks surged, a crimson tide of memory and shame. I had forgotten my soul purpose from the night before. I was no longer chaste, no longer the prince's weapon. If Sagar had some sort of motive to use me, this would gain the prince nothing.

My hands flew to my face, wrapping the blanket tight as I buried myself in the folds of fabric. "Goddess," I breathed. "I'm sorry. I've been stupid."

A laugh, deep, amused, and infuriating, rumbled from Sagar's chest. He leaned forward, peeking into my blanket cocoon, mischief dancing in his eyes.

"Come out of there," he teased, his voice a velvety growl. "Or I'll make you."

My eyes narrowed. "How will you—?"

Before I could finish, he grabbed me with practiced ease, lifting me off the ground and tossing me gently onto the cot. I let out a startled grunt as I bounced, the blanket slipping from my fingers, baring me to him again.

I glanced down, heat blooming across my chest as I scrambled to retrieve the fabric, fumbling to cover myself. But he was already crawling over me, his movements slow, deliberate.

"Don't be shy now," he murmured, his voice low and hungry. "This is the first time I get to see you like this in the daylight. Your bedhead is breathtaking."

I should have pushed him away. I should have been angry. But his distraction, his warmth, his nearness, was maddeningly effective. The defiance inside me cracked beneath the weight of longing. With a frustrated sigh, I let the blanket fall away once more, meeting his gaze head-on.

He looked at me like I was something sacred, like the sun had risen just for this. I felt my resolve crumble further.

He leaned in and kissed me, soft, slow, and worshipful. His lips moved against mine like he was memorizing the shape of my soul, and I hated that it made me want him even more.

His touch felt different today, more ravenous than it had been the night before. I could feel his hands squeeze me tighter to his body as he stiffened beneath me. A part of me wanted to continue our rendezvous from the prior night, the other half wanted to curl back up into his arms forever.

"I really do have to go," I admitted, the words came out sadder than I had wished.

The smile faded from Sagar's face, and the atmosphere in the tent shifted. I immediately regretted my words.

"Silvia..." Sagar grasped my wrist delicately. "I know you do, it's just..."

His brow furrowed as I could tell he yearned for the right words to say in that moment. I pressed my lips to his cheek, instantly feeling his muscles relax with the movement.

"You'll have to choose someday," I whispered, pulling away from his touch. My voice was steadier than I felt. I rose from the bed and resumed my search for the discarded nightgown.

Somehow, likely in the heat of the moment, my gown had ended up draped across Sagar's desk, lost in the clutter of books and parchments. I plucked it delicately from the mess, only for my elbow to knock into a precarious stack beside it. Books tumbled with a loud clatter, echoing through the stillness of the tent.

"Oh!" I gasped, falling to my knees. "I'm sorry!"

Sagar laughed, already crouching beside me to gather the mess. "It's my fault, really," he said, balancing a pile of tomes in his arms. "I shouldn't have borrowed half your library."

He moved to place the books back on a shelf, and as I pulled the gown over my head, something on the desk caught my eye.

A stack of letters scarred with the dark emerald seal of Calbraxia. My family's crest glinted faintly in the soft morning light. I hesitated, then reached for them. My fingers trembled as I read the top one.

The parchment was familiar. The handwriting, more so.

It was an invitation. To my name day celebration. Signed with my name.

Confused, I reached for another.

A formal request for a private meeting with the Crown Prince of Etheria, again signed with my hand. My breathing stilled as I sifted through them. One by one. Letter after letter. Invitations, personal notes, verses of poetry, romantic sentiments.

Each has been dated over the past year.

Each requested an audience with the Crown Prince.

Each one something I never wrote.

"What are these?" My voice came out thin, frayed with disbelief.

Behind me, Sagar stilled. He had just tugged his shirt over his head, but now it hung loose, forgotten. He exhaled, his brow creasing as he stepped closer.

"Tell me!" I snapped, holding up the letters like evidence of some great betrayal. "I didn't write any of this!"

He nodded slowly. "I know. At least, now I do."

He reached for the papers, gently taking them from my grasp. His eyes moved over them as if memorizing each stroke of ink.

"We've been receiving them since the King died," he said quietly. "Letters, invitations, poetry, all from you. Or at least, signed in your name."

My knees weakened. I dropped back onto the edge of the bed, bracing myself against the wave of nausea curling in my stomach.

"All this time?" I whispered. "But, why didn't you tell me?"

Sagar sat beside me, folding the letters in his lap. He hesitated a moment, as though weighing how much to say.

"The Prophecy. I didn't know you knew about it, but I was—"

"Hold on!" I yelled. "What prophecy?"

Sagar flashed a quizzical expression. "The reason I'm here, the reason I came to Calbraxia. You said you knew…"

"You're here because the Prince was planning to propose to me! That's what I was told!"

Sagar shook his head solemnly. "No. That was never part of the mission. The Prince had no intention of proposing to you. Think, Silvia. You were the one who proposed to him."

"But he did propose!" I burst out, scrambling to my feet. "At my name day. In my last—" The words caught in my throat. The blood drained from my face. In my last life. "Tell me of this prophecy, tell me what you know."

Sagar dug through the letters, pulling out a lightly tattered piece of parchment and placing it in front of me.

"We received this letter right before your name day. It wasn't signed by anyone, but the handwriting is still the same."

When moonlight weeps upon the crimson tide, and the fawn stands where the stag has died, the eternal throne shall burn to dust, by fate's cruel hand, by broken trust.

"What...What does it mean?" I asked.

Sagar sighed, running his fingers through his hair. "I don't know, we think it's a warning of some kind. Threatening the Etherian throne. We were able to match the handwriting. I came to ask about it."

He stood, walking to a small leather-bound box near the foot of his bed. He opened it with care and drew out a charred piece of parchment.

"Then, that night, in the library, this is what I pulled from the fire."

I stared at the singed letter, barely legible, but there was a bit I could fully make out.

...My heart burns for you, unlike anyone I have met before. I want to see you again, even if you don't feel the same.

Sagar knelt before me, his expression softer than I'd ever seen it, full of pain, protectiveness, and something deeper I didn't yet dare to name.

"Silvia," he said gently, "It's the same handwriting. The same parchment. Whoever forged those letters, whoever sent us the prophecy, and possibly whoever orchestrated your kidnapping, they are in the palace with you. You're not safe there, you haven't been."

"The prince..." I whispered.

Sagar laughed incredulously, raking his fingers through his hair. "The Prince had nothing to do with this. He sent me here to save you. I was under strict orders to bring you back to Etheria, no matter what." He squatted in front of me, gripping my face in his hands. "Silvia, I don't know what I can say to make you believe the prince doesn't want you harmed."

I stared at him, my pulse thudding in my ears. "I-I didn't write those letters," I whispered, though the truth of it had already settled like stone in my chest. My voice trembled with disbelief, with the quiet horror of what it all might mean.

"I know," Sagar said, nodding slowly. "I see it now. They were forged. All of them. That's what I've been trying to tell you, you're in danger here, Silvia. Real danger."

His words clanged through my mind like a dropped sword. If someone had been sending forged letters in my name, letters that lured Etheria closer and closer to Calbraxia, then this was more than manipulation.

Heat flooded my cheeks in a wave of humiliation and confusion. My thoughts from this life and the last crashed into one another, tangled threads unraveling into something raw and terrifying.

Had none of it been real? Had my fate, this entire twisted path, been written by someone else's hand? Had it started not with love or politics, but with deceit? And then a deeper fear settled into my chest like poison: What if this is why I was brought back?

To uncover the truth.

A sharper, darker thought pierced the fog. The war.

If the letters were forged, if the alliance had been fabricated, then who had truly started the war?

My knees gave out as the realization struck, memories colliding like a thousand shattered mirrors in my mind.

The faces of the soldiers I'd slain in battle. Etherian knights. Their blood on my hands. Their hollow eyes locked on mine, even in death.

I saw the kingdom I had crushed beneath my heel in my past life. The throne room was bathed in fire. The screaming. The silence after. The control I had over the rebellion. How I had believed I was serving justice, only to find my hands soaked in it, drenched in it.

Maybe this was the true reason I was sent back, to atone for the sins I hadn't known I committed.

I staggered toward the desk, gripping it for support as my body shook.

"Silvia!" Sagar's hands grasping my shoulders, grounding me. His voice was laced with panic. "Gods, you're burning up!"

Only then did I realize the heat flooding through me, blistering just beneath my skin. My breath came in shallow gasps. I felt as though I was being ripped in half from the inside, one part of me in this moment, and another trapped in the horrors of what had come before.

"I-I don't know what's happening," I stammered, though my lips barely moved. My words felt like smoke on the air, fading as fast as I spoke them.

I couldn't stop shaking. The tent twisted and shifted around me. The walls melted into flames. The shadows became corpses. The scrolls and maps unfurled into battlefields soaked with blood.

Sagar's voice came through the haze. Calm, firm, trying to pull me back. But I couldn't hear him anymore.

All I could see were the dead. My death. The ones I couldn't save. The ones I had slaughtered.

"Help me..." I whimpered, clutching him as darkness began to creep in from the edges of my vision. "Please, help me."

His arms wrapped around me tightly, shielding me from the cold that shouldn't have been there, from the ghosts, from the weight of it all. His voice was in my ear, soft and desperate.

"I've got you, Silvia. I swear by the gods, I won't lose you."

Chapter 22

Only the heat remained. It wrapped around me like a shroud, curling along my spine, sinking deep into my bones. Each breath was a battle, the air too thick, the weight on my chest unbearable. I felt like I was being pressed beneath the surface of some invisible sea, drowning in fire.

My limbs refused to obey me. My skin burned, my thoughts came sluggish, hazy. The world was little more than shifting colors and noise. Somewhere above me, a cloth dabbed gently at my forehead, but it felt distant, like it belonged to someone else's body.

"Silvia," a soft voice murmured, close to my ear, calm but trembling. "You have to drink this."

I forced my eyes open. I wasn't sure how I had made it back to my chambers, but the familiar canopy was unmistakable. Had Sagar brought me back? Had June come looking for me?

The room spun, then slowly settled on June's face. Or was it? Her features were haloed in a golden blur, and for a moment, I wasn't sure if I was in the present or reliving something lost to time.

She held a small cup to my lips. I tasted bitterness, but I swallowed without protest. My throat felt raw, my lips cracked.

Was this June? Or was this Margaret?

My vision warped again, and the face before me changed. Darker hair. Softer eyes. My sister's face, Margaret, full of quiet grace and the kind of silence that always spoke volumes.

My heart clenched as sorrow overwhelmed me.

"I'm sorry," I rasped, reaching out to touch the sleeve of her dress. My fingers curled weakly into the fabric. "Margaret, you never got the same attention I did. I know that. I always knew. And I told myself, this time I would be better. This time, I'd be the sister you deserved."

She stilled. For a long moment, the only sound in the room was my labored breathing. Then arms wrapped around me, gentle, steadying, warm. She didn't correct me. She didn't pull away.

I let myself believe it was her, just for a moment.

She smelled different. Her voice wasn't quite the same. But I didn't care. I clung to the illusion because if it wasn't the truth, my words were meaningless.

"It's okay, Silvia," she whispered, rocking me gently. "Everything will be okay."

Tears slid from the corners of my eyes, cooling my fevered cheeks for the briefest of moments.

"I did terrible things," I murmured, my voice breaking with regret. "So many terrible things, and they need to know how sorry I am. The blood, the war, I should have never—"

She pulled away slowly, her expression unreadable as she rose from the bedside.

"You did nothing wrong," she said firmly, though I heard the tremble in her voice. "You're strong, Silvia. You'll make it through this."

Her hand brushed mine one last time, a quiet promise pulsing through her touch.

Darkness claimed me again, and in that darkness, the visions returned.

Worse than fire. Worse than pain. Worse than death.

I saw cities burn. I saw soldiers screaming for mercy, their cries drowned in steel. I saw my hands, bloodied, cracked, trembling. I saw the moment I raised my hand against the Etherian men. I saw myself atop a throne I had carved out of ashes, weeping.

I didn't know if this was punishment or purification. Perhaps this was Goddess Leticia's final cruelty, a divine reckoning meant to break me piece by piece.

"Princess," June's voice returned, now distant, like an echo down a long corridor. "I'm going to leave for a moment. I need to fetch more water."

"No, please don't leave me," I whimpered, forcing my eyes open again.

She poured another trickle of water into my mouth. I swallowed, the liquid like ice against the fire in my throat.

"It's just a moment, Silvia. You'll be okay. I promise."

"You can't!" I cried, my voice shrill and panicked, clinging to the last thread of lucidity. "June, please!"

But she was already gone.

The moment the door closed behind June, the silence returned like a tombstone slammed into place. And the fever, it surged again. Fiercer this time, clawing its way beneath my skin. It dragged me down, down into a spiral of memories that were no longer just memories; they were curses, visions, warnings, truths tangled in fire.

Prince Gerraint's voice rang in my ears, as if he were right beside me, whispering poison against my throat.

"When moonlight weeps upon the crimson tide, and the fawn stands where the stag has died..."

The words twisted through my mind like thorns. The vision crashed over me again. I was no longer in my bed; I was back there, on the battlefield, at the end of the world.

The final battle of Etheria.

The smoke choked the sky. The air reeked of blood and scorched earth. I heard the cries of soldiers dying, killing, begging for gods who had never listened. And I was at the heart of it all. My body ached with fatigue, my armor splattered in red. I stood with my hands outstretched, flowing with divine retribution, every movement weighted with grief and fury.

Then I saw him. At the edge of the battlefield, making his way towards me, the head of the Etherian army. Shrouded in his thick gold armor, bow drawn, ready to fire.

But not the man I knew, not the charming knight who stole my breath in stolen glances. This Sagar was older. Hardened. His armor was dented, his jaw clenched tight with sorrow.

"The eternal throne shall burn to dust, by fate's cruel hand, by broken trust."

I charged. I remembered charging. My powers shifted the air between us in a deep green blaze. The impact was so vivid I could feel the vibration in my fevered bones. It struck his helm, loosening it.

Only when it fell away, It wasn't Sagar at all.

I gasped, bolting upright in bed, as if waking from a nightmare I had lived before. My chest seized, breath hitching in jagged sobs. The room spun. My hands fisted the sweat-drenched sheets. I was suffocating in my skin.

"Sagar!" I cried out, the name torn from me, desperate and raw. "Sagar, please!"

A hand closed over mine, real. Warm, steady, grounding.

I blinked. He was there. Kneeling at my bedside, hair tousled, eyes filled with so much worry it made my throat close.

"Shhh, I'm here, beautiful," he whispered, his voice the one constant in a world that wouldn't stop spinning.

"You came?" My voice cracked. "Or, is this another dream?"

From the doorway, June gave a soft smile. "You wouldn't stop asking for him. I thought he should be here."

She stepped away quietly, and the door clicked shut behind her. The silence that followed pressed against my ears, louder than thunder.

"It is a dream," I breathed, sinking back against the pillow.

A cool hand cupped my cheek, gentle but firm. "Silvia, you're hot."

I blinked. "No, *you're* hot," I mumbled with a laugh, delirium dragging my words.

Sagar chuckled softly, his laughter like kisses on my soul. "No, I mean you're really burning up." He pressed a kiss to my forehead, slow and lingering, as if he could draw the heat from me with his lips. "I shouldn't have let us be outside that long. I should've been more careful."

He was warm. Too warm for a dream. Too vivid. His presence wasn't a memory; it was now. So I decided if it was a dream, I didn't care. I would live in it anyway.

"Since we're being honest with each other now, I'm going to tell you the truth," I said, reaching up and tapping his nose with my fingertip. "I would've done that with you anywhere. Anytime."

"Don't tempt me with a good time," he said with a grin, capturing my hand in his and lifting it to his lips. He kissed my knuckles as if they were holy.

"You like me, don't you?" I asked, searching his eyes, their rich honey hue glittering in the low light. He looked too beautiful, too real to be imagined.

Sagar's expression shifted, all mirth swept away like sand before a wave.

"What a foolish question," he said, voice suddenly soft. "I knew from the moment I found you in the garden, in that torn dress, terrified and trembling, that you were going to ruin me. You were the truth I hadn't known I was waiting for. From that day on, there was no version of my life where I didn't want you, all of you."

His words sank into me like a blade, sharp, deep, and irrevocable.

I sat in silence, trembling, the fever still pulsing through me, the world teetering between dream and reality. I wanted this to be real. I needed it to be real. That this man, this fierce, tender man whom I cared for so deeply, had found me at my worst and stayed anyway.

But something dark clawed at the edges of my thoughts, something I had buried too long. My lips moved before I could stop them.

"Except, there is a version of you that doesn't..." The words came softly, broken. I barely recognized my own voice. "In fact, there's a version that despises me. A version that I may have—" I couldn't finish. The weight of the memory lodged in my throat like ash.

"What are you talking about?" he asked gently, dabbing my forehead again with a cool cloth, his movements steady despite the tremor in my words.

"You've always thought my fear of the prince was irrational," I whispered. "But if I told you the truth, you'd understand."

Sagar's brow furrowed. His hand found mine, his thumb brushing my knuckles. "So tell me, help me understand."

I took a breath, deep and shaky. And for the first time, when I closed my eyes, I was met with memory.

"I've lived this before," I said. "Well, most of it. It was different then. I was sent to Etheria to marry the prince. On the day of the wedding, something happened. I was locked away in that cursed tower until my divine power awakened."

His eyes widened, but he stayed silent.

"I lived, I died, I—" my voice cracked "I killed so many. I thought I was doing the right thing."

"Silvia," he murmured, concern threading through his voice, "this fever, it's taking so much out of you—"

"It's not the fever!" I snapped, my voice ringing through the room like thunder. I shoved his hand away, my body shaking. "Why do you think I've been so terrified of marrying the prince? Why do you think I tried to find another suitor? Sagar, I spent ten years trapped in a tower, convinced that he locked me away to be used as a weapon!"

I could barely breathe. The walls closed in. My hands trembled violently as I stared at him, begging him to see me. To believe me.

"And now," I whispered, "to find out it was all a lie..."

He was still for a moment. His expression shifted, soft concern giving way to something darker, something colder. Then, wordlessly, he pulled me into his chest. His arms wrapped around me like iron and warmth.

"If what you say is true..." he whispered into my hair, "then the prophecy is real."

I leaned back to look at him, my heart thudding in my ears. "I'm the cause," I breathed. "The destruction of Etheria that the prophecy speaks of. It's me. I thought I was liberating the empire, setting things right. But now, I don't know what to believe anymore."

His eyes were shadowed with something unreadable. "A tower," he said slowly, almost to himself.

I nodded, trying to push myself upright. "Ten years. I was kept there, alone, until my power manifested and could be used. I only went there because I was told it was my wedding day. That I was going to meet my husband."

He paused. "Wait, so you never even met the crown prince?"

"No. Never," I said, exhaling shakily. "Not until this life. He looks exactly like I imagined he would." I turned toward Sagar and gave him a weak smile. "Though I'll admit, he's nowhere near as handsome as you."

A chuckle broke from him, warm and real, as he leaned forward and kissed my cheek. "You're delirious, but I'll take the compliment."

Then, without warning, his expression sobered. "Silvia, I have to go."

Panic shot through me like ice. I grabbed the front of his shirt, clutching it tight. "What? Now? No, don't leave me."

"I need to go to the library," he said, voice gentle but firm. "There may be something, records, journals, anything about the prophecy, or your powers."

"No." I shook my head, already moving. "I can come with you. Let's just—let's go now."

I threw off the covers, my bare legs trembling as they hit the floor. I tried to stand. The world lurched sideways. Darkness flared at the edges of my vision, and I fell forward with a gasp straight into waiting arms.

Sagar sighed, wrapping me effortlessly in his arms. "Silvia," he muttered, more to himself than to me, "you're going to be the death of me."

With practiced tenderness, he lifted me back into bed, his touch careful. The sheets felt cool against my flushed skin, but it was the loss of his warmth that made me shiver. He tucked the covers around me with maddening precision, like I was something fragile he didn't quite know how to hold without breaking.

"You need rest, my dear," he murmured, brushing damp strands of hair from my face. He pressed a quick kiss to my fevered forehead, the touch so light it might've been imagined.

I stared up at him, dazed, blinking slowly. His face hovered above mine like a vision, soft and glowing at the edges, unreal in the dim light. He looked like something out of a story, a dream conjured from the depths of my fever. I was terrified to blink, afraid the moment I did, he'd vanish into mist.

"Don't go," I whispered, the words no louder than a breath.

He froze at the end of the bed, fingers curled around the edge of the blanket. "Tell me to stay," he said, voice low, "and I'll stay."

My throat tightened. I didn't want to be selfish. I didn't want to keep him from the answers we both needed. But I was tired, so tired, and the thought of being alone again, of falling back into the dark spiral without him...

"Stay."

Without another word, he slipped beneath the covers and drew me into his arms. My body curled instinctively against him, my head resting just over his heart. It beat steadily and strongly beneath my cheek, a rhythmic promise that he was real.

His warmth bled into me, it was different than the heat that burned through me. It wasn't suffocating, it was soothing. Solid. I clung to it, my fingers curling into his tunic like a child afraid of the dark.

"You're safe," he murmured, his lips brushing the crown of my head. "I plan on keeping it that way, no matter what."

His voice melted into the hum of the storm in my blood. I wanted to speak, to tell him everything I hadn't yet said, but the weight of exhaustion was pulling me under fast.

As sleep wrapped around me like a heavy fog, I let myself believe this was all a dream. That I was tucked safely in the arms of a man who loved me, that the past hadn't happened, that there was no tower, no prophecy, no future lined with fire and ruin.

But if it was a dream, I never wanted to wake up.

Chapter 23

When I opened my eyes, the world around me thrummed with life.

It was as if someone had peeled a foggy layer from reality. Everything; the air, the light, the sounds, felt too sharp, too clear. The haze that had weighed me down for what felt like an eternity was gone, and in its place was something startlingly vivid.

I could feel the softness of the sheets brushing my skin, the cool breeze sneaking through the windowpanes, the distant flutter of wings in flight. My breath no longer caught in my throat, it flowed easily, filling my lungs like I hadn't tasted air in days.

Birdsong spilled through the open window like a symphony. Not background noise, not the idle chirping of nature going about its business, but vibrant, joyous notes that seemed to dance along my nerves and call me back to the world. The scent of smoldering embers still lingering in the fireplace warmed me. Smoky, rich, faintly sweet, it stirred a strange sense of longing, like a memory I hadn't made yet.

I couldn't help but wonder, could this be what my existence boils down to, now that I'm not filled with divine energy? Things felt different, raw, real, relentless, a true feeling. Did all that power somehow hide the simple but strong beauty of just being normal? This new, unfiltered reality was so different from what I knew, but it thrilled me.

It was then that I was interrupted by the warmth.

Not the oppressive, burning heat of the sickness, but a quieter warmth. Steady. Intimate. It sank into my skin like sunlight through layers, spreading into my limbs, anchoring me to the here and now. It made my skin tingle and my heart stir, though I didn't yet know why.

A pair of hands wrapped tightly around me, squeezing me closer to the source of the heat.

I turned my head. Sagar lying perfectly on the pillow next to me, breathing softly, barely awake.

I stopped breathing. His tousled blonde hair, his bare chest peeking from beneath the disheveled tunic, that lopsided smile creeping across his infuriatingly handsome face. He looked so out of place in this fragile morning light, like something carved from a dream I hadn't meant to keep.

I couldn't help but wonder, why was he here? Had he heard me in the night? Had I shouted his name as I dreamed?

My thoughts blurred in panic. The line between memory and illusion twisted in my mind, leaving me grasping at half-formed moments, flashes of a fevered confession, soft touches, truths I never meant to speak aloud.

"Sagar," I breathed, my voice weak as I tried to pull away from his hold.

"Mmm." His grin widened, lazy and utterly unbothered. He buried his face against my neck, his lips brushing my skin with a featherlight touch. "Good morning to you, too."

My heart stuttered painfully in my chest.

His body was flush against mine, one arm looped casually around my waist as if it had always belonged there. His skin was warm and damp with sleep. I could feel every line of muscle, every inch of him as he shifted closer, and my body responded before my mind could catch up. I wanted to stay wrapped in that moment, forever, but I couldn't. Not until I knew.

"How long have you been here?" I asked, trying to sound nonchalant, though my breath was still catching on every syllable.

"Long enough." He brushed my hair gently behind my ear, his fingers trailing down to my cheek. "Your fever's gone." His hand moved to rest on my forehead. "You're cooler now. Are you feeling alright?"

"Much better," I whispered, though the answer wasn't just about my body.

I lifted my hand to his face, tracing the edge of his jaw. He leaned into my touch without hesitation. His skin was soft, with the faintest sheen of perspiration. He stayed this time, and that meant everything.

I opened my mouth to speak, to thank him, to question him, to beg him to tell me this was real, but the words withered on my tongue.

"Silvia, was what you told me last night the truth?" His voice was quiet, but the intensity in his gaze held me in place. There was no judgment there, only a desperate need to understand.

Reality surged over me like a crashing tide. The weight of everything I'd revealed, everything I hadn't meant to say, pressed down on me. I swallowed, my face burning with embarrassment. My throat felt too tight.

"I-I'll be honest," I said softly, "I don't remember everything I said."

A half-smile tugged at his lips. "Well, for starters, you admitted you're actually seventy years old." His tone was teasing, but the gentleness didn't hide the gravity underneath. "And you told me you caused the end of Etheria. That the prophecy is true."

I nodded slowly, a lump catching in my throat. "It is. At least, it was. You have to understand, I was made to believe it was Etheria's fault. I was manipulated. I held onto that resentment for decades."

The tears came without warning, soaking into my pillow before I even felt them on my cheeks. A sharp sob threatened to escape, but before it could, Sagar wrapped his arms around me, tucking me tightly into his chest. The scent of leather and pine enveloped me. His lips pressed to the top of my head as he whispered, "Shh. You didn't know. Silvia, whoever did this to you, whoever did *that* to you, they were counting on that. They wanted to use you. They wanted to bring an end to Etheria."

"Who would want to do that?" I murmured, pulling back just enough to see his face.

His expression darkened. His gaze drifted toward the far wall, as if he were seeing through it. "I don't know. But it would have to be someone close to you. Someone who knew enough about your life to manipulate it, someone with access to your mind, your trust."

My lip trembled.

"I don't think I should be alone with anyone but you today." I whispered the words like a confession. "You're the only one I can trust now."

Sagar shifted upright, his hand resting protectively on my waist. The weight of my words settled between us. His brows furrowed, and I could see the silent war playing out behind his eyes. Shock, suspicion, something like fear.

Then his mouth opened as if to speak, but before the words could fall, the door creaked open.

Panic jolted through me like lightning. I shoved at Sagar's chest, motioning frantically toward the side of the bed. "Hide!"

Sagar blinked once, then dove under the bed with alarming grace for a man his size.

"Silvia!" June's laughter rang through the air like bells as she leapt onto the bed with me. "I hope you're feeling better, because you'll never guess who's here!"

I shifted uncomfortably, wrapping my sweat-soaked sheet tighter around me. "By your reaction, I'd guess the Goddess Leticia herself has descended upon the palace!"

But my gaze snapped to the figure standing in the doorway.

"Madame Levior," I said softly.

She sat like a shadow come to life. Her wild curls had been pinned back with delicate silver clips, exposing the weary hollows beneath her sharp cheekbones. She looked smaller somehow, thinner, as though the weight of her craft had worn her down to the bone. Her skin was paler than I remembered, kissed by exhaustion, and her lips, painted in a bold crimson rouge, looked like the last trace of defiance she could muster.

"Pardon me, but what are you doing here?" I asked. June stood and twirled beside her still in the doorway, a blur of excitement.

"The Queen sent me," Levior sighed, retrieving a letter from the folds of her coat. "I'm to make you, and I quote, 'the most beautiful bride Calbraxia has ever seen.'"

I forced a smile as I took the letter. Lovely. The most beautiful lamb to ever be led to slaughter.

June squealed with delight, wrapping both arms around the Madame as though they were the best of friends and not two people who could not be more temperamentally opposed. Madame

Levior visibly tensed beneath the embrace, giving June a look of such withering disdain it could have curdled cream.

"That means she'll be here until the wedding!" June beamed. "Isn't that exciting?"

"Thrilling," I muttered, cracking the seal and unfolding the parchment with a sigh.

Silvia,

I know the past few days have been a struggle, perhaps the hardest in your life, but I hope you take this time to reflect. Marriage is hard. Being a queen is harder. But the most difficult thing of all will be leaving home.

I do not know the fashion trends of Etheria, but I've sent Madame Levior so that you can bring a bit of Calbraxia with you, even if it's just in the form of a few dresses.

I've shared my thoughts on the wedding gown. I trust she will make something exquisite. You will be a radiant bride and an even more radiant queen.

—Mother

I let out a small, humorless scoff and handed the letter back to Madame Levior. "Were you aware you were also expected to craft me an entirely new wardrobe in under a week?"

Her eyes widened in horror as she snatched the letter from my hands, scanning the contents like a woman betrayed by fate itself.

"In five days?" she hissed. "Does your mother think I run a factory? What am I supposed to do, summon the spirits of Saint Doria's tailors from beyond the grave?"

Before I could reply, June's eyes lit up with something dangerous. That look she got when a bad idea bloomed fully formed in her mind. "I mean, I could—"

"No!" Madame Levior snapped, spinning toward her like a viper. "I'm sure Silvia desperately needs you for wedding planning."

"Actually..." I said slowly, rubbing the back of my neck, "June would be an excellent help to you, I'm fine fending for myself."

June gasped, as if I had just handed her the crown itself. She dropped to her knees in front of Madame Levior, clasping her hands in melodramatic desperation.

"Please," she begged. "I'll be quiet! I'll be good! I'll organize beads or steam hems or, goddess help me, I'll even hand-sew sleeves. I promise I have very steady fingers. Just let me help!"

Levior groaned so deeply I thought she might collapse backward onto the chaise. She held a hand to her temple like she could already feel the incoming headache. But eventually, she let out a sharp exhale and straightened her spine, returning to her usual clipped, no-nonsense demeanor.

"Fine," she muttered, waving her hand. "But if you so much as breathe too loud, I'll banish you back to working for the princess."

June squealed and clapped her hands in victory.

"I hope you don't mind," Madame Levior ventured. "But I could use the space in the dining hall as a temporary studio."

I flashed a grin, "Of course not! Margaret and I can take our dinners elsewhere, the space is yours."

The corners of her mouth tugged just briefly upwards for a moment before she turned to June. "We have work to do. This won't be easy, I can promise you that."

June nodded, a resilient soldier going to battle, "You lead the way, Madame!"

The two trotted out of the room, arm in arm, excitedly discussing the fabric choices of the gowns that would be my companions as I headed to Etheria, leaving me in silence.

However, a shuffle from under the bed reminded me I wasn't alone.

"Sagar," I whispered, just as he rolled out from beneath the bed like a shadow shedding its hiding place.

I leapt up, only for my foot to catch his side, and in a graceless tumble, I landed right on top of him. My palms smacked the floor, but his chest caught the worst of my fall.

"Sorry," I muttered, breathless.

He shifted slightly, guiding me into his lap with maddening ease. "You know," he said quietly, "your maid has a very dramatic way of saying good morning."

I tried to rise, but he held me steady, his arms warm around my waist. His expression darkened slightly, the playful glint replaced by something more serious.

I rolled my eyes, but the warmth in my chest returned just from the sound of his voice. He leaned closer, the faintest hint of teasing still in his expression. "Last night, I told you I wanted to visit the library. If I wanted to say, follow the lineage of some Divinials, where would I look?"

I didn't have to think about it. "The hall of saints."

Sagar's grin widened. "Then that'll be our first stop."

He leaned in and kissed me gently, like a promise. His warmth wrapped around me like a memory I didn't want to let go of. I gave in, letting my lips separate so I could get a taste of his hot breath.

Sagar's tongue twisted around mine, and I couldn't help but let out a muffled sigh. At this rate, we would get nothing accomplished, but I wasn't going to argue.

"Excuse me," came a deliberately loud voice.

We both turned to see June standing in the doorway, arms crossed and an amused smirk on her lips. She had entered so quietly that neither of us noticed.

"You two are adorable," she said, striding in. "But I do need Silvia for just a quick fitting, a request straight from Madame Levior herself."

Sagar sighed dramatically and stood, lifting me effortlessly with him. "I know I said I wouldn't leave your side," he said, brushing a hand down my arm, "but I think you're in good hands, for now."

He winked at June, who winked right back like they were old friends conspiring. Then he turned to me, cupping my face for just a second, grounding me with that ever-steady presence.

"Meet me in the library for lunch?" he whispered, lips brushing my temple.

I nodded. And just like that, the moment broke. He dropped his hands and stepped back. The sudden loss of his warmth made the room feel ten degrees colder.

June gently pushed me into the chair by the dressing table, fingers already reaching for a hairbrush.

At the door, Sagar paused. "Oh, and Silvia?"

I looked up.

"Last night..." His voice softened. "I meant what I said."

And then he was gone, the door shut quietly behind him.

Something had shifted. Whether it was fate, or prophecy, or the fire within me beginning to rise again, I didn't know, but part of it frightened me.

Chapter 24

I arrived at the library, my heart drumming a steady rhythm of anticipation against my ribs. The rest of the fitting had flown by, I hadn't paid any attention to what June or Madame Levior prattled on about.

Part of me wanted to beat him there, to order everyone to leave and surprise him with my body sprawled in front of the fire, but I knew our time was limited, and if we were successful in our findings, we could spend plenty of nights together.

The grand oak doors groaned as I pushed them open, spilling dim golden light across the marble floor. The familiar scent of old parchment, beeswax, and a faint trace of mildew curled in the air. This place had begun to feel like a sanctuary, like truth nestled among dust and time.

There, in the far corner, was Sagar, looking every bit the part of a brooding scholar: elbows deep in ancient tomes, brows furrowed, jaw tight, the flicker of candlelight dancing across his face. He hadn't noticed me, so lost in the world of the past. A shadow of ink and prophecy. My shadow.

A smirk tugged at the corner of my lips as I sauntered over and leaned casually against the table. I tossed my hair with an exaggerated flourish, making sure he saw the gown June had chosen, an emerald green number that cinched perfectly at the waist and caught the light when I moved.

Still no reaction.

Finally, I nudged his arm with playful impatience. "I hope you're not ignoring me for a book," I said with a mock pout. "That would be quite the insult."

Without glancing up, he replied dryly, "You are definitely more interesting than centuries-old script on Divinial lineage."

He yawned. "However, you only have decades of history. This lot spans eras."

I huffed dramatically, placing a hand to my chest like I'd been struck. "You wound me. Deeply. I might never recover." I leaned closer. "Anything worthwhile yet?"

At last, he tore his gaze from the book, tilting it so I could see. The aged parchment crackled slightly, ink faded but still legible, elegant calligraphy filled the pages, accompanied by strange sketches of women, each draped in a shroud.

I traced a finger along the margin, pretending to be intrigued. "Hmm. I assume you're not looking for Saint Partrice the Kind's work with the elderly?"

"Surprisingly, no." He rubbed his temples, his eyes weary. "I've combed through half the Saint Archives and haven't found anything that may have to do with the prophecy."

His frustration pulsed in the air around him. The crease between his brows had deepened, and I instinctively reached out, smoothing it with my fingers.

"Have you been here all day?" I asked softly.

He blinked, surprised by the gesture. "No, I bathed this morning," he said, then glanced ruefully at the mountainous pile of books beside him. "But otherwise, yes."

Without another word, I gently closed the book in his hands and, with deliberate grace, slid into his lap.

He let out a breathless, amused noise as his arms instinctively wrapped around me.

"You deserve a break," I whispered, brushing my lips just under his jaw. "Maybe we could revisit that book from last time? You know the one..."

His eyes narrowed with a mixture of amusement and warning. "You're incorrigible."

I grinned. "And you're enjoying every second of it."

His gaze burned into me for a brief moment, as if he were contemplating it himself. Then, he let out an exasperated sigh. "Silvia," he murmured, his voice low and rough, "while any other time I would burn the heavens and earth to do *that* with you, now's not a good time. We have work to do."

I exhaled heavily, letting my head fall to his chest with theatrical defeat. The heat of his skin beneath the fabric, the thud of his heart beneath my ear, it was maddening. My body remembered every kiss from the other night, every touch, and now it cried out for more.

"I suppose so," I said, lifting my head and brushing his ear with my lips. "But I know you would if I told you to."

His body stiffened. I knew he was thinking the same thing I was, and if we weren't in the library this early in the day, I would have gotten what I wanted. The corner of his mouth twitched, fighting a smile, before he gently shifted me off his lap. "You're a wicked thing," he said with a husky laugh. "Are you sure you were a saint?"

"Unfortunately, I can confirm," I replied breezily as I sauntered toward the nearest bookshelf. "You gave me a taste of the forbidden fruit. I have decades of repression to make up for."

A devilish smirk played across Sagar's face as he picked up another book from the stack. "Well, I'm trying to get us plenty more time to do just that."

I glanced over my shoulder at him, fingers gliding along the cracked leather spines of old tomes. "Then let's find what we need," I said, a teasing edge in my voice. "The sooner we solve the mystery, the sooner you can corrupt me properly."

His low laugh followed me down the aisle, warm and dark, curling inside me like smoke. I turned back to the shelves, heart fluttering in a way that felt reckless and far too dangerous.

I scanned the bindings, though truthfully, I doubted there was a single volume on these shelves Sagar hadn't already poured through. Still, I let my hands wander, tracing the edges, brushing against dust-heavy volumes as if some answer might reach out and grab me.

I caught a glance of him over my shoulder, head bowed, focused, and determined. That intensity in his eyes, that quiet ferocity in the way he searched, as if Etheria's future rested on his shoulders. It made something in me ache. My feet stopped moving. My hand lingered on a book I hadn't even registered.

Was this love?

The question curled itself around my heart, pressing in. My skin prickle with something sharper than the cold, more intimate. Was it love, or was it simply the undoing of years spent coiled in loneliness? Could it be both?

My thoughts scattered as our eyes met, his gaze lifting just in time to catch mine.

I turned back to the shelves with almost childish urgency, pretending to focus, heart thundering like a war drum. It was *some-*

thing. Whatever it was, it was powerful. It consumed me from the inside out. It unstitched all the quiet, practiced stillness I'd built over the years and left me raw and breathless.

June had once told me what love was, and now I couldn't help but wonder if it was different for everyone, that it didn't always come in the ways you expected. Sometimes it came softly. Sometimes it came with claws. I wasn't sure what mine had yet, but I could feel it scraping through my bones.

My fingers stilled on a thick, familiar, ornately bound tome. I knew this one.

I pulled it carefully from the shelf, its weight heavy in my hands, and brought it back to the table. With a loud thump, I let it fall open in front of Sagar.

"What's that?" he asked, peering over the top of another book.

"The royal family history," I murmured, thumbing through the first few pages. "My governess used to show me this when I was little. I couldn't read then, but I'd make up stories for each of the portraits."

Sagar stood and wandered over, curiosity overtaking his irritation. He leaned close, eyes scanning the stained parchment and fading sketches as I flipped through them. The book smelled of pressed flowers, wax, and time.

"Who's that?" he asked, pointing to a particularly striking young man clad in elaborate armor.

"King Brixbane the Great," I said with a grin. "Yes, named after the Etherian god. He was supposedly a terrible rake, fathered more bastards than they cared to admit. But I used to make him a hero in my stories. He saved a girl from an evil dragon. Married her, too."

Sagar chuckled and rested his chin lightly on my shoulder, his presence both weightless and binding. I kept flipping pages, telling him each little tale I had once imagined as a child, tales of bravery, of tragic romance, of fools and saints.

Then I stopped as I turned the page and saw him.

My father.

His portrait was still intact, still vivid. Strong, steady features. The same rounded cheeks and fiery hair that looked far more endearing on Margaret. I reached out and traced the delicate ink lines that shaped his jaw, his eyes, the firm set of his mouth.

He looked proud. Regal. Alive.

In my short years with him, I had only been allowed to see him once. He looked so old, so fragile, as if a whisper would send him crumbling.

I found myself missing him. I had dreamt of what it would be like, living with a Mother and Father who weren't shackled to their duty, who could truly care after their children with their entire hearts. The ache wasn't for him, it was for the idea he left. The quiet pain that had settled somewhere permanent inside me. A missing piece I'd long since stopped expecting to find again.

Sagar slid his arms around my waist from behind and gently pulled me closer. I leaned back into him, grateful for the silent comfort.

"That's your father?" he asked, his voice low against my ear.

I nodded slowly. "Yes. He was a good king, at least that's what I was told. I didn't know him, really."

Sagar studied the image beside me. "Margaret has his hair, for certain," he murmured. "But the eyes, no. You got his eyes."

I turned, confused. "Everyone says I'm my mother's double."

He met my gaze. "I don't mean the color. But the way they look when you want something, or when you're holding back. The intensity, it's the same. You have eyes born to rule, Silvia. You'll be a great Queen."

I blinked, caught off guard. For so long, I'd been told I was little more than a reflection of the Queen, a mirror made flesh. But in that moment, he gave me something precious. Something of my own.

My fingers lingered on the page before I finally let them fall. "He died before Margaret was born. I was only six, maybe seven."

Sagar's arms tightened briefly.

That time in my life had always felt foggy, as though the palace itself had conspired to shield me from the truth of his death. I remembered my mother's pale face, the hushed voices, the way the halls grew darker overnight.

I remembered wandering for days afterward, asking servants if they'd seen him. Each time I asked, they would lower their heads, unable or unwilling to meet my eyes.

"... I think Margaret suffered more than I did. My mother didn't even know she was pregnant when he died." I swallowed. "She took his death hard. Shut herself away. Even after Margaret was born, she didn't come out for months. Margaret called her wet nurse 'mother' until she was nearly five."

There was a pause. Sagar's hands slowly fell away from my waist. I turned to face him, only to find his expression twisted in something between curiosity and alarm. His eyes scanned the page with sudden urgency.

"That's... eerie," he murmured. His finger shot toward a paragraph near the bottom of the page, just beneath my father's portrait. "Silvia, read this."

I followed his gesture, eyes narrowing. The text was partially scratched out, as if someone had taken a blade to the parchment. But the ink lingered beneath the abrasion, faint yet legible.

Married to Queen Elanore, who possesses the Divinial blood, just as her mother Ashera, her grandmother Poppiri, and her great-grandmother, Saint Cyradil.

The words clung to the page like ghosts refusing to be buried. I blinked, rereading them. "What am I looking at? I know we all have Divinial blood. That's hardly new."

Sagar didn't respond; he was already on a mission, muttering curses under his breath. Books clattered as he swept them aside, rifling frantically through a heap of parchment.

"That name..." he growled, hands flying through brittle pages.

"Who?" I demanded, irritation flaring at being left behind in his whirlwind of thought.

"The Saint," he said, almost to himself. "There's something off about it..."

I frowned, glancing back at the family record. "Saint Cyradil?"

He leaned back, scanning the chaos he had created across the table. Eight books, all opened and splayed like wounded birds. "See!" he suddenly exclaimed, pointing down.

I leaned in, squinting. "Sagar, what exactly am I supposed to be seeing? There's nothing about Cyradil."

"Exactly." He pushed away from the table and began pacing. "Nothing. Not a single mention. These tomes list every saint, every one. Even the ones no one remembers. From Saint Abigail the Scribe, who wrote one holy verse and then vanished. To Saint Zenith, who, by every account, did absolutely nothing. But Saint Cyradil? Not a word. She's missing."

I froze. Slowly, I turned back to the family book and ran my fingers over the text. There it was. A name no one wanted us to see.

"She's not just missing," I whispered. "She's been erased."

Sagar nodded grimly. "Deliberately. And sloppily, in some cases."

He reached for one of the older books and slid it across the table toward me. The binding cracked beneath his fingers as he opened it to the middle section. There, on the right page, was the frayed edge of a torn-out leaf, ragged and thin, like someone had yanked it free without care. Only the faint shadow of ink remained.

I touched the space where the paper had once been. A sudden sting bloomed on my fingertip, and I drew my hand back to see a thin line of blood.

"She was here," he said. "Whoever she was, she was recorded. And someone wanted her forgotten."

I stared at the empty space, the phantom page. My blood still shimmered faintly against the paper's edge. "Why erase her from every record except the one in my family book?"

"Because they missed it," Sagar said. "Who would think her name would appear in the royal family history? They weren't thorough enough."

We exchanged a look. A shared understanding passed between us like lightning: this wasn't just historical erasure. It was personal. Someone, somewhere, had wanted Saint Cyradil buried. Forgotten. Hidden from every trace of the past.

My mind raced. Who would benefit from hiding a Saint? From concealing a direct line of Divinial descent that reached the current royal bloodline to me?

"What is so important about Saint Cyradil?" I asked, the words catching in my throat. "And what are they—whoever *they* are— willing to do to keep this hidden?"

"Anything." Sagar looked at me with a gravity I hadn't seen in him before. "Maybe even destroy kingdoms..."

A chill rippled down my spine, but I didn't let it show. I straightened my shoulders and met his gaze. "Then we need more answers."

He nodded, already reaching for another book. I lingered near the table, my eyes drawn once more to the portrait of my father. His gaze, frozen in ink and time, seemed to see right through me.

There were entire pieces of my history I had never questioned. But now? Now I couldn't stop questioning.

I inexplicably found the copy of A Winter's Eve sitting on the table where we left it. I glided over, a giggle rising in my throat as I tossed it to Sagar, watching it tumble and flop open.

He shot me a quick glare, picking the book up and glancing at it. "I don't think we'll find anything holy in this book."

"Oh, I wouldn't be too sure about that," I teased. "There are plenty of holes in chapter twenty."

I frowned, turning over, expecting another smart remark. But instead, I saw Sagar gripping the book, his face stern and filled with a fierceness I hadn't seen.

"Sagar?" I called softly, a knot forming in my chest. "What is it?"

He didn't answer immediately. He looked up slowly, and the look on his face made my blood run cold. The teasing gleam that usually danced in his eyes had vanished. His brow was furrowed, and his mouth was set in a tight line.

"Hey I was just joking—"

"It's not that," he interrupted, his voice tight. He picked up something from the table and stared at it, turning it over in his fingers. His jaw clenched.

"Who told you to read this book?" He asked.

I moved towards him, taking the book from his hand, and scanned the pages. "June did, she said it would *inspire* me. Why?"

He snatched the book back, flipping to the front cover where there was a brief handwritten note.

My dearest,

May our nights together be as beautiful and loving as those shared by Eve and the Duke, just without either of us dying from the lung. (Sorry for the spoiler.)

—June

"That explains how she knew about the book, but what does that have to do with anything—?"

"Read it again," Sagar instructed. "Really look at it, each word."

I did as he commanded, staring at the lines, studying. Only then did I realize what he was telling me.

The book slipped from my grasp and clattered to the floor. My breath caught in my throat as Sagar nodded grimly.

"The letters..." I whispered, a cold wave crashing through me. "June wouldn't—"

"She had access to your parchment, your seal," Sagar cut in, his tone hard and sharp. "How long has she worked for you?"

I blinked, trying to think. "She was just assigned to me last season. This doesn't make sense. How could she copy my handwriting so perfectly?"

"She didn't learn it overnight," he muttered, eyes scanning both pages again. "She was practicing. And by the looks of this, she's been doing it long before she ever got near you."

A sickening twist unfurled in my gut. My mouth went dry. My thoughts tripped over one another, racing too fast to catch.

"I need to know..." I said suddenly, voice cracking. "Why would she do it?"

Sagar's jaw tightened. "I don't know. But if this is real, if this is what it looks like, then she knows about the prophecy, she knows you are the end to Etheria, and she wants to bring it down."

The room tilted slightly. I sat down hard in the chair, clinging to the edges to stop the shaking. A different kind of cold sank into my bones now, the unmistakable shiver of betrayal.

"I trusted her," I muttered, more to myself than to him. "All this time."

Sagar didn't move. The flickering firelight painted hard lines on his face, but something else was in his eyes now, something wary and wounded.

Finally, he stepped forward, keeping his hand in mine. "You can't trust anyone, Silvia. Not anymore. From now on, no one can know anything. Not your friends, not your staff, not even your sister. No one."

I stared at him, heart squeezing tight. There was something final in the way he said it, something heavier than frustration. This wasn't just about espionage or sabotage.

It was fear.

"Sagar..." I began.

He turned to me, cupping my face in both hands. "We'll figure this out," he murmured, his thumbs brushing along my cheekbones. "I swear it. But you can't let your guard down anymore. Not with *anyone*."

Before I could object, he kissed me.

It wasn't like before. This kiss was grounding, steady. A tether in the storm. Something to hold onto before everything else unraveled. And for a fleeting moment, I let myself believe him.

"I have to go," he whispered at last, his forehead resting against mine before he pulled away.

"You're leaving me alone tonight?" I asked, already knowing the answer. But hoping foolishly that he might change his mind.

"Yes, just for now," He smiled. "I'll sneak back into your room tonight, it may be late though."

A reluctant smile tugged at the corner of my mouth. "Fine, but you'll just have to make it up to me later."

He smirked and leaned in to kiss my forehead, soft and lingering. "Gladly."

I caught his hand before he could fully step away. "Wait, before you go."

Sagar's brows rose slightly, amused. "What's wrong?"

"No secrets," I said, more serious than I expected. "You're the only person I can trust now. I need to know that works both ways."

For a breath, he didn't move. His smile faltered, just barely, a stutter in his expression so small I might've missed it if I weren't looking for it. But I saw it. I felt it.

He reached for me again, gently lifting my chin until my eyes found his. The fire behind him painted gold along his cheekbones, casting flickering shadows across the hard planes of his face. In that light, he looked like something carved by fate itself. Too beautiful, too sharp, too dangerous.

"I promise," he said, voice steady. "No more secrets."

Chapter 25

My feet moved on their own as I marched my way to dinner. My mind spun in a million directions at the discovery of June's betrayal. Why did she do this? She wanted Etheria destroyed. What reason could she possibly have?

I pushed the doors to the dining hall open mindlessly, excited for the distraction of Margaret to pull me back to earth.

Scraps of fabric lay strewn about the room. Pieces of skirts and sleeves pinned to mannequins stood like haunting soldiers. I felt the confusion wash over my face as I remembered; June and Madame Levior were building me a new wardrobe.

Only, the room was suspiciously empty now.

Had they left? Had they needed more fabric, gems, or bobbles?

My thoughts were smashed when I heard a giggle from across the room. I nervously approached the floral-patterned sofa as I peered over the edge.

June simpered passionately as her head fell back in ecstasy. Her blouse was unfastened, leaving her nearly exposed in just her chemise and skirts. A mysterious figure lay hidden beneath the layers as the laugh turned into something far more sensual. It was a moment so intimate, so unexpected, that I felt like an intruder in my own space.

I froze, too stunned to run.

They didn't notice me at first, too caught up in each other. But when June shifted slightly, her gaze flicked toward the door, toward me.

Her eyes widened in horror. "Oh!"

"Was that too much?" Madame Levior asked, popping her head up from beneath June's dress. She then locked eyes with me. "Oh..."

I took a step back, heat rising to my cheeks. "I-I'm sorry!" I stammered, my voice higher than usual. I turned sharply, covering my gaze.

"Silvia!" June shouted, quickly covering herself and pushing the Madame's body off of her own. "I-I thought we told you we were using the dining room!"

"I forgot!" I yelled, desperately wanting to escape my own skin.

"This isn't what it looks like!" June squeaked, simultaneously trying to pull her blouse back on and straighten up her hair.

"It very much looks like what it looks like!" I sputtered, shielding my eyes with a hand but failing to hide the grin creeping up my face.

"Silvia I—" The Madame started.

I twisted a grin onto my face as I eyed her up and down. "Now I understand why you needed such...*steady fingers.*"

Madame Levior's face dropped as she pressed it to the couch. "Please, don't fire me."

"I wouldn't dream of—" My words fell short as I locked eyes with June. My moment of surprise had blinded me to her betrayal. I backed up, lurching towards the door. "I uh…I have to go."

"Silvia, please, I'm so sorry." She pleaded.

I slipped out the door and let it shut with a final thud. What had just happened? I didn't want to risk seeing that again. I shook off the thoughts as I devised a new plan of where to go.

The marble beneath my feet was cold, the air sharp with the scent of stone and old candle wax. My steps were quiet, cautious, as I drifted through the palace like a shadow. I didn't stop until I stood before an unfamiliar door.

Margaret's room.

I hovered for a heartbeat, uncertain, then slowly pushed the door open.

A soft glow greeted me. One candle burned on the far table, casting flickering amber light across a room that felt too large, too still, for someone so small. Dolls sat in a neat row against the wall, untouched. Racks of old gowns hung in perfect order, their silks and satins undisturbed. A layer of dust clung faintly to most surfaces, except the books.

Dozens of them, stacked with almost reverent care. Worn spines. Creased pages. Their only reader sitting cross-legged on the floor, hair still curled in neat little pins, a pale gown folded perfectly around her like a storybook princess who'd never stepped into the real world.

Margaret's eyes squinted at me in the dimness. "Silvia?" she asked, her voice so soft it wrapped around my name like a lullaby.

The ache in my chest returned, sharper this time. When had I last come to her like this? When had I last stepped into *her* world? Every meal we shared was on my terms. And here she was, alone, surrounded by all her pretty little things, waiting.

I swallowed hard as guilt bloomed into something uglier. Shame.

Margaret tilted her head. "What are you doing here?"

"I..." The words nearly caught in my throat. But then I crossed the room and sank beside her. "I guess I came to get you for dinner," I said, barely above a whisper. "I promised, didn't I?"

She grinned like I'd just handed her the stars, slamming her book shut with a satisfying thud and scooting closer until our knees touched.

"What were you reading?" I asked, trying to summon a smile that didn't feel fragile.

"Some old tome about the last great war," she said proudly. "Did you know Etheria and Calbraxia were in a near-constant war for hundreds of years? I'm glad we've found peace since."

"Oh, how history repeats," I muttered under my breath. Fortunately, she didn't catch it.

"Did you also know that back then, Saints were born with their power? They were born pure, kissed by the gods they say."

"That seems a little advanced for you," I added, eyebrows lifting.

Margaret just shrugged and stood, returning the book carefully to the shelf. "My tutor says I should focus on practical things, you know, needlework, etiquette, things that'll help me find a husband someday. But one day in the library, I found this..."

She pulled another volume from the shelf. Its cover was cracked leather, the spine less broken than most. She flipped carefully through its yellowed pages, stopping halfway and gently sliding it toward me.

"It's not the book," she said, voice hushed. "It's what someone wrote in it."

I leaned in.

There, in the margin, scrawled between dense lines of historical fact, were words etched in deep, resolute ink. The handwriting was slanted, elegant, and vaguely familiar.

History is not a script, nor is it a chain. It is a fire, wild, consuming, ever-changing. Those who wait for it to shape them will find themselves turned to ash, remnants of another's design. But those who reach into the flames, who dare to grasp the embers of their fate, will find that they are the ones who forge the future. Power is not inherited; it is taken. And destiny is not followed; it is made. When the time comes, we must remember this. No title, no prophecy, no bloodline can decide the course of our path. Only our own hands will shape it.

I stared at the words, my fingers hovering over the page like they might burn me. The ink had bled slightly in places, as if whoever wrote it pressed the pen too hard, like each word cost something to say.

"Mother wrote that," Margaret exclaimed, a smile blooming across her face like the first light of dawn. "When I found it, I kept reading history books, hoping I'd find more. Did you know she was quite the scholar before she had us?"

My heart sank in my chest. I couldn't look away from the words, reading and rereading them as if they might say something different the next time. But they didn't.

"There were hundreds of annotations, but only few survived," she added softly, her voice tinged with sadness as she gently took the book and slid it back into its place. "I think most of her books were destroyed after Father died."

My throat tightened. "Does Mother ever tell you stories about him?" I managed, quickly swiping at the tears forming in the corners of my eyes before she could see.

"Mother doesn't talk to me much," she replied with a little shrug. "Well, not unless she has to." Her voice held no bitterness, just a quiet longing before a yawn slipped past her lips.

I glanced toward the shelf again, one particular spine catching my eye. An old, leather-bound tome, one of the same ones Sagar had been reading earlier. Except this one was nearly crumbling at the edges. I pulled it free and sat on the edge of Margaret's bed.

"Here," I said, motioning for her to get in.

She climbed in eagerly, curling into my side as I settled in beside her and drew the blanket over us both. The bed was small, but warm. Familiar. Comforting in a way I hadn't felt in a long time.

"It's because you look like him," I said suddenly. "Father, I mean. You look just like him. His death—it was hard on her, so I've been told."

I flipped carefully to the page I was looking for. "Did you know you were named after Saint Margaret the Noble?" I asked, pointing to a portrait of the saint draped in a sheer silk veil.

Margaret nodded with pride. "Yes, she freed the people of Calbraxia from a twenty-year drought. She brought rain with just her hands and prayers."

I laughed. "Wow, you really have read all those books."

"Of course I have. Oh!" she said excitedly, flipping ahead to another page. "And you were named after Saint Silvia, the First Mother! Did you know she started the first orphanage in Calbraxia?"

"I did know that," I smiled, letting her energy soothe some of the tension in my chest.

Margaret paused then, tilting her head. "Why are you showing me this?"

I was quiet for a moment before I answered. "Because whenever I feel lost, or like maybe I wasn't meant to be born into this family, I remind myself that we're not just royalty, Margaret. We're more than that. We come from a line of women who changed the world." I flipped another page, tracing the ink with my fingertip. "Most of these women didn't get a choice about if and how to use their gifts. But we do. That means something."

She grew thoughtful at that, staring at the saints' portraits. "I'll be honest," she said after a long moment, "I've never really felt connected to the Divinial heritage." She flipped to the next page and smiled gently. "But thank you."

I pulled her closer and kissed the crown of her head.

She continued turning pages slowly, mindlessly, until my breath caught.

A name had flashed across the paper. One I had never seen before. One that was conveniently missing from the other books.

"Wait!" I gasped, flipping back. "Who's this?"

The title loomed in bold, black ink: Saint Cyradil, the Unholy.

Margaret leaned over to glance, then jumped up and shuffled across the room to grab the book she'd left on the floor. "Oh, She was part of the war I told you about. I think she was our great-great-grandmother."

My eyes stayed locked on the page. "Unholy?" I repeated. "Why would they call her that?"

Margaret jumped back onto the bed, her face glowing with fascination as she flipped to a specific passage in her book, one she clearly had memorized.

"She broke every one of the Seven Heavenly Virtues," she said with wide eyes.

"Seven Heavenly Virtues?" I asked, staring at the page. "What are those?"

Margaret smiled, I'm sure proud to be able to teach me something new. "People knew the only way to make a Saint was to have Divinial blood, but they argued why our powers weakened over time. Eventually, it was decided that the only way to preserve the powers was to remain pure in the eyes of the gods. Charity, modesty, justice, temperance, solitude, honesty, and chastity. Saints had to embody all seven or else lose their Divinial powers."

"So... she lost them?" I asked.

Margaret shook her head solemnly. "No. That's the strange part. She remained a saint. In secret, at first. But..." her voice lowered, "it's hard to hide a pregnancy. Still, according to this," she tapped the book methodically, "she received a prophecy from the gods. A rare exception. They called her unholy not because she lost their favor, but because she defied the system. And kept her power anyway."

A shiver traced down my spine as my eyes dropped to the page. The illustration of Saint Cyradil wasn't like the others. Cloaked in both light and shadow, her outstretched hands crackled with energy that seemed to bleed off the page, something ancient, volatile. A power that didn't feel divine at all.

It felt dangerous, yet the eyes on the page were familiar, my own.

My chest tightened. Something inside me stirred. Sharp, instinctual, like a truth I had always known but buried too deep to name.

"Do you know what the prophecy was?" I asked, my voice nearly lost to the pounding of my heart.

Margaret flipped carefully through the fragile pages. "It's in here somewhere... Ah! Here it is."

She cleared her throat and read aloud, her voice strangely steady. "When the moon is swallowed by shadow and the stars weep silver, A saint shall bear a child untouched by mortal hands.

Born beneath the veil of divinity, shaped by both light and shadow, they shall be the harbinger of death the gods themselves fear."

The words fell like thunder in the quiet room.

It wasn't the prophecy Prince Gerraint had received, but it was something. A thread. A beginning. A key to the world Sagar had spent so long trying to unlock, and maybe, just maybe, a door to the truth I had been too afraid to open.

"The only thing I don't understand," I murmured, "what happened to the other child? Did they turn into the harbinger?"

Margaret brightened. "Well, she became our great-grandmother, didn't she? Saint Cyradil's daughter. By all accounts, she was normal."

"Maybe—maybe it was the wrong child," I said slowly. "Did she ever have another one?"

Margaret's expression darkened. Her hands folded the edge of the blanket as she gently closed the book with a soft thud.

"She died in childbirth," she said quietly. "Only twenty years old. That was her only child."

Twenty. She was my age.

I stared into the candlelight, unease twisting through me like a serpent. There was more to this story, more than anyone had dared preserve. Why go to such lengths to erase her unless...unless the prophecy hadn't failed at all?

"Say, Margaret," I said, lifting the book from her lap. "Where did you find this?"

She looked up with a curious tilt of her head.

"It's just that Saint Cyradil isn't in any of the books I've read. Not to mention. It's almost like—"

"She was erased on purpose," Margaret finished, hopping off the bed to return her war book to the shelf. "I have a knack for finding things people want forgotten. Mother's books. This one. Even the war histories. All of them hold pieces that no one wants to survive.

I guess where you find solace in the Saints, I find it in preserving what others would rather forget."

I stared at her, a smile tugging at the corner of my mouth. How much of her had I missed in all these years? Had she always been this insightful, this perceptive, this grown?

I clutched the book tightly to my chest. "May I borrow this? I promise I'll keep it safe."

"Of course!" Margaret said with a bright grin. "As long as you promise not to lose it."

"I'll guard it with my life," I said with a wink. "Now, I'm not sure the kitchen will stay open this late for us…"

Margaret gave a dramatic sigh and eyed the bed longingly. "I'm not very hungry. But will you stay with me? Just until I fall asleep. I swear I won't talk your ear off."

I laughed, slipping beneath the covers. "I wouldn't dream of leaving."

She beamed, curling up beside me as she opened the book, carefully sounding out the stories of Saints and their sacred trials.

Her voice, steady at first, began to soften with the weight of sleep. Eventually, she paused mid-sentence, and I glanced over, half-expecting to find her asleep. But then, in the hush of the room, her quiet voice broke the silence.

"You don't want to marry the prince, do you?"

I froze, sucking in a breath of confidence. I was not going to hide the truth from her anymore. "No, I don't."

She didn't respond right away. Instead, a long, thoughtful pause settled between us, thick with unspoken fears.

"Do you think I'll have to marry someone she picks for me?" she whispered. Her voice was smaller than I'd ever heard it, fragile and cracking at the edges. "Someone I don't even like? Just because she wants me to?"

Her chartreuse eyes locked onto mine, eyes too young to be asking that question. Eyes that deserved joy and choice and freedom. I brushed a soft curl from her forehead and pressed a kiss there.

"So help me, Goddess, you will find someone who truly makes you happy, Margaret," I whispered. "You'll be beloved. For who you are. Not who they want you to be."

She let out a tiny hum of relief, the tension melting from her body as she nestled closer. For a long moment, neither of us moved.

"You should be beloved too," she murmured against my shoulder, her fingers absently flipping back to the page with Cyradil's likeness. "You deserve that."

I smiled sadly, trailing my fingers down her arm. "Maybe I will be. Some day."

But my thoughts turned to my past life. Another battlefield. Another throne. The Calbraxian people had adored me and once called me their savior. I had ended a fifty-year war drenched in blood and grief.

But to the Etherians? What was I to them? Destruction? Chaos? A weapon.

"Do you think..." Margaret's voice broke through my thoughts again. "Do you think fate can be changed? If Cyradil somehow managed to change hers, even just a little, who's to say you can't change yours?"

I looked at her. Her face was open, hopeful, utterly sincere. She still believed in the impossible. I wanted to believe with her.

"I think it's time for sleep, my dear Margaret," I whispered, sliding the book from her tired hands.

She didn't argue, didn't resist the ache of sleep as it beckoned her eyes shut. I found her warmth intoxicating, so much so that my own eyes started to feel heavy. I couldn't prevent myself from falling into its whim.

But even as I drifted into the dark, my hand still curled protectively around the book. And somewhere, deep in the echoing caverns of my mind, the prophecy whispered back to me.

Chapter 26

The warmth of Margaret's body was still curled against mine when I awoke. The room was dark, steeped in shadows, save for the soft, dying glow of embers in the fireplace. For a moment, I didn't move. I just listened to the rhythm of her breathing, the quiet flutter of her lashes as she slept, the peaceful rise and fall of her small frame pressed against me.

I didn't want to leave. Not yet. Not when the room was still wrapped in the comfort of sleep and the world outside hadn't begun to stir.

How long had she been suffering in silence while I was too distracted, too absorbed in my spirals to see her clearly? I searched my memory, trying to conjure what Margaret had been like in my past life. Had she been as lonely then as she seemed now? Had I failed her before, too?

But I couldn't find the memory.

With a deep breath, I carefully untangled myself from her, pressing a soft kiss to her forehead. She murmured something unintelligible, turning over as I gently tucked the blankets around her shoulders. A smile tugged at my lips despite the heaviness holding onto my heart.

I slipped out of the room in silence, my bare feet gliding over the cold wood floors as I pressed the book tightly to my chest. The palace at this hour was unsettlingly quiet, the kind of silence that didn't feel restful, it felt suspended, like the whole place was holding its breath. Only the torchlight guided my path, its flames flickering wildly in a draft I couldn't feel.

I knew where I was heading. I was now holding the information that Sagar desperately needed to help me escape this life, and more importantly this marriage. I wasn't sure what all the pieces meant, but I knew he would be able to put them together, make them whole and understandable.

As I stepped outside, snow fell in silent sheets, a relentless hush draped across the kingdom. Every flake felt like a warning, delicate and damning. I pulled my cloak tighter around my shoulders, but it did little to shield me from the chill that gnawed at my bones. The determination I carried burned hotter than the frost, but even that heat began to feel fragile, flickering like a candle's last gasp in a bitter wind.

Each step toward the Etherian encampment was slow, trudging through a landscape smothered in snow. Ankle-deep, then shin-deep, then deeper still. It caked against my skin like icing, deceptively beautiful in the moonlight. A pristine mask over treacherous terrain. I hated how perfect it looked, how peaceful. It reminded me of the palace, of the way everything rotten was covered in gold and rose petals, dressed up to fool the world.

I bit the inside of my cheek hard enough to taste iron.

My feet slipped on a patch of frozen moss hidden beneath the snow. I caught myself before falling, breathing hard, my exhales blooming like petals in the air. This was madness. I should've waited until morning. Should've at least worn proper boots. But something inside me screamed that I couldn't afford to wait anymore. Not another moment. If I didn't face him now, I never would.

The storm was only growing stronger, gusts of wind lashing through the trees, tearing through the woods like a living, breathing thing. Branches creaked and groaned in protest, and every now and then, a distant crack split the silence like a whip. But I pressed on.

And then, through the swirling snow, I saw it.

The crimson stain on the pure white sheet. The Etherian encampment glowed faintly in the distance, golden firelight flickering like a heartbeat behind each canvas wall. Sagar's tent stood on the outskirts, a warm light indicating that he must have been in. It looked so warm. So inviting. So easy to step inside and pretend everything could be fixed with a single kiss, a whispered apology, a touch of his hand. That was his greatest power, making me believe he could protect me from the storm, even when he was the storm.

But tonight, I didn't come for comfort. I came to give answers.

I stood outside the entrance, the tent looming tall and taut before me, every seam casting long shadows against the snow. I reached out to lift the flap and felt the heat kiss my fingers before the fabric even parted.

But there was something that made me freeze in my tracks. Voices. Low and murmur-soft. One roughened with command, the other smooth as silk dipped in venom.

My breath caught in my throat, every nerve in my body lighting up like the storm above me. My pulse pounded in my ears, louder than the wind. I couldn't make out the words, not clearly, but there was a tone to them, sharp, clipped, something strained just beneath the surface. Not the easy hostility of enemies, but the grim, measured intensity of two men who knew each other far too well.

My hand hovered at the flap, fingers trembling. I took a quick peek and spotted Sagar, sitting at his desk, eyes fixated on the Prince standing in front of him. His expression was cold, unlike anything I had seen from him. I was equally intrigued and scared.

I stepped back, just a little, enough for the cold to rush in and replace the warmth I'd been so close to touching. My mind reeled with worry.

The wind howled louder now, furious and relentless, tearing through the camp like a beast unchained. It clawed at my cloak and tangled my hair, whispering that I had no place here, that I should run. But I didn't.

I slipped quietly from the entrance of the tent, boots crunching softly in the snow, and crept around the side. The canvas walls billowed with each gust, fluttering just enough for voices to trickle through. I pressed myself against the side, my breath held tight in my throat.

"It's happening," Gerraint said. His usual charm was still there, but it was buried under something colder, weightier. "I can't believe your silly little plan worked. Congratulations, how does it feel?"

I heard the slow glug of liquid poured into a glass, followed by a quiet sip.

"Bittersweet," Sagar finally murmured.

Gerraint gave a soft, humorless laugh, and I imagined his usual smug smile, that twisted glint in his eye. "She is a fine woman, Sagar. You should feel proud. You've played your part beautifully."

Sagar muttered something inexplicable before a long silence hushed the tent. I could hear footsteps; someone was pacing.

"I hate it too, the sooner we're out of this cursed cold kingdom with her, the better." Gerraint chuckled, taking a long sip from his glass. "Snow before a wedding, isn't that supposed to be good luck?

"I never wanted it to come to this," Sagar replied, voice heavy, tired. "But we're in too deep now. The switch will take place during the wedding ceremony. If we're going to make this work, you're going to have to make a scene. Can you handle that?"

The switch. The words sank in slowly, like poison through the bloodstream. My body locked up, cold turning to ice in my veins. What switch? What did that mean?

I could hear my heartbeat thundering in my ears, so loud I feared it would drown them out. I pressed in closer, willing the canvas to vanish between us.

"Oh, I can manage that." Gerraint chuckled, more fox than man. "But do you think it's wise she still knows nothing?"

"She *suspects* nothing," Sagar said sharply, almost defensively. "She's been too busy researching and finding a way out of marrying you. She won't see it coming."

There was a dull thump, a hand, probably his, landing on Sagar's shoulder. Sagar's voice was low, too low for me to catch what he was saying.

"Except her eyes," Gerraint mused, the sound of another glass being poured echoed from within. "She's the real deal. Etheria may finally have its Divinial after all."

I stumbled back, breath punching out of my lungs, a strangled sound caught in my throat.

It couldn't be.

"No," I whispered. I felt my stomach twist as the words slipped past my tongue. I clasped a hand around my mouth.

"Did you hear something?" Gerraint asked, creeping closer to my side of the tent.

"It's just the wind," Sagar muttered.

Sagar, the man who held me like I was made of starlight, who brushed snowflakes from my lashes with such reverence, who whispered that he wanted me, not my crown, not my powers. He couldn't have tricked me. This had to be a mistake.

I collapsed to my knees in the snow, one hand clutched to my chest, the other digging into the icy ground like it could anchor me to something real. But even the earth felt foreign now, soft and slick and sliding out from under me. I felt the betrayal crack through me like thunder.

Still, desperation dragged me forward again. I crawled back to the tent like a moth to flame, seeking warmth, seeking clarity, seeking him.

Inside, the conversation continued.

"...I still think it's silly," Gerraint said more quietly now, his voice taking on an oddly sober tone. "Maybe you should tell her the truth."

Then, the sound of something crashing, sharp and sudden. A glass, maybe. A bottle. Something thrown with force.

"And tell her what?" Sagar snapped, his voice stripped of its usual calm. "That I've been lying to her this whole time?"

I flinched. It felt like he'd struck me himself.

"I mean, I think it's better she learns *now* than on her wedding day, Sagar. What if this pushes her over the edge? What if she declines?"

"We can't trust *anyone* here, Gerraint. Not until we're back. Not until we're safe with her."

I clutched the canvas tighter, my breath fogging the air, mixing with the frost gathering at the edge of the tent. Who were they talking about? With her, did that mean me? Or someone else? Every word only birthed more questions. Every second cracked the fragile hope still beating in my chest.

"Besides," Sagar muttered. "It was *you* who decided to agree to the marriage. Let's not forget that, Gerraint."

"Yes well, it was all just a bit of fun watching the two of you squirm for so long, wasn't it?" Gerraint sighed, boots shifting in the tent. "You'll have to tell her at some point. Otherwise, before you know it, she'll be walking down the aisle with a knife at her back."

The flap rustled as Gerraint moved closer to the exit. I backed away just in time, slipping behind a stack of crates and barrels. I watched his silhouette pass, tall and sharp-edged, the storm peeling at his cloak as he disappeared into the snow.

I stayed hidden, trembling, unsure if I was more afraid of being caught or being wrong.

The pain in my chest twisted tighter, a knot of grief and disbelief. What if I'd misunderstood? What if the words I'd heard were out of context, part of some strategy I couldn't begin to understand? And yet, what if I hadn't? What if I had heard the truth, and it was exactly as it seemed?

Another gust of wind shrieked past me, clawing at my exposed skin, but I didn't flinch. The cold had seeped so deep into my bones that I welcomed it now. I wanted to freeze. I wanted something, anything, to make sense.

Numbness crept up my limbs as each extremity began to shake. I didn't know how long I'd been crouched there in the snow, just a thin cloak around my shoulders like it could protect me from the weight of betrayal. The storm whirled around me, snowflakes collecting like diamonds on my skin, but it was the sound of my sobs that filled the air, low and hollow.

Or so I thought, until I heard his voice.

"Who's there?"

It was faint at first, cautious. The fabric rustled as someone exited the tent. I didn't move.

Sagar rounded the corner. He looked like something from a dream, his breath curling in the frozen air. The flush in his cheeks bright from the liquor. He held a bow in one hand, lowered now in confusion and alarm.

When he saw me, he dropped it entirely.

"Silvia!" he gasped, stumbling through the snow, falling to his knees at my side. "I was looking for you! What are you doing out here? Gods, you're freezing."

His arms wrapped around me like a vice, scooping me into his chest. I didn't resist, I didn't have the strength. I reached out, brushing his collarbone, half-convinced he wasn't real. That I had already died, and this was just some fevered dream.

"Shhh, you're okay," he muttered, holding me tighter. "You're okay now."

He carried me into the tent like I weighed nothing. The warmth hit me instantly, almost painfully. My skin prickled, nerves twitching awake after being numbed near to death. He set me down, wrapping me in thick furs, his hands rubbing furiously up and down my arms to force the blood back.

"What were you thinking?" he said, panic hidden behind mock-scolding. "It's a bloody blizzard out there. You could've—" He cut himself off, not letting his mind go to such dark places.

I couldn't respond. My gaze drifted across the tent, familiar but warped. The maps looked like lies now. The weapons, like threats. Then my eyes landed on the table. Two empty glasses. A bottle half-drained.

His hand cupped my cheek, thumb brushing just under my eye. A smile slithered across his lips, soft and gentle, and it made my heart ache. I should've pulled away, screamed, demanded answers, but instead, I leaned into his touch like I always did, as if my body still hadn't gotten the message my heart had.

He kissed a trail from my forehead to my ear, his hands found my waist, pulling me close until I could feel the heat of him through every layer of cloth. I wanted to believe him. I wanted to fold into him and let it all fade away.

But the truth was still waiting outside that tent. Buried under snow. Waiting to drag me under again.

"I found information on Saint Cyradil," I murmured, stiffening.

He paused. "Oh yeah?" His tone was casual again, like he hadn't just carried me in from the brink of death. "What did you find?"

"She put her trust in the wrong people," I said, voice steadier now, more pointed. "She thought they would protect her. Instead, they used her. Turned her into a symbol. A martyr." I looked up at him then, meeting his gaze. "It's funny. History has a way of repeating itself."

He paused, just for a second. His fingers still tangled in my hair, breath catching in his throat. His eyes searched mine, desperate, pleading, but I didn't blink. I didn't give him a way out.

I watched as his face shifted, no longer soft, no longer composed. Conflict flickered there like a storm cloud caught between thunder and lightning.

"She died at twenty," I said, voice low, almost numb. "Saint Cyradil. Strange, isn't it? We're the same age. She died in childbirth. And here I am, preparing for a future I never chose, in a body that doesn't feel like mine anymore. At least she had her powers. I've got nothing. I'll never be her. But I guess Etheria will finally get its Divinial... right?"

Sagar stood sharply, the blood draining from his face as understanding hit him like a blow.

"You heard?" he asked, voice hoarse.

"I heard."

"How much?"

"Every word."

He ran a hand over his face, dragging it down in slow agony before looking up at me again. But there was no guilt in his eyes. No shame. Only relief.

"I've been trying to find a way to tell you," he said quietly, falling to his knees in front of me, his head pressing into my lap like a broken man. "Silvia, I swear. I never wanted to lie. It's been so hard. You—you're the only one who could possibly understand."

I shoved him off, disgust rising like bile in my throat. "Understand what, Sagar?" My voice shook with restrained fury. "How you manipulated me? How you used me? You wanted me distracted, and you succeeded. You made me trust you. Even—" My voice cracked, and I choked down the sob threatening to spill. "I was so stupid."

Sagar reeled back like I'd slapped him. His face crumpled in horror. "So you *didn't* hear everything."

"I heard enough," I hissed, standing.

He rose with me, towering like a shadow, but there was no threat in his stance, just heartbreak. "Silvia, I swear to you, it's not what it sounded like. You have to believe me."

"You promised me," I whispered. "No secrets." My gaze dropped to the ground, too ashamed to meet his. "You promised, and I believed you."

He stepped forward and gently tilted my chin until our eyes met. His fingers were tender, trembling.

"Please," he said. "Let me explain—"

I pulled away like his touch burned. "Explain what? That I've been a means to an end this whole time? A vessel? A sacrifice?"

"Don't say that," he said, desperate now.

"I don't even know who you are," I breathed. "Everything I thought I knew is all a lie."

Sagar's hands found my arms, gripping them tight, the warmth of him searing through the layers of betrayal between us.

"Silvia, please, just listen! I'm trying to explain—"

"No!" I tore away from him, bursting into the frigid night air outside the tent. The wind caught my hair, dragging it around my face. "Don't touch me! You'll never get to touch me again!"

He followed me into the snow, the moonlight casting silver streaks along the angles of his face. He looked like a statue, like something carved from myth and frost. But his eyes burned with fire. That same fire that had always undone me.

And gods help me, my body still ached for him. My skin still remembered his hands, my mouth still remembered the taste of his kiss. Every inch of me longed to fold back into his arms and forget everything.

I halted as a hand caught my shoulder, strong, unyielding.

"Let me go!" I yelled, twisting, but his grip only tightened.

"Silvia! Please," he begged.

I spun, shoving him back, staring into those honey eyes that once felt like home. Now they just felt like a trap.

"I want to—no, I *need* to tell you everything," he said, words tumbling like broken glass. "But not out here. Just come back with me. We'll talk, we'll scream, cry, break everything if we need to. Gods, I don't care. Just let me explain."

I took a trembling step back.

"How am I supposed to trust you?" I demanded, voice shaking but firm. "You've been behind everything. You've sabotaged my marriage prospects, you turned me against the only person who cared for me, and you took my power from me. It's done, Sagar. You win. I'm marrying the prince." My lip quivered just the slightest. "But if you think I'll sit quietly in some tower, waiting while you and Gerraint turn me into some weapon for Etheria..." My voice rose with each word, cracking under the weight of it. "I'd rather—"

Before I could finish, he surged forward and crushed his mouth to mine.

It was feral, furious. A war between anguish and longing. Between love and betrayal. His hands tangled in my hair like he was afraid I'd vanish if he let go. His lips moved against mine with a desperation that shook me to the core. I gasped against his mouth, my body betraying me completely as my fingers clutched the front of his tunic, fisting the fabric like it was the only thing tethering me to the earth.

I hated him. Gods, I hated him.

And yet I wanted him.

I wanted to scream. I wanted to sob. I wanted to melt into him, just for a second, and forget everything.

His tongue brushed against mine, coaxing. Demanding. And I let him in. Just for a breath, just for a heartbeat, I let myself drown in him. In the heat of his mouth, in the scent of fire and winter on his skin, in the way his body curved into mine like it belonged there. Like we were made to break together.

With a sharp gasp, I tore away, breath ragged, lips swollen. My body buzzed with heat and horror.

My hand moved before I could stop it.

Crack.

The sound echoed into the night air, sharp and merciless.

His head snapped to the side. A red streak bloomed across his cheek, angry and immediate. But he didn't move. He didn't flinch. He just stood there, frozen, stunned, his chest rising and falling like he'd just taken a blade to the gut.

Silence fell. Heavy. Suffocating.

My throat tightened. My heart screamed.

"I love you," he whispered, still not meeting my eyes.

The words sliced through me like a knife.

His jaw trembled. His fists clenched at his sides.

"It's too damn late for tricks," I spat, and this time, I made sure my voice didn't crack.

His gaze shot to mine, burning, furious, as if he was pleading.

"It's not a trick, Silvia." His voice broke. "I loved you from the moment I laid eyes on you. I love every stubborn, sharp-edged, beautiful inch of you. Even when you told me your past life, it didn't change a thing. Remember that?" His voice softened. "Even when you told me the worst of it, I loved you. And I still do now."

My head shook slowly, my vision blurring at the edges.

"Gods, every second I'm not with you, I think about the next time I get to see you, smell you, taste you, touch you. I dream of you every night. When I wake up and you're not there, it's agony, the worst I can bear. I never meant for it to happen, never thought I could feel this way, but I do. I love you, and I hope that somewhere inside, you love me as well."

"No," I whispered, shattered. "No, you don't get to say that now. Not after everything."

He took a half-step forward, but I lifted my hand to stop him. To draw a line he could no longer cross.

"I have one question left, remember?" He asked, his voice laced with ferocity. "One question that you have to answer, truthfully. I'm using it now, you have to be honest."

"It's too late for truths!" I snapped, wishing the distance between us was greater.

"You don't understand how important it is that you answer this." He ignored my request, the heat from his body was palpable in the night air. "Tell me, do you love me too?"

My chest heaved as if my lungs had forgotten how to work. I searched his eyes, desperate for some crack, some mercy that might let me slip past the question unscathed, but the fierceness there held me in place like a hand at my throat. There was no room to lie. No room to pretend.

Memories surged unbidden. Every stolen breath pressed into the dark, every kiss that tasted like defiance, like choosing myself for the first time. Every reckless, beautiful mistake I had made in this life traced itself back to him. I saw it all at once: the nights I laughed too loudly, the mornings I woke without dread coiled in my stomach, the intoxicating freedom of choosing my own life, my own fate.

He had been the hinge on which my world swung open. And knowing that, feeling it still lodged in my ribs, terrified me more than the answer.

"I loved you," I said, barely audible. And it was the truth. That was what made it hurt so damn much.

Sagar's face crumpled at the past tense. At the finality. But I didn't wait for him to respond.

I turned and ran through the snow, through the cold, through the ache of his touch still burning on my skin. The night swallowed me whole.

By the time I reached the palace, my lungs burned, my skin numb. I didn't remember the halls. I didn't remember getting to my door. I only remembered silence.

I let the door close behind me with a soft click. My steps faltered. And then my knees gave out.

I crumpled onto the bed like a broken doll, the mattress catching me as I curled inward, my arms around myself like they could hold all the pain in.

My breath came in uneven gasps. Then the tears came. Hot. Silent. Endless.

I had tried. I had fought so hard to write a different story for myself. To escape the chains that had bound me once before. But no matter what choices I made, no matter how many times I clawed for freedom, the outcome never changed.

I could feel fate's hands again, cold and merciless, tightening around my throat. I was going to be trapped. Again. And what was worse, I let my captor lead me to my new cage.

A hollow laugh escaped my lips, bitter and cracked. Had I ever really had a choice? Or had every step just led me back to the same end, dressed in different robes?

Perhaps fate was never meant to be rewritten. Perhaps all I'd done was loop the tragedy into a prettier noose.

I rolled onto my back, staring up at the ceiling until my vision blurred. My hand drifted into the air, palm up, fingers trembling. This body, this second life, was supposed to mean something. A second chance. A rebirth. But it was just the same story, the same pain, wearing a prettier mask. I let my arm fall limp beside me. And I exhaled.

No. No, not this time. If I couldn't escape my fate, then I would claim it.

A stillness settled over me. Cold. Steady. Clear. They would not chain me again. They would not dress me in linen and parade me like some sacred lamb, groomed for slaughter. I would not wither behind gilded bars until nothing remained of who I once was. After the wedding, once I was far from Margaret, far from my mother, far from Sagar—once everyone I loved was safe. I would end it myself. And I would take the prince with me.

I would not die forgotten, late in my years, and filled with regrets.

This time, I was going to die free.

Chapter 27

My dear Margaret,

I wish I could give you all the time in the world. A thousand lifetimes spent at your side, watching you grow into the woman and queen I know you will become. But fate, cruel as ever, has other plans.

In every life beyond this one, I will find you again. I swear it.

We will run through the gardens, barefoot and laughing beneath the golden sun. I'll braid flowers into your hair, read you bedtime stories, and kiss your forehead goodnight. Nothing, not duty, not destiny, not the weight of kingdoms will take me from you again.

Until then, be strong, my little star. Let your light shine even when I am gone.

With all the love in my heart,

—Silvia

A soft knock at the door snapped me back to the present. I flinched, fingers tightening around the parchment as if it were the only real thing in the room. With trembling hands, I folded the letter with precision, slipping it into the envelope before tucking it under my pillow.

"Come in," I said, wiping hastily at my eyes.

The door creaked open, and June stepped inside, her face drawn, worry etched into every line of her brow. "It's time."

The past days had blurred together. I hadn't left my room. Had barely spoken. I had spent hours lying on my back, staring at the ceiling as I calculated my death like a blueprint.

Poison had been my first thought. Swift. Painless. But the prince deserved pain. Besides, where could I obtain poison in such short notice without rising suspicion? A fall from the palace balcony? Dramatic, but uncertain.

Then, the idea struck me. A dagger to the heart. Clean. Direct. Obvious. And poetic, in the most tragic sense.

The cold sting of the knife I had hidden beneath my corset was the only reminder I had of my plan. The moment I was alone with him, I would end his future reign of terror then and now, and take myself along with it.

I had chosen silence, told no one of my plan. If I had spoken it aloud, it might've lost its power. Or worse, someone might've tried to stop me.

I forced a smile, the same way I had every morning since the truth of her betrayal. "It's my wedding day. They can't very well start without me, can they?"

June let out a breathy laugh, more sad than amused. She crossed the room and sat on the edge of my bed, her eyes scanning my face like she was trying to memorize me.

"You know," she said softly, "you don't have to go through with this. Sagar's been—"

I looked away, my stomach twisting. "I don't want to see him."

She hesitated, lips pressed together as if she was holding back more words than she dared speak. But in the end, she only stood, crossing to the vanity where my wedding gown waited, a haunting reminder of the day ahead.

Madame Levior entered the room with quiet grace, her eyes immediately catching the tension crackling between us like a stray storm cloud.

"It's time to get you ready," she said softly, almost tenderly.

I nodded, the numbness settling back into my bones like an old friend.

June approached with the gown draped delicately in her arms, her face lit with forced brightness. "Are you at least ready to admire our work?" she asked, trying to keep her voice light. "I think you'll look—"

"June," I snapped, sharper than I intended. "Ruffles and lace may solve your problems, but they won't solve mine."

She flinched, the words landing too hard. Her smile faltered, and she lowered her head, blinking fast to keep tears at bay. "I-I'm sorry, Silvia. If this is about the other day—"

"June, perhaps you could fetch the Princess some water," Madame Levior interjected smoothly, though her tone held no judgment. Then, with a side glance in my direction, she added quietly, "Make it a wine. White."

June nodded, her shoulders hunched as she hurried from the room.

Silence fell again, thick and aching.

Madame Levior stepped forward and began to dress me with practiced care. No words. Just the sound of silk whispering against skin, of pins being fastened, of breath being held.

The gown shimmered like moonlight on still water, ethereal and impossible. Pale silver silk draped around me in fluid sheets, cool to the touch, soft as a sigh. Roses, painstakingly embroidered in thread that shimmered like starlight, bloomed across the bodice and hem, catching the candlelight like they were lit from within.

It was beautiful. Too beautiful for what it was meant for.

"It's stunning," I murmured, forcing the words past the knot in my throat.

Madame Levior finally smiled just a little, admiring the gown like a mother gazing at her firstborn. "Yes," she said, her voice softer now. "It is."

She moved behind me again, her hands cool as she made the final adjustments. The silence stretched for a moment.

"It's none of my business," she said lightly, never missing a beat, "but I can't help but wonder if this gown wouldn't look better beside a different groom."

I blinked. The words hit harder than they should have. "Who?"

She caught my gaze in the mirror, one brow arched with unmistakable clarity. "You know who."

Of course, she knew. Maybe not everything. But enough.

I hesitated. "What does it matter?"

She paused, her fingers briefly stilling at my waist. "Love matters to fools and dreamers. But women like us? We have to think practically."

I frowned. "That's... rather depressing."

She smiled at that, but it didn't reach her eyes. "The truth can be, sometimes. And honestly, you need the truth right now."

Something flickered across her face then. Regret, maybe. Resignation.

"You speak as though you have experience," I said carefully, turning to face her.

For a long time, she was silent. Her hands rested against the window frame, still and unmoving, her eyes distant and fixed on something far beyond the palace walls, lost in a memory only she could see.

Finally, her voice returned. Low. Brittle. Like parchment cracking under time. "I was in love once. Or I thought I might be."

The admission hung in the air between us, fragile and unexpected.

"I-I'm sorry," I murmured, my voice small, uncertain. "I didn't mean to—"

"Oh, don't you worry." She gave a short laugh, one that didn't quite reach her eyes. "I was married. My first—well, my *only* marriage."

Her voice softened then, as if something warm and wistful had settled into her chest. "It wasn't for love or anything like that. I needed out of the house, and he needed an heir. It was transactional. Convenient. He was respectable. I was expected to be a respectable wife. So I did what I was told. I kept my head down. I played my part."

Her fingers twitched, gripping a swath of discarded fabric a little tighter. The silk creased in her hands. "Then I got pregnant. And for a moment, I let myself believe maybe this was how love began. In quiet glances. In shared duty. In hope." A smile tugged at the corners of her mouth, but it was thin and sad. "But I never got the chance to find out."

A lump formed in my throat. I stepped closer, reaching out to place a hand on her shoulder. "Madame, I'm so sorry."

She nodded, but didn't look at me. Her gaze remained locked on the shadowed rose garden below.

"I miscarried late," she said, the words heavy with memory. "My husband had to make a choice. Save me or save the baby. And I'm still here, so..." She trailed off, then straightened the hem of my gown with a swift, practiced tug. The motion was firm. Controlled. But her hands were trembling. "In doing so, I lost the ability to carry another. No heir, no use for me anymore. He never said it, not with words, but I knew. That kind of silence speaks louder than screaming."

My heart ached for her, for the girl she once was, for the woman who had survived it.

Madame Levoir exhaled softly. "Don't pity me. He left me with a little money. I bought my shop. I started again. Now I make the most beautiful dresses in the world." She stepped back, wiping her palms against her skirt before nodding at my reflection. "In a way, I still give birth. To beauty. To art. To something that makes me feel alive. And now, I get to experience *real* love."

I turned toward her, the ache in my chest pressing harder. "I'm sorry," I said again, and this time I meant it, not just for her pain, but for how much I had taken her strength for granted.

She shook her head, her smile real this time, tired, but honest. "He loved me, I think. Just a little. Enough to choose me over his legacy. That's something, isn't it?"

I nodded, blinking back the heaviness behind my eyes. Then, quietly, I walked to the bed and sat down, the weight of everything settling in. Madame Levoir had always seemed immovable, like stone carved by war and time. I felt unworthy to see this softened side of her.

She joined me with a small grunt, settling beside me and gazing at our reflections in the mirror. Two women, worlds apart in many ways, yet bound by survival and secrets.

"I only tell you this," she said, her voice softer now, almost motherly, "because I want you to understand tragedy isn't always the end of the story. Sometimes, it's the beginning of something else."

Her words settled in my chest, like warm embers stirring in a hearth that had long since gone cold.

"Even so," I whispered, eyes still fixed on the mirror, "you have June. I'll have no one."

Madame Levior frowned. "You *still* have June. She loves you, Silvia, more than anyone. You're like a sister to her. Maybe it's not my place, but what happened? You've been cold to her lately. Distant. Don't think she hasn't noticed."

My stomach knotted.

I could name every one of Sagar's betrayals. But June's? Hers remained a foggy riddle. I didn't know her reason for forging the letters, for playing a part in Etheria's downfall. And maybe a part of me didn't want to. Knowing her motive might make her forgivable.

And if Sagar had been right about anything, it was this: I couldn't trust anyone. Not even her.

As if summoned by the weight of our silence, June entered the room quietly, holding a silver goblet filled to the brim.

"Here," she said, offering it to me with a smile that didn't quite reach her eyes. "For the nerves."

I took it and drank, the sharp liquid burning down my throat. I stifled the cough, but the taste brought back too many memories. My first night home, the bitter ache of betrayal, the bone-deep exhaustion.

Still, I drank. Because I needed something, anything to help me survive the ceremony.

"Silvia, are you sure you don't want me to come with you to Etheria?" She quietly asked. Her eyes had gone red, puffy with tears.

My chest ached. She had offered plenty of times in the past week, pleading with me to bring her with. I plastered a smile on my face, I had an excuse ready, something that would keep her here in the palace, something that would keep her away from me and what I was about to do.

"I need you to stay," I said softly. "I have a much more important job for you here," My voice trembled only slightly.

June tilted her head, confused. I hesitated, then reached beneath my pillow, fingers curling tightly around the folded parchment. The letter still held the faint warmth of my hand. My heart.

"While I'm gone," I continued, "I need someone to keep an eye on Margaret. She's already so lonely. I can't imagine how she'll be once I leave."

June's brow creased as she looked at the envelope I offered. Her gaze flicked from the parchment to my face, something uncertain settling in her eyes. "You'll write to her, won't you?"

I forced a smile that tasted like ash. "Of course." I placed the letter into her hands, folding her fingers around it gently, firmly.

"But once you get word I've made it to Etheria," I added, "I think you two should read this together. Just some words of encouragement until the honeymoon is over."

June held the letter like it was made of glass. Her knuckles whitened as her grip tightened, her silence louder than any question. She looked at me, really looked, her eyes searching the planes of my face like she was trying to solve a puzzle that terrified her.

And I knew then that she felt it. The wrongness. The finality.

Her lips parted, a thousand unspoken pleas caught behind them. Her breath hitched like she wanted to scream, to beg me not to go through with whatever I was planning.

I exhaled and stood tall, letting my fingers brush down the length of my gown. The silk was smooth, cold, and heavy against my skin. Like armor. Like a burial shroud.

"Alright," I said, my voice stronger than it had any right to be. "Let's get this over with."

Chapter 28

The walk to the throne room was eerily peaceful, the kind of calm that settles just before a storm tears the world apart.

The palace had been transformed overnight, cloaked in crimson blooms. Roses, in this time of year, were a rarity, but my mother always had a thing for them. Petals lined the corridors like a trail to the gallows. The scent was dizzying; sweet, cloying, relentless. I wondered if they would still smell as lovely when they dried and fell, brittle and dead.

The throne room had been repurposed into a makeshift chapel. No churches, no temples, just golden columns, high windows, and a floor polished until it reflected the lie I wore like a crown. Only nobles had been invited. Only those close to the crown. It was to be intimate, prestigious, controlled, like a performance.

June walked beside me in silence, carrying the long, delicate train that swept from my gown like fresh snow across marble.

She would not be allowed into the ceremony itself, but she had promised to stay with me until the final moment she was permitted. I begrudgingly accepted.

Today I felt nothing. No, that wasn't true. I felt calm. Cold, sharp, calm. My heart didn't thunder. It didn't ache. No nerves were fluttering in my stomach.

The dagger I had hidden in the folds of my corset pressed lightly against my ribs, a steady, silent companion. My salvation. My freedom. I would not be caged again. I would not let them lock me in a tower, drape me in solitude, and call it a privilege. I would not grow old watching my reflection fade behind glass, wondering who I might've been.

I reached the entrance of the throne room, and there she was.

My mother, draped in Calbraxian green velvet and gold, her hair pinned into an elaborate twist, every inch of her styled to reflect the image of power and grace. Her eyes welled with tears when she saw me, the faintest tremble in her lips betraying a softness she rarely showed.

"Silvia," she whispered, reaching up to place a hand on my cheek. Her palm was cool, but it trembled slightly. "You look so beautiful, my dear."

I didn't smile. Didn't flinch. Didn't react.

I simply nodded, cold as the marble beneath our feet, my gaze locked on the heavy oak doors in front of us. Through them, I could hear the muffled murmur of nobles gathering, whispering, waiting.

"I'll be walking you down," she offered, a forced lightness in her voice, as if this was just another tradition, not a calculated betrayal. I turned to her and gave the smallest of nods. "Are you nervous?"

"No." I scoffed, eyes never leaving the twisted grain of the wood. "I've never been more ready for something in my life."

There was silence, broken only by her exhale.

"I'm sorry, Silvia," she said at last. "Sorry that it had to come to this."

Before I could respond, I felt hands grasping my shoulders. I turned, startled, and saw June.

She was shaking, visibly trembling as sobs wracked her small frame. Her eyes were red, her face blotchy and streaked with tears. The moment she saw my face, her composure crumbled entirely.

"Silvia," she choked, "I'm sorry."

She collapsed against me, and I caught her, wrapping my arms around her and holding her close. Her sobs soaked into the fabric of my gown. I ran a hand through her hair, smoothing it gently.

"Shhh," I whispered, my voice steadier than it should've been. "It's okay, June. This isn't your fault. None of it is."

She nodded, hiccupping through her grief. Her eyes found my mother's, something unreadable flickering there. Then she dropped into a quick, shallow curtsey.

"I-I'll see you in the reception," she said, her voice barely audible.

I watched her go, watched her disappear around the corner, my last real tie to the world I knew. When I turned back to my mother, something inside me shifted. My composure cracked, just enough to let the fury slip through.

My voice came low, gravelly, quiet enough that no one else could hear. But she heard.

"I'm doing this," I said, "not for you. Not for duty. For Margaret. And if you ever pull this shit on her, if you try to mold her into your perfect little pawn the way you did me, may the Gods have mercy on you. Because I won't."

My mother's eyes widened. Her lips parted, but no sound came out. She was afraid.

Good. Let her be.

If I hadn't been walking to my own execution, I might've felt extraordinary.

Instead, I smiled. That hollow, dead smile I had practiced so well. "Brides smile, right?" I said, offering her my hand.

She took it reluctantly. Her hand was shaking. Maybe from my words. Maybe because she knew, deep down, that I would do something to ruin her perfect, polished ceremony. That I would find a way to taint it forever.

She looped her arm around mine as the doors began to creak open, golden light spilling into the corridor. Trumpets sounded in the distance. The music swelled like a tide, too grand, too final. It had begun.

The massive doors swung wide, and the heat of a hundred candles surged forward like a wave. I stepped into it, into a sea of stares, jewels, and judgment. The nobles turned as one, a thousand painted faces shifting toward me like flowers seeking the sun. But their eyes remained cold, glinting, calculating.

The chamber reeked of roses. Hundreds, maybe thousands, clustered in vases and garlands. Red and white, lining every pew, draped over every column. Their cloying scent clung to the air like smoke, sickly sweet and overwhelming.

"Destiny is not followed; it is made." I whispered, remembering the words my mother wrote so long ago.

My mother stiffened at my side. I felt her flinch like I'd slapped her. She didn't respond, but I didn't look at her. I didn't need to. I could feel her eyes boring into the side of my face, trying to read me, to restrain me with nothing but will.

My gaze locked forward, straight to the end of the aisle to the Prince.

Draped in jet-black velvet that shimmered like obsidian under the candlelight, adorned in gems of red and green, blood and envy,

Calbraxia and Etheria. He looked carved from marble, every inch the princely figure. Regal. Perfect. Dead-eyed. And waiting.

A sea of red roses coiled at his feet, thick and lush and suffocating. More blood than bloom.

I hesitated, a flutter of nausea twisting in my gut. Then I took a breath, small, tight, but enough, and stepped across the threshold.

One step.

A hush fell across the room like a ripple on still water. Whispers broke free, soft as moth wings, sharp as knives. My name passed between painted lips and powdered hands. Silvia, so graceful. Silvia, so pale. Look at her veil. Look at her eyes. Look at that dress.

The silk hem of my dress whispered across the stone, its brush as soft as a sigh, cruelly gentle against the riot inside my chest.

Ten steps.

The murmurs grew louder, bolder. A noblewoman tilted her head and leaned toward her husband. Why does the queen look so pale? Another voice, male, clipped and skeptical. Is the princess crying?

I wanted to rip the veil from my face, to scream at them, to be the storm I felt inside. But I didn't. I couldn't. Don't fidget in public, Silvia. Don't make a scene. Even now, Mother's voice haunted me.

Twenty steps.

The music swelled again, a triumphant crescendo that felt more like mockery than celebration. Lutes and viols, too bright, too sharp. The melody pierced the chamber like a crown of thorns.

My fingers tightened around the bouquet. White roses. Purity. Obedience. Sacrifice. All wrapped in a satin ribbon, destined for a lover I would never truly know.

Thirty steps.

A voice broke the spell.

"Silvia!"

My head turned, just slightly, peering through the gauze of my veil.

I locked eyes with Margaret. She stood at the edge of the pew, her hands gripping the carved wood so tightly her knuckles had gone white. Her face, so open and innocent, was stricken. Her green eyes were wide and glistening.

"You look so beautiful," she whispered, and in her voice, there was something more than admiration. There was grief.

A single breath escaped me, trembling, cracked. Tears I had tried to suppress broke loose, trailing silently down my cheeks. They hit the white petals in my hand, blooming there, tainting the roses.

I stopped.

The steps to the altar towered ahead, just a few feet more. My legs refused to move. The gown clung to me now, heavy as stone. My heart beat like a war drum.

"Who gives this woman to this man?" the Cardinal asked.

"I do," my mother said.

She released my arm and stepped back into the crowd, her words booming through the still air. My spine stiffened as I watched her retreat.

I stared up at the altar, blinking the veil of tears from my eyes. My hand trembled as I reached down, gathering my skirts to ascend the steps. But before I could lift my foot, a gloved hand extended toward me. White. Pristine. Strong.

I followed the arm to its source and met Gerraint's gaze. My future husband.

His deep brown eyes glittered like shards of glass beneath the candlelight, a grin stretching across his face, mocking, indulgent, wrong. He looked like a man who thought he had already won.

I hated him. Every word we shared, every glinting ruby stitched into his robes, every strand of hair slicked back to frame his smug expression. He was a lie made flesh. A performance wrapped in velvet. I wanted to claw that smile off his face, dig beneath the surface, and see what blood and filth lay underneath.

Yet, I reached for him.

My hand slid into his, and he pulled me up beside him with ease. His fingers, despite their elegance, were unnaturally strong. It caught me off guard. For someone so thin, so willowy, there was weight in his grip, a strength that felt foreign like something hiding in plain sight.

"You ready?" he whispered under his breath, his grin tilting into something darker. "This will be quite the show."

I grimaced, turning away from him to face the Cardinal. I gave the old man a curt nod, signaling him to begin.

He opened his book, and his voice echoed across the stone hall. "Welcome, people of Calbraxia. For the first time in almost two hundred years, we are pleased to bring together both our kingdom and Etheria in holy matrimony. Both the God and Goddess smile upon us on this day..."

His words blurred, muffled, and hollow, like they were being shouted across a canyon. I couldn't hear them, not really. All I could hear was the rush of blood in my ears and the pounding of my heart, heavy as thunder.

And still, somewhere inside, I had hoped that Sagar would storm through those doors. That he would pull me from this altar, from this nightmare. That his loyalty, his love, if it had truly been love, might still mean something.

But he wasn't there.

I scanned the crowd from beneath my veil, my eyes darting across rows of nobles and dignitaries. The ache in my stomach deepened. No amber skin. No sandy hair. No quiet fire burning at the back of the room.

Was he gone? Had he truly walked away? Had I been nothing but a task?

The world narrowed. The gilded chandeliers overhead seemed to spin, the air thickening with incense and heat and the weight of hundreds of gazes. I couldn't breathe. My chest tightened, the corset now a vise squeezing me from the inside. My lungs scratched against my ribs, panicked and fluttering like trapped birds.

Not here. Not now.

I dug my nails into my palm, trying to keep from unraveling, but the floor shifted beneath me. My vision wavered, blurring into streaks of color and shadow. The voices blended, the whispers rising and falling like the tide.

My knees buckled. I stumbled. A hand caught my arm, firm, steady.

And then came the voice.

"Breathe."

Familiar. Deep. Controlled. I turned, eyes wide, heart slamming against my ribs.

Sagar stood just behind me, dressed in Etherian crimson, his usual guard uniform pressed neatly and looking immaculate on him. Only now he wasn't my knight, or my protector. He was my warden.

His expression was carefully neutral, but I could see it in his eyes, the flicker of concern, the flicker of something else. Regret. Or guilt. Or worse: duty.

My panic dissolved into cold fury. He wasn't gone. He was watching me. Waiting. Ready to act if I made a run for it.

I turned sharply back to Gerraint, who flashed a knowing, cheeky grin like the two of them had just shared a joke at my expense. A secret I wasn't part of.

I didn't know what was coming, but I knew it wouldn't end at this altar.

"Your Highness?" the Cardinal asked gently, drawing my attention. "If you would like to continue..."

I cleared my throat, forcing composure into my voice.

"Apologies, Sir." My eyes flicked back to Sagar, who was now smirking under his breath. "Continue."

The Cardinal straightened and lifted his ceremonial book once more.

"As I was saying: We are here to unite Princess Silvia Stephan of Calbraxia and Prince Gerraint Petris of Etheria in holy matrimony. May the God and Goddess bear witness to this joining of blood and crown, and may peace blossom between our lands…"

I tuned him out again.

Instead, I let my eyes find Margaret. She sat near the front, her hands folded tightly in her lap, her lower lip trembling. She looked impossibly small in her seat, like a flower trapped in a vase too tall for it to bloom.

This was for her.

I reminded myself that every step I took, every lie I told, every ounce of pain I swallowed was for her future. For her freedom. For a life I would never get to live.

"Prince Gerraint, do you take Silvia, to have and to hold, in the eyes of the Goddess Leticia, as your wife and queen of Etheria?"

Gerraint smiled at me, all smug affection and glittering teeth, as if he were savoring a secret I didn't yet know. He took my hand in his, his fingers wrapping around mine with what I assumed was supposed to be reassurance. But I couldn't feel it. My skin was ice, my heart stone.

"Silvia," he said, voice warm, too warm. "You are a remarkable woman, and you will make a perfect queen for Etheria."

A hollow pang echoed through my chest. Was this it? Was I truly about to be bound to this man? To this lie?

Then, with maddening poise, Gerraint turned to the audience and spread his arms as if addressing a theater.

"But I cannot marry you."

His words cracked through the throne room like a thunderclap.

Gasps rippled across the chamber. The Cardinal took a stumbling step backward, his mouth agape. My mother rose to her feet with a furious rustle of velvet and lace, her eyes snapping between me and the prince.

My fingers stiffened in his grip, but Gerraint didn't release me. He held on, like a puppeteer milking the last note of his grand finale.

"I—" I whispered, not even sure what I was about to say.

He finally turned back to me, still grinning that maddening grin. "You look stunning, by the way. Unfortunately for me, I haven't been honest with you, or with anyone here."

"What are you talking about?" my mother demanded, her voice sharp and rising. She stepped out into the aisle like a serpent about to strike. "What game are you playing?"

Gerraint bowed, still holding my gaze. "My deepest apologies, Your Majesty. While your daughter is a dazzling choice for a bride, I can not continue this ruse. It's time the truth came out."

He straightened, then turned fully toward the crowd, his voice ringing clear across the vaulted ceilings.

"I am not the Crown Prince of Etheria."

The throne room erupted. A roar of confusion, accusations, and disbelief surged through the nobles, a cacophony of outrage and curiosity. Some stood, others remained frozen, caught between loyalty and shock.

My eyes darted to Sagar, who still stood behind us. Calm and unreadable, but alert. Watching.

My mother's face twisted into disbelief. "That's impossible! You're the King and Queen's son, are you not?"

"I am," Gerraint replied smoothly. "But I am not the heir."

She scoffed, rounding on me as if I should have known, as if this betrayal had somehow originated from my hands. "Then who is?"

A hush fell over the chamber as Sagar stepped forward. He bowed low before my mother, then turned to face the sea of nobles, his voice strong, steady.

"I apologize for the deception, Your Majesty. And to all those present. My name is Sagar Petris. I am the firstborn son of King Ronen of Etheria and rightful heir to the Etherian throne."

The silence that followed was maddening.

My breath caught. I looked at him as if I were seeing him for the first time again. The man who had once protected me from assassins in the dark, who had held me in the cold and kissed me like I was his last breath. The man who had lied.

The Queen's voice pierced the silence again. "What the hell is going on?!"

"I second that." I muttered.

Gerraint chuckled softly beside me. "Sagar just explained it to you. Though I understand it's a bit much to process. We do so love our dramatic timing."

Sagar stepped closer to me, his eyes never leaving mine. Slowly, deliberately, he reached for my hand.

His palm was warm. Steady. His heartbeat thundered beneath his skin.

"My mother," Sagar began, his voice quieter now, more personal, "was not of noble birth. She and my father loved each other long before court alliances were arranged. She raised me far from the palace. After her death, I was sent to live with the king. He kept his word to me and her."

He glanced briefly toward Gerraint, who nodded solemnly.

"The king vowed two things. First, that I would inherit the throne when the time came. And second..." His grip on my hand tightened slightly, his eyes burning into mine, unwavering. "That I would never be forced into a political marriage. That I would marry only for love."

Something caught in my throat, sharp and sudden. My lip trembled as I searched his face, unsure if I was dreaming or falling headfirst into something I couldn't escape.

"I didn't intend on finding it," Sagar continued, his voice softer now, raw with honesty. "But wouldn't you know it, I fell in love with the princess. Before I even knew who she was. Before she knew who I was. I had to be sure she felt the same."

He glanced over his shoulder. "My brother here stepped in to help with that—"

"And I played my part perfectly, if I do say so myself," Gerraint chimed in with a grin and an exaggerated bow. The bastard looked pleased with himself.

"This is ridiculous," my mother snapped, storming to the edge of the dais. Her voice cut like a whip. "The Etherian kingdom is making a mockery of us!"

"I understand your anger, Your Majesty," Sagar said, bowing slightly in her direction, "and I truly apologize for the deception. But this was never meant to insult you or your house. Today, I'm lucky enough to fulfill both my father's wishes and my own."

Sagar turned to me, reaching up to brush back the veil that clung to my face. His fingers were warm, trembling slightly from something deep within, hope.

"If you'll let me," he whispered.

"Sagar..." My voice cracked as I whispered his name, thick with disbelief. "Is this true?"

"No more lies. Remember?"

His smile bloomed, soft, vulnerable, real.

Standing in front of me was the man who had fallen in love with me. The one who had come to save me now, even if it was too late.

My knees wobbled, barely holding me up as my heart tried to wrench free from my chest.

"So," he murmured, "what do you say?"

Before I could answer, my mother lunged between us, grabbing my arm and yanking me back with enough force to send my balance teetering.

"No!" she barked. "She will not marry you. This union is built on lies!"

I pulled free from her grip, my voice rising in a roar that surprised even me. "You told me I had to marry the crown prince. Well, Sagar is the crown prince! So, unless you'd like to revise your orders, I suggest you sit down and enjoy the wedding you so desperately orchestrated."

The Cardinal, still pale, blinked at us. "So... the wedding is... back on?"

"No!" my mother shrieked.

"Yes!" Sagar and I shouted at the same time.

We turned to each other, equal parts shock and excitement bubbling between us. For the first time in what felt like an eternity, I smiled, and not the rehearsed kind.

Sagar reached up and gently cupped my cheek. His thumb brushed away a tear I hadn't realized had fallen.

"The 'I's have it!" Gerraint clapped, stepping forward with theatrical flair. He offered a sly grin to my mother as he gently guided her back toward her seat. "Let's all enjoy the second act, shall we?"

I turned back to Sagar, my fingers threading through his.

He squeezed once.

"I love you," he mouthed, no sound needed.

The Cardinal cleared his throat, attempting to salvage his place in the ceremony as his voice rose again above the quiet murmur of the room.

"Do you, His Highness, Prince Sagar of Etheria, take Princess Silvia of Calbraxia to be your lawfully wedded wife?"

Sagar beamed. "I do."

The words fell like sunlight through storm clouds. And then the silence stretched again, this time waiting for me.

"Do you, Princess Silvia, take Prince Sagar of Etheria to be your lawfully wedded husband?"

Every instinct in me tensed. My mind reeled, flashing with doubt, betrayal, heartbreak, and the shadow of the dagger still tucked inside my gown.

But then I looked at him.

And I realized if he was standing here, marrying me, then something had shifted in the heavens. Some cruel plan had failed. The tower would remain empty. I would never be locked away again.

I had my choice back.

I lifted my chin. My voice rang clear.

"I do."

B eside me, Sagar sat with his hands in his lap, the flickering lantern between us casting soft gold across his features. His presence was a steady heat, but not yet comforting. He was the closest thing I had to safety now, and that thought terrified me as much as it steadied me.

The grand reception my mother had planned had been cancelled of her own accord. I had said my quick, silent goodbyes before being whisked into the carriage with Sagar off to Etheria, off to our new life.

For a long while, neither of us spoke. We simply listened to the steady rhythm of hooves striking stone, the low murmur of the cold wind threading through the trees, and the soft rustle of the velvet curtains as they swayed with each bump of the carriage.

Eventually, I felt him glance my way.

I turned to meet his gaze, finding his expression shadowed in thought. Eyebrows knit, jaw clenched, as though he were debating something with himself.

"Don't worry, we have left behind soldiers to keep an eye on June. She won't even take a step without somebody knowing her location."

I felt a twinge of anger rise within me. "That wasn't my concern at the moment, but thanks... I guess."

His gaze didn't falter, even with another uncomfortable silence that stretched between us.

"What?" I asked, panic lacing my voice.

"You might get uncomfortable dressed like that," he said, voice cautious, eyes flicking toward the mass of silk and lace still pooled in my lap.

"Sorry," I muttered, tugging at the layered fabric self-consciously. "Is it taking up too much space?"

A corner of his mouth quirked. "That's not what I meant."

My fingers fidgeted with the hem of my veil. "Everything just happened so fast. Should I have changed?"

Sagar leaned forward, resting his chin in his palm, a playful gleam breaking through the solemnity of his face. "I could always fix that."

My eyes widened. "Don't you *dare!*" I hissed, swatting at his arm. "You promised not to ruin any more dresses, remember?"

He chuckled, eyes dancing with mischief. "A promise I've *mostly* kept."

I rolled my eyes, but a reluctant smile tugged at my lips. "You're impossible."

"Well," he said, leaning back and stretching his long legs out toward mine, "you can change into something more practical when we make it to the inn tonight."

I blinked. "The inn?"

Sagar nodded, casually brushing a speck of lint from his sleeve. "It's a two-day ride to Etheria. The horses need rest. We'll stop for the night halfway."

"Oh..." I turned back to the window, pressing a palm to the cool glass.

The thought of being alone with him at an inn, without an audience, without protocol, without anyone interrupting, sent a wave of anticipation fluttering through me. My pulse quickened. Firelight. Quiet. His hands. It should have been thrilling. Instead, it felt like teetering at the edge of something dangerous and uncertain.

I let out a breath, too long, too shaky, and before I could catch it, the fantasy tangled with memory and snapped back into something sharp.

Sagar shifted beside me, then placed a hand gently on my thigh. "Should we have *that* conversation now?"

I froze. My gaze dropped to where his hand rested and I swallowed the tight lump rising in my throat.

"I suppose so," I whispered. I inhaled deeply, forcing air into my lungs until they ached, hoping the words would stay buried. They didn't. "Sagar, I don't even know who you are!" I exhaled, the confession cracking on its way out.

His hand stilled. Slowly, he withdrew it. He looked at me then, fully, openly. Regret taking over his usual aura of flirtation and charm.

"I'm sorry," he said quietly, his voice stripped bare.

I laughed, a bitter sound that tasted like salt on my tongue. "Sorry? You married me without telling me. I woke up this morning expecting to marry Gerraint, then there you were. The prince. The *real* prince. And you had been, this whole time. I feel relieved, don't get me wrong, but I also feel like such a fool."

His hand reached for my face, hesitant. When I didn't pull away, his thumb brushed across my cheek, sending a shudder through my nerves.

"Silvia..." he murmured. "I would do anything to keep you safe. You have to understand—"

"What I *don't* understand," I snapped, louder than I meant to, my voice ricocheting off the narrow walls of the carriage, "is why you didn't just *tell* me. You had every opportunity. Every chance to be honest. Why wait until I was at the altar with your brother?"

"We knew that there was someone inside the palace behind your letters; we didn't know who we could trust, we couldn't risk *anyone* finding out. We had a plan, we just needed to get you out of there, get you somewhere safe. Then, I was going to tell you."

"That's not good enough." My words spat like poison. "You could trust *me*. You knew you could! I told you everything, and still you couldn't trust to tell me the biggest part of you? I don't believe it, not for a second."

He exhaled sharply and raked a hand through his sandy hair, the tension in his shoulders so tight I could see it in the way his fingers trembled. "Because," he whispered, almost to himself, "if I told you, then it would be real."

I blinked, stunned by the simplicity of the answer.

"Tell me now," I said, softer. "Please. I'll listen."

He turned, his profile shadowed in the moonlight slipping through the carriage window. For a moment, I thought he might shut down again. But he spoke slowly, carefully, like peeling back a wound.

"My father was the King of Etheria," he began. "And my mother... she was his childhood friend. He wanted to marry her. Loved her, even. But his father, the former king, would never allow it. She wasn't a noble. So the court arranged another match. Someone 'appropriate.'" He paused, eyes growing distant. "It didn't matter.

They were together anyway. She raised me in a quiet village outside the capital, away from court politics. I didn't even know who my father was until she was on her deathbed."

My heart tightened as I watched his face drop, the boy he had been flickering beneath the man he'd become.

"I was seven," he murmured. "Too young to understand, but old enough to know what it meant to lose the only person who ever made me feel safe."

I reached out, my fingers resting gently on his thigh. A quiet gesture. I didn't speak, there was nothing I could say that would undo the pain, but I needed him to know I was here.

"She made me promise to be brave before she passed," he continued. "And then I was sent to the capital. To him. The king welcomed me in secret. I was a bastard, sure, but he never treated me like one. He placed me with the royal guard and trained me. Groomed me. And he told me I'd be king. Someday."

"But the Queen never knew?" I asked.

"She knew I was his bastard," he said, voice low. "But her whole focus was on Gerraint. He was born frail. Sickly. She wrapped her entire life around him like a noose." His eyes met mine, guarded now. "She believed—well, everyone believed—that he would inherit. Until my father fell ill. Then he made it clear, in no uncertain terms, that I was his successor. He left letters. Witnesses. His seal. Everything. All he wanted was the future king to love Etheria as the people do."

I swallowed hard, trying to piece together the past with the present. "Sagar, I'm sorry. You didn't ask for this."

"No," he admitted. "I never wanted to be king. But when I met my father, I saw how much he loved Etheria. How much hope he had for me. And I couldn't walk away from that."

I nodded slowly. This wasn't the life he chose, either.

"And Gerraint?" I asked, the knot in my stomach twisting tighter. "Why did he go along with all of it? He accepted the proposal. He *flirted* with me."

Sagar's mouth curled into something between amusement and annoyance. "Because he enjoys playing games. Just because he's not a bad person doesn't mean he's not an asshole." He chuckled warmly. "He likes attention. Likes chaos. And he likes pushing people's buttons, especially mine. When you proposed, he was kind of testing me in a way by saying yes."

I sighed, scrubbing a hand over my face. "That explains so much."

"Don't worry," he said with a smirk. "You'll have plenty of time to get revenge."

Somehow, I didn't doubt that. But still, the bitterness lingered.

"You could have told me," I whispered again, this time quieter. There was no venom in it now, only a deep, raw sting. "I would have understood."

His smile faltered. "I wanted to. A dozen times, maybe more. After I saved you from the bandits. In the carriage. At the hot springs..." He let out a low breath. "Every time I got close, something stopped me. Or someone did. And when you told me about your past life..." He trailed off, his voice catching.

"What about it?" I asked, brows drawing together.

"I got scared," he admitted. "You said you were used by whoever the Etherian King was. That your power made you a weapon. And I started to wonder, what if that was *me* in that past life? What if *I* used you back then? What if this was just history repeating itself? What if I were doing the same thing now?"

The ache in his voice was palpable. Tangled in guilt. In fear.

"I needed to be sure," he said, eyes searching mine. "That I loved you, that I would never become the monster from your past life. And if I were the one responsible, that you could still love me now."

I should've been furious. Should've thrown every accusation I could muster at him. But instead, I leaned my head against his shoulder and let the silence settle over us like the snowfall. My eyes stung. My chest ached. But I felt steadier.

Sagar turned, just slightly, and pressed a kiss to the top of my head.

"Silvia," he murmured, his voice barely more than breath, "I will spend the rest of our lives apologizing for lying to you. But only if you give me that chance. Otherwise, I will get you home safe, and you can live apart from me. Marriage in name only."

His words struck something sharp and sudden in me, something deeper than fear. A bone-deep ache. The thought of leaving him, of walking away from the one person who had both broken and rebuilt me, sent a hollow chill through my entire being.

I clung to his chest, my fingers twisting into the fabric of his jacket like it might tether me to him, to this moment, to the fragile new hope beginning to bloom between us. I looked up at him, my eyes burning, the words catching in my throat.

"If you think for even one second that I won't love you with everything I have," I said, voice tight, "you are *highly* mistaken."

He gave me that smile. The one that reached his eyes. His hand rose to cradle my cheek, his thumb brushing lightly across my skin as if I might vanish if he didn't touch me gently.

The tension between us shifted then, no longer sharp, but magnetic. That same energy that had always pulled me to him, even when I tried to fight it. The warmth of his palm against mine was no longer enough. My heart thundered as our silence turned into something deeper, heavier, electric.

We were past words.

The moment our lips met, I melted.

The kiss was slow at first, deep and savoring. He kissed me like he had all the time in the world, as if he knew I wasn't going anywhere. His hands slipped around my waist, holding me to him, and I went willingly, sliding into his lap as if I'd always belonged there.

I sighed against his mouth, the noise escaping me before I could stop it. For the first time in this and my past life, I felt safe. Truly, completely, utterly safe.

"Sagar," I whispered, breath catching as his fingertips ghosted along the curve of my waist, sending a shiver through me. "Do you remember the first time we kissed?"

He pulled back just far enough to rest his forehead against mine, his breath warm against my lips. He chuckled, low, velvet, wicked. The sound curled down my spine and coiled somewhere deep in my belly. "How could I forget?" he murmured, voice rough with hunger. "That night in the carriage."

"We never got to finish what we started..." I whispered, lips brushing his.

This kiss wasn't soft. Nor shy. It was fire, it was fury, it was every suppressed want finally being unleashed. My lips crashed against his in a way that cracked open every place inside me I had once armored shut. There were no more questions. No more fear. Just him and me, in the dark belly of the night, with nothing left to hide behind.

He responded instantly, arms tightening around me like he couldn't bear another inch of space between us. His mouth moved over mine with a ferocity that was searing, worshipful, devastating. I felt him in every nerve, every pulse point. And I kissed him back just as fiercely. Because I was done running. Done doubting. Done pretending I didn't want him with every cell of my being. I had tasted what taking control of my life was like, and I wasn't going to stop any time soon.

I took his hands, sliding them up my waist, and slowly working their way above his head. I held them there—or maybe he just let me—with a single hand. I let my fingers tangle in his hair, threading through the soft waves and tugging gently, tilting his head just enough to deepen the kiss. He groaned into my mouth, a deep, raw sound that made my knees go soft and my breath stutter.

This was my husband.

The word echoed inside me like a prayer. *My husband.* The thought struck like lightning. Equal parts awe and heat, sending a rush through my blood, fluttering in my chest, then crashing low in a swirl of want.

I leaned down and kissed along his jaw, slow and tasting, savoring. His stubble scratched softly against my lips, and beneath it was the warmth of his skin, leather, pine, and something else entirely *his*. Something I'd already begun to crave.

I traced a path to his throat, teasing my tongue across the hollow just above his collar. He exhaled hard, his knuckles bleaching as I sucked gently at the place where his pulse pounded fast and steady. He tilted his head back, a moan escaping him, rough and desperate against my ear.

I released his hands. "Take off my dress." I commanded.

His hands moved without hesitation, finding the lacing of my corset, fingers brushing the taut ties. He tugged with an infuriating patience, loosening one at a time, each shift of fabric drawing a dangerous sound from my lips.

"See?" he murmured, lips brushing against my collarbone, his voice thick with teasing heat. "I'm being careful this time."

I arched into him as his mouth lingered just above the swell of my breasts, brushing silk and skin with featherlight reverence. Each kiss was a vow, every inch of me he touched was a new page of a story written just for us.

But then—*click.*

"Wait," I breathed, blinking out of the haze of heat, and reached down between us.

He stilled immediately, concern flaring in his eyes as I reached into the bodice of my gown. My fingers found warm steel. I drew the dagger out in a slow, practiced motion, the metal catching flickers of moonlight.

He blinked, then tilted his head and let out a stunned, amused breath. "Well," he said, "that's a fun party trick." His gaze flicked downward, then back to me, eyes gleaming. "What was *that* doing in there?"

I laughed, the sound unsteady, breathless. "Plan B."

I twirled the knife between my fingers as an idea bloomed in my mind. Something dark and wicked but thrilling enough to make my pulse quicken. And gods help me, I wanted it.

Sagar," I said softly, "do you trust me?"

"With my life," he replied without hesitation, though his gaze flicked to the dagger. A corner of his mouth curved. "Though I'd prefer to keep it intact for now."

I smiled and drew closer, unsheathing the blade. The lantern-light caught along its edge as I pressed it to his tunic, not cutting, just enough to make him inhale sharply. His breath stuttered beneath me. "My turn to ruin something of yours," I whispered.

I dragged the blade upward, slow and deliberate. Fabric gave way with a soft tear, parting beneath my hand. His shoulders tensed with anticipation and the sound seemed impossibly loud in the small, lantern-lit carriage. I felt his breath hitch, felt the way his body leaned instinctively into the threat of the steel, as if the danger itself was a promise.

The knife traced a languid path, never cutting skin, only skimming close enough to make the point unmistakable. Heat radiated from him, steady and alive, and I reveled in the way control shifted so easily between us. Every inch of revealed skin felt like a confession, like he was offering himself piece by piece without ever saying a word.

His gaze never left mine. It darkened, sharpened, the playful edge replaced by something deeper. Something hungrier. One hand curled into the seat beside him, knuckles whitening, while the other hovered uselessly at his side, resisting the urge to grab, to claim. I could feel the restraint in him, coiled tight, and it sent a shiver straight through me.

"You enjoy this," he murmured, voice low and rough, as if it scraped its way out of his chest.

"I enjoy *you*," I replied, letting the knife pause at his collarbone, the cool metal a stark contrast to what lie beneath it. "And the way you look when you're waiting."

His lips parted on a breath that sounded dangerously close to a groan. The lantern light caught the sharp line of his jaw, the rise and fall of his chest, the quiet desperation in his stillness. It was intoxicating—this moment stretched thin, trembling with everything we weren't yet doing.

He was beautiful. Strong, real, and mine. Not a fantasy, not a dream, but *mine*.

I shifted closer, flush against him now, and I felt it. I felt all of him, hard and wanting beneath me. Clearly, he liked this side of me. My hands braced against his shoulders, fingers digging into the firm line of muscle as my body arched instinctively against his.

I lifted the knife again, tilting my head. "I still seem to be fully dressed."

His hands moved with purpose now, gathering the heavy layers of my gown, pushing the silks and lace up and around my waist. The cool air kissed my thighs and made me shiver, but it was nothing compared to the shiver that followed as his fingers brushed bare skin.

I caught his hand when it moved again, stopping him with a playful lift of my brow. "Did I say you could touch me yet?"

A feral spark lit his eyes, but he obeyed. I slid back, bearing myself to him as my hand slowly crept down, making their way to the ache between my thighs. I traced the swollen flesh, letting myself cry out with relief as the satisfaction rushed through me with every flick of my fingers. The entire time, I refused to break eye contact.

He simply sat, hungry and waiting for me. I felt myself become slick with desire as I coated my fingers with my arousal. When I felt satisfied enough, I brought them to his lips.

"Would you like a taste of what you've done to me?" I asked.

He nodded.

I brought them forward, watching as he licked them slowly, deliberately, savoring every last drop of me.

"Gods," I breathed. "You *are* hungry for me."

"I love tasting you," he murmured. "You're so Addictive."

I wanted him, *gods*, I wanted him. I wanted him to feel how he made me feel. But even more than that, I wanted him to worship me. I wanted him to *beg* for me.

I tipped his chin up with the knife's hilt, smiling. "I'll let you touch me," I said. "If you ask properly."

"Please, princess." He whispered. "Can I touch you?"

I leaned in, my lips grazing his ear. "It's *Your Majesty* now."

That was all the permission he needed. In one smooth movement, he eased me onto my back, his frame poised above mine, like a storm about to break. His gaze burned into mine, dark, wild, utterly devoted.

He started exploring my skin with slow, searing kisses. When his mouth reached the curve of my neck, he nipped lightly, then soothed the sting with his tongue. I arched into him instinctively, my breath stuttering as his path continued down, across my collarbone, lower still.

His tongue flicked over a peaked nipple, teasing it with maddening slowness until I trembled. He circled, tasting, teasing, his free hand tracing down the center of my body with unbearable tenderness.

I reached between us, undoing the ties of his trousers, my fingers slipping beneath the fabric to free him. The sight of him made me wince in anticipation, and I took him in both hands, stroking gently, carefully, watching his head fall back with a low groan of approval.

I positioned him at my entrance, rubbing the thick head of his cock against me.

"Do you want me?" I asked, burning into his gaze.

He nodded.

"I want to hear you say it," I whispered, stroking slowly and tightening my grip.

"Silvia, I want you."

I released my grasp. "Then take me."

When he finally pushed forward, I cried out, the stretch sharp and perfect. He paused, breath ragged, his eyes locked to mine. For a heartbeat, we were suspended there, frozen in something truly holy.

Then, with a low grunt, he sank into me, inch by aching inch.

I reveled in it, overwhelmed by the sensation of being split open and made whole all at once. Another thrust and he was buried to the hilt, stretching me so deeply I could barely breathe. It was too much. It was *exactly* enough. I clawed at his back, wanting him impossibly closer.

He started moving at an agonizingly slow pace, his hand pressing down on my lower belly, forcing me to tighten around him with each lunge.

I loved every inch I took, every movement he made. I loved *him*, and that made this even better than the first time.

Before I could reach my peak, he flipped me over with practiced ease, pressing my front into the velvet seat, my body trembling beneath him. His hands gripped my hips, pulling me up, guiding himself back inside me.

I had thought it couldn't get any better. I was wrong.

I screamed, raw, instinctive, biting down on the pillow to keep from shattering. He filled me so completely I felt undone, each drive pounding through me with maddening precision.

His grip tightened, bruising in its desperation, his fingers digging into the soft flesh of my thighs as he pulled me back to meet him. The sound of our bodies meeting echoed through the carriage, filthy and divine. The slick heat between my thighs was relentless, a flood that drenched the bench and left me trembling.

"I'm never letting you go," he rasped, his voice like fire in my ear. His hand fisted in my hair, dragging my head back from the pillow. "You're my wife—my *queen*—and I'm never letting you go."

My moans spilled freely, rising with the crashing wave of my second climax. It stole the strength from my limbs and the breath from my lungs, but Sagar wasn't finished. He held me upright by my hair, still moving, still *claiming*, even as my body trembled and gave out beneath him.

It was too much. It was perfect.

He followed with a groan of my name, his body locking up as he spilled inside me, warmth spreading between us. His arms wrapped around me tightly, holding me as we both caught our breath, his lips pressed against my hair, my shoulder, my jaw, any part of me he could reach.

The silence that followed was thick with emotion, our bodies still tangled together in the afterglow. I glanced up, catching the blush that colored his ears, the faint smile that tugged at his lips.

He pulled out of me, the warmth of our shared climax slipping down my thighs as he shifted us, lifting me into his lap with gentle, practiced strength. His arms curled around me, cradling my head against his chest. The pounding of his heart echoed against my ear, steady and solid, like the beat of something ancient and ceremonial. I could feel it through his skin, through mine. The rhythm of a man who loved me. Who had chosen me.

"I never want to stop feeling like this," I whispered.

Sagar let out a lazy chuckle, pressing a kiss to my temple. "Enjoy that, my love," he mused, his voice thick with satisfaction. "We both have a lifetime to keep going."

I laughed softly, curling into his side. "Well, hopefully the next time we will actually get to enjoy a bed."

He brushed my hair behind my ear, cupping my cheek in his hand. "I promise, we will *only* enjoy the comfort of our bed from now on."

His words filled me with a warmth I hadn't expected. I felt the heat rush to my face. "Well," I muttered. "Maybe not *only*."

For a fleeting moment, I let myself believe the night might stay perfect. But, as if in answer to the thought, the carriage jolted violently to a halt.

Sagar's body tensed beneath me in an instant. Gone was the warmth, the languid ease of our shared bliss. He was alert, cautious. His hand moved to the floor, grabbing his discarded coat as his eyes flicked to the small window.

"What's wrong?" I asked, the air suddenly cold despite the lingering heat still trapped beneath my skin.

"We must've made it to the inn," he murmured, but something in his voice didn't sound convinced.

I pulled myself together, watching as he slipped his coat over his shoulders, not bothering with the buttons.

I caught his hand as he reached for the door. "Wait," I whispered. "Something's not right."

He paused, placing a quick kiss on my cheek. "Don't worry. Just stay in the carriage until I come to get you."

Before I could object, he pushed open the door and stepped into the night. The door clicked shut behind him.

Silence fell. Thick. Suspicious. Suffocating. I waited. First patiently. Then not.

The wind howled softly outside, brushing the side of the carriage like ghostly fingertips. I shifted, suddenly too aware of how exposed I still was. I tugged my dress back on, fumbling with the laces, fingers stiff with nerves. Seconds stretched. Then a full minute. Then another.

"Sagar?" I called out. No response.

The carriage, once warm and intimate, now felt like a prison.

With a curse under my breath, I grabbed my discarded knife and cracked open the door, stepping out of the carriage. The night air slapped my skin, sharp and bitter. Snow fell in delicate flurries, the lanterns from the carriage throwing long, flickering shadows across the ground.

But there was no inn. No buildings. No lights. Nothing but trees and snow and silence.

"Sagar!" I called again, louder this time, desperation creeping into my voice.

The crunch of snow beneath my feet was the only reply. I moved forward, scanning the darkness, and that's when I saw them.

Footprints. Several sets, all leading away from the carriage.

And then red.

A bloom of blood stained the white snow, stark and jarring. My breath caught.

"No," I whispered.

Just beyond the prints, something pale jutted from the ground like a broken branch. A hand.

I ran.

The closer I got, the more real the nightmare became. The driver. Face down, his limbs twisted at unnatural angles. Blood soaked through the snow beneath him, already beginning to freeze. I staggered back, bile rising in my throat. This wasn't a robbery. This wasn't bandits. This was targeted.

"Sagar!" I screamed, spinning wildly. My breath fogged the air in frantic clouds.

No response.

I turned and sprinted back to the carriage, slipping on the ice, my fingers numb as they grasped the handle. The world tilted sideways, panic crashing through my chest like waves. We had been separated from the convoy. There was no inn. No safety.

I would find my cloak, I told myself. Run. Find help. Disappear into the trees if I had to. And if Sagar came back, we'd find each other again. We had to. But then I froze.

The carriage door was shut. I had left it open.

My fingers hovered over the handle, heart thudding in my ears. I knew. In that moment, I knew. Still, I opened the door.

A hand slammed into my back, shoving me forward. Another caught my arms. I gasped, trying to twist away, trying to slice whatever I could with the knife, but I was off balance, too slow, too stunned.

Something rough and scratchy yanked down over my head, muffling my scream. Fabric closed around me. Darkness fell.

I thrashed, clawed, kicked, anything I was lifted, dragged. A voice hissed something I couldn't understand. I didn't recognize it. It wasn't Sagar.

No.

No. No. No.

I had just tasted freedom. Love. Victory. And just like my consciousness, it was already slipping through my fingers.

Perhaps my fate couldn't be escaped.

Chapter 30

W hen I awoke, it was with a scream caught in my throat, stifled by the thick, damp air and the crushing weight in my chest. My arms and ankles were bound with wiry rope that bit deep into my skin every time I so much as twitched.

Panic surged like a tidal wave, crashing into my ribs as I thrashed. The cold stone beneath me scraped my spine, and the sickly-sweet scent of mildew and stale snow clawed its way up my nose, clinging to everything.

I looked around the dimly lit room, being struck with familiarity. I knew this room; I had spent ten years alone in it, and it haunted me in every nightmare.

The tower.

The realization cracked through me like lightning. But this wasn't a dream, or a nightmare. This was real. I was back.

The rope burned my wrists raw as I fought it. My breath came in shallow gasps, tears slipping down my cheeks before I could command them not to. I'd been here before, helpless, scared, and alone. I swore I'd never come back.

But I was here. Again.

A scream finally tore loose, hoarse and raw. "Sagar!"

It echoed off the stone walls, unanswered. The silence that followed was heavy, suffocating. I coughed violently, my lungs spasming against the stagnant air. Each cough turned into a sob until I was heaving, crumpled in my now tattered and dirt-streaked wedding gown.

A sound cut through the stillness. Footsteps. Slow. Deliberate.

I stiffened, instinct dragging me upright as best it could. My body screamed in protest, muscles aching, blood sticky against my skin.

The door creaked open, and a figure stepped through.

"You're awake," a voice said, calm, smooth, maddeningly familiar.

I froze. *No. No, it can't be.*

The figure moved forward, her presence like a ghost sliding across marble. She stepped into the moonlight spilling through the narrow slit of a window high above, and her jeweled silhouette glittered like a serpent's smile.

My stomach turned to ice.

The Queen. My mother.

She looked regal as ever, as if she hadn't orchestrated my kidnapping or slammed me back into a nightmare I thought I'd escaped. Her dark gown shimmered with hints of violet and steel, and every inch of her radiated cold triumph.

"Where is he?" I choked out. "Where's Sagar?"

Her smile vanished. She dragged a wooden chair toward me with a screech, the sound of it on stone scraping into my bones.

"Don't worry," she said, her tone suddenly glacial. "When we find him, he'll be dealt with."

Relief bloomed in my chest like spring through snow. Sagar had gotten away. He wasn't caught.

I smiled with my teeth. "Sagar will come back for me. And when he does, he'll bring Etheria with him."

She smiled, too confidently. "Good, I hope he takes out half of our army on the way in. You can't have a revolution without spilling some blood."

My smile faded, shifting into fury. "When he does come, you'll have to pay for what you've done."

She arched a brow, unimpressed. "You foolish, deluded girl." She knelt beside me suddenly, fast and sharp. Her hand gripped my chin, nails digging into my skin like claws. "You always jump to conclusions, just like you did with the prince, just like you did with June..."

"You..." I hissed, breath ragged. "It was you this whole time, wasn't it?"

Her nails pressed harder, and I winced. "Of course it was me. Silvia, darling, did you really think the prince was the one pulling the strings this whole time? He's a man, not even a man, he's a boy. You think he has any real power? I thought I raised you to know better."

I curled tighter into myself, the rope biting into my skin, grounding me in pain. "Why?" I rasped, tears drying on my cheeks. "Why are you doing this to me?"

She tilted her head, that eternal beauty now an eerie mask of grief and madness. Her voice softened, not gentle, but fragile, like she was speaking through a cracked window into a memory.

"I'm sorry," she said, though there was no sorrow in her eyes. Only something older. Sadder. "Truthfully, you never should've gotten involved in such trivial matters. But you're the only one who could possibly be of use."

I bit my lip, tasted blood. Let her talk. Let her ramble. The more she spoke, the more time I had to think. To plan. To escape.

"This wasn't always the plan," she went on, almost wistful. "You were such a bright little girl... just like her."

"Her?" I asked carefully, confused.

"My twin," she said. "Eden. She was everything I wasn't. Lively. Effortless. Adored. Father's favorite. But she didn't have the eyes. I did."

I blinked. "You... had a sister?"

"She was beautiful," my mother said with a soft smile. "But useless, in our father's eyes. He needed a Divinial heir, and Eden wasn't it. So he devised a plan. He hid us from the world, dressed us alike, and presented us to both kingdoms as one girl. One daughter, rare and magical, perfect for sale." Her voice dripped with bitterness. "Two buyers. One girl. A lie he could profit from."

I stared at her, stunned.

"He made us choose," she said, eyes going glassy. "And of course, Eden got to pick first. She always got whatever she wanted. She chose the sweet, naïve prince. I got the aging king with no heir. Father said if I didn't take the offer, he'd sell me to the streets. I could take a thousand men instead of one. I was only twelve."

She looked at me, then really looked, and for a heartbeat, she wasn't a queen. She was a child. Broken. Abandoned. Terrified.

"I prayed the king would be kind," she said. "But the gods don't listen to girls like us. He took everything away from me. All I had left were my books, my lovers, and shortly after, I had you. My beautiful little doll. My Silvia. You were the only good thing to come from that horror."

For the briefest flicker of time, her eyes softened. But it passed. Her expression hardened again, something wild and cruel glittering just beneath the surface, sharp as shattered glass.

"I didn't want him near you, couldn't bear to think of what horrors would await you once you came of age. I couldn't imagine a world where you had to go through what I had." A longing smile crossed her lips. "Did you know he was allergic to roses," she added, almost absently. "*Deathly* allergic. So I planted them. A whole garden. My sanctuary. A place he couldn't touch me. A place where I could plan."

My stomach clenched, a knot of ice forming in my gut.

"It was so easy, slipping the rose petals in his tea. Part of me thought perhaps, he wanted to die."

"So, you murdered him?" I whispered, trembling.

"I saved you!" she snapped, eyes flaring. "Do you have any idea what would have happened if I hadn't? Fathers were put on this earth to disappoint their daughters, you would have ended up just like I had..." She sucked in a breath, as if re-centering herself. "But then I found out the awful truth. The King had been allowing the churches to tax the people to the point they had almost nothing left. We—our kingdom—was desolate. Our people practically starving in the streets. Sure, I was free, but being queen of the slums is worse than not being a queen at all."

I didn't answer. Couldn't. The heat of rage and the chill of revulsion warred in my chest.

"Then I found out I was pregnant with Margaret."

I froze.

"She was trouble from the very start," she murmured, her voice drifting. "I was sick for months. Weakened. Near death by the time I delivered her. I wasn't even sure if she was his, not until I saw her. That mouth. That hair."

Her hands curled into fists. "I thought I was going to die in childbirth. And in those moments, lying there, bleeding and broken, I realized I was going to die bearing the child of the man who violated me. The man I killed. It was as if he were laughing at me from beyond the grave."

I watched her closely, my heart beating like a war drum. She wasn't just unraveling, she was confessing. Like a sinner trying to claw her way out of damnation.

"I cursed the gods that night," she said, her voice low and venomous. "I told them I would burn the heavens down if they let me die like that."

Her eyes lost their focus, slipping into something otherworldly.

"And then someone answered."

My blood turned to ice.

"They came to me," she whispered. "Not Leticia, nor Brixbane. Something older. Stranger. It had no face. It told me I had a role to play, that it would give me the power to save our kingdom. All I had to do was accept my fate." She stepped forward, lowering her voice as if sharing a secret not meant for mortal ears. "When moonlight weeps upon the crimson tide, and the fawn stands where the stag has died, the eternal throne shall burn to dust, by fate's cruel hand, by broken trust..."

"How do you know the prophecy?" I demanded, my voice shaking despite myself.

She laughed, bitter and knowing. "My fate, as told to me by the god itself."

Her eyes glazed, unfocused, as if she were staring back through decades instead of at me. "I understood it immediately. The child. The fawn mirrored by the stag. The echo that would undo me." Her lips twisted. "After everything I endured, I refused to let fate have the last laugh. Not my father. Not my sister. Not the king. And certainly not Margaret. No, I needed to escape this fate, one way or another..."

Cold spread through my veins, sharp and absolute. The realization landed with sickening clarity.

She and I were the same.

"I simply passed the prophecy along to Etheria," she continued calmly, almost fondly. "I knew it would reach the prince eventually. I knew he would misinterpret it's meaning. All it takes is a whisper placed in the right ear. A spark in dry grass. You think kings and knights shape history?" She scoffed. "Please. It's always women in the shadows who decide when kingdoms fall."

I shook my head, horror dawning slowly in the marrow of my bones. "You manipulated everything. You made him come."

She smiled then. "The lack of response to the letters I had June forge told me all I needed to know. She's quite talented, isn't she? I never realized we housed such a skilled forger." Her eyes glittered. "She refused to continue after a while, of course. Morals are so inconvenient. So I adjusted. Encouraged things along. The bandits were... effective."

I surged against my restraints. "That was you? You sent them after me?" My voice broke. "I could have *died*!"

"Shhh." She knelt beside me, fingers brushing my hair with false tenderness. "Sweet Silvia. I was protecting you. Protecting everything you could become." Her voice softened, poisonous and intimate. "You truly think I would allow you to be handed over to that sickly creature my sister birthed all those years ago? Of course not. I was going to keep you safe. Hidden. Untouchable. I may be too late to kill her, but killing that wretch—taking away the thing she loved most—is enough for me."

The room seemed to tilt as the final pieces locked into place.

"Why?" I whispered. "Why do any of this? Was it revenge? On the king? On your father?"

She laughed again, hollow this time, as she rose. "No," she said quietly. "I did it because I want to see it all *burn*. Calbraxia. Etheria. The gods themselves." She turned her back to me. "I had enough reason to despise this kingdom long before your birth. And when my sister built her perfect little kingdom across from me? While I was left destitute with a future certain in ruin? That only gave my hatred direction."

She paused, turning away from me now. "The idea came to me, one day as I read through one of my books."

"Cyradil..." I breathed.

She spun, eyes flashing. "Yes. Though clearly I failed to destroy all records of her." Her smile was sharp. "The last great war nearly tore the world apart. Why not make it happen again? All I needed was something the people of Calbraxia could rally behind." Her gaze locked onto mine. "Or *someone*."

"Me," I said, the word tasting like ash.

Her expression softened. "Yes of course. Their beloved, sweet, innocent princess. Tragically kidnapped. Betrayed. Broken by the evil monster of a prince." She spread her hands. "How could the people not demand blood? All the while, I just had to feed you exactly what I wanted you to hear. I know how deep my hatred grew in isolation, and it only got worse with time. I would have made you hate them all. The Etherian court, the throne, even Sagar. Slowly. Sweetly. Like fruit left to rot. One rumor. One betrayal. One loss at a time." Her voice dropped to a whisper. "You would have emerged hollowed by grief and rage. A beautiful weapon ready to destroy with an army at your back, listening to every command."

I hated how true it all was. How neatly her words aligned with the memories of my first life, still humming now, restless and alive, like a nest of hornets under my skin. I had been exactly what she wanted then: hollowed out, sharpened by grief, wielded by devotion and rage.

Her plan had worked once. But things were different this time around.

I was different.

I let out a sharp, bitter laugh. "Do you honestly think I would let you do this to me? Now, after everything?"

"Now now," she cooed, stepping forward, brushing her fingers over my cheek as though I were a frightened child. "Sweetheart, you'll see it my way. Eventually."

Her touch burned.

I met her gaze, steel in my voice. "You really have no idea."

She blinked, the smile faltering.

"I'll never get those powers," I said. Calm. Cutting. "You're too late."

Something flickered behind her eyes. "What?"

"I'm not a virgin, Mother," I said, my voice laced with bitter triumph. "Haven't been for a while now. I chose Sagar. I chose *love*. You can keep me here, chain me, beat me. But you lost the moment I decided to live for myself."

Her face twisted first in confusion, then in fury.

"You foolish girl," she hissed, yanking her hand back as though burned. "You would throw everything away for him? For lust?"

"For freedom," I spat.

She turned from me, pacing the stone floor like a caged predator. Then she stilled, spine straightening.

"You think I've lost?" she said, her voice suddenly eerily calm. "You think denying me your powers changes anything?"

My gut clenched. "What are you talking about?"

She turned, that same cold smile on her lips, composed now, horrifyingly serene.

"When the beloved princess of Calbraxia is discovered dead, abandoned by her Etherian husband on her wedding night, how do you think the people will respond?"

My blood turned to ice. "You wouldn't."

She tilted her head. "Peace makes people weak, Silvia. A martyr inspires rage. And war—war brings unity. Once no word comes from you for a few weeks, a search party will be sent. They'll find your body in this tower, cold, violated, murdered. And the new king of Etheria will be nowhere to be found."

My mouth went dry. "You're planning to kill me."

"No," she said sweetly. "You're going to die, Silvia. Whether it's quietly in this room or found half-frozen in the mountains, it doesn't matter. The ending remains the same."

"So I stay here as your prisoner, or die and start a war," I said, barely able to believe the words coming from my mouth.

She beamed. "Exactly. And now that you've thrown away your only value to me, there's no choice left, darling."

I stared at her, the truth of it crashing over me like a tidal wave. I had never had a choice. Not in this life, not in the last. My first life ended in this tower. And now, it would again. Only this time, there would be no sainthood. No rebirth.

I felt the hot tears streak my cheeks, finally letting the reality crash inside me. She won, and I wouldn't be able to save Margaret, or June, or even Sagar.

"You have let this grudge haunt you for over twenty years; you'll destroy both kingdoms," I whispered. "Including yourself."

It was then that a deep rumbling knocked through the door, exploding through the room. Stone and splinters flew in every direction. A figure burst through the smoke, sword drawn, voice hoarse with rage. I could barely make out his typical chiseled features until his soft voice pierced the silence.

"Silvia!"

"Sagar!" I called.

His silhouette was bathed in firelight, eyes wild as he took in the scene. His face and neck were sopping with sweat and what I could only hope was other people's blood; however, the cuts I spotted peppering his arm told me otherwise. He hadn't waited for backup.

I had seen him like this once before, when he saved me from the bandits. His eyes glowing with fury, his jaw set in stone, his aura thick with something primal, something dangerous. His gaze shifted to my mother, who stood over me like a specter of death as I tugged furiously at the rope binding my wrists.

"Touch her," he snarled, his voice so low it was nearly inhuman. "And I swear to the gods I'll kill you."

The queen raised her chin, regaining her composure. "The gods won't help you here, your Majesty."

Without hesitation, Sagar swung his blade at me and the Queen. He fumbled; he was no swordsmith, but it was enough to get a rise from her. I watched the horror twist across her face as she leapt out of the blade's icy point, stumbling across the crooked stones. Her head connected with the chair, and her body slumped to the floor.

The sword connected with the wooden beam I was tied to, slicing the rope with a satisfying snap. I lifted my hands away from my back, my fingers finding their way to Sagar's face as I felt his warm cheeks begin to thaw my hands.

Both of our eyes flashed to my mother, but only for a brief moment, making sure she was, in fact, unconscious. Sagar pulled me close, wrapping his thick arms around me and cradling my head in his chest.

"At least it wasn't me who ruined your dress this time, right?" He laughed, relief warming his voice.

I pulled away, staring into his tear-streaked eyes. "I thought...I was worried you weren't coming to get me." I admitted, letting the lump in my throat rise. "I thought maybe you did have something to do with this."

Sagar furrowed his brows, brushing his thumb across my cheek. "Silvia, after everything?"

I wiped at the tears staining his cheeks, only to smudge a sick mixture of blood and dirt away. Guilt rattled me in a new way, but I knew I would have to be honest.

"I know it was silly, but you left me there."

"When I stepped out of the carriage, I found the coachman already incapacitated by some bandits. They asked if I was traveling alone, and I assured them I was. I let them gag me and take me to their hideout. We were almost in the clear, but they heard you calling for me. If you had stayed in the carriage even just a few minutes longer, you could have been safe."

I let my forehead press against his chest. His heartbeat strummed against me, loud and steady, somehow remaining calm amongst all of the chaos that we found ourselves in.

"I'm sorry," I whispered.

He lifted my chin, forcing our eyes to meet. "Silvia, I would let the world burn for you, but I would never be the one to strike the match."

There was something in his eyes. Fierce, unshakable, mine. The moment stretched, time slowing until I could feel the weight of every choice that had led us here.

I surged upward, closing the distance between us.

Our lips collided in a breathless, frenzied kiss. A kiss born not just of love, but of survival. Of two souls that had been tested, stretched, torn, and were still choosing each other in the end.

His hands wrapped around my waist, pulling me into him like he couldn't bear the space between us. I clung to him, my fingers tangling in his hair, holding on as though the world might fall away beneath our feet, and I wouldn't care as long as he was there to fall with me.

He kissed me like he had nothing left to lose and everything left to protect.

His mouth was warm, hungry, tasting of hope and fury and devotion. My body melted against him, the storm around us fading to nothing. For one single moment, there was no tower. No prophecy. No gods. Only us.

Only him.

Behind us, a raspy voice broke through the silence. "Well," my mother muttered from the floor, voice dripping venom, "isn't that sweet."

Sagar pulled away just enough to press his forehead to mine, breathless, a crooked grin twitching at his lips.

"Hold that thought," he murmured.

My mother managed to pull herself to her feet, a thick streak of crimson blood fell from her head like loose hair. She pressed her hand to it, pulling back and grimacing at the sight.

He turned, drawing his blade in a single fluid motion, and stepped in front of me.

Before she could respond, a surge of movement came from behind her. Guards who were not in royal Calbraxian nor Etherian armor, but in something darker, older, like they had crawled out from beneath the earth itself. Their faces were half-covered by cloth, but their eyes glinted with the kind of devotion that only came from blind loyalty. Or fear.

Sagar didn't hesitate.

With deadly precision, he struck the first through the throat. Blood sprayed across the stone floor in a sickening arc as the body dropped without a sound. Another guard lunged, blade gleaming, but Sagar turned with brutal grace, parrying the strike before slamming the hilt of his sword into the man's temple. A swift spin, a downward stab, steel met flesh, and the next one crumpled to the ground with a strangled gasp.

He moved like a creature possessed, like a storm given form. Love and rage surged through his limbs, driving each blow. His jaw was clenched, his eyes locked in that singular, feral focus that made him seem untouchable. Every movement was a promise. Every strike screamed she is mine to protect.

"Get him!" my mother commanded, her voice strained as the blood trickled down toward her collarbone. Her hand pressed weakly at the wound on her head.

Two more men surged forward, knives drawn, flanking Sagar with practiced efficiency.

Sagar ducked beneath one of the swings, catching the man's arm mid-strike and twisting it until bone snapped. The guard shrieked, his weapon clattering to the ground before Sagar finished him with a clean thrust to the chest. But the second one was fast, too fast, and managed to slash Sagar's shoulder.

I cried out as the blade cut through his coat, red blooming across the fabric. Sagar stumbled for half a second.

That was all the time the last guard needed.

He pounced like a jackal, knocking Sagar to the ground and raising his blade for the kill.

But I was already moving.

Before I knew it, my hands had found a jagged piece of stone from the broken wall behind me. I gripped it tight and drove it down into the attacker's back with everything I had. He screamed and twisted, trying to shake me off, but Sagar used the distraction to grab his sword from the ground and plunge it through the man's side.

The guard fell limp between us, blood pooling around him.

Silence returned, thick and stifling. Only the sound of Sagar's labored breathing and the crackle of distant torches remained.

I stood, shaken but steady, and stepped beside him. My voice, though trembling, carried all the weight of truth.

"Is that all?" I spat at my mother, pride radiating through me. "You have no power now,"

But she only smiled a wicked, bone-deep grin that chilled the blood in my veins.

"Oh, sweet girl," she purred, stepping forward. "Did you really think I had nothing this whole time?"

I helped Sagar to his feet as he shakily pointed his sword towards her. Her eyes shifted to him, but locked into mine.

"You see, our family holds a secret. While our people were being bought and sold as commodities, weapons, for centuries. One of us managed to find a loophole..."

"Cyradil..." I muttered.

"There's still a chance for you yet, my sweet Silvia." Her eyes shifted back to Sagar as she raised a single hand towards me. "The path to power doesn't lie in purity..." Her smile twisted further, crueler. "The true path to power is death."

Before either of us could react, her hands lit with green light, the same light that I had seen in my nightmares from my first life. This was the Goddess's blessing, the divinial powers that had once made me a great Saint, and also a weapon.

She thrust them forward, and from her palms, a streak of energy, sickly and vibrant, shot toward us like a bolt of lightning.

"No!" I screamed, closing my eyes and bracing myself for the light flying towards me.

But instead, I felt a warm pair of hands grip my shoulders, and soon I found myself tumbling to the ground. I smacked the stones with a sickening thud, twisting and turning over myself as I flew across the room.

When I finally stopped, I wearily opened my eyes, seeing Sagar standing where I was, a smile on his face, but pain stung in his eyes. He gasped, then crumpled to the floor.

"Sagar!" I scurried to him. His blood was warm, soaking through the fabric of his coat, staining my hands.

"No, no, no, no—" I pressed against the wound, desperate. "You can't leave me, not now!"

I moved my hand to his chest, shaking feverishly, hoping he would regain some movement.

"Sagar! You promised!" I yelled, ripping at the fabric as my eyes caught the true horrific sight.

Thick black soot marked a strange X shape over his heart as twisting vine-like singe marks stretched across the rest of his chest. His body remained stiff and cold. I tried squeezing his hand, only for it to fall back to his side, lifeless.

"Please... Stay."

But it was too late. He was gone.

I was surprised by the soft sound of my mother's footsteps as she approached me, placing her hand on my shoulder.

"Well, that was... unexpected." She muttered, prodding Sagar's body with her foot. "Maybe he did love you after all."

"Why—why did you do that?" I demanded as hot tears streaked my cheeks.

My mother stiffened. "It's the only way now. You need to see it, Silvia, see the true power you can accomplish. The gods have chosen this path for us!"

"Fuck the gods!" I yelled, swatting her hand away.

Something inside me cracked.

I stood, facing my mother, watching her face twist in horror at whatever expression I was radiating.

"I don't care if it takes me two, ten, or one hundred lifetimes. I will never serve the gods again!"

Heat surged through me. Something far more violent than the warmth of passion, or the ember glow of love. It radiated outward in white-hot waves, boiling in my veins, seizing every nerve until I thought my body might tear apart from the inside. This wasn't the power my mother had waited for. This wasn't divine. This was fury. This was mine.

"And I will never serve you," I spat, every syllable drenched in finality.

Her eyes narrowed. "Then die."

I planned to, I hoped she would end it, right then and there. If death was the only way to power, I would play right into her trap, and gain whatever I could to get Sagar back.

Her hand reeled back and then slammed into my chest with a force that cracked through bone and soul. I flew backward, crashing to the stone floor with a sickening thud. The air left my lungs in a single, broken gasp.

Then came the fire.

Twisting green flames erupted around me, engulfing everything. My skin blistered, my eyes felt as though they were boiling in my skull. I screamed, raw and unholy, the sound tearing through the tower like a death knell. Somewhere in the distant corners of my mind, I thought: This is what I get for forsaking the gods.

As my vision blurred and the pain peaked into something transcendent, the shadows lengthened. They peeled away from the walls, dancing across the chamber like they'd been waiting for me all along. And soon, there was nothing else. No flame. No tower. No mother.

Just me and the shadow.

Then a voice echoed, soft as winter wind through dead trees.

"Silvia."

It spoke like it knew me. As though it had spoken my name a thousand times before. Across hundreds of lifetimes. The tone was not cruel. It was not kind. It simply was.

"Come to me."

I turned, closing my eyes and embracing it. I felt myself sink into the numbness. Into the dark.

Then I was gone.

Chapter 31

I awoke to nothing. No walls. No ceiling. No light. No air. Just an endless, oppressive void pressing against my skin like wet velvet, soft and suffocating. My breath caught, but there was nothing to breathe. My voice stuck in my throat. And yet I wasn't dead.

I wasn't alive, either.

Then I heard it. A voice—no, *voices*—layered and spiraling, eerie and hollow, as though they came from a distance and from inside my skull at the same time. It was like hearing a thousand whispers echo through a cathedral of shadows, each one saying the same thing, but slightly out of sync. A chorus of secrets brushed against my mind.

"Hello, Silvia." The sound slid along my skin like lace dipped in ice. Gentle. Intrusive. Intimate. "I'm so excited to finally meet you."

The words weren't spoken. They arrived, like breath against my ear, like the softest fingers tracing the edge of my spine. I shivered from the sense that I was no longer alone. That I had never really been alone.

I clutched my chest, fingers pressing into the place where my mother's power had struck me. The memory of the pain still pulsed there, not physical now, but spiritual, a scar etched beneath my skin. My heart pounded beneath my palm, as if trying to escape the echo still lingering in the dark.

"Who are you?" I demanded, or maybe I just thought it. I wasn't sure anymore what was real in this place.

The void shifted. A ripple of smoke and shadow twisted into form before me. A body began to take shape, tall and ambiguous, skin like onyx dust and eyes swirling with galaxies.

"I'm sorry, does this form suit you?" the figure asked, its mouth unmoving.

The figure shimmered, then changed. Twisting and turning like a drop of ink in a water glass, until I watched in horror as my sister's face stared back at me.

"How about this one?" it asked. Its face wrinkled as it took in my horrified expression.

I watched as it twisted and morphed into various people from my life, all of whom stood before me. June's warm grin, Madame Levior's tired face, even Gerraint's sharp and pale features made a brief appearance, only each more uncanny than the last.

While the shape was an exact replica of the real thing, the eyes never changed. Two black circles so dark and endless, it struck a new fear inside of me. I was no longer watching the faces, only looking into the sinking pools.

"I know!" It called, dispersing one last time.

I stumbled back as it shifted and twisted until finally it settled into a shape that mirrored my own. My same face. My same mouth. But two black voids where the eyes should be.

"I guess that's better," I whispered. "Who are you?"

The creature smiled. My smile but wrong.

"I have been called many things," it said, "Death, Time, A God, a Demon, but you may call me Noire." The name settled over me like ash. "I am the beginning and the end. The space between breath. The bringer of life and death. I am everywhere and everything. And I have waited a very long time for you, Silvia."

My knees wobbled, and I sank to the nothingness below me, cradling my arms around myself. "So I'm—?"

"Dead?" They asked. "Not yet, you're awfully close though. Everyone passes through here when they teeter on the brink."

"What do you mean you've been waiting? What do you want from me?"

"It's not what I want, Silvia. It's what you already are." Noire sat beside me, mimicking the motion perfectly. "A saint and a sinner wrapped in one pretty package, one who serves the Gods and refuses them. You are a very intriguing person."

"A saint?" I coughed. "I'm far from a saint."

"I'm not talking about this life, my dear," the voice cooed, silk wrapping around iron. "I'm talking about your past."

I stood still, the words hanging in the air like a blade at my throat.

"How do you know about my first life?" I asked, my voice barely more than breath.

Noire laughed, the sound both musical and fractured, like a harp being played underwater. They let their strange, shifting form fall back as if admiring the unseen stars in the abyss above.

"I see everything here...when I want to." they said, stretching the word with delight. "I've been watching for centuries. Reaching out. Testing your kind. Looking for someone worthy, someone who might finally set me free. A few have managed to reach back... none succeeded."

My mind raced. "Mother..." I murmured.

Noire's head tilted, their swirling features knitting into something like confusion.

"Mother?" they echoed. "Ah... yes, I suppose that would make sense. Though she was awfully young. Quite the liar too."

"So it was you," I snapped, realization setting fire to my voice. "You gave her the prophecy."

Noire's grin twisted wider, inhuman, gleeful, unrepentant.

"She told me she was the great saint Silvia," they crooned. "She begged for a way to escape death. I gave her your prophecy, thinking she was you." They chuckled darkly. "A simple mistake. You mortals all blur together after a few centuries."

I froze, my stomach dropping.

"*My* prophecy?" I said slowly. "What do you mean by my prophecy?"

Noire sighed with mock regret, lifting a hand as if to bless me. "It was meant for you, child. Crafted by fate, shaped by your many lives. But I guess your mother intercepted it and well, what's done is done. Still," they smiled, "I intend to make it right. I promise."

That word hit me like a slap.

"Promise." I spat. "You made that same promise to my mother. What did you promise her?"

Noire's eyes, bottomless and shifting like smoke over mirrors, locked onto mine.

"The only thing I can ever offer," they whispered. "If you try to help me escape, I'll give you your powers. All of them. And if you succeed, so much more."

"Escape?" I echoed. "You're trapped here?"

Their expression soured, lips curling like something spoiled. "Unfortunately," they muttered, "yes. I've been locked here a long, long time. Too long."

I let myself fall back beside them, mimicking their posture, feigning ease as my mind whirled. "Why not ask the gods for help?"

At that, their face twisted, rage, sorrow, and contempt melting into one unholy mask. "Who do you think trapped me here?" they snarled. "You should understand, Silvia. *Family* will do that to you."

I turned my head toward them, my heart knocking painfully in my chest.

"Family?" I repeated.

Noire's voice dropped to something ancient, something tired. "Yes," they said. "You might call them my children."

My blood ran cold. "You're saying..." I hesitated. "The gods we worship, they're your children?"

Noire shrugged, gaze unfocused, distant. "I was the first. The original voice in the dark. I came to this world before it knew its own name. I was the cycle: life, death, rebirth, endlessly churning. The conductor of time. I took on forms: a shadow behind a candle flame, a question in a dream, the voices you hear when you're alone in the dark. I watched your kind bloom like petals in a field, then wither again. And I loved them." Their voice grew wistful, almost tender. "They entertained me. Their worship gave me shape. I used their faces to give myself life. But they died so quickly, flickering out before I could ever truly know them. So I made companions."

My pulse quickened. I already knew the names. "Leticia and Brixbane," I murmured.

"Yes," Noire's voice dipping low like a lullaby wrapped in ruin. "Two souls unlike any I had ever seen. Brilliant. Flawed. Hungry. One born from flame, the other from ice. They created factions in my name, shaped faith into war, and war into worship. And still, they were lonely. Just as I had been."

Their grin faded, something colder settling across their face. "So I gave them each a piece of my spark. Split the divine fire, hoping they would carry it with purpose. Hoping I would never have to walk this world alone again." A long pause fell between us, heavy with the weight of centuries. "But power," they murmured, "always divides."

Noire's gaze drifted to the dark expanse, their voice soft with longing. "I hoped they would seek answers. That perhaps, together, we could unravel the purpose behind the cycle: life, death, rebirth. But purpose proved... elusive. And temptation is far more immediate."

"They succumbed," I said quietly.

"They indulged," Noire corrected, tone turning bitter. "In lust. In envy. In pride. With each mortal lover they touched, with each child they bore or sired, the spark passed on, thinned, diluted. And thus, the Divinials—your kind—were born."

I blinked. "So, we were an accident?"

Noire laughed, the sound dry and razor-sharp. "Most humans are."

They turned to face the vastness again, and their eyes dimmed with something like regret. "But even accidents have consequences. Leticia and Brixbane adored their worship. They built temples of gold, let their names become legend. The mortals made them gods. And when I confronted them, when I said I would take back what I had given, they panicked. Turned on me."

Their fingers grazed mine, almost comforting. Almost. "They were human at heart," Noire said. "And humans love power. They cling to it. Breathe it. Kill for it. They told the world I was chaos incarnate, a threat to their 'divine order.' They turned your kind against me, and then trapped me here. Sealed me away like a forgotten myth."

My voice trembled. "And the gods? What happened to them?"

"They played their games," Noire said, eyes narrowing. "Two kingdoms formed, one for each of them. A divine game of thrones played with mortal pieces. The war between them shaped your histories, your myths. Leticia built Calbraxia in her image, order, purity, devotion. Brixbane shaped Etheria with passion, freedom, and fire. Their children carried on the madness, dividing the spark further and further."

A chill crawled up my spine.

"But time wore them down. The Divinials thinned. Mortals grew forgetful. And eventually, they grew bored." Noire leaned in, voice dropping to a whisper. "The last I saw of them, they retreated into the Godswood. Planning something new. Another experiment."

I swallowed, the words catching on something heavy in my throat. "But why me? Why am I here with you now?"

Noire smiled, and I hated how it warmed me.

"Because you, sweet Silvia, you called to me," they said. "When fate asked you to kneel, you spat in its face. You could've surrendered. You could have let this life pass you by like the last one. But instead, you chose to indulge it. To live. To love. To defy."

Their eyes darkened as they drew closer, their breath cold against my skin. "You broke every one of the Seven Heavenly Virtues. You let injustice guide your hand. Deceit rule your tongue. Lust claim your heart. Gluttony, dependency, immodesty, greed, you danced with them all. And then, you vowed to destroy the gods. To burn it all down."

They pulled back slightly, their gaze cutting through me. "So now, as you float between life and death, I ask you this..." They extended a hand, long fingers wrapped in starlight and shadow. "Would you do it again?"

I was caught off guard. "W-what?"

"You heard me," Noire said, voice soft and dangerous. "Would you live it all again if I sent you back?"

I staggered to my feet, every nerve screaming. "You—you can send me back?"

They grinned. "Who do you think sent you back the first time?"

"No," I said, shaking my head. "No, that was Leticia! She showed me—she told me..."

"No," Noire snapped, rising in a sweep of shadows. "Leticia is powerful, but she cannot undo death. She plays with fate, bends it. I break it. I tore you from the cycle. I ripped your soul from the void and forced it back into your broken body." Their grin widened. "And now... You must choose."

My mind was spiraling. The truth pressed down on me like a falling sky. It hadn't been Leticia who saved me. Not some merciful goddess of light who had just been ill-willed with her intentions. It had been this—this being. This twisted god of gods. This shadow in the shape of salvation.

Every pain I'd suffered, every choice I thought was mine, how much of it had been mine at all? The fury bubbled up, hot and sharp. But then another thought broke through the noise.

If Noire had the power to rip me from death, to bend time and fate, then maybe...

"Sagar," I whispered. "My soul—" I choked on the words. "It's like I've lost half of it. There is no life for me without him. I don't want to return to a world where he's not in it. So yes. I would do it again, but only if I have the chance to save him."

They said nothing for a moment. Just watched me, their gaze dark and bottomless. I felt myself being weighed, measured.

"You would give anything for him?" Noire asked softly, honestly.

I paused. The weight of the question settled deep in my bones. I understood what they meant. I knew this was not a question of metaphor, but of cost. Of sacrifice.

I inhaled slowly, feeling the fracture in my soul widen and solidify. "Yes," I whispered. "Whatever it takes."

Noire's lips curved into something between a smile and a sigh. "I can give you power; you can save him. But I need you to understand, Silvia, it's not as simple as snapping my fingers and bringing him back. Your fate, his fate, were sealed long before your first breath. You've tried to defy it more times than you know."

My pulse quickened. "Then help me succeed. Just this once."

They moved closer, their voice a low murmur in the hollow between us. "I will. But first, I need something from you."

I swallowed, heart thudding hard enough to shake me. "What is it?"

Noire's lips curled, but it wasn't cruel; it was tired. "I want to find Leticia and Brixbane. I want to end the madness they left behind in your world. The false gods have played their game long enough."

I tensed. There was more. Always more.

"To do this," they continued, "I will need a vessel."

A chill licked down my spine. I took a slow step back. "What do you mean... vessel?"

"You are Divinial, Silvia. Your soul is not like most. It holds a piece of me. It's like a door," Noire said gently, almost reverently. "You have the power to let me through, there's a chance, just a chance, that I can escape this prison for good."

"What happens when you escape?" I asked, barely able to get the words past my tongue.

Noire hesitated. It was the first time I'd seen them falter. "I'll stay in that vessel, using it to track down Leticia and Brixbane, and ending this with my own hands."

My mind reeled. There was a reason they weren't telling me more; their vague language made the hair on the back of my neck stand up. "Who is the vessel?"

Their face cracked, just for a moment. "I can't tell you, I have a feeling you won't like the answer."

"Why not?"

"You just have to trust me on this..." They whispered.

"It's me, isn't it? I'm the vessel. You want to possess me."

Noire paused for a brief moment, contemplating their answer. "I'm not your enemy, Silvia," They said softly. "But I must return. With your help, or not at all. I have no connection to anyone else in your universe. Not even the faintest tether. You are the only one left who can help me."

They reached for my hands and took them in theirs, cool and dry, but trembling with something fragile. Desperation. "I have watched you for lifetimes," Noire whispered. "And you—you are the only one who still has the will to fight fate."

I closed my eyes.

Sagar's face rose in the dark behind my eyelids. His warmth, his fierce loyalty. The way he whispered "I love you" like a vow carved into the stars. I saw him as he had been, lying still and broken on the stone of the tower floor. I felt that ache all over again, the shattering of my world. If there was even the smallest chance to save him, I would take it. I knew he would do the same for me, without hesitation.

"I'll do it," I said, voice steady despite the quake in my bones. "Take me. Use me. Just let me bring him back."

Noire's expression changed, less glee, more awe. Their eyes shimmered like mirrors catching firelight.

The room began to tremble.

"Silvia," Noire whispered, stepping forward, reverent. "You have done it once. You shall do it again."

They leaned forward, pressing their forehead toward mine. I felt their breath against my skin, cold, ancient, electric.

The room folded inward. Darkness pressed in, like being wrapped in every night sky I had ever seen. My body tensed, then softened, the world slipping away in streaks of violet and gold. I knew this would change everything. I had no idea what would come next, how long I'd have, whether I'd survive it, but it didn't matter.

I would break the chains of fate. For me. For him. For all of us.

"Let us begin."

And just before their lips touched my forehead, the world split.

White light exploded behind my eyes. It was a blaze, a wildfire ripping through my flesh and bone, turning me inside out. I screamed, but it wasn't pain. It was transformation.

Heat poured through me, filled me, lit my veins with divine fire. I was burning, reborn, rewritten. And as the darkness faded, as the stars themselves seemed to pulse within me, I heard Noire's voice echo through the new silence in my mind, this time warmer, familiar, like an old melody finally remembered.

"Oh... how I've waited for you..."

As I opened my eyes, the world rushed back like a scream underwater.

I let out a cough, hoarse and ragged as I sucked in the air, begging for it to relieve my burning lungs. It bit as I gasped, dragging in each breath like it might be my last. My chest burned, the scar tissue tight and raw beneath trembling fingers. I pressed my palm against the raised ridges, feeling the evidence of what had happened, what I had survived.

Noire was gone. The shadowy warmth of their voice, once wrapped around me like gossamer, now felt like a memory burned to ash. There was no darkness now, only the dull gray light of dawn leaking through a high window, casting everything in a sickly pallor.

"Did it work?" I whispered, voice sandy and dry.

Then I turned, and my world shattered again. Sagar lay beside me. Still, eyes open. Unseeing.

"No," I choked. I crawled to him, ignoring the ache in my limbs. "No, no, no. Please—"

I clutched his hand. It was already cold.

"You're back," came a voice, smooth and sharp as a knife. My mother stepped from the shadows like she belonged to them, every inch regal, even in the dim. "I almost thought you had given up for a minute there."

"He's—he's still dead," I choked, leaning over Sagar's body, my forehead pressed to his. "They were supposed to save him. That was the deal."

"Yes, well," she said, with a flick of her hand, "the gods like to lie, don't they?"

I looked up at her, a strangled sob catching in my throat. She wasn't triumphant. She wasn't mocking. She looked tired.

"I was promised a new life too, once," she said, her voice quieter now. "A prosperous kingdom, my revenge exacted. But instead, I woke up to a child I could never love. A life I didn't choose. And powers I had to hide like a disease."

Her words slithered under my skin. My grief was a storm, but something colder crept in alongside it. Rage.

"But I was already sent back once," I said slowly. "That can't be all this was. There must be more to it. There has to be a reason."

"Life is cruel and unfair, Silvia," she said, stepping closer. "If you're searching for purpose, let me give you one."

She knelt beside me, brushing hair from my face like I was still her little girl. Her hand was soft. Her touch was warm. "Help me," she whispered. "Fulfill the prophecy. *My* prophecy. Together we can destroy Calbraxia, destroy Etheria, destroy everyone who ever tried to control us."

I stared at the tear stains on Sagar's red coat. The silence between us was thicker than stone, pressing in on all sides. "The eternal throne shall burn to dust..." I looked up at her. "By fate's cruel hand. By broken trust."

Her face paled.

"This wasn't *your* prophecy," I said, voice growing stronger. "It was mine. You stole it. You tried to rewrite fate in your image, but it wasn't meant for you."

Emotion crashed over me. Sagar's stillness. My mother's lies. Noire's riddles. My own hands, once wrinkled with age in a different life, now trembling with power and guilt.

"I know what will happen if it comes true. I know what I will become," I said, balling my hands into fists. "These hands will bring kingdoms to ruin. These hands that were supposed to save them."

I stood, pulling myself together and straightening my spine despite my screaming joints. "It's not your purpose I need. I have a purpose. Destroy everyone who tries to control us, you say?" My eyes flashed with something new, something wicked. "I believe that would include you."

She was shaking now, whether with rage or grief, I couldn't tell. Her hands clenched at her sides, trembling.

"I sacrificed everything for you," she hissed. "I carried you in a body ruined by a man I hated. I gave you a crown, my blood. And this is how you repay me?"

"I never asked for any of it!" I snapped, steadier now. "I never wanted the throne, the power, the prophecy. All I ever wanted was freedom!"

"Freedom?" Her laugh was shrill, unhinged. "There is no freedom for women like us. Only survival. Only control."

"I'm not your tool. I'm not your weapon," I said coldly. "I'm not *you*."

Something snapped.

She stayed silent for a while, too long. It filled the room with an uncomfortable air until she finally let out a featherlight whisper. "If you won't be my weapon..."

She screamed, a sound raw and guttural, her composure shattering like glass. Her hand lifted, glowing with a sick green fire, and in the same breath she hurled it toward me.

I dove to the side, the blast of energy tearing through stone and splintering the wall behind me.

The look in her eyes was madness, betrayal, heartbreak, rage, twisting into something monstrous. Her skin shimmered with magic, and shadows began to rise around her like a storm.

"You're not leaving this tower alive," she snarled, voice laced with venom. "If I can't use you, I'll bury you here with your dead king!"

I took a trembling step back, hands still raised in front of me. "Mother, you don't have to do this," I pleaded, my voice cracking with emotion. "You don't have to become the villain in your own story. You can still turn back."

"Villain?" she hissed, eyes glowing brighter with every syllable. "I want this, Silvia. I've prayed for this. For Etheria to burn. For every arrogant, bloated noble to choke on their last breath. No one, and I mean *no* one will take this from me now."

"You think this is revenge, but it's suicide," I snapped, louder now, firmer. "You won't just destroy the kingdoms, you'll bring everything down with you. Margaret. The people. Even yourself. Everyone will die."

A manic, guttural laugh tore from her throat. Her head rolled back as if the idea delighted her. Her laughter bounced off the cold stone walls like the screech of a crow.

"My sweet, naïve daughter," she crooned, stepping toward me with that same twisted grin. "You still think love can stop your fate. You still think you can save me."

I glanced down. Sagar's blood had dried against his skin, his lifeless face like a dagger to my heart. Rage coiled in my chest. If I were going to burn in this place, I'd make sure she burned with me. For him, I would strike the match.

Her head tilted, as if she heard the thought. That eerie green light flared across her body, pulsating from her fingertips, veins glowing like molten cracks in the earth.

"Tell your husband I say hello," she sneered, and with a flick of her hand, the room exploded into light.

A storm of sickly green energy ripped toward me, thick as smoke and sharp as glass. I threw myself sideways, skidding across the floor as the blast shattered the stone wall behind me. Pebbles and ash rained down in my hair.

"Please—" I gasped, raising my hands instinctively.

She laughed. "Oh, Silvia. I've had a decade to master my gift. You haven't even used yours!"

She was right. I hadn't trained. I hadn't honed. I had no idea what I was doing.

Not in this life, but in your last...

The realization struck me like a bolt of lightning. This was why Noire sent me back. This was why I had suffered through a life I couldn't escape. My mother thought I was still the girl she had raised, the girl who obeyed, who cowered.

She didn't know I had lived another lifetime. She didn't know what I had done. She may have had time, but I had a *lifetime* of practice to hone my skills. She didn't know what burned inside me now. I stood, hands trembling with something deeper than fear. Something older. I closed my eyes, took a breath, and whispered the name that now echoed through my blood.

The air shifted. It bent to me. A violet shimmer rippled across my skin like fire and water all at once. The shadows in the corners of the tower twitched, then surged. They poured from beneath my feet, coiling up my arms like smoke made solid. My fingertips crackled with darkness. The green magic hurtling toward me collapsed, consumed in an instant by the swirling void that hungered for more.

My eyes snapped open. I felt it. The pulse of the ancient power. Not that of the goddess. Mine. A force older than bloodlines, older than kingdoms. It wasn't gifted, it was claimed. A magic born of sacrifice, pain, fury, and choice. A magic that remembered every betrayal, every lifetime.

My mother staggered, her eyes wide and unseeing. Her lips parted in a silent breath, one trembling hand lowering as if she were touching something sacred or profane.

"That's not Divinial magic," she stammered. Her voice had lost its iron.

Then she turned and ran.

Coward.

But I was faster. I didn't even raise my arms this time, just thought, and the shadows obeyed. They surged past her like a rising tide of night, slamming into the archway with a bone-deep thud. Inky tendrils exploded outward, threading into the stone and sealing the exit in a living wall of darkness, jagged and snarling.

"No," I said, my voice low and shaking, but no longer with fear. "We're not done."

She whirled back toward me, desperation overtaking rage. Her hands slapped against the void where the door had been, nothing but darkness now. Endless, impenetrable.

"What *are* you?" she whispered.

I took a step forward. The floor groaned underfoot like it feared me. The very tower trembled not from her anymore, this time it was from me.

"I'm what you made me," I said. "Your daughter. Your weapon. Your sacrifice."

She raised her hand again. It trembled, but the spark was still there. A thread of green flickered in her palm. She wasn't giving up. She never would.

But still I tried. "If you surrender now," I said, softer this time. "I can end this. I can make sure you live. The Etherian guard won't touch you. You'll have a cell, a name, a future. You don't have to die."

She stared at me like I'd just asked her to bleed willingly.

"I've spent my whole life as a prisoner," she spat. "I'm not spending my life in a cage."

And then she screamed. Magic erupted from her palms like wildfire trapped in a hurricane. It shattered stone, tore through the air like thunderclaps made solid. The tower wailed in protest.

I didn't move. I answered. Violet and black magic bled from me like a tempest unleashed. The air cracked as the two powers met, collided, and howled. Light burst between us, twisting and writhing, shaking the very bones of the tower.

We were no longer mother and daughter. We were gods. Or monsters. Or both.

She screamed again, pouring everything into the spell. Her hands trembled as her magic frayed at the edges, unraveling like silk caught in fire. The green light flickered.

I stepped forward. My shadows answered the call, ripping from the floor, the walls, even the corners of her power. A wave of darkness shot from my hand, striking her shoulder with a sickening crack. Her body crashed into the far wall, dust and stone raining around her.

She stood. Somehow. Barely. Her hair clung to her face, wild and tangled. Blood dripped from her lip. She looked like a ghost, familiar, but wrong. Like a memory that had lived too long in the dark.

Still, she fought. Her hands lit up again, wild and erratic. She fired one blast. Two. A third.

I raised a single hand, catching them in my palm. They fizzled out like sparks in a thunderstorm, consumed by the void now living in me.

She roared. Again. Again. Again. Her fury boiled into desperation. Her magic was flailing now, wild and unfocused. Her hands shook. Her knees buckled.

And then, she stopped. Silence rang through the tower like a bell. Her shoulders dropped. Her hands fell to her sides. Her chest rose and fell with ragged, human breaths. And when she looked at me, truly looked at me, and I saw her. Not the Queen. Not my Mother. Just her. Just a girl who never had a chance in life.

Her voice was a threadbare whisper. "Silvia..." she gasped. "My sweet Silvia, you don't have to do this. We could run away. Just you and me, somewhere quiet. We could start over."

The words struck something deep within me, something raw, trembling, half-buried beneath the wreckage of every lie I had once mistaken for love. My magic faltered. The shadows, once snarling and alive, hesitated, then slowly withdrew into my skin like frightened animals.

"Just you and me?" I breathed, my voice paper-thin. "What about Margaret?"

Her smile faltered. She blinked, once. Twice. Then the sneer returned.

"Her?" she spat. The word dripped with venom. "That little parasite was never meant to be part of the plan."

That was it. The spell broke. Not just the one in the air, but the last fragile thread that had tethered me to any illusion of who she once was, or who I had hoped she could become.

She wasn't just broken. She chose to be cruel.

"You never loved her," I said, disgust curling in my throat.

She watched my face change, saw the certainty settle in, and with a tired sigh, she dropped the act.

"I see," she murmured. "Then let's end this, shall we?"

She twisted, flinging her arm out. Light screamed through the air. I wasn't fast enough.

One bolt struck me directly in the shin, searing through flesh and nerve. I hit the stone with a cry, agony ripping up my leg as I clutched it, watching the burn pulse with an unnatural, shimmering green before it faded to black.

Pain bloomed, and with it, fury. I gritted my teeth, rising with trembling limbs, dragging air into my lungs like it was fire itself.

"You wanted a weapon?" I roared, voice thick with wrath. "Then watch what you've built."

The shadows exploded from me like a tide breaking free from a dam. I hurled everything, every heartbeat, every scar, every life, into the spell and unleashed it.

The blast struck her squarely. She flew across the room, her body a ragdoll against the far wall. The crunch echoed like thunder. She collapsed in a heap, magic flickering around her like dying embers caught in a windstorm.

Silence.

I stood, chest heaving, legs shaking beneath the weight of everything I had become. Her fingers twitched. I watched, frozen, as she tried to lift her head. Blood poured from the corner of her mouth, staining her teeth red. Her limbs trembled with the effort to move, and for a long, breathless moment, she said nothing. Just the soft rasp of her breath.

I stepped forward. Then fell to my knees beside her. She looked up at me, her eyes hazy, the rage gone. What remained was tired. Broken. Human.

Her mouth moved, barely forming words. "It's funny…" she whispered. "All this time I thought Margaret… She was the fawn… The thing that would bring me to ruin." She sucked in a deep breath. "But it was… you."

Her eyes fluttered. I reached for her hand, squeezing her cold fingers between mine. She had never felt this fragile. Never seemed so small.

My voice cracked. "Mother—"

But the breath caught in her throat. And then nothing. Her head tilted back. Her eyes stared past me, unseeing. Her hand slipped from mine like water through trembling fingers.

Queen Elanore, the architect of my torment. The ghost behind every whispered command. The mother who had birthed me into duty instead of love was gone.

I sat frozen. Wind howled through a crack in the tower wall, stirring the silence like a funeral hymn. My breath stilled, my magic crackling softly beneath my skin, now dim, now dying.

I didn't know what I was supposed to feel. Victory? Justice? All I felt was grief.

I cradled her in my arms for one last moment, brushing a strand of bloodied hair from her face. Her skin was already cooling.

"I'm sorry," I whispered, choking back the flood rising in my throat. "I really tried to be the daughter you needed."

A sob ripped from me, jagged and raw. I didn't know if I cried for her or for the little girl I used to be. The child who had once clung to every rare smile, who had begged to be seen, to be held, to be loved, and had only ever been weaponized. But I couldn't stay there.

I forced myself to move, dragging trembling limbs away from my mother's still body. My feet slipped on shattered stone and scorched marble as I scrambled to the other side of the room. To him.

Sagar lay where he'd fallen. Unmoving. Too still. The sight knocked the breath from my lungs.

In my last life, my healing had been meager at best. I couldn't bring someone back from the brink. Not really. Let alone bring someone back from the dead. But this time was different. This power wasn't just mine; it was older, deeper. It bled with Noire's promise. With sacrifice.

"Wake up," I begged, voice shaking. "Please, just wake up. It's my turn to save you."

I pushed everything I had into him: grief, desperation, hope. The magic poured from me in waves of violet light, wrapping around him like a cloak. I didn't even know what I was doing, only that I had to try. My body ached with it, my soul stretched thin from holding so many lifetimes.

Please, let this work. Let me have this one thing.

The power surged. Then stillness. I held my breath as I waited for something, *anything*. A sign, a whisper, a breath.

A groan broke the long silence. It was A low, rasping sound that barely escaped his chest. His body twitched. My heart stopped.

His brow furrowed. He inhaled sharply, chest rising with a gasp like the first breath after drowning. His eyes fluttered open.

"Sagar?" I breathed, disbelief threading through my voice.

He blinked slowly. "...Silvia?"

A broken sound escaped me, half-sob, half-laugh, all relief. Tears blurred my vision as I gripped him tighter, as if I could anchor him to this world with the force of my love alone.

"You're okay?" I whispered, barely able to believe it.

He sat up, slowly, cautiously, wincing with each movement. "I... think so?" His voice was hoarse. "Last thing I remember, I saw your mother raise her hand, and I—"

"I know," I interrupted, my throat tightening. "You pushed me out of the way."

I threw my arms around him, burying my face in the crook of his neck. He was warm again. He was breathing.

"You're okay," I murmured, my voice cracking. "You're really here."

His arms wrapped around me a moment later, strong, solid, trembling.

"I'm here," he whispered. "Gods, Silvia. I-I thought I'd lost you."

"No," I said, pulling back just enough to look him in the eyes, to really see him alive, breathing, warm beneath my hands. "Not this time."

He pulled me closer, burying his face in my hair. "I told you I'd protect you."

"And yet here I am protecting you," I replied, a breathless laugh slipping through my tears.

But the moment's sweetness soured in my chest. Because now the weight of what I'd done pressed against me, cold and unrelenting. I was the vessel. The gate. A ticking hourglass dressed in flesh. I still felt like me, but for how long? Was this some twisted mercy Noire had granted me, to let me feel whole before I lost everything?

I pulled away gently. Sagar's brows knit in concern, his hand brushing a loose strand from my cheek. His eyes searched mine, already sensing the truth I hadn't yet spoken.

"What's wrong?" he asked, fingers tightening around mine as if he feared I might slip away.

I looked back, just once, at the broken body of my mother. Then I returned to him and spoke the words like a confession.

"Sagar..." My voice shook. "To save you, to save us, I had to make a deal."

His eyes didn't blink. "What did you do?"

"I had to promise myself away," I whispered. "I-I sold my soul. In a sense, I gave my body to a god. I'm their vessel now. When the time comes, I won't be *me* anymore."

He stilled, his breath catching. I felt the sob trapped in his throat. Or maybe it was fury. Or grief. His body shook faintly beneath my hands, but still, he didn't let go.

"I understand," I began, my voice breaking, "if that's not a risk you want to take. If you can't—"

"Enough!" he said, sudden and firm, cupping my face between both hands. "Silvia, don't ever say that. I don't care if we have one day, one month, or a hundred years. I don't care what fate has planned for us. You are the only thing I will ever choose."

My eyes burned with new tears, and he leaned in closer, resting his forehead against mine.

"Any moment I get with you is a gift," he murmured. "I will spend *every* second of it loving you, fighting for you. And when the time comes, if you're taken from me, I will tear through realms to find you. I'll drag you back with my bare hands if I have to."

He kissed me. Not desperate. Not frenzied. It was slow. Steady. Solid. A promise. A lifeline. His heartbeat thundered against my palm. His lips were warm against mine, no longer still. No longer cold. Alive.

When we broke apart, he rested a hand over mine, guiding it to the center of his chest.

"I love you," he said softly, fiercely.

"I love you too," I whispered, the words raw with meaning. "More than anything."

He tucked a strand of my hair behind my ear and smiled, though his eyes still shimmered with worry. "Then believe me when I say I won't let anything take you from me. Not even a god."

I smiled, tears slipping silently down my cheek as I rested my head against his shoulder.

Outside the shattered window, the first rays of morning spilled across the tower. The sky burned with lavender and gold, the world reborn in the hush of aftermath.

We sat there in the wreckage, the silence not empty but full of meaning. Full of promises and ache and the stubborn, desperate hope that maybe, just maybe, we had earned this peace, if only for a little while. The future was still a storm. The gods still stirred in shadow. But in this moment, beneath the sun's warm kiss, we were just two souls who had endured.

And that, somehow, felt like the beginning of everything.

Epilogue

The pain came in waves, sharp, all-consuming, and yet somehow comforting. Anchoring me to the present as the past reeled through my mind like a storm I'd only just stepped out of.

Nine months. That's all it had been. Nine months since the tower. Since blood-stained stone and magic tore through the air like lightning. Since the day time rewrote itself. Nine months since I chose love over destiny, rewriting my own fate.

More importantly, it had been nine months since I made the deal with Noire, and somehow I was still here, still myself.

I gasped, the pressure mounting again as the midwives urged me to push. My body was drenched in sweat, muscles quivering, breath shallow, but my mind, it was elsewhere. Weaving through memories like threads of silk, tugging gently on the smallest shifts that had unraveled centuries of war and manipulation. Such small choices. Such little changes.

If Sagar hadn't found me in the gardens that night. If I hadn't cursed the Gods. If I hadn't bargained with Noire.

Would I be here now?

"Almost there, Your Majesty," the midwife said gently. Her voice cut through the haze like a lantern in the dark.

A scream ripped from my throat, primal and raw. My hands clawed at the sheets. Sagar's were wrapped around mine, steady, gaurding.

"You're doing so well, my love," Sagar whispered against my sweat-slicked forehead, his hand gripping mine like it was the only thing tethering him to the earth. "You're almost done."

Almost. Whatever that meant anymore.

As the pain swelled through me again, I let my mind drift backward, away from the sting and the pressure, into the quiet aftermath of chaos.

After the battle, the world didn't collapse the way I once feared it might. It healed. Etheria extended its hand to Calbraxia, not out of pity, but out of something far rarer, hope. Its new King and Queen made sure of that. The people began to sing again. To smile. And in time, to believe.

With my mother gone, it was Margaret who would take her place on the throne. I knew she would rule with heart, with mercy. With the kind of strength that does not need to shout to be known. She will be everything Calbraxia never let me become. And when she comes of age, I know she would wear the crown like it had always belonged to her.

June stayed close, of course, ever watchful, ever loyal. We were able to reconcile her deceit quickly, of course a new gown helped speed the process along. She and Madame Levior were now guarding Margaret with the kind of devotion only love can breed.

And Sagar, gods, Sagar. He took the Etherian throne with grace I could only marvel at. The people adored him. And they welcomed me too, not just as their queen, but as one of their own. Our Etherian wedding ceremony spanned nearly an entire month, every street alive with color and music and wine. On those nights, I held him like I might lose him all over again. I kissed him until the past couldn't find us.

We lived as though every sunrise was a stolen thing. And shortly after, we created something new from it, something perfect. Which is what brought me here. To this room. To this moment. To the agony that wracked every inch of me like lightning. I cried out once more, my body fracturing in the heat of it, until—

A wail. Small. Sharp. Utterly alive. Piercing and perfect.

"It's a girl," the midwife breathed.

My heart stopped. A girl. A daughter.

"A girl! Silvia!" Sagar cried, pressing his lips to my forehead.

Tears sprang to my eyes as I slumped back, dizzy and trembling. The world spun. My limbs felt distant, waterlogged. The last thing I whispered before the blackness took me was a promise.

"Sagar." I breathed, looking into his eyes. "I promise, she will get to choose her own fate..."

Darkness wrapped around me like fur, thick, suffocating, sweet. It clung to my skin like a second womb, warm and wet with memory. Somewhere in the distance, something pulsed, a low hum, like a heartbeat not my own. It reverberated through the space between breath and death.

I drifted in the silence for what felt like hours, or days, or maybe no time at all. There was no weight to my body, no edge to my being. Just a vast nothingness, waiting. Watching.

"Silvia," came a voice I had not heard since her final breath.

I turned. There she was.

My Mother stood in the darkness like a statue carved from memory. Regal, unbroken, beautiful in the way winter was beautiful; distant, sharp, deadly. Her hair was bound back from her face in a way I had never seen, almost child-like. Her eyes, once endless wells of power and control, now glimmered with something far more terrible. Knowing.

"You look just like I did when I first gave birth," she said softly, stepping forward. "Angry. Terrified. Alive in all the wrong ways."

I wanted to run. Wanted to scream. Wanted to remind her that she was dead, that this was over, that she had no power over me anymore. But my mouth stayed shut. My feet, rooted.

Her voice wrapped around me like a chain. "You thought you could escape fate? That's laughable."

"I did." I spat. "The kingdoms remain intact, my prophecy—"

"Silvia, that was never your prophecy..." She laughed, stepping forward. "That prophecy was for me."

"Noire said you stole my prophecy!" I called.

She shook her head, a smile spreading across her face. "Silvia, always finding answers before thinking. Did Noire ever say *my* name specifically? Who else do you know spoke with Noire, received a prophecy?"

My breath caught. The memory surged up like a tide I couldn't hold back. The book, Noire's words. "Saint Cyradil..." I gasped.

"When the moon is swallowed by shadow and the stars weep silver..." My mother murmured.

"...a saint shall bear a child untouched by mortal hands," I whispered, the words spilling from me like blood. "Born beneath the veil of divinity..."

Elanore nodded. "You did always love to jump to your own conclusions, didn't you?"

"No," I said, voice trembling. "Noire was supposed to take me. I was supposed to be the vessel, not—"

I reached down, grasping at where my bump used to lie under my dress, but now it was gone.

She stepped closer, her figure flickering like flame. "Who else but you, my daughter born of light and shadow? Soon to be known as the saint who bore the child that even the gods feared."

I shook my head, retreating a step. "No. No, it couldn't be. She was supposed to be able to choose her own fate, not this."

She smiled, and it was the saddest thing I'd ever seen on her face. "And who said they wouldn't?"

"You lied to me," I hissed. "You knew. All along."

"I didn't know," she said, voice thin with regret. "Not until the end. The longer I spent here, the more I re-watched our lives…"

A pulse echoed through the darkness, like a heartbeat made of stars. Mother smiled, her gaze sharper now. "And now you thought you were smarter than the gods? Smarter than fate? Fate, sweet Silvia, always collects. Even when it pretends to forget." She reached out, brushing a phantom hand against my cheek. "And when she opens her eyes, you'll see the truth."

The darkness cracked open behind her like glass shattering.

I gasped, lungs dragging in air that tasted of blood and salt and lavender. I woke slowly, caught between worlds, between nightmare and breath. The edges of the dream clung to me, sticky and slick like afterbirth. How long had I been under?

The moonlight bled through the window in a sharp sliver, illuminating the room in cold silver. It was quiet, too quiet. I shifted, summoning the midwives with my alert presence. I could feel the tone in the room. They were hushed, whispering. Urgent. Uneasy.

"Where is she?" My voice was hoarse, barely audible. "Let me see her."

The midwives froze, exchanging nervous glances. One of them stepped forward, clutching the bundle tightly to her chest.

"Please," I said again, voice firmer now, more mother than queen. "Bring her to me."

She hesitated, eyes flicking toward the others, as if asking for permission. Then, slowly, carefully, like one offering a relic to a god, she stepped forward and placed the bundle in my arms.

And I saw. She was perfect. Dark curls clung to her damp forehead, her cheeks flushed with the effort of simply existing. Her tiny body radiated heat. Her tiny fingers curled instinctively, as if searching for something to hold. My heart flooded with something. Love, yes, but something darker, too. Dread.

She moved, curling into me instinctively. Her eyes blinked, batting her thick dark lashes at me and smiling. I felt my soul catch in my throat. Her eyes were open. And I saw them. Black. Not just dark, black. Endless. The kind of black that didn't reflect light but consumed it. The kind of black that watched. That waited.

My body went still. Those were the eyes that haunted my dreams for the past nine months. The ones that stared back at me as I begged for Sagar's life. The eyes of something ancient. Something unknowable. Something I had bargained with. Those were Noire's eyes.

"Silvia…" Sagar whispered, shifting next to me. "You saw."

My mind raced, searching for the right words. Instead, I smiled. It was not a smile of joy, nor fear. It was the smile of someone who understood what had been set in motion. Sagar wrapped his arm around me as he looked down at her with such pure wonder it made my heart ache.

"She's beautiful," I whispered, shooting a glare at the murmuring midwives.

"She's perfect," Sagar whispered. "I hadn't chosen a name, I know we spoke of naming her after June, but—"

"No," I cut in. "I know the perfect name."

I looked at him. Then at her. The vessel. The future. I would tell her the truth someday, but until then, she could carve her own future. She would know love, freedom, and life. Far beyond the reaches of what she was destined to do.

"Noire," I said softly. "Her name is Noire."

He blinked. "That's... unusual."

"It's fate," I whispered. "And we'll make sure hers is perfect."

Because *she* was perfect, and she was everything. Light and dark. Life and death. The past and whatever came next. Perhaps I couldn't escape what fate had in store for me, but I had all the hope in the world that she would be able to. And now, the world would change again, one choice at a time.

Just as it always had.

Acknowledgements

There are so many people I want to thank for helping bring *The Saint's Second Life* into existence.

First, to my beta readers: thank you. Your feedback was unbelievably helpful at every stage of this journey. From early ideas that barely held together to later drafts that finally began to resemble a real story, your insight shaped this book in ways I could never have managed alone. This project went through something like seven or eight versions, and if you had told me back in version one what it would eventually become, I wouldn't have believed you. Your patience, honesty, and willingness to dive deep into this world made all the difference.

Next, to my better half, Paige. Your support throughout this entire process is what pushed me to actually finish this thing. On the days when I doubted myself, when the story felt impossible or unfinished, you were there (no literally I saw you in the google doc) encouraging, and believing in this world even when I struggled to. Truly, *The Saint's Second Life* wouldn't exist without you, and I'm endlessly grateful that you were there to witness it grow from its very first idea to its final page.

I also want to thank the writers who inspired me to write this series. From breathtaking works of fiction to the nastiest, worst smut I've ever read, this book is my love letter to the genre and to everyone who came before me and everyone still writing alongside me now.

Lastly, to you, the reader. Thank you for choosing to step into this story. Without your time, curiosity, and willingness to turn the page, this book wouldn't exist at all. I hope you had as good of a time jumping into Silvia's world as I did writing it, and I'm grateful you gave this story a chance.

About the Author

Abby is a non-binary loving parent of three little furballs, a skillful cosplayer, and a long time lover of books. They have been writing stories since elementary school, starting with silly little horror tales far beyond what was appropriate for their grade and graduating to fan fiction on *The Sims 3* forums and various fanfiction websites. After reading one too many "villainess was transported back to their life to better themselves" novels, they decided to take a crack at it themselves. Somewhere along the way, this turned into a real published piece, much to their own surprise. While they never planned on writing a fantasy smut novel, fate (and poor self-control around morally gray characters) had other ideas. Abby now thrives off of tales filled with magic, romantic tension, and characters who desperately need therapy.